An Heir Unraveled

Jane Maguire

An Heir Unraveled

Copyright © 2025 Jane Maguire

Cover design by Holly Perret

ISBN: 978-1-7382727-6-1

www.janemaguireauthor.com

Also by Jane Maguire

THE INCONVENIENTLY WED SERIES

Book 1: **Secrets and a Scandal**

Book 2: **Rumors and a Rake**

Book 3: **Longing for a Lady**

THE ROCKLIFFE DYNASTY SERIES

Book 1: **A Study in Desire**

Book 2: **A Duke Once Lost**

Book 3: **The Marquess Returns**

Book 4: **His Christmas Rose**

Book 5: **An Heir Unraveled**

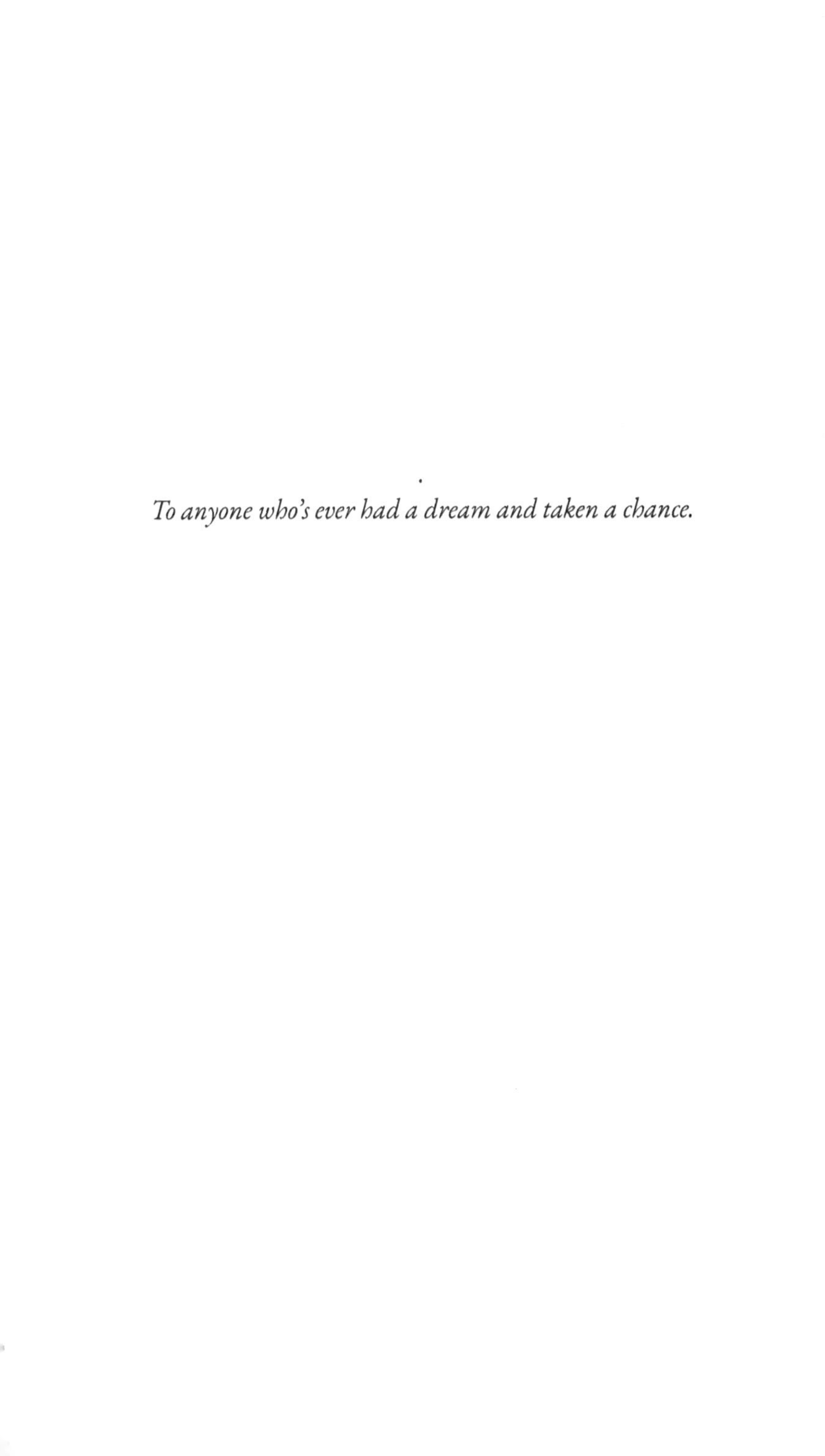

To anyone who's ever had a dream and taken a chance.

An Heir Unraveled

By Jane Maguire

1

Benedict Prescott tried to endure whatever misfortunes came his way with a steady countenance. However, doing so proved considerably easier when he wasn't up to his ankles in sheep shite.

His top boots sank into the spongy ground with each step he took, progressively undoing his early morning efforts of shining them to a glossy black. But what difference did that make now? He would bemoan his defiled footwear, and the unfortunate odor his boots emitted, once he was seated before a blazing hearth at Aldercombe Grange with a steaming mug in hand. At present, his only concern should be seeking cover from the steadily increasing rainfall.

Fortunately, a shepherd's hut stood in the field up ahead, and although the wooden structure appeared somewhat rickety, it would serve his purpose as he waited out the rain. And determined where in hell he was.

He plodded along at a half-run, grimacing at the pungent

aroma of the air surrounding him. Grimacing even harder at his own inanity.

He'd always liked to think of himself as a man of some intelligence, having taken several firsts at Cambridge prior to his expulsion. He'd spent the entirety of his carriage ride from London reminding himself of this fact, assuring himself that if he could excel with his studies, he could surely succeed with estate management, too. Therefore, when one of the horses had thrown a shoe just as they'd passed through the final village before arriving at Aldercombe, he'd opted to get out and walk the remaining distance rather than wait at the blacksmith's. After all, it was a fine day, and going the last few miles on foot would allow him to better survey the land under his domain.

Yet the clouds had rolled in quickly, and in advising him that he'd arrive at the grange if he simply kept heading north, the coachman had neglected to mention the fork in the road and whether it was necessary to veer left or right.

Ben had chosen left, which was looking increasingly like the wrong selection. He'd passed nothing but a cottage or two and then fields, and had spotted no creatures besides some sheep far in the distance.

The rain took the last of his precarious confidence and dissolved it like salt. Yes, he was good with books and exams, but what did that have to do with rural life? *Nothing*.

Perhaps this was a sign that in complying with his uncle's request that he travel to the Wiltshire estate, he'd chosen wrong. A sign he wasn't meant to reside here. Had betrayed what mattered most.

He gave his head a brisk shake to push the thoughts—and the subsequent stab of guilt—away, abandoning all efforts to choose his foot placement carefully and sprinting the remaining distance to the hut. The place had a look of desertion, but just in case, he gave the door a sound knock before bounding up the two steps, flicking the latch, and pushing his way inside—

Where he came face-to-face with a woman, her breath shooting out as a gasp as she startled backward, her eyes becoming huge. Bewildered.

They stayed that way only for a moment, though, before she narrowed them, crossing her arms tightly across her chest. "You cannot be here."

He blinked, fighting to adjust to the hut's dim interior. The floorboards were worn and dusty, the furniture sparse and basic. But this woman ...

This woman stood in contrast to all of it. Her gown was the pearly pink of an iced confection, adorned with cheerful yellow flowers embroidered across the bodice and hem. Her slippers, which had fared far better than his boots, were each decorated with a floppy mint green bow, the same shade as the ribbons dangling from her wide-brimmed bonnet. Her eyes were blue, the curls framing her face a sunny blonde. For everything drab in the hut, she offered color; for everything crude, she was elegance and refinement.

The incongruity of her presence threw him off balance and made his body tense with surprise. What other reason could he possess for saying, more sharply than he intended, "And who are you to make that judgment? You do not look like a shepherdess."

She arched a golden brow. "I'm no shepherdess, but ..." Her indignant speech stopped short, and she caught her lower lip between her teeth, her face flickering as if she were in deep contemplation.

He knew that look. It was the same one his brother Alexander had worn as a child when he misbehaved and pondered how best to avoid getting scolded. But unlike Alex, the woman accompanied her expression by the continued worrying of her lip, nudging the plump, rosy flesh back and forth in a manner *most* distracting.

"I don't plan to stay long," he said brusquely, turning his attention to his damp coat and giving it a few tugs to smooth it. "Only until the rain stops."

"Oh, is it raining?" Her voice sounded unnaturally light, tinged with a hint of disingenuous laughter. "Surely, not more than a sprinkle. You shouldn't let it hinder you."

Ben gave a pointed glance at the window, where thick raindrops streaked the murky glass. She'd made her message explicitly clear: she wanted him to leave, *now*, regardless of what the elements and the pasture covered in sheep excrement had in store for him.

Yet why should he? While the location of Aldercombe Grange remained a mystery to him, he was *reasonably* certain this field was Rockliffe land. *His* land. At least, it could be if he wanted it. Why should he begin his tenure upon it by taking orders from a stranger and trespasser?

He planted his boots more firmly against the floorboards —ignoring the way her nose scrunched up when he moved his feet—and mimicked her position, crossing his arms over his chest. "Let me ask a question of you first, Miss ..." He paused to give her the opportunity to supply her name, but when none was provided, he continued anyway. "What, pray, are you doing here?"

Her face flickered again, although she neglected her lip this time, fortunately. "Some friends and I were picnicking on Skylark Ridge," she said with sudden nonchalance. "I care little for archery, so when they began a competition, I decided to take a walk."

Ben's brow furrowed. He hadn't grown so ignorant that he failed to notice when he was being lied to. "To the scenic environs of a musty hut?"

She gave a tiny sniff, her cheeks coloring to a similar shade as her dress. "Perhaps I ... wanted to explore."

"Alone?"

She hesitated for a beat too long. "Yes."

Ah. Suddenly, so many unknowns of the situation became clear. Miss—Miss *Nameless*, with her honey-gold curls, fine shoes, and jaunty dress that highlighted generous curves, was planning an assignation. A clandestine one, certainly, for why else would she remain in the hut while so adamantly insisting he leave? For some reason, the thought created a knot in his stomach.

"I regret to inform you, Miss"—again, he waited for her name, and again, none was forthcoming—"that since the time you departed the picnic, the weather likely put an end to it."

"No, no, the rain won't be a problem." She shook her hand dismissively, her words accompanied by the steady patter of droplets upon the roof. "We brought along a canopy."

He paused, his jaw tightening. He hadn't intended to allude solely to the picnic, but to ... but to ... there was no delicate turn of phrase to be had, so he may as well just come out and say it. "Regardless, the person you planned to meet here, far beyond the shelter of the canopy, is likely to have judged the rain a deterrent."

Understanding deepened the pink in her cheeks, and the abrupt flash in her eyes told him he hadn't erred in his assumption.

"Very well, you've discerned the truth." She dipped her chin in concession, although the gesture lasted only an instant before she squared her shoulders, her gaze boring into his without compunction. "But in one thing, sir, you're mistaken. George may be a little late, but I know he wouldn't let a small shower stop him. It's only your presence, I fear, that will prove a hindrance."

He bit back the impolite noise that rose in his throat,

grinding his teeth as he spun from the astute blue gaze and looked for guidance amidst the endless fields beyond the window. He could lecture her on the folly of such an undertaking, but it was hardly his concern. If Miss Nameless derived pleasure from rendezvous in dank, malodorous spaces and had found a gentleman who shared her predilections, why should he stand between them? Already, the angry downpour had eased, the sky once more showing traces of muted sunrays through the clouds. Why shouldn't he depart and pretend this whole encounter had never happened?

There was simply one problem.

"If I'm to leave ..." He cleared his throat, which grew dry as sand as his focus came back to his own predicament. His own folly. "I wonder if you might point me in the direction of Aldercombe Grange."

"Of course," she said, motioning eagerly toward the door. "There's a shortcut from here. Simply walk all the way to the northwest edge of this pasture, where the fence ends and the trees begin, and turn left. There's a little path that leads through the wood and straight to Aldercombe's back garden."

"Thank you." He straightened his wet top hat and bowed stiffly, then pivoted to reach for the door.

"Aldercombe Grange hasn't been occupied for years." Her voice did the very thing she didn't seem to want and caused him to halt in his tracks. "Is that to change?"

"Yes." He glanced over his shoulder at her, and perhaps he would have left it at that and been on his way if not for the fact she was biting her lip again. A simple action that somehow had the power to transfix him.

Her eyes clouded with uncertainty, and he could tell she was thinking again, calculating. Until all at once, her mouth gaped, and her words rushed out in a flurry. "You're the new land agent, aren't you?" Another burst of color flooded her face, sweeping away her air of confidence and leaving guilt in its wake. "I'm terribly sorry for trespassing, I—"

"No, not the land agent." He shook his head, ridding her of the misconception before her worry had a chance to spiral. Yet how was he to explain his position without keeping her another half hour and providing details far too intimate to share with a stranger?

"I'm family," he settled on after a moment, because despite the years of estrangement, the years of separation from country estates and peerages, he couldn't change the blood running through his veins.

She cocked her head, almost like a foxhound who'd picked up an unexpected scent. "Family? To ... to the Marquess of Rockliffe?"

"Yes. His nephew." *The heir presumptive, the accidental successor, the man who was never supposed to have any of this.* All these new titles he didn't know how to sort, didn't know how to own, rushed through his head, convoluted and strange. And so, he uttered the only thing that gave him certainty, the name that had been his since birth. "Benedict Prescott."

"Oh!" The woman stumbled, her hem catching in her slipper, and she emitted another of those breathy gasps just like when he'd thrown open the door to discover her.

He acted instinctively when he saw her body pitch, his arms shooting out to secure her in his grip. However, he took a split-second too long, and she was on the floor before he could do a damn thing to stop it, her skirts tangled amidst the leg of a wobbly-looking chair.

"Are you all right?" He dove to the floor beside her, quickly scanning up and down her body for signs of injury. Although first glances revealed that the worst of the damage had been done to her pride.

"I'm well," she huffed, attempting to wrench her foot from behind the chair leg. "I'm perfectly fine."

However, her foot remained where it was, caught up in the ruffle that had torn at her hem. She tried anew, tugging impatiently, but the only effect was the loud rending of fabric.

"Allow me." Ben spoke just as she let out an aggrieved cry, and he approached her cautiously, waiting for the brief glimmer of assent in her eyes before taking hold of her silky hem. The material slid over his fingertips like butter as he worked to disentangle it from the chair leg, then slipped the ruffle free of her foot.

She winced. Only for a moment before wiping the expression away, but not so swiftly that he failed to notice it. And before he could ponder the wisdom of what he did, he took her ankle into his grasp, cradling it within his palm.

"You're certain you haven't hurt yourself?" He peered down at the feminine limb and the stocking that covered any evidence of bruising. He wasn't prepared for how very *warm* she would be. How very soft she would feel when he let his fingertips brush against her. Perhaps he should fetch his spectacles from his pocket so he could observe the site more thoroughly for signs of injury. Except suddenly, he seemed incapable of movement.

"I ..." Her voice trailed away; all that remained was her blue gaze upon him, not wounded or aggrieved but ... pensive.

He took a quick breath, his nostrils prickling. In this hut smelling of mildew and sheep, on this floor full of dust and Lord knew what else, he could also detect the scent of something floral. Something fresh and sweet, which one would be apt to find only in the countryside. Or perhaps, only in close proximity to a woman—

The door crashed open, and a bracing gust of wind pervaded the hut, along with a deep, caustic voice. "What's this, then?"

Ben whipped his head around, his eyes falling upon the gentleman in the doorway. He was a young man, finely dressed, with features displaying a potent mix of shock and bewilderment—along with a heavy dose of anger.

"George?" The mystery woman spat out the name as if she didn't quite comprehend it, and her ankle shuddered within Ben's palm—a reminder he was still holding it. He set it gently on the floor, the one bit of carefulness he managed before jerking his head back toward her.

"What in hell is the meaning of this, Violet?" the gentleman's voice boomed from behind him, his boots making the floor creak as he took another step into the hut.

Violet. Ben should have known she'd possess such a name —both a color and a flower, bright and fragrant.

Presently, though, she looked less like a delicate blossom and more like a provoked adder, ready to strike. "I could ask the same of you." She glared at her errant suitor, any trepidation she held turning to blazing-eyed fury. "You said you'd be just five minutes behind me, but I'm certain an hour has passed."

"Denham cajoled me into joining the archery tournament, and I could hardly say no." For an instant, the young man almost sounded sheepish, although when Ben turned to him, any hint of remorse was quickly replaced by a scowl. "What does it matter? Apparently, you found someone else to take my place."

"You're mistaken, I assure you," Ben bit out, just as Violet cried, "That's not what this is!"

She took hold of the chair, using it to help herself clamber to her feet. "This gentleman and I stumbled upon one another by accident, and I fell, and—"

"I have no interest in your excuses and falsehoods. My eyes have already told me everything I need to know." The gentleman—*George*—cast a final scathing look around the hut before giving her a brusque nod. "Good day, Miss Collingwood."

And then, before either of them could utter another word, George stormed back into the elements, slamming the door behind him.

Violet stood in stunned silence, almost as if her suitor had dealt her a blow. It lasted only an instant, though, before she took hold of her damaged skirts and rushed toward the doorway. "George, wait!" she yelped, grabbing the latch and shoving the door open once more. "You're being unreasonable, you—"

"Miss Collingwood." Ben found his voice at precisely the same moment he realized he was still crouching on the floor, watching the scene as if it were a farce on Drury Lane. He scrambled upright, hastily brushing the dirt from his trousers and darting over to the doorway beside her before she could run away.

"Miss Collingwood," he repeated softly, using the name the gentleman had uttered just prior to his departure—although truth be told, Ben would have far preferred testing *Violet* upon his tongue. And then ...

And then, he didn't know what else to say. Didn't know why he'd kept her there. So he could tell her he'd noticed her flinch when her feet hit the floor, and she should stay to rest a while longer? So he could share his observation that, at the risk of judging too hastily, he deemed George a veritable jackass who wasn't worth her time?

None of the words felt right; out of myriad possibilities, he didn't know how to form an appropriate sentence.

Nor did he have the opportunity. She remained in the doorway with him, letting silence linger, for merely a beat before bursting out into the field, leaving only the echo of her breathless words behind her. "*Apologize, Mr. Prescott, for the intrusion ... cannot stay ... George, come* back *here*!"

Ben couldn't help but cringe a little as her feet hit the muddy grass, struggling to catch up with her irate suitor, who had the advantage of sturdy boots and an advanced start. Her flimsy white slippers, with their elaborate green bows, didn't fare well now that the ground was wet.

Yet once again, it was none of his concern. The pair were having a lovers' quarrel that they alone needed to sort. His interference wasn't needed, nor did he particularly desire placing himself in the middle of such volatility—especially when George's ears seemed to be stuffed with cotton wool.

Besides, he had troubles of his own to sort, starting with successfully making his way to Aldercombe Grange. If nothing else, the unfortunate encounter in the hut had granted him the directions he required.

He stepped out into the field, heading toward the northwest corner where the fence met the trees, just as Violet had instructed. His boots squelched against the ground, but he tried not to think about where—or in what—he was stepping. He tried not to think about anything except that soon, at long last, he'd arrive at his destination.

But even though Violet and her suitor had run off in the opposite direction and were now well out of earshot, he couldn't stop replaying the scene from the hut in his mind. Couldn't shake the slight sense of unease that tugged at his gut.

A sense that, maybe, he couldn't wash his hands of the matter as cleanly as he would like.

2

By the time Ben located Aldercombe Grange, tidied himself in his new bedchamber, and went downstairs to await a meeting with Mr. Hayward, the land agent, he'd *nearly* convinced himself that he could forget the day's prior mishaps and enjoy a return to order.

Nearly, until a plaintive wail floated out from the kitchen, followed by a woman's stern bark.

He paused with his foot partway between two steps on the servant's staircase, his not-quite-relaxed muscles promptly squeezing themselves into knots. After the various sources of tumult he'd encountered already today, he hadn't imagined that going to the kitchen and ensuring ample food was prepared, should Mr. Hayward wish to stay for dinner, would provide another of them. However, when he prompted his feet back into motion, descending the remainder of the staircase and hurrying down the basement corridor, it became clear the servants were in an uproar.

He halted at the threshold of the kitchen, peering in to discover that the cook, kitchen maids, and housekeeper had all abandoned their tasks in favor of gawking at the scene unfolding by the back door. Namely, one of the chamber-maids—*Molly*, he seemed to recall from his earlier introduction to the staff—was being dragged off by an irate older woman with a reddened face and eyes that bulged.

"You can't make me leave, Mum!" Molly cried, wrenching her slender arm free and throwing her body against the door like a barrier. "I don't want to return to the farm."

Her cry only made the woman's—her mother's—scowl deepen, and she set her hand back on her daughter's sleeve without missing a beat. "Tending livestock and threshing corn was good enough for me and will be good enough for you, too. It's honest, *wholesome* work."

Molly shook her head urgently, holding her position despite how her mother had a clear advantage in size. "Mrs. Wheeler says I'm one of the best. She says I could even be promoted to lady's maid someday."

"Lady?" Her mother let out a snort. "I'm not sure you should count on any *ladies* entering this house of ... of ... of ill repute!"

"I'm certain it's not bad as all that." The housekeeper, Mrs. Wheeler, stepped forward to intervene, although the sound that escaped Ben's throat caused her to whirl around, her words faltering and her brows shooting up in horror as she took him in. "Mr. Prescott." The spry, middle-aged woman stumbled into a curtsy, quickly schooling her features into impassiveness. "What may we do for you?"

But Ben couldn't answer. He was busy studying the chambermaid and her mother—the former diffident and quivering, the latter turning purple with indignation. For a long moment, the woman glowered at him as though she'd never seen anything so revolting in her life. And then, before any of them pieced together a sentence, she pushed past her daughter to fling open the door, hauling the startled girl out with her. "Come along. You'll not set foot in this house again."

The door slammed closed, cutting off Molly's answering protest and leaving the kitchen in weighted silence.

After an indeterminate number of seconds passed, the kitchen maids began muttering amongst themselves, and Mrs. Wheeler repeated his name. Ben, though, was impervious to everything but the chatter within his own head.

What in hell had just happened? What had he done, after a mere afternoon at Aldercombe, to so grievously offend a servant's mother that she would remove her daughter from the house while giving him the cut direct?

Could she have somehow discovered his expulsion from university and the reason behind it? The thought caused his skin to prickle with unwanted heat. But no, she had no way to discover such things—did she? Surely, a farm woman in Wiltshire wasn't privy to the goings-on at Cambridge.

Her displeasure must be because of something else—a conflict already in place before his arrival. Maybe there was trouble amongst the male and female staff for which he, as new head of the house, was now considered responsible. Whatever it was, he would need to remedy it immediately.

Yet just as he moved to reply to Mrs. Wheeler and beg her assistance in sorting the matter, a raspy throat cleared, and a male voice came from behind him. "Mr. Prescott? Mr. Hayward has arrived to see you."

He spun abruptly to find Pearce awaiting him, the seasoned butler showing not a trace of discomposure. That was a promising sign, at least—the turmoil from the kitchen must not have made its way elsewhere in the house. As for the nature of the turmoil, it turned out he'd have to wait until later to discover it, after all. He'd summoned his land agent for a three o'clock meeting, and as the main purpose of Ben's being at Aldercombe was to assess the man's management skills and see what improvements they could implement with the estate, he didn't wish to keep Mr. Hayward waiting.

After instructing Pearce to show Mr. Hayward to the study, and informing Mrs. Wheeler he'd like to speak with her as soon as his meeting concluded, he started back into the corridor and up the stairs, trying to put the scene in the kitchen aside. He needed to focus on ledgers. On the discussion he and Mr. Hayward would have on profits and losses. On the questions he must pose regarding land use.

However, the incensed words of Molly's mother kept returning to him like a gnat buzzing in his ear. *I'm not sure you should count on any* ladies *entering ... House of ill repute ...*

He gave his head a brisk shake as if to force them out, smoothing down the folds of his cravat and pleats of his waistcoat. Then, ignoring the knot that had settled in his stomach, he pushed into the study, where a man stood by the desk awaiting his arrival.

"Mr. John Hayward, I presume." Ben nodded in his direction, motioning for him to take one of the leather chairs alongside the desk. "I'm Benedict Prescott."

"A pleasure, sir." Mr. Hayward accepted the proffered seat as Ben strode to his own chair on the opposite side of the desk, studying the land agent out of the corner of his eye.

At first glance, he appeared respectable, with a smart double-breasted tan coat and neatly clipped gray-brown hair. Ben estimated him to be about two decades his senior, which placed him at an ideal age: old enough to possess plenty of experience, but not so old that his memory should be at risk of declining like that of the previous man to hold the position.

The only trouble was ... Mr. Hayward didn't seem quite comfortable while he sat. Nor did he look Ben directly in the eye, the edge of the desk seeming far more interesting to him.

Ben brushed invisible wrinkles out of his trousers, trying to shake off his sense of unease. Mr. Hayward's malaise was likely a figment of Ben's imagination, brought on by the unanticipated contempt he'd encountered in the kitchen.

There was no reason for the land agent to scorn him. No reason aside from his youth and inexperience, perhaps, although he was determined to prove those were surmountable obstacles.

"Let's get right to it, shall we?" Ben reached for the account book he'd placed at the top of the pile on his desk, flipping it open to the first page. "I understand that last year's lack of true summer created unfavorable growing conditions, and that the man you're replacing made some omissions in reporting, but I wonder if ..."

He trailed off, an overloud feminine whisper in the corridor interrupting his train of thought. *"Everyone will know about it by nightfall. He had no care for her reputation at all, nor did she have much care for it herself, it seems. The lady is ruined."*

The knot in Ben's gut pulled tight, his teeth clenching as his gaze darted upward. Through the partially open door, he could just make out two chambermaids sauntering along, their frilly caps pressed close together while the women animatedly conversed.

Blast it, why must they gossip here, at this precise moment? Then again, perhaps he should be grateful the house still *had* chambermaids and that no more incensed mamas had come to remove their daughters from his employ.

He bit back a sigh and returned his attention to the ledger, trying to shut out everything beyond the perimeter of his desk. "I wonder if, assuming more satisfactory weather this year, we could—"

"And he really acted that quickly?" the second maid exclaimed in a whisper no more subtle than her companion's.

"Yes! He didn't even come to the house first before he—"

"Mr. Hayward." Ben pushed aside the ledger, his voice coming out far more clipped than he intended. He had only to look at the mottled face and pinched mouth of the man sitting across from him to realize Mr. Hayward, too, had heard every word from the corridor.

There could be no more ignoring it, for this situation was growing worse by the minute. "Something is amiss at Aldercombe," Ben said tightly. "Something that's causing disorder and gossip, and at the risk of sounding over-anxious, I'm starting to believe myself the cause. Might you know what it is?"

"I ..." Now it was Mr. Hayward's turn to trail off, his hand running agitatedly over his brow. "I couldn't say for certain, sir."

A lie. It wouldn't take a keen observer to determine as much. Ben cleared his throat, forcing himself to hold the nonplussed man's gaze. "Even if you have an inkling, I'd be much obliged if you shared it with me."

Redness spread all the way up to the roots of Mr. Hayward's hair. "Uh." He shifted in his seat, wringing his hands against the desktop. "There's been some trouble at the neighboring estate, Watley Hall. It seems a young lady—a, uh, local viscount's daughter—who's a guest at the home was caught in an ... *untoward* position with a gentleman when she wandered onto Aldercombe land during a picnic today."

"A gentleman." Ben repeated the word thickly, his heart slamming against his ribs. Everything was falling into place now, one awful piece at a time, but he still needed to hear it confirmed aloud. "What gentleman?"

"Well." Mr. Hayward coughed, peering fixedly at the bookcase just beyond Ben's head. "Based on the timing of the incident ... Based on the description of the gentleman provided by a witness ... There's speculation it was, uh, you."

There it was, the truth laid out in all its horrifying glory. A truth that made Ben's blood run cold and his chest throb.

"There's been a grave misunderstanding, I assure you," he snapped, jumping up from his chair and hurrying to the window to peer out at the greenery. He'd hoped the view would prove calming—a vast improvement to the sight of his flustered land agent. Instead, his mind swooped back to the rolling hills beyond Aldercombe's garden. The hut in the muddy pasture. The ankle within his palm.

Damn it, how had things gone so appallingly awry?

"I'm afraid our meeting will have to wait," he said to the window, because he was now the one incapable of making eye contact. "I must quell these appalling rumors at once."

"Certainly, sir." The sound of Mr. Hayward's chair pushing back, along with boots hitting the carpet, followed instantly. "Whenever you have need of me again, just say the word."

It was a remarkably polite farewell given all the uncomplimentary things the land agent must think of him. So polite that it nearly eased the sting over how quickly the man fled his presence, taking all Ben's good intentions about remedying the estate with him.

Ben pressed his forehead to the cool glass, a colorful assortment of curses tumbling from his throat. Perhaps he should be relieved that his disgrace had nothing to do with the scandal at Cambridge. But if anything, this was worse. Much, much worse. Mere hours in Wiltshire and he'd become a bloody *rake*.

He dug his fingers into his temples, trying to find order within his spiraling thoughts. His entire household—the entire *neighborhood*—thought he'd debauched a viscount's daughter, for Christ's sake, and he couldn't let that stand. He needed to devise a way to set things right before the situation grew even worse and he had yet another irreversible smear on his name.

The great irony of it was, he'd always been the one to stay back when his classmates at Cambridge went off to establishments in search of carnal activities. Unlike them, he hadn't felt an interest in sharing a fleeting moment of passion with someone he'd never see again. It was as if that component, present in every other male of his acquaintance, was missing in him.

As for the concept of a lasting relationship—a marriage— it had proved far too slippery to grasp. How was he to envision a future with a woman when he didn't even have a clear path forward for himself? How was he to imagine belonging with another person—*loving* another person—when he himself didn't belong anywhere finite?

Yet when a gentleman needed to repair a slight to a lady's honor ... what other option was there but marriage?

Despite his bloodline, he had little experience dealing with high society and remembering all its unspoken rules. Nonetheless, he knew how these matters worked. He knew the solution to a ruined reputation. And wasn't a solution worth any cost?

"Mr. Hayward!" He spun away from the window, bolting out of the study and toward the entrance hall. His pulse was too quick, his head too skittish. Every rational part of his being insisted that a decision this momentous required weeks of careful planning and consideration.

But desperate times, desperate measures. He *would* fix this at once, for both himself and the lady.

Fortunately, Mr. Hayward was still in the entrance hall when Ben arrived, accepting his beaver hat from Pearce with a look of mild trepidation.

Ben ground to a halt and took a breath, pulling his spine as straight as it would go. "Before you leave," he said to the land agent, forcing himself to push past his consternation, his humiliation, and anything other than what he needed to stop this scandal in its tracks. "I wonder if you might give me directions to the home of Miss Violet Collingwood."

3

"Fetch my vinaigrette. *Immediately.*" With a hand clasped to her chest, the viscountess Collingwood collapsed against the settee, shooting her daughter Violet a pitiable glance from beneath her puckered brow. Thus providing Miss Violet Collingwood with another reminder of the spectacular mess she'd made.

"I'll get it, Mama," Violet's sister, Arabella, cried, stepping out from behind her to offer their mother a reassuring nod. Yet the placid gesture promptly turned to a scowl when she spun to face Violet before rushing from the room.

Violet blew out a long breath, her forehead becoming strained. She'd attempted to explain herself to Arabella. She'd even uttered several apologies, although it was difficult to make them heartfelt when the blame seemed so unfairly cast. After all, she'd hardly *tried* getting caught tangled on the floor of a shepherd's hut with a gentleman. Not with an unknown gentleman, in any case.

"How could this have happened?" Her mother's wail cut into the momentary quiet in the drawing room, creating a plaintive yet accusatory echo. "And just when I thought our fortunes had changed for the better. Lord Frederick had all but proposed to Arabella. I was certain Mr. Metcalfe would do the same for you. And now—oh, my nerves cannot bear it!"

Violet gritted her teeth, silently willing her sister to hurry with the vinaigrette before the viscountess spiraled into full-blown hysteria. Again.

Upon arriving home far earlier than expected, Violet had done everything in her power to break the news of the afternoon's mishap with delicacy. Had she been given the choice, she wouldn't have breathed a word of it to their mother until tempers had a chance to cool.

Unfortunately, keeping silent hadn't been an option. Not after she'd stepped into Meadowleigh House with a ripped hem, thoroughly defiled slippers, and a tear-stained Arabella in tow. And all because George—that blasted George, who'd suggested the meeting in the shepherd's hut in the first place—had been so quick to spread gossip and render her a pariah.

The memories of what happened wouldn't stop burning a hole in her chest. The way she'd been only minutes behind George in arriving back at Skylark Ridge after the mishap, yet it was enough time that the other picnic-goers whispered behind their hands and avoided looking her in the eye. How the chaperone, Lady Kingsland, had declared the picnic to be over, frostily informing Violet that the dinner and dancing at Watley Hall were also canceled for the evening so she and her sister had best return home. The way, worst of all, these people she'd so recently called friends now shunned Arabella by association. Particularly their neighbor and host, Lord Frederick—the object of Arabella's affection—who'd ignored his intended's cries as though they were naught but a whisper of wind in the trees.

Each slight proved more rage-inducing than the last! But Violet couldn't let anger take over or they'd never solve anything. She refused to believe there wasn't a way this could all be put right.

"Try not to fret." She unclenched her teeth long enough to give her mother a poor semblance of a smile. Then, she approached the settee as if creeping toward a buried explosive, silently praying it wouldn't detonate. "As I said, this is just a misunderstanding."

"A misunderstanding? A *misunderstanding*?" Her mother's voice rose an octave, causing Violet to fear for the delicate jasperware vase on the end table beside her. "You snuck away from your chaperone and an afternoon of perfectly respectable entertainment, only to be caught on the floor of a shepherd's hut while a stranger handled your *ankles*!"

"I didn't ... It wasn't ..." Violet's voice broke off, frustration rendering her throat too tight to continue. Blast it, she'd already revealed the truth of what happened more times than she could count. Why would no one *listen*?

"Here it is, Mama." Arabella burst back into the room, and for once, their mother didn't criticize the lack of refinement in her hasty footsteps. Instead, the viscountess extended a limp hand, waiting until her younger daughter set the opened vinaigrette in her palm and then shoving it beneath her nose.

She inhaled deeply, the creases on her face displaying every mote of her chagrin. "Oh, I shall swoon," she moaned, the flowery yet acidic smell emanating from the silver box strong enough that Violet's eyes began to sting. "I shall—"

"My lady?" Davis, the house's long-serving butler, appeared in the doorway and took a tentative step into the room, looking very much like he wished he were already making his retreat. Especially when he received only a series of exaggerated sniffs in response. Ever the dutiful servant, though, he squared his shoulders, swallowing visibly before saying, "There's a gentleman here to see Miss Collingwood."

The vinaigrette flew to the floor with a clatter as the viscountess bolted upright upon the settee, her eyes becoming huge, glittering saucers. "A gentleman, you say?"

The announcement gave Violet's chest a jolt—shock, followed by airiness that radiated to her limbs. "See, I *told* you." Her gaze flitted between her mother and sister—for she was unsure of who needed the reassurance more—and she couldn't help but give her foot a little stamp in triumph. "All it took was several hours of reflection before George realized how silly this all is. He's now come to his senses, and there's no reason things cannot go back to the way they were—"

"Yes, yes, send him in," her mother cried, giving her hand an impatient flick and turning her attention to smoothing the wrinkles in her skirt.

Davis hesitated for just a moment, his pinched mouth opening but then snapping closed without a word before he fled into the corridor.

"You really think all is forgiven?" Arabella rushed to Violet's side, sinking her fingers into Violet's arm as sharply as if they contained claws. Yet her expression had brightened. "You believe Lord Frederick and I still have a chance?"

Of course you do. He'd be a proper jackanapes not to propose. You shall have exactly what you desire. Violet intended to utter all those words and more, anything it took to widen her sister's eager smile and to make herself feel as though she hadn't ruined everything.

But instead, Violet said nothing, for Davis had returned, his sturdy baritone taking command of the room. "Mr. Benedict Prescott."

Mister ... Whom? Her heart lurched, a deep pit forming in her stomach. She'd misheard; there could be no other explanation.

Yet the aforementioned gentleman filed in without delay, clad in fresh attire—and boots that didn't smell to the high heavens—but still very much the same person with whom she'd become entangled in the shepherd's hut.

She blinked rapidly, for her eyes had started to burn. *There's no way ... He's in my house ... How did he find ...*

"What are you doing here?" she hissed, feeling the uncomfortable weight of her family's gaze upon her.

For a moment, the look Mr. Prescott gave her suggested he didn't quite know the answer himself. Indeed, something flashed in his eyes that made him seem rather lost. Even so, and despite the harrowing circumstances behind the encounter, she didn't fail to notice his handsomeness. He was slender but tall with a straight, aristocratic nose, sharp jawline, and eyes the color of rich chocolate. If only he didn't appear so continuously ... *stiff*. As if he had a stone in his boot or the knots in his starched white cravat were too tight.

But regardless of any uncertainty he felt, he was quick to draw his shoulders up even more rigidly and give her a curt bow. "Good day, Miss Collingwood." He turned to her mother and Arabella and offered them the same, his face washed of everything but perfect neutrality. "Ladies."

"Mr. Prescott." The viscountess inclined her head cordially, showing no trace of her earlier distress. "I don't believe we share the pleasure of an acquaintanceship. Am I correct in assuming you are a relation of Lord Rockliffe?"

He hesitated an instant before nodding, the motion causing a carefully slicked-back dark lock to dare inching toward his forehead. "His nephew."

Her mother's lips twitched, her entire countenance becoming instantly more alert. "His eldest nephew?"

"Yes."

His heir. The words remained unspoken, although there was no denying they'd all made the connection. And then, the viscountess bestowed on him the brightest, kindliest of smiles. "How nice to have you in the area. I'm Lady Collingwood, and these are my daughters, Miss Collingwood and Miss Arabella. Although you already addressed Miss Collingwood. Do you know one another?"

Violet shot him a warning glance. At least, as much of one as she was able with her mother and Arabella observing her every move. She'd told them all they needed to know about the afternoon's incident. There was no need for them to discover the name of the gentleman with whom she'd been caught, nor to learn she'd been a trespasser who ordered the Marquess of Rockliffe's nephew out of a building on his own property. Surely, he would take pity on her and hold his tongue. For he must see how much the revelation would complicate—

"We became unexpectedly acquainted this afternoon, which is the reason for my visit," he said, promptly taking any hopes for discretion she harbored and casting them out to sea.

She bit back the oath that rose on her tongue, although she couldn't contain her frown or stop her eyes from shooting daggers.

Nonetheless, Mr. Prescott took several steps closer to her, his spine as unyielding as ever. "Miss Collingwood, it has been brought to my notice that our encounter garnered a great deal of unsavory attention. You and I both know nothing untoward happened, but it doesn't change the gossip or the fact that your reputation has suffered a stain." He paused to clear his throat and take a breath. "Therefore, I've come to do the honorable thing and make you an offer of marriage."

"You've come to *what*?" Violet's knees wobbled, and the air surged from her lungs as if she'd been punched. Once again, her ears must be deceiving her, for this wasn't right; it couldn't be—

"She'll accept," the viscountess exclaimed, the eager ring of her words slicing into Violet's haze of stunned disbelief.

Violet's jaw slackened, and a little cry rushed out. How could her mother so readily fling her into the arms of this ...

this *stranger*? Yes, yes, Violet knew: her father's scandal in London, followed by the scandal she'd just created, had rendered them desperate. But even so ...

"This is absurd," she snapped. "We don't even *know* one another."

Mr. Prescott's brows drew together, making him appear especially sober. "Given the circumstances, I'm not sure we can allow that to matter."

"Quite right, Mr. Prescott," her mother chimed. "The sooner we have the banns read and put all this malicious gossip to rest, the better. Indeed, it may be best to procure a common license so we needn't wait for—"

"No! I will do no such thing." Violet spun away from her mother, unable to listen to another word. Everything was happening far too fast, hurtling toward her like an unruly stallion who'd broken free of his reins. She wouldn't stay and submit to it, wouldn't allow herself to be trampled.

"Violet?" Arabella's voice, little more than a wavering whisper, trailed after her as she stomped toward the door. "Violet, where are you going?"

To the kitchen, perhaps, to dump a bucket of cold water over her head and awaken herself from this nightmare. Or ideally, to the past, so she could dissuade herself from leaving the picnic for a tryst with George in a dingy old hut.

Even in her state of shock, she recognized the impossibility of such things. However, that didn't mean there was nothing she could do. She would *not* let a misunderstanding change her entire future.

"I'm going to talk some sense into that pudding head George Metcalfe," she said, her footsteps becoming faster, more resolved. Now that she'd gained momentum, she refused to look back. "Good day, Mr. Prescott. I'm sorry to have wasted your time."

"Violet!" Her mother's admonition chased after her,

returning to a pitch that could break glass. "Violet, come back here this instant. You're being unthinkably rude. You still need to give Mr. Prescott your acceptance, and we must plan, and —*Violet*!"

But Violet wouldn't be stopped. She stormed out of the drawing room and straight through the front door, not slowing to collect her bonnet.

She'd made a mistake, and the world had proceeded to go mad around her. It was time to set it back in order.

4

In the late afternoon sunlight, Watley Hall, with its honey-colored stone and rows of mullioned windows, looked as pleasing as ever. The same abode that, through a stroke of unexpected good luck, had welcomed Violet and her sister when they were at their lowest and caused them to believe things could turn bright again.

Curse the place, anyway, Violet inwardly grumbled as she climbed the steps leading to the stately front door. *Curse the mutton-headed gentlemen who reside within.*

She took a moment before reaching for the door knocker to give her skirts a few hasty swipes and push back the errant curls that refused to stay contained in her chignon. As for the redness she felt marring her face—both from exertion and her unrelenting indignation—there wasn't much she could do.

She'd hoped the walk to Watley would help clear her head and bring her a sense of tranquility before she approached George, but it instead seemed to have the opposite effect. Each step she took, each little jolt that shot through her wrenched ankle, reminded her just how *unfair* life could be.

The first disappointment of the year—her father's scandal,

which had caused the viscountess to take her daughters and flee from London in humiliation a full three months before the Season ended—had been bad enough. Violet found it no easy feat to sit in the country while everyone else remained in town enjoying parties and entertainments, and Arabella, whose debut Season had been ruined, felt the loss even more deeply.

However, this second disappointment—this blunder, this setback, this calamity—proved worse again. Perhaps because in the time directly preceding it, they'd allowed themselves to feel so much joy. To garner so many expectations and hopes.

They hadn't been wrong to do so, had they? What was it, if not a cause for hope, when their dashing neighbor, Lord Frederick Denham, tired of London before the Season's end and brought a group of like-minded friends to his estate for a spring house party? Why would they consider themselves anything other than fortunate when Frederick—and for propriety's sake, his widowed older sister, Lady Kingsland—invited Violet and Arabella to join the merriment?

Arabella, who'd developed quite a tendre for Frederick during the Season, had delighted at their reunion. As for Violet, she'd been beyond pleased to encounter George Metcalfe, one of her favorite dance partners who never lacked a witty remark. Their lonely days had suddenly become full, their bleak prospects once more filled with promise.

All until Violet had been foolish enough to agree to a private rendezvous with George, thinking it would solidify their relationship. Imagining he took the risk of being caught alone with her because he planned to propose. Believing he valued their time together more than a blasted archery tournament.

Stupid.

She slammed the knocker against the door, her fingers tight around the cool brass. No sooner had metal hit wood than the door flew open, causing her to stagger backward beneath the butler's stony regard.

"Miss Collingwood." The butler, Andrews, spoke her name as though it left a vile taste in his mouth. "The household is not currently accepting visitors."

"Please." She rushed forward, wedging her foot in the doorway before he could slam the sturdy slab of oak in her face. "This isn't merely a social call but a matter of grave importance. I must speak with Mr. Metcalfe, just for a minute."

"As I said, Miss Collingwood, the household isn't accepting visitors." He glanced at her slipper in distaste, and she wondered if he meant to shut the door on her regardless of the obstacle she presented.

She huffed out a breath, planting her feet more securely against the ground and drawing her spine tall. "And as *I* said, Andrews, this is a matter of grave importance!"

They stared at one another icily, neither of them willing to move. She may be forced to resort to desperate measures. What if she were to take inspiration from her mother and fall into a swoon? Or what if she feigned a sudden burst of weakness in her ankle? Andrews couldn't be so cold that he would allow a viscount's ailing daughter to languish on the doorstep.

She was just about to throw a hand to her forehead and start trembling when a male voice rang out from the entrance hall. "What's going on, Andrews? I thought I heard shouting."

Violet popped onto her tiptoes to peek around the butler's shoulder, and she was met with the sight of Lord Frederick coming down the stairs. *Oh, thank heavens.*

She'd spent many years with a finishing governess and had been raised to exhibit genteel manners and feminine grace. Yet the moment had come when she could afford to display neither. Instead, she used Andrews's brief distractedness as an opportunity to push her way into the entrance hall and reveal herself to its owner.

"Lord Frederick," she said, trying to ignore every bit of her trepidation, her outrage, her shame. Trying to ignore how beneath her skirts, her knees really had started quaking. "Might I have a minute of your time?"

"Miss Collingwood." He bounded down the last few steps to meet her, his lips curving into a frown. "I thought my sister made it clear that this evening's entertainments are canceled." *At least for the likes of you.* He didn't need to utter the last part to make her understand it as plain as day.

"I haven't come looking for dinner or dancing." All the steps she'd run suddenly seemed to catch up with her, and she took a few quick breaths, willing her voice not to falter. "I must speak with Geo—Mr. Metcalfe."

Lord Frederick's scowl deepened. "That's impossible. Metcalfe is upstairs seeing that his bags are packed. He'll return to London on the morrow and has no wish for an audience with you in the meantime."

"I ..." A thousand different words and emotions rushed through her head, but none of them would fully materialize. Was she sorry? Angry? Heartbroken?

She couldn't claim to love George in the way Arabella loved Frederick. Couldn't claim to have wanted a betrothal at all during her first two years on the marriage mart. Most gentlemen, in her estimation, were ne'er-do-wells. *Faithless.* She'd do much better to enjoy her time in society without being tied down to anything so cumbersome as a husband. But in the midst of her third Season—when both her father's scandalous antics and her mother's fretful hypochondria worsened—she'd begun to view the matter differently. While sitting in isolation in Wiltshire, she'd started to think of how a husband, if chosen wisely, could be beneficial. As a married lady, she'd acquire her own household, where never again would she be forced to the country because of her father's poor behavior and her mother's frayed nerves. A husband would give her a new name, a new start. A husband such as George, who was a respectable second son with no rumors of mistresses or other vices attached to his name.

But that future was gone now, and she couldn't deny it: the loss of him stung. Yet if he was so willing to doubt her, to cast her aside without another word ... well, perhaps that was every bit as bad as parading about London and causing scandals with a paramour.

"I regret that his visit to Watley ended so abruptly, especially if today's misunderstanding is the reason for it," she said at last, her tone coated in ice. "I wish he were more inclined to listen to the truth, but if his mind is made up, I won't beg him to change it."

A deep line formed in Lord Frederick's brow. The lone imperfection on a countenance that had known little hardship, for the man's greatest sorrow in life was being born a third son instead of a first. "If that's all, Miss Collingwood," he said, matching her frostiness, "I'll bid you good day."

He pivoted away from her in a single beat, leaving her with a view of the back of his coat.

"Wait." She scrambled forward, rushing to catch up with him at the bottom stair. "You must see that Arabella is blameless in all this."

He did her the courtesy of stopping and turning to her, but the groove in his forehead deepened, and his gray eyes were like steel. "Blameless, perhaps, although by sullying your own good name, you've also defiled hers."

The retort jabbed her chest, but she refused to back down. Refused to shy away from the truth, no matter how uncomfortable. "You were willing to overlook our father's scandal."

He scowled at her gaucheness. "That's different."

"How so?" She looked him up and down, glaring at the

pursed lips and foppish wheat-colored locks that were often the subject of Arabella's poetry. Except without him saying a word, she *knew*. Her father's misdeeds could be swept under the rug. After all, carrying on with mistresses was what peers did. Violet, however, was a *woman*. Therefore, she was automatically hauled over the coals for every slight misstep, every hint of a rumor attached to her name. It was so blasted unjust!

"My father is the Duke of Hawkesbury," he said levelly, as if he hadn't already declared that fact a good three dozen times throughout the course of the house party. "I can hardly stay involved with a woman whose unwedded sister has behaved so shamelessly. Our family must remain above reproach."

How could Arabella stand kissing that mouth? Violet was more of a mind to slap it. Yet this was whom Arabella had chosen. The man to whom she'd devoted countless diary entries. The man she'd sought before all others at every London soiree because he made her smiles brighter.

"Do you love my sister, Lord Frederick?" Violet blurted out the question, then fixed him with another hard stare.

He started, his face taking on a reddish tinge and his eyes pointing to the floor. *Good.* She was glad she'd unsettled him. However, he recovered himself quickly, angling his chin high and meeting her gaze. "My affections for her run very deep, indeed."

"Yet you're willing to let a situation in which Arabella is in no way at fault keep you apart?" It took every bit of restraint Violet had left not to stomp her foot in aggravation.

"Alas. I can do nothing else while scandal taints your name, as much as it may pain me."

Her hands became tight fists, shaking at her sides. It wouldn't pain him nearly so much as a knee to the—

No. Once more, what would she accomplish if she let ire get the better of her? Nothing. She'd best leave while she still had a few shreds of dignity intact.

"Good day, Lord Frederick." She folded herself into a curtsy that was almost ridiculously low. "I thank you for your time."

And then, she spun on her heels and flounced out of the entrance hall, not daring to slow or look back until she was far away from Watley Hall.

Only when she'd reached a solitary field on her own land, and the lone oak tree that grew within, did she allow herself to stop to catch her breath. She leaned against the rough bark, chest heaving, eyes stinging at the corners.

She'd tried to set things right, but she'd failed. Would her mother and sister ever forgive her? Or would the viscountess's anxieties and woefulness grow by the day? Would Arabella's heart break?

She swiped at her eyes, refusing to let tears fall. Sorrow would do her no more good than fury. She needed to keep a level head, for if everyone cared more for appearances than the truth, she required another plan.

She took the rest of the journey back to Meadowleigh slowly, and once there, she claimed a severe headache and fled to her bedchamber. Her mother, who considered health complaints with the utmost seriousness, postponed her torrent of questions and admonitions and left Violet alone to rest.

She didn't rest, though. Instead, she noiselessly paced the floor until the sun sank below the horizon, a collection of faces flashing through her mind. George, shocked and offended. Frederick, contemptuous and smug. Arabella, tearful and distraught.

And then ... then, another visage stared at her, the eyes dark and solemn. The mouth set in a straight line that showed no trace of good humor. *I've come to do the honorable thing and make you an offer of marriage.*

She crawled into bed, wishing she could push every one of

those images away. But as she tossed and turned beneath the bedclothes, *his* was the face that wouldn't disappear. His words were the ones that rang through her head.

Had he meant them sincerely? Would he still mean them now after the reaction she'd given him? He seemed so measured and reserved, yet his proposal was nothing short of rash. But if rashness wasn't a typical part of his character ... did that mean honor was?

A lady could do worse.

Oh, how ridiculous. Why did she pay so much heed to a man she didn't even know? To an offer spoken out of obligation, in haste? *Because he could provide the solution you need.* As much as she didn't want it to, the idea kept sparking to life, a tiny flame nurtured by the winds of desperation.

There was no salvaging her relationship with George—and she no longer wished to salvage it. But what if there was still a chance for Arabella and Frederick?

Somewhere in the blackest hours between dusk and dawn, she made up her mind about what she needed to do. She'd hoped that planning a new path forward would give her even a tiny scrap of comfort, but instead, she grew more restless than ever, and sleep wouldn't come.

Her stomach ached. Bitterness flooded her throat.

The taste of humble pie was unpleasant, indeed.

5

Ben took yet another sheet of paper and tore it into bits, scattering the remnants into the fireplace so the flames could turn them to ash. That accomplished, he slunk back to the desk in the middle of his study and sank into the leather chair, taking up his quill for perhaps the twentieth time.

But it was no use. The words he needed wouldn't come;

there was no explaining a situation that continued causing him a great deal of uncertainty and, frankly, confusion.

He slumped back in his chair with a sigh, surveying the stacks of literature that cluttered his desktop. There were account books to peruse. Farming pamphlets to study. Estate correspondence in need of replies. Yet for all that he'd been a dedicated scholar, he could focus on none of it.

He leaned to the side where his bulldog, Achilles, lay curled up by his feet, and he absently scratched the sleeping animal behind the ears. There was something calming in performing the rhythmic motion. In a world that kept changing and throwing him off balance, the dog at his heels was the one constant.

Achilles had happened upon him by chance when Ben was a mere boy of eleven, providing a much-needed companion to both Ben and his brother Alex when they'd become fatherless children adjusting to life in their stringent grandmother's home. Many years had passed since then, but although Achilles grew slower and a little grayer about the muzzle, he remained ever the faithful friend.

He'd been there waiting at the door upon Ben's unexpected return from Cambridge several weeks ago, wagging his tail while the rest of the family looked on in bafflement.

He'd been there the day when Ben's uncle, the marquess, had shown up at his home on Buckingham Street, looking to give Ben a fresh purpose.

And now, Achilles was here as Ben sat in the countryside, pondering how swiftly and abysmally he'd erred in his new role.

He'd *tried* to right a wrong in the best way he could imagine. How was he to know that Miss Collingwood would receive his proposal as favorably as if he'd asked her to go to London and stroll about Hyde Park in the nude? How could he have predicted that her cheeks would turn very pink, and her eyes would look very blue, and she'd storm away from him while shouting her intentions to revisit the house that had cast her out?

There'd been nothing for him to do in the period following but go home, despite Lady Collingwood's frantic assurances that if he only stayed for dinner, her daughter would return and come to her senses. He may not know Miss Collingwood—*Violet*—well, but he'd discerned enough to suspect that once she made up her mind on something, she didn't easily back down.

Which left him with an unsolved problem. He sank his fingers deeper into the dog's glossy coat, his gaze wandering to the vibrant green fields beyond the window. Unless Violet's darling George—the mere thought of the man made Ben somewhat dyspeptic—had a change of heart, how would she rid herself of the scandal? In turn, how was Ben to salvage his own good name? He could ill afford another smear on it.

"Sir?" His butler's voice drew his attention to the door, eliciting a soft whine from Achilles when the ear scratches stopped. "Forgive the interruption," Pearce said, "but there's a young lady here to see you. A Miss Collingwood."

Ben stiffened in his chair, the name jolting him as if he'd touched his palm to a hot poker. What did this mean? A deluge of possibilities began forming in his head, each one fighting for purchase. However, he pushed them aside, offering a brusque nod. "Thank you, Pearce. Please show her in."

The butler shot him a knowing glance—which should perhaps come as no surprise—before bowing and making his retreat. Rumors seemed to travel in the countryside even faster than if they were printed in a London gossip rag.

But what of it? Ben sprang to his feet, running a hand through his hair and smoothing the sides of his trousers. He would get back to lamenting the virulent spread of gossip *after* his meeting with Violet.

He was just returning his reading spectacles to his pocket when the woman in question walked in, halting a few steps before his desk and standing there like a portrait on display. She'd seldom left his thoughts from the time of their first encounter, but his memory failed to do justice to how bright she appeared. Her gown today was vibrant yellow, the striped fabric subtly highlighting the plushness of her curves. The sun caught the corkscrew curls that hung below her bonnet, making the golden swirls shine. Her eyes were the same clear blue as the afternoon sky, her lips the same soft pink as the peonies blooming in the garden.

Lips she began biting as her eyes fixed uncertainly on the creature at his feet.

Not that Ben could blame her—the dog did have origins in a blood sport arena. However, it was a place for which he couldn't have been more ill-suited because he didn't have an aggressive bone in his body. Presently, Achilles lifted his substantial head, sniffing the air in Violet's direction. Maybe he smelled sweetness.

"Come in, Miss Collingwood." Ben quickly cast away all postulations about feminine scents as he bent to give the dog a few pats, then motioned to the chair on the other side of the desk. "Achilles is harmless, I assure you. He does little these days beyond sleeping."

As if proving Ben's point, Achilles finished his evaluation and, seemingly satisfied, rolled onto his side to doze.

Violet almost smiled at that. He caught the quirk of her mouth and the tiny crinkles at the corners of her eyes. Yet before it fully developed, she rushed forward, accepting the proffered chair with merely a nod. "Thank you. Good day, Mr. Prescott. And Achilles."

"Good day." He returned to his chair, giving his waistcoat

a swift tug to ensure it remained straight and folding his hands against the desktop. And then, when she made no attempt to say anything else ... he waited.

The lady had obviously come for a reason, and he had no wish to play a guessing game as to what that reason was. Especially because his recent assessments weren't particularly sound. Instead, he sat in silence while she adjusted her bonnet. Smoothed her skirts against the chair. Twisted the edge of the airy material within her fingertips. Until finally, her attention returned to him, and words tumbled out. "I fear I was impolite during your visit yesterday."

His brow twitched. Had she come to apologize, then? He gave his head a single brisk shake. "You needn't trouble yourself over it."

She pursed her lips, drawing in an audible breath that made her chest rise and her shoulders tauten. "I fear I was hasty." She exhaled, but the tension didn't leave her body. "When you made me the offer of marriage, did you really mean it?"

Marriage. The mere mention of the word caused him to feel ... he didn't know. Relieved? Terrified? He didn't try to sort it; he made himself focus only on facts. "I wouldn't have extended the offer otherwise."

"But why?" She leaned forward, her elbows hitting the edge of the desktop as she gazed at him. "Why would you choose to spend the rest of your life leg-shackled to a perfect stranger?"

He eyed her levelly, reciting the truth he'd gone over so many times in his head. "Because after what happened yesterday, I'm honor-bound to see that your reputation is restored. It's unfortunate our paths collided when they did and that the situation should have been so misconstrued, but due to the appearance of impropriety between us, I have an obligation to—"

"Yes, very well. You'd best not continue lest your passionate speech cause me to swoon." She returned her spine to ramrod straightness and folded her arms across her chest. "Are you aware that my father, too, is currently embroiled in scandal?"

He blinked, the sudden change of subject enough to make his head spin. "I don't read the gossip rags."

"Let me enlighten you, then. He was caught in flagrante delicto at the Theatre Royal with both his mistress *and* an actress. Simultaneously."

No, Ben certainly hadn't known that. How ... *adventurous*. Yet if Violet thought the revelation would make him rescind his offer, she'd miscalculated.

He blew out a short exhale, pressing his knuckles more firmly into the desktop. "I'm not sure how familiar you are with my uncle, the Marquess of Rockliffe, or the rest of the Prescott family, but there's been plenty of scandal attached to us over the years. My name hasn't remained clear of it." Which was true this month more than ever. Ben could still recall every detail of the day he and Alex had been called to the provost's office. The way Dr. Thackeray had clutched the offending literature in his palm and grimly relayed his discovery. *I'm certain one of you is responsible.*

"As my mother enjoys gossip rags, I know a little about your family," Violet said, causing the memory to shatter and pulling him back to the study. "But to quote another of your amorous declarations, *Given the circumstances, I'm not sure we can allow that to matter.*"

He paused, a small knot tugging at his chest. It was all very well to decide he'd ignore feelings in favor of facts. When it came down to it, though, he couldn't overlook the shadow that passed over her features or the tight lines that formed at the edges of her mouth.

He cleared his throat, suddenly feeling as though he'd

swallowed a spoonful of sand. "I'm not trying to force you into something you find abhorrent. If we married ... I wouldn't wish for you to be unhappy."

She made a little sound at that, her eyes becoming especially wide. Especially sharp and blue. Until suddenly, the tension in her limbs seemed to melt away, and she slumped against the chair back. "I wouldn't wish you unhappiness, either." She let out a long sigh. "Did you not hope for a love match?"

His head spun anew, and though he remained planted firmly in his chair, he felt as if she'd pulled a rug out from beneath his feet. *A love match*. Like his mother had found with his father and later his stepfather, Jeremy. Like his uncle, the marquess, had found with the marchioness.

The type of match that made a person gad about all day as if walking on air and retire each evening with a smile on their face.

The type of match a person could seek if they knew where they belonged and had nothing holding them back.

Yet when a person's future was uncertain, when one was tugged in two different directions and neither seemed right, such a thing stayed well out of reach. In cases such as those, there was no alternative but to remain at university and concentrate on one's studies because anything beyond that proved far too difficult.

"It's not something I've given much consideration," he said tightly, opting for the truth in its simplest form.

"Do you have a mistress, Mr. Prescott?"

The woman was nothing if not blunt. "No."

Her cheeks colored, a rosy pink that spread toward her temples, but she didn't look away or relax her gaze. "I realize I'm in no position to make demands, but even so, on this I must insist. I refuse to have another woman paraded before me. I will not tolerate that humiliation."

He gritted his teeth, swallowing thickly before his face could mimic hers and redden. An image cropped up in his head: Violet's name bound to his in the parish register but some faceless woman—*not* Violet—upon his arm. The thought caused his stomach to churn.

"You have my word, Miss Collingwood." He tugged on his cravat, which had become tight about his throat. "I would never do such a thing."

She gave him another moment of assessment before, at last, the light in her eyes softened, and her voice turned quieter than it had been previously. "No, you wouldn't, would you?" Her palm returned to the desktop, and he didn't know what was happening beyond that her fingers were inching toward his, and he could detect the honeyed scent of flowers.

He stared at her glove, at the absent-minded movement, and he could already envision the moment their hands collided. Could almost feel what would surely be softness.

Except then, she retreated instead of moving forward, folding her hands tightly upon her lap. "I suppose there's nothing left, then," she said, "but for me to give a sentimental discourse of my own. My sister desires, above all else, to marry Lord Frederick Denham, something the *charming* man will not abide while I continue to sully the family name. As our father's scandal has made her other prospects bleak, and I don't wish to be the cause of her heartbreak, I can see no way to remedy the situation but my own marriage. And because George Metcalfe refuses to hear reason, it seems my marriage will need to be to you."

Ben appreciated plain speech and logic. Nonetheless, something about her declaration felt so ... empty. Enough to create a pang in his gut.

But why was he getting caught up on such a thing now? He and Violet each had a problem, and they'd devised a solution. There was no need to involve sentimentality.

"Shall I write to your father?" he asked, carefully inhaling *away* from the woman across from him. "If he gives his consent, I can inform the local vicar of our intentions."

"Write to my father if you want to ensure my dowry is to your liking, but the *consent* part is a mere formality. I turned one-and-twenty last month so do not require his permission, and he's so zealously occupied in London that I doubt he cares either way. Besides ..." She peered at her skirt. Bit her lip. Brought her eyes to him once more. "I wondered if we should forgo the banns and wed by license before the gossip surrounding our union has a chance to grow."

A license. A document that would see them wed within a week. He hadn't considered anything quite so precipitous. As a man of three-and-twenty, he didn't require permission to wed, either, but what would his mother and stepfather say when they found out? His younger brothers? And what would Uncle Rockliffe say? To marry in such a timeframe would mean doing so without the knowledge or blessing of those Ben valued most. And yet ...

Why did he need to trouble them with another scandal? Why subject them to his fears and uncertainties, to his distinct sense that without Cambridge, he was inches from being caught in an ocean current that would tow him beneath the waves? Wouldn't it be better for him to approach them all with a solution instead of a problem?

"Quite sensible, Miss Collingwood," he said before deliberations on the matter plagued him any further. First and foremost, it *was* sensible to quell slanderous talk before it got out of hand. "I'll seek the bishop tomorrow."

"Very good." She shifted in her chair, pressing her palms against the carved wooden arms. "All is agreed upon, then, and I'll not keep you any longer. Thank you, Mr. Prescott."

He watched her push to her feet and hastily followed suit, stepping around Achilles's prostrate body. Should he join her on the other side of the desk? A decision this momentous seemed to require a gesture of some sort. A handshake? The type two business partners would share to solidify an agreement.

If this were the love match she'd alluded to, perhaps she would throw her arms around him, and he'd return her enthusiasm by sweeping her into a kiss. An action that would be rough and passionate, in contrast to her mouth, which he knew beyond a doubt would be soft.

As matters stood, he settled on a bow. The same stiff inclination of his head that he gave to the vicar on Sundays. She offered a curtsy in return, decorous enough to greet the queen.

There were no more words after that. She simply spun on her heel and exited the study as hastily as she'd entered it. Leaving behind only a faint floral scent and the memory of all that had just transpired.

He returned to his chair and perched his spectacles on his nose, but he didn't attempt reading or correspondence. For instead of tiny black words on a white page, all he could see was color. Cerulean eyes. Golden curls. A yellow gown.

A stranger.

A spot of light.

His future wife.

6

"The pearls or the amethysts?" Arabella stepped in front of the mirror in which Violet had been gazing, holding out an ornamented bandeau in each palm.

"The ..." *I don't care*, Violet had been about to say, but seeing her sister's eager face, she listlessly pointed at the purple gems. "The amethysts, I suppose."

"Excellent choice." Arabella darted behind her, pulling the bandeau over Violet's coiffure and arranging it artfully atop her head. "There. You're going to make the prettiest bride. Are you pleased?"

Violet returned to peering in the mirror at the corner of her sister's bedchamber, surveying her finery. The lilac gown with the lacy overskirt and bodice. The small pendant at her throat that glinted beneath the candlelight. Her mass of hair that, with great effort from her lady's maid, Edith, had been contained in a series of elegant knots.

The image staring back at her was her own, most assuredly. But at the same time, she felt a sense of detachment. As if the girl preparing for her wedding tomorrow was someone else entirely.

"Oh!" Arabella's cry snapped Violet away from her musings, and her sister released the bandeau, pressing her hands together in delight. "Do you know what would make you even lovelier? If we added flowers to your hair. I'll go down to the garden and cut a few irises."

"There's no need to trouble yourself at this hour." Violet shook her head, the mirror image copying the motion. Reminding her that *she*, in fact, was the one soon to get married.

"Nonsense. It will only take a moment, and I'll bring a lantern. It's best you try them now so you can see what you think, and your ensemble will be exactly as you wish it when you get ready tomorrow."

Any further protests Violet thought to make were vanquished by Arabella's rapid departure. Her sister had grown particularly light of foot over the past few days, flitting about almost like one of the springtime butterflies that appeared in the garden.

And why shouldn't Arabella be happy? A mere two days after news of Violet's impending nuptials spread, Lord Frederick had written to his sweetheart to invite her for a game of pall-mall as if no rift had ever occurred. Since then, Arabella had been at Watley Hall for two luncheons, three dinners, and a musicale, her smile growing brighter each time she returned home to relay all the charming things Lord Frederick had said and done. Her dreams of a betrothal had been restored. Consequently, their mother hadn't complained of a single megrim or ague all week.

Violet frowned into the mirror, giving the bandeau an impatient tug to the side. She couldn't begrudge Arabella some happiness. Only, she was tired of dressing up this evening. She knew Arabella meant it as a kindness, that she'd summoned Violet to her bedchamber and inundated her with a selection of jewelry and other fripperies because she wanted her to experience the same excitement over her wedding that Arabella would surely feel when it came time for hers.

However, Violet's stays—which their mother had instructed Edith to tie tighter when she'd popped in earlier—pinched, and she'd had enough. She *knew* her hips were wider than the fashion, that her bosom was overlarge, and she wouldn't protest tomorrow as she was finagled and laced into her gown. Tonight, though—her last night in her mother's country house as an unmarried woman—was another matter altogether.

"Edith?" she called, kicking off her satin slippers with the too-tight toes and spinning away from the mirror. After helping Violet dress and completing the hard-fought task of making her hair look presentable, the lady's maid had removed herself to Violet's room to turn down her bed and ensure her trunks were packed. But while her bedchamber was situated directly across the corridor from Arabella's, she received no answer.

"Edith?" She tried again, padding out to the corridor in her stockinged feet and easing open her partially closed door. However, her bedchamber sat vacant, the bedclothes still tucked tight over the pillows. *Drat.* Where had the maid gone? If she didn't return soon, Violet would be forced to wait for her sister to come help her, and Arabella seemed disinclined to bring their fashion endeavors to an end.

She slunk back to the threshold of the corridor, peering up and down the frustratingly empty space.

Which was the precise moment a giggle emerged from the direction of the stairway.

She bounded toward the sound, her eyes darting in all directions, trying to adjust to the low light from the sconces. Had she not been so intent, perhaps she wouldn't have noticed Edith tucked into a shadowed alcove with a chamber-maid hovering beside her, a tiny glow emerging from the candle they shared. Their backs were turned, and they left just enough space between their bodies for Violet to see they each held something that commanded their attention. Pamphlets, it looked like. And amusing ones at that, for another stifled peal of laughter broke out between them.

Violet gave her foot a pointed tap against the floorboards, and when that did nothing, she cleared her throat.

At once, the two women whirled around to face her, their giggles becoming startled gasps.

"Miss Collingwood." Edith's voice had a strange, wobbly quality, and though she was quick to bend into a curtsy, she nearly tripped over her feet while doing so. "Did you require my assistance?"

Violet said nothing, merely studied the two maids, who both stared back looking like a pair of foxes who'd been caught pillaging a henhouse. For a moment, no one moved a muscle.

Until suddenly, the chambermaid shoved the candle and papers into Edith's hands, then bobbed an ungainly curtsy of her own. "B-begging your pardon, miss," she said, the words ending on a noise that was part hiccup, part squeak. And then, she fled down the stairs before Violet could so much as blink.

Edith's mouth opened. Closed. Her face turned from the color of whey to that of a summer strawberry, and Violet was no longer certain whether her lady's maid looked like a fox caught scavenging or the hen that was about to be made into the fox's dinner.

She placed her hands on her hips, eyeing the pamphlets within Edith's trembling fist. "What do you have there?"

"I ..." The blood drained from Edith's cheeks once more. Yes, she'd definitely become the hen.

"I insist on seeing it at once." Violet wedged herself into the alcove to take the place the chambermaid had just vacated, her chest burning with an equal mixture of impatience and curiosity. Fortunately, when she reached for the collection of pamphlets, they slid from Edith's fingers without resistance.

She leaned toward her lady's maid, bringing the open pamphlet close to the candle until the flame illuminated a passage in the middle of the page. *His hand glided over skin smooth as cream, slipping between glistening thighs and traveling to her netherlips—*

"Dear Lord!" She coughed, choked, and spluttered all at the same time, her side hitting the wall as she gave a startled jump. Her hands, like Edith's, became shaky, and she tightened her grip, adjusting the pamphlet's position in the sparse light so she could read another passage.

She moaned her desire, her cries intensifying as he circled the heart of her pleasure—

Violet nearly tore the page in her haste to close the pamphlet, her attention going to the large letters upon the cover. "*The Scandalous Scholar?*" She shot Edith an incredulous glance, then rifled through the remaining pamphlets in the pile, each one containing the same bold typography to denote the title. "*The Naughty Vicar, The Illicit Earl, Mrs. Rumpteaser's Footman, Three Merry Kitchen Maids ... and a Groom?*"

Her eyes went wide. Cheeks grew hot. Belly became even hotter. She'd known things like this existed, but she'd never read ... never seen ...

And now, she was standing in the corridor holding a whole collection of erotic literature when Arabella might return at any moment, as could their mother.

"Come with me," she hissed, tugging Edith's arm. Fortunately, the startled maid followed her rapid footsteps without missing a beat, all the way back to the safety of Violet's bedchamber.

She threw the door closed with a noisy click, then let her weight sink against it, taking several deep gulps of air. "It's fortunate my mother didn't choose this time to come up from the drawing room, for had she been the one to discover your activities in that alcove, she may well have had an apoplexy." She tried to make her expression stern, although she didn't doubt she looked flustered. Flushed. Besides, she had much less interest in chastising Edith than in satisfying her curiosity. "Where on earth did you get these?"

"From Lord Frederick's valet," Edith blurted out, then clamped a hand over her mouth. Her complexion reddened beneath Violet's shrewd gaze, but Violet refused to relent. Not until Edith made free with the rest of the story.

She waited with all the patience she could summon while Edith slowly lowered the hand from her face, giving in to Violet's silent demand that she continue. "I suppose I should say from Lord Frederick's cousin's valet," Edith said, "who got them while serving his master at Cambridge. He gave them to Lord Frederick's valet when they all met in London at Easter, and Lord Frederick's valet then gave them to Lady Kingsland's lady's maid when they journeyed to Watley. He's sweet on her, you know. She told me all about it because we've grown to be friends, which is why she shared the pamphlets with me so I could—"

"I see," Violet mumbled, trying to keep straight the deluge of names hurtling her way. She was feeling a touch dizzy. Also, why had she asked for a fire to be lit in her room? The evening's sunset had brought with it an unseasonable chill in the air, yet her bedchamber had turned stifling.

"I'm so sorry, miss," Edith said earnestly. "Please don't be angry. I know we all did wrong, but we didn't mean any harm, I swear. We just couldn't help but be curious when we discovered the author."

"The author?" Violet quirked a brow, taking another hasty look at the text on each pamphlet's cover. "These were published anonymously."

"Yes, but ..." Edith's words faded to silence, and her mouth became an *o*. "You don't know?"

Violet bit back a frustrated sigh. "No." Since when had her lady's maid developed a penchant for talking in riddles? "Kindly enlighten me."

Edith hesitated for an aggravatingly long moment before leaning toward her ear, her voice becoming an overloud whisper. "The author was recently determined to be Mr. Benedict Prescott."

Violet's body jerked, and her fingers reflexively loosened, sending the pamphlets fluttering to the carpet in a disordered, salacious pile. "That's impossible."

Edith shook her head intently. "No, no, it must be true, miss. It's the whole reason he was sent down from Cambridge last month. Like I said, Lord Frederick's cousin is also a Cambridge scholar, which is where he got the pamphlets to give his valet, and his valet gave them to ..."

Edith continued speaking, but Violet could no longer decipher a word. Her mind raced with too much other information to reconcile. Such as the fact that Benedict Prescott had been expelled from university. For writing erotic pamphlets.

The same Benedict Prescott who used excessive starch in his cravats. Who probably considered a treatise on foot rot titillating literature. Who'd agreed to their betrothal as detachedly as if he were arranging for the purchase of a flock of Cotswold Lions.

"Violet?" Arabella's singsong voice rang through the corridor. "Violet, where have you gone?"

Panic froze Violet's limbs for a single instant before she dove to the floor, scooping up the pile of pamphlets and racing across the room. Her eyes darted around wildly from her bed to her night table to her vanity. In a split-second decision, she shoved the pamphlets beneath her pillow and rushed to the vanity in the corner, plopping herself upon the bench and pivoting to face the mirror.

"I'm in my bedchamber," she called, forcing her shoulders to straighten and motioning for Edith to open the door.

"I've brought the irises, along with some ..." Arabella trailed off, her approaching footfalls halting in the middle of the room. "Are you both well?"

"Yes, of course." Violet's declaration sounded a touch pinched, but it was the best she could do. Without turning around or even seeking Edith's reflection in the glass—for she didn't think she could face her lady's maid again without her skin becoming crimson—she said, "Thank you, Edith, for your assistance. I won't require anything else this evening, so you may go."

She assumed the subsequent rustle came from Edith's curtsy, which was quickly replaced by the sound of her footsteps flying into the corridor and fading away. Not that Violet faulted her for her wish to escape—she'd do the same if she could.

She picked up a perfume bottle—anything to prevent her fingers from fidgeting, to keep from remembering how it felt when she held the pamphlets within her grasp and read the words they contained—and turned to face her sister.

Luckily, Arabella's eagerness to plan wedding attire over-shadowed any suspicion she may feel that something was amiss, and Violet let her pin flowers as she wished, managing an appropriate reply to her exclamations when required. Violet no longer even noticed her tight stays. Nor could she be certain, when at last the primping and coddling ended, what arrangement of flowers she'd agreed to.

She had Arabella stay to help her change from her wedding finery to her nightgown, then bid her sister good-night for perhaps the last time she would ever do so under this roof.

With Arabella gone, she was free to climb into bed and embrace the thoughts that had inundated her from the moment Edith leaned in and whispered, *Mr. Benedict Prescott.* Thoughts of stiff bows and even stiffer cravats. Thoughts of caresses, nude flesh, *pleasure.*

She lifted her head so she could slide the pamphlets out from beneath her pillow and sank back down with one of the scandalous works in hand. Thinking herself helpful, Arabella had extinguished Violet's bedside lamp and the sconces before departing, which left only the flames in the grate for light.

Flames that remained strong enough, though, to illuminate the title. *Mrs. Rumpteaser's Footman.* How provocatively named. Yet the title was secondary to the letters beneath. She traced them with her finger, following each line and curve. *By an author who shall remain anonymous.*

She flipped to the first page, squinting so she could make out the smaller print within and beginning to read. Wondering whom, exactly, she was marrying come morning.

7

Dear Ben,

I fear my eyesight is failing me. For I __thought__ your latest missive revealed you were to be married, and no matter how many times I stare at the page to rectify my misunderstanding, I cannot make your words say otherwise.

Which cannot be correct. When you left London, you gave no indication you were so much as considering a courtship, let alone something more.

Timothy has an ague, which is the only reason I have not yet boarded a coach bound for Wiltshire so I can gain some insight into what, exactly, is going on. There's clearly much you haven't told me, and I think we should have a discussion before you do anything rash. Please write to me at your earliest convenience— actually, hang convenience. Write to me __immediately__ and tell me what in blazes has transpired.

Your loving (but utterly perplexed) mother

Ben sank into his desk-side chair, running the letter between his fingertips. Trying to reconcile himself with the fact that, despite his mother's entreaties, he was now a married man.

How in hell would he pen a satisfactory reply explaining that the wedding had already taken place? Frankly, he hadn't a clue.

He cast the letter aside, squeezing his eyes closed and drumming his fingers against the desktop. It was difficult to find the right words when, truth be told, his status as husband had yet to feel real.

When he discovered this morning that the rustling in the adjoining bedchamber came from chambermaids preparing a room for his *wife*, he'd felt as though he were a guest looking in on someone else's home.

When he'd first encountered Violet at the church— covered in lace and flowers, with golden spirals framing her face—and watched her walk to the altar, he'd felt like he was viewing a pantomime rather than living out a pivotal moment.

When he'd spoken his vows, the voice seemed to come from somewhere other than his own throat, and the feminine replies had echoed as if from far away.

Hours had passed, twilight fallen, and the house had grown so quiet he could almost think himself the only person in it. As if he, and not his young brother Timothy, were the one with the ague, and delirium had caused him to imagine the day's events.

Yes, he could *almost* think that. Almost, except for the little details that kept springing up in his memory, too vivid to be false. The deep purple of the irises in her hair. The coolness of the gold wedding band, the warmth of her skin as he'd slipped it onto her finger. The scratch of the quill as she'd signed the register. All proof he had a wife.

A wife who'd ridden home with him in the landau in near silence, taken a tour with the housekeeper, and retreated to her bedchamber, declining the need for dinner. Even though she'd consumed little besides champagne during the wedding breakfast at Meadowleigh.

For that matter, Ben had been disinclined to eat much at the breakfast either, despite the food being well-prepared and plentiful, and he'd requested nothing since beyond a strong cup of tea and dry toast. His throat was gravelly, his stomach unsettled. A natural reaction, he supposed, when one had the sense of drifting deeper into the ocean in a rowboat with no paddle.

He didn't know what he was doing here. What the eventual outcome of his time at Aldercombe would be. What he wanted from the future. And if he didn't know his own place in the world, how was he to offer a happy, prosperous future to another? Especially to a woman who'd dreamed of marrying elsewhere.

He opened his eyes to relieve the tension in his brow and pushed his spectacles up his nose. He'd had little success concentrating on ledgers and agricultural pamphlets over the past week, or even the novels he typically enjoyed, but he may as well try again.

He selected one of the lengthier books on his desk, an in-depth tome about farming, and flipped it open at random, attempting to focus on the words within. *Turnip crops ... strong soils ... fermentation ...*

"What are you reading?" The sharp voice wrenched his attention away from the page, and he looked up to find Violet hovering near the other side of the desk, studying him intently.

She'd changed from her wedding gown to her nightclothes and removed all the adornments from her hair. For the first time since he'd met her, she wore no color, only white. Yet that only made her golden hair shine brighter in the candlelight and her eyes seem even purer a blue.

"A farming manual," he supplied after clearing his throat, although his words came out more like a question than a statement. Did he imagine things, or had her query held an accusatory ring?

"May I see?" Without waiting for his reply, she scurried around to his side of the desk, leaning over his shoulder to peer at the text. He watched her lips part and brows rise. "*The Treating of Dunghills.*" Her nose wrinkled, and she quickly took a step back. "Fascinating."

He snapped the book closed, pushing it beneath a stack of ledgers. It wasn't as if he'd derive any knowledge from it tonight. Especially not now, with her standing so near. She was close enough that he got a strong whiff of her floral perfume—lavender, perhaps—and he wondered if she'd recently been in the bath, for the curls around her face looked damp.

A skittish sensation shot across his chest. He hadn't expected to see her in his study, and now that she was here, he felt ... unnerved?

No, that wasn't right. Well, yes, it was, because having her in his study in her dressing gown certainly proved unnerving, but at the heart of it, he also felt ... *glad*. He hadn't liked thinking of her shut away in her bedchamber, refusing to eat. Hadn't known what to make of her wan face and near-silence as he'd conveyed her to Aldercombe Grange after the wedding breakfast, as if the fiery spirit he'd witnessed during their previous encounters had been doused.

The fact that she'd emerged from her room and sought him out was a promising development. He had no illusions that her disappointment over their circumstances had waned, nor did he have any idea how to rectify matters. But at least her presence here was a start.

"Did you require something?" he asked. He may not be able to give her the marriage she'd envisioned, but he could at least ensure she had every comfort while she was under this roof. Whatever money could buy.

She straightened her shoulders, her chest rising as she took a breath. "Yes. I wanted to ask ..." All that followed was a stuttering exhale, and she bunched her fingers around the belt of her dressing gown, twisting them in the fabric. "Never mind. Perhaps we could have a drink to toast our union."

That much, he could provide. In part, anyway. He rose from his chair, going to the cabinet in the corner that had been stocked with spirits prior to his arrival. "What's your drink of choice?" He crouched down to rifle through the bottles, searching for whatever would prove most suitable. "Sherry? Orange wine? Madeira?"

"Do you have brandy?"

He glanced over his shoulder to where she remained by his desk, arms folded across her chest. Eyes upon him, holding a hint of challenge. Was she waiting for him to deny her? He couldn't imagine she imbibed brandy while out in society. But rather than make a comment to that effect, he turned his attention to selecting a glass and filling it from the bottle at the front of the cabinet. The one placed there for his use. The drink of gentlemen.

"Would you like to sit?" He stood abruptly, motioning to the pair of leather armchairs positioned beside the hearth. Although it wasn't a cold night, a low fire burned in the grate, providing an extra bit of comfort to Achilles, who lay stretched on the rug before it to absorb the warmth.

Violet accepted the invitation, her hips swaying gently as she crossed the room to take the glass from him and her dressing gown rustling softly as she lowered herself into a chair. He followed behind her, giving Achilles a cursory scratch on the ears before taking the other seat. He allowed himself a moment to smooth his waistcoat and place his reading spectacles back in his pocket.

Only to find, once he'd finished, that Violet was gazing at

him, her mouth twisted into a frown. "You don't have a glass for yourself."

"No." He swallowed, the same long-ago recollection assaulting him the way it always did when the topic arose. The stillness of the dusky study. The heavy, stringent odor. The overturned bottle, the limp hand hanging from the desktop.

He shook his head, forcing himself away from the room in his memory and back to the study at Aldercombe. With Violet. "I don't partake of alcohol. But please, drink to the marriage on behalf of us both."

She paused, her brows giving the slightest twitch. But then, with a little shrug, she raised the glass in the air and tipped it to her lips.

Her face contorted instantly, and a strangled sound emerged from her throat.

"Is it not to your liking?" It was rude to gawk, but he couldn't help but stare at the deep flush coloring her skin and the hand she pressed to her chest as she tried to stifle a cough.

"It's splendid," she choked out in a voice that relayed the exact opposite. Nonetheless, she returned the glass to her lips as if proving her point, taking another brisk swallow. She was better prepared this time, enough that her momentary grimace was hardly distinguishable. "Thank you, Mr. Prescott."

"You needn't call me that," he said more gruffly than he intended. He didn't know why her words unsettled him the way they did. She'd always addressed him as such. It was the proper title to use. Yet given their newfound status as husband and wife, wasn't it also a touch formal? He inhaled, taking care to gentle his tone. "It's Benedict."

"Very well. *Benedict*." She said his name with a hint of breath, and a lick of warmth snaked through his gut. "In that case, I must ask you to call me Violet. Assuming you're comfortable dispensing with the formality of *Mrs. Prescott*."

"I prefer Violet." He let himself answer honestly, to utter

the name by which he always referred to her in his head. As he suspected, it had an agreeable ring on his tongue. "Mr. and Mrs. Prescott are my parents. At least, they were at one point …"

His momentary pleasure faded and his throat seized, the tightness radiating down his chest and deep into his abdomen. Why had his mind wandered in such a direction? Furthermore, why had he alluded to it out loud? While he'd spent little time out in high society, he was well aware that the rise and fall of his parents' scandalous marriage had been a talking point amongst the ton for years. After all, there were few things more shocking than a marquess's second son forsaking his family so he could marry a lowborn woman and become a poet. Few things, perhaps, except the aristocrat-turned-poet dropping dead a decade later, leaving behind such copious debts that his widow was forced back to his estranged family for help.

Violet had said her mother enjoyed the gossip rags; therefore, the viscountess had likely recounted the sordid tale. He'd accomplish nothing by speaking of it, nothing but letting her into a place within him that was raw and vulnerable, and that was something he couldn't abide.

But if his veiled reference to the scandal had piqued Violet's curiosity or made her eager to glean additional fodder for gossip, nothing in her countenance suggested as much. In fact, she simply looked … thoughtful.

"I understand that your mother is Mrs. Clare now," she said after a pause, the firelight making her features bright and illuminating a few drops of brandy upon her lips. "She's made quite a name for herself in London."

So, Violet was familiar with that part of the saga, too. The way his mother, after another falling out with the Prescott family matriarch—the fearsome dowager marchioness—had found success and independence as a book illustrator and portrait artist. How she'd remarried a novelist—and Ben and Alex's former tutor, of all people—and they'd proceeded to establish a thriving printshop. The situation suited them well, even though it kept them far removed from being considered equals amidst the ton.

Ben bristled, his gaze turning from her firelit face to the flames themselves. He'd received no small amount of taunting on the subject during his first months at Eton, and he was used to people with pure blue blood thinking him inferior. However, he detected no judgment or condescension in Violet's tone. On the contrary, she sounded awed.

"Yes," he said, knowing he should offer more. He could tell her he was proud of his mother's strength and determination, and that he considered himself fortunate beyond measure for the devoted stepfather—and later, two half-brothers—he'd acquired. Their terrace house on Buckingham Street wasn't luxurious, but he'd never wished for anything different, for they'd all been happy there.

Happy until the time came when they could no longer ignore the truth. When life had tugged him in another direction, into a world of peerages and estates. In other words, the exact things his father had sworn to avoid and wanted his children to stay clear of.

Perhaps Violet deserved more of a conversation, but how was Ben to speak of all this to his new wife without one thing leading to another? How was he to explain that he was part of the ton yet not part of it? That he didn't truly belong on Buckingham Street *or* behind a marquess's desk. That he could either accept his responsibilities as his uncle's heir or honor his father's memory and wishes, but it was impossible to do both.

The topic wound him in knots, a problem without a solution that kept him awake late into the night. Presently, it made his throat turn dry—and for a flash of a moment, he wished he, too, had a glass of brandy in hand.

And so, while Violet's comment may warrant more than a one-word answer, that was all he gave. All he *could* give, for everything else was his alone, locked deep inside.

"Might we visit London?" Her question broke the silence between them, floating above the quiet pop of flames and Achilles's soft snore.

He turned to her, and for a few seconds, he imagined it. Strolling in Hyde Park, visiting the family printshop on Fleet Street, getting ices at Gunter's, all with Violet on his arm.

Yet he doubted she had the same things in mind while posing the question. If he returned to London, he would no longer be the boy who rambled through parks and stained his fingers with printer's ink. He would be there as the husband of a viscount's daughter. As a future marquess. His whole purpose would be to immerse himself in society events as if he belonged there. Thus, bringing him back to his primary dilemma.

"Someday, perhaps." He didn't quite look her in the eye while giving the vague answer. "The estate business will take at least until the end of the London Season, if not longer. And given your desire to rid your name of scandal, I think it would be unwise for you to travel there alone."

"Of course." She raised her glass again with a jerky motion, swallowing the remainder of the brandy. "How silly of me to have brought it up."

Had he disappointed her? She clenched her fingers around the edge of the glass, quietly tapping the crystal with her nails. She peered at the amber droplets that remained on the bottom rather than at him.

"Are you certain there's not something you need?" He changed the subject abruptly, straightening his already rigid spine against the chair back, forcing himself to look at her and not shy away. He couldn't talk about the past or future, his family or his fears. He could, however, gift her updated furniture for her bedchamber. A new mare. Trinkets for her sister. Whatever she desired.

She bit down on her lip. "No. Yes." Her hand went back to her dressing gown, looping the belt around her fingers, and her face took on the same hesitant cast as the first time he'd posed the question. "I wanted to ask you ... That is, I wanted to say ..."

She trailed off, but he didn't prod her. He sat and waited, wanting her to understand she had nothing to fear by asking for something that would add to her comfort.

"I plan to go to sleep soon," she burst out, "but I wondered if I should wait up for you."

The wheels in his head turned like cogs in a poorly oiled machine. Violet hadn't requested he *buy* her anything. Rather, she was going to bed, and she wondered ... *oh*.

"I mean, to perform my wifely duty," she mumbled when his silence lasted too long.

Yes, he'd arrived at that conclusion. Albeit a beat later than what was ideal.

Of all the things she could have asked, he hadn't expected *that*. Although perhaps he should have. They hadn't discussed the nature of their union, but given the circumstances, he'd just assumed it would remain a marriage in name only. However, it was natural for her to conclude that a marquess's heir would want heirs of his own.

He tried to picture it. Violet sprawled atop crisp sheets in the darkness. The belt of her dressing gown in his fingers instead of hers so he could pull it open, leaving her bare. The warmth of her beneath him, flesh against flesh. Cries of pleasure, a yearning within him that heated and swelled—

But he didn't even *know* her. Didn't know how to summon that sense of yearning with a stranger.

Besides, she didn't want him. She wanted *George*.

"No, that's unnecessary." God, his voice sounded thick. Almost as if it were about to crack. He clamped his lips together before he did anything embarrassing.

As for Violet, he could just make out the sharp intake of her breath. The slight tremble of her chin. Had he been a betting man, he would have wagered a large sum that his declaration would give her relief. However, the glint in her eyes suggested something different, something he couldn't name. Surprise? Anger? *Hurt*? Surely not.

Whatever it was, it lasted only an instant before she shuttered her features, her lips becoming a tight line. "Good. I needn't be inconvenienced, then."

The words hit him like an ice shard between the ribs. But there was no time to analyze them, no time to form a reply, before she sprang to her feet, giving him a curt nod. "I'm going to bed. Goodnight, Mr. Prescott."

He opened his mouth, but no sound came out. He could do naught but observe as Violet pivoted away from him and marched across the study, stopping just long enough to deposit her empty glass atop his desk.

Wait. I didn't mean … I don't want … So many half-formed thoughts raced through his head, but none would materialize into a coherent sentence. And so, not for the first time, he watched her disappear, the hem of her gauzy dressing gown trailing behind her.

Only when her footsteps faded into nothingness and he allowed himself to slump forward, pressing his fingers into Achilles's fur, did his voice return.

"Call me Benedict," he muttered to her vacant chair.

8

As much as Violet wished to stay in bed with her head buried beneath the covers for, oh, another three decades or so, she forced herself down to the breakfast room early the next morning. Prepared to face her husband.

However, when she entered the sunny room with the large, oblong table and well-stocked sideboard, it was empty of anyone save for a footman.

"Good morning, madam." The footman—*Thomas*, she remembered, from her introduction to the servants yesterday—bowed courteously. "Would you like me to serve you?"

Delicious smells wafted from the sideboard, but she hesitated, the tentative confidence she'd summoned while dressing dissolving like sugar in a teacup. "Perhaps I should wait for Mr. Prescott."

Thomas's brow gave the slightest lift. "Mr. Prescott has come and gone, madam. He said he had an early meeting with his land agent."

"Right. I must have forgotten." She conjured a semblance of a smile, taking mechanical steps toward the sideboard. Above all else, she wouldn't give the staff additional cause to speculate on what must already appear a sham of a marriage. "I'll serve myself, thank you. But perhaps you could get me a fresh pot of tea. I like it especially hot."

"Of course. I'll return with it directly." Thomas bowed again and disappeared through a door that blended with the wainscoting.

With the room well and truly empty, she released a shaky breath before hurrying to the sideboard and tossing a slice of toast and a spoonful of eggs onto a plate. She wasn't particularly hungry, nor did she have a true desire for piping hot tea. Her real craving was for a moment of solitude while she reworked her expectations of how breakfast was to proceed.

She sank into a chair at the foot of the table, taking a nibble of toast that turned to sawdust in her mouth. Wasn't it a good thing that she could avoid seeing her husband after their mortifying encounter last night? If anything, she should be flitting about the breakfast room with a weight removed from her chest.

However, she'd spent the better part of a sleepless night, and then the entirety of her time getting ready at her vanity this morning, quelling her anxieties and steeling herself for how she would act when they came face to face. How she would look him in the eye and comment on the weather, and it would be as if her question in the darkness of his study, and his subsequent rejection, didn't matter in the least. The fact that the man she'd envisioned—slicked back hair, tightly knotted cravat, ironed newspaper in hand—wasn't here, and that their next meeting would take place at an undetermined time, meant she had to undergo another agonizing, lonely stretch in which her worries built right back up.

She abandoned her toast, turning to peer mindlessly at the garden beyond the window. Drat Benedict Prescott. Drat him! He'd made it clear how he viewed her: as an obligation, nothing more. And even so, she'd been foolish enough to go to him. To suggest ...

Her cheeks burned, and not from the sunlight streaming through the glass. Why should she have expected anything from him beyond aloofness? Beyond the strictest propriety? He'd met most of her questions with non-answers. The mention of intimacy clearly horrified him. And yet ...

And yet, there'd been that one easy moment where a single brick in the wall that sequestered him crumbled away. *It's Benedict*, he'd said.

Benedict. The name she pictured in print, taking the place of *by an author who shall remain anonymous*. The name that mixed with the other words in the lines of those pamphlets, for she'd brought them with her to her new home, flipping through the pages before shoving them into the drawer of her bedside table. *Caress. Crisis. Cunt. Cock—*

"Here's your tea, madam." Thomas burst back in through the hidden door with a silver tea service in hand, causing Violet to startle to attention.

Heavens, her face was hot. Her entire body was hot. But somehow, she had the presence of mind to summon an artificial smile and nod her thanks as Thomas set down the tray before her. She even managed to unclench her fists—for it would seem she'd bunched her fingers into the folds of her skirts.

The tea tray contained milk and sugar, but she ignored them, pouring herself a steaming cup of the dark liquid and bringing it directly to her lips. Unsurprisingly, she scalded her tongue, felt fire in her throat. That didn't stop her, though, from taking another sip. And then another.

She'd drink the whole blasted pot if it distracted her from pondering her mystery of a husband.

~

Ultimately, Violet decided to spend her afternoon taking a lengthy walk.

After breakfast was through, she'd done her best to focus on menu planning for the week with the housekeeper, Mrs. Wheeler. She'd also let Mrs. Wheeler show her all the fine china and silverware. However, when the housekeeper suggested they move on to take inventory of the linen room, she'd drawn the line.

Violet *tried* to be a good mistress of the house—after all, what else did she have to occupy her time? Yet when every slight creak in the floor put her in mind of Benedict's polished boots approaching, when every shadow that hit the periphery of her vision became a suggestion of *him*, she knew she had to escape.

She turned down the offer of a horse and groom, or even a footman to accompany her. If she was going to clear her head, she needed to walk. And she needed to do it alone.

Fortunately, the sun continued to blaze high in the sky, and she didn't go twenty paces into the garden before pulling off her bonnet so warmth could wash over her skin. With no mother around to lecture her about the risk of freckles, why shouldn't she? She could stay outdoors as long as she liked, letting sunlight and fresh air soak deep into her veins until they pushed everything else out—the uncertainty, the frustration, the apprehension.

Having undertaken that small act of rebellion, she continued her journey with a little more lightness in her step. Not knowing where she went, but not caring, either.

The land was both familiar and unfamiliar. Prior to the day of the shepherd's hut incident, she'd never been to Aldercombe during any of her visits to Wiltshire, for the property had remained vacant since before her birth. However, it bore natural similarities to Meadowleigh given its proximity.

Gentle emerald hills. Air scented with freshly turned earth and blossoming hawthorn. Limestone walls bordering corn fields.

It certainly wasn't London. No, she was far removed from the bustle of the Season and didn't know when—*if*—she would get that part of her life back. Yet there was beauty in the countryside. Some people, perhaps, found happiness here.

She took a long breath, then quickened her pace before the ache in her chest could take hold. Her half-boots tramped over meadows of primrose and cowslip. Past a field of grazing sheep and alongside a riverbank, where a group of laborers were hard at work with plows and spades amidst the channels on the other side.

She nodded a brief greeting before following the river's path into a copse of trees, breaking into a near-run until the din of animated chatter was drowned out by the water's steady trickle. Until the knots in her stomach were caused by exertion, nothing more.

This was what she needed: fresh air. Solitude. A space where nothing existed beyond the river, birdsong, and new-grown oak and beech leaves.

Except suddenly, another round of voices emerged. Not the same amicable hum as back at the water meadow but indistinct words that were terse and harsh.

Her feet crept forward as if of their own volition, silently padding atop the underbrush until the voices grew louder, and two men materialized from behind a massive beech, each gesturing indignantly toward the river.

"I'm telling you, there's too little clay," said the man with the scuffed twill coat, his voice painted with a note of urgency. "Suppose we get the same rains as last year. It will never hold."

"And I'm telling you," the other snapped, his vowels rounded and polished, "it will suffice. Last year was an anomaly, and I have both a survey and an architectural plan. Do you presume to know more than your betters?"

"No, m'lord, but ..."

Violet startled backward, shielding herself behind the nearest tree trunk. Whatever else they said became a discordant whir, for she could hear nothing beyond *my lord*.

She should have known the moment she laid eyes on him. The aristocratic set of his shoulders. The fine pair of Hessians. The glimpse of wavy, wheat-colored hair beneath his top hat. Wherever the boundary lay between Aldercombe and Watley, she'd apparently crossed it.

Blast, why would nothing go right today? Her heart thumped skittishly against the wall of her chest, and her body suddenly felt too conspicuous, too exposed, as if she were a beacon in the dead of night.

No. *No.* This was no time to lose her head and get in a flutter. Lord Frederick hadn't seen her, which meant she still had the chance to remove herself without detection. He and the other man remained facing the river, absorbed in their disagreement, so if she just backed away slowly—

A twig snapped beneath her boot, and Lord Frederick whirled around, his eyes frantically scanning the coppice and landing on the worst place possible. Upon her.

"What are you doing here?" He marched toward her with indignant strides, ruffling up dirt and old leaves before grinding to a halt mere inches from her face. "Did *he* send you to spy?"

She took a rapid step to the side, freeing herself from the shadow of his body and the unwelcome heat of his breath. "I don't know what you're talking about." She frowned, reminding herself that this was her future brother-in-law, even though she saw little more than a snake in the grass. And since when had he become so combative? "I was out for a walk and must have lost my way. My presence on Watley land is unintentional, I promise you."

Lord Frederick gave his hand a dismissive wave, sending

the man who'd accompanied him fleeing in the opposite direction. Then, he turned his attention to glaring at her, the eyes Arabella rhapsodized about growing beady. "See it doesn't happen again. You may have cajoled yourself into marriage, but that doesn't mean you're welcome—"

"Violet?" A familiar, airy voice rang out, and her gaze darted beyond Lord Frederick to land on a cluster of people coming through the trees. Two of Lord Frederick's gentleman friends from the house party. His sister, Lady Kingsland. But most importantly, Arabella, who dropped her parasol and sprinted forward, her face breaking into a wide grin.

Violet ran, too, heedless of land boundaries. She couldn't have predicted how good it would feel to spot a friendly face. A remnant of her life from before everything had been turned upside down.

"Oh, Vi, I'm so glad to see you!" Arabella stopped just short of colliding with her, reaching for her hands with a little laugh. "Meadowleigh is lonesome without you already."

Violet eagerly squeezed her fingers against her sister's, taking in Arabella's poke bonnet with the pink ribbons, the little curls that hung fetchingly on the sides of her face, and the becoming flush in her cheeks. How pretty she looked. How joyful.

Yet Arabella's brow furrowed as she peered at Violet, and her lips twisted uncertainly. "Are you well, darling?"

Violet swallowed, the crisp, woodsy air becoming cloying in her lungs. She needed to say yes, to tell her sister the comforting lie that everything was fine. However, the ache she'd tried to outrun had returned, and so many unpleasant truths hovered on the tip of her tongue. She hadn't a clue whom she'd married. She might never be happy again. Lord Frederick Denham was a cork-brained coxcomb—

"Arabella?" Lord Frederick's voice sliced into the silence as sharply as a poison-tipped dagger. And here Violet was hoping he would vanish into the woods or turn into a frog or *something* so she needn't look at him any longer. He remained, though, as haughty and un-amphibian-like as ever, with a gloved hand extended to her sister. "Are you coming, dearest?"

Arabella's frown deepened, and she ignored the proffered hand, even when he took a step toward where the rest of the group observed silently from the more distant trees. "But you said we were going for a walk along the river and then would stop to play charades in the meadow." She nudged her head in Violet's direction as if trying to reestablish her bearings. "It's this way, I'm certain. And now that we've run into Violet, she can join us."

He did a poor job concealing his sneer. "I've changed my mind. We'll finish our walk in the gardens at Watley and then have libations on the terrace. I'm sure Violet, as a newly married woman, has other things to keep her occupied."

"But ... but the dust," Arabella muttered weakly, her eyes becoming forlorn pools that traveled between her sister and her beau.

Violet clamped her lips together, trying not to let her vexation show. No one would enjoy a stroll in Lord Frederick's parkland, which was undergoing extensive remodeling and had turned to little more than dirt and uprooted trees. However, the unfavorable locale was apparently preferable to spending time with an undesirable woman such as herself.

She wished she were strong enough that the realization didn't faze her. Better yet, she wished she could tell Lord Frederick and all his gawking houseguests to go hang. But as Arabella's gaze continued darting back and forth, Violet saw where it lingered the longest: upon her beloved's outstretched palm.

"You should go," Violet whispered, trying to make the words for her sister's ears only. There were few things less palatable than having Lord Frederick listen to her admit defeat.

Arabella kept hold of Violet's hands a moment longer, her lovely face darkened by doubt. Only a moment, though, before her grip slackened and a smile returned, bringing the cheery light back to her eyes. "Of course, you must be very busy in your new role. I've been thoughtless; don't let me keep you." With a skip in her step, she approached Lord Frederick, sliding the fingertips of her dainty cotton gloves between the sturdy leather of his. "Goodbye, dear Violet," she called over her shoulder. "Promise you'll come visit Mama and me as soon as you find the time."

"Goodbye," Violet said, although the word was thin, drowned out by the swish of Arabella's skirts and the returning lull of conversation as the group continued on their way. They wasted no time departing, for the quicker they left, the quicker they could pretend the disagreeable encounter had never taken place.

For an instant, Violet stood transfixed, watching Arabella's embroidered hem flutter in the breeze. Listening to the sound of her coquettish giggle as Lord Frederick murmured something in her ear.

No more. Violet spun abruptly, taking clumsy, hurried steps back in the direction she'd come. Upon insisting that she wanted no one accompanying her for the walk, why hadn't she at least taken the trouble to determine where the property line lay? What a foolish oversight. *So* foolish.

She dug her nails into her palms, trying to erase the memory of Lord Frederick's smug, infuriating face—along with the entire group of faces who'd given her the cut direct and disappeared without a word. It was misery having to think of them all drinking lemonade and playing games while she returned to a strange house, alone.

I did it for Arabella. That's what she attempted to focus

on as she made her way out of the shady trees and back into the sunshine. Arabella was so happy, she glowed. Arabella had everything she wanted. Violet had no one to blame but herself —and another of her incredibly foolish decisions—for the fact that the price of that happiness was her own marriage to a stranger.

She blinked as the brilliant sunlight stung her eyes—for it was brightness that caused them to water, *not* tears—and glanced over to where the laborers remained busy digging along the channels, just as she'd left them. Except something was different.

Her footsteps faltered, her eyes widening despite the burn. Two additional men had arrived on the scene, not dressed in workman's attire but in the finely tailored clothing of gentlemen. One of middle age and middling height, with thick gray-brown hair peeking out beneath his hat. And the other ...

The other was tall and lean, with perfectly polished top boots and tan trousers that hugged his thighs, displaying each muscle. He had a crisp gray coat sculpted to rigid shoulders, a starched cravat, and a head of black hair with not a strand out of place.

So. It would appear Benedict did, in fact, have plans with his land agent. She'd half-wondered if he used the meeting as an alibi while he shut himself away to pen another erotic story.

She watched as the presumed land agent pointed at something in the grass with his walking stick, and Benedict's gaze followed the movement, his lips pursing as he made an indistinguishable comment in response. His dark brows rose in question.

Lord, why was she staring at him so? She diverted her eyes, her body giving a sharp twitch like she'd just awoken from a trance. Rather than ogling, she should go over there and make herself known. Wasn't that what she'd wanted since early this morning: to get their next meeting over with so it ceased weighing heavy on her mind?

No. Not anymore. This morning, she'd been brave, prepared to face whatever awkwardness, whatever aloofness, came her way and let it run off her shoulders. However, she no longer had it in her to act as though everything were well. As though she weren't lonely, mortified, and unsure how she would ever dig herself out of such a colossal hole.

Fortunately, Benedict and the land agent remained absorbed in their discussion, their gazes fixed on one of the channels. And so, before that could change, she sprinted away without looking back, the bright sun continuing to make her eyes water.

9

For all his proper demeanor and irreproachable manners, Benedict Prescott played with his food.

From her seat at the opposite end of the dining table—an absurdly far distance for a couple dining alone—Violet tracked the motions of his spoon as it cut through the surface of his white soup and swirled through the viscous liquid. Around and around it went, giving the appearance it would dip to the bottom of the bowl and emerge, ready to rise to his lips. Except instead of making its final ascent, the spoon sank as if the weight of the rich broth were too much for it to bear, thus capturing it in an unproductive limbo.

Interesting. Indeed, it was almost satisfying to see him commit a slight faux pas. Not that she could in any way fault him for the misstep. While there was nothing outwardly objectionable about the soup, she did little more than stir hers, either.

Why would her stomach not settle? After spending the afternoon in her bedchamber licking her wounds, she'd answered in the affirmative when Mrs. Wheeler came to ask whether she'd be joining Mr. Prescott for dinner, once more ready to face what she'd been avoiding. The meal had started as well as could be expected. He'd risen as she walked into the dining room and bowed to her. She'd looked him in the eye without a single blush and curtsied. He'd inquired after her well-being, and she after his, and just like that, it was as if the night before had never happened.

But it did *happen*, her brain insisted on reminding her with each infrequent spoonful of soup she pressed to her mouth, only for it to glide unappetizingly down her throat. Just as her accidental visit to Watley had happened. The stares. The terse words. The rejection.

She abandoned her spoon in favor of her wine goblet, continuing to watch Benedict over the rim. His spoon dipped and swiveled, while his dark eyes studied the broth like it contained secrets to the universe. *Dip, swivel, dip, swivel—*

Suddenly, those eyes weren't on the soup but on her. Catching her in the act of ogling.

Wine hit her throat the wrong way, and she coughed, rapidly diverting her gaze to the napkin in her lap. She sank her fingers into it, waiting for the burn to subside, willing herself not to sputter, not to flush, not to do anything that would paint her as less than composed.

"Did you pass a pleasant day?" she asked after a moment, forcing herself to bring her eyes back up to meet his. She tried to appear as if the question had been her reason for looking at him in the first place.

"I did." His spoon made another swirling motion, and she prepared herself for a return to silence. Yet instead of bringing his attention back to the uneaten soup, he continued looking at her, and his speech didn't stop. "Mr. Hayward—the new land agent—and I made progress with the water meadow. Apparently, some of the drainage channels sustained damage during last year's heavy rains, and the repairs were never completed. But thanks to Mr. Hayward's efforts, we now have a proper team of workmen in place."

While it was hardly an enthralling topic of conversation, it appeared to please him, for his shoulders grew less stiff than usual, and the set of his mouth didn't seem nearly as tight. Why, if she squinted a little and used her imagination, she could almost see what he would look like when smiling.

An action he wouldn't want to perform in real life, of course, lest he strain facial muscles weak from disuse.

An action that, if performed, would make him very handsome, indeed ...

"That's good news," she said, shaking off the wayward direction of her thoughts. Ideally, she would say something else. Ask him a question before their fragile conversation lapsed into nothingness. However, the words to follow deserted her, and she busied herself with taking a mouthful of soup.

"I saw you by the river." His matter-of-fact comment filled the void she'd left, and the weight of his gaze continued resting upon her, allowing her no place to hide. "You were running."

Drat, he'd *seen* that? And here she'd deluded herself into thinking she was so inconspicuous that no one had witnessed her blotchy face, flyaway hair, and awkward sprint. Heat crept toward her cheeks, and she stiffened her spine, trying for all the dignity she could muster. "I was merely out for a walk."

"Ah." There was no way he believed her, surely. But all he said was, "You passed a pleasant day as well, I hope."

No. "Yes."

He considered the word a moment, as if it contained so much more than a simple affirmation. As if he were formulating a much more detailed response to give back to her, and it rested on the tip of his tongue. Ultimately, though, he returned to his bowl, dipping his spoon into the thick white broth. Lifting it ... Dropping it ... Lifting it ...

"Is something the matter with your soup?" she blurted out, unable to keep the exasperation from her tone. If he continued at this speed, they'd be here at the dinner table until Michaelmas.

His body tensed, the sudden tightness of his fingers making the spoon clink once against the side of the bowl before he brought it under control. "No, not at all." As if proving his point, he filled the spoon, letting it rise above the surface this time and travel toward his lips. However, his face had taken on an ashy cast, and the lines around his mouth had grown pinched.

"Not at all?" She mimicked his words, her brows lifting. "I've seen children eat mouthfuls of mud with more enthusiasm than you're displaying."

He sighed, interrupting his spoon's journey and abandoning it on the edge of his bowl. "I confess, I don't have a particular fondness for soup of any kind."

She tossed down her spoon, pushing her bowl to the side. "For heaven's sake, then why are we eating it?"

He blinked, looking as though she'd just uttered something nonsensical. "Because dinner is supposed to start with a soup course. Because you planned for it on the menu. Because it is proper—"

"Thomas?" She turned her gaze abruptly from Benedict, catching the attention of the familiar footman who stood in readiness near the doorway. "Mr. Prescott and I are finished with the soup course. Please clear it away and bring out dessert."

From across the table, Benedict made a sound of mild alarm. "But we haven't yet had—"

"The dessert, please, Thomas," she repeated, giving the perplexed-looking footman a reaffirming nod.

Fortunately, that was all it took for him to disappear from the dining room, and the other footman was right behind him, stopping just long enough to scoop up their bowls before hurrying away.

There. That was better. She reached for her wine glass, coolly taking a sip to wash down the taste of soup she hadn't wanted.

Meanwhile, Benedict shifted in his chair, the lines in his forehead making him appear more pained than ever. "We cannot eat dessert without first having the meat course."

She shrugged. "The duck will keep until later if you're inclined to have it."

"Even so, we cannot."

Lord, she was sick of denials. Sick of expectations, and rules, and society's judgments on what was and wasn't acceptable. "*Why*?"

"Because ..." His voice sounded tight. Unsteady. "Because it isn't *done*."

"Is a magistrate going to burst in and stop us?" She leaned in to rest her elbows on the table, mainly because her mother had always told her she *shouldn't*. "We're not on display before the queen. Not trying to impress the patronesses at Almack's. We're in the privacy of our own home, beholden to no one's rules but our own, and if I wish to eat dessert first, I don't see why I shouldn't bloody well do it!"

His lips parted. Snapped shut again. Had she grown a pair of horns? Sprouted a head of purple hair? He was staring at her as if she'd done both, and he was consequently determining what should be said when one's wife became cornuted and purple. But before he could arrive at an appropriate conclusion, Thomas swooped back in with the dessert tray, laying a dish of lemon ice before each of them and a plate of biscuits in the middle of the table.

She nodded her thanks and partook of her dessert without delay, savoring the blend of tart and sweet that rushed over her tongue. Lo and behold, the room didn't burst into flames from her scandalous act of skipping dinner in favor of dessert. The ice didn't turn noxious and choke her when it hit the back of her throat.

And whether Benedict was satisfied with the visual proof she provided or simply too afraid to contradict a wife whom he may well consider deranged, he cautiously lifted his spoon to his mouth and swallowed a morsel of lemon ice.

The change on his face was instant—no more furrowed brow or pallid skin. Indeed, as he helped himself to several more bites, his mouth loosened enough that she could almost envision his smile again.

"No one dislikes ices," she muttered, feeling her own lips twitch in kind. There was something fundamentally satisfying about eating lemon ice for dinner. Something even more satisfying about watching her pedant of a husband do the same.

Perhaps from now on, they should devote their time together to the sole task of eating ices. Maybe then, he'd loosen his cravat and let down his guard, and she truly *would* see him smile. Maybe she'd even smile and laugh herself, because surely it was impossible to get crushed by misery while enjoying such a delicious dessert.

She ate right to the bottom of her crystal dish, ignoring the slight churn in her belly. Should she finish the meal with an iced biscuit? She was nowhere close to being able to reach the plate, but she could take a little jaunt to the center of the table, he might feel inclined to follow, and they'd have a biscuit-filled reunion that was as joyful and sunny as their dishes of lemon ice.

She bit her lip to keep from giggling at the ridiculous notion. Which was the precise moment a water droplet hit the bottom of her empty bowl. *Odd.* She glanced upward, although it didn't make sense that the roof would leak when it wasn't raining.

Another fat droplet splashed against the crystal, and she unthinkingly put a hand to her cheek.

Oh.

Oh, no. The droplets came from *her*. As if a dam behind her eyes had sprung a tiny leak.

She concentrated on her dish and gave her eyes a few hasty swipes, suddenly glad for the vast distance between one end of the table and the other. What in blazes was wrong with her? One moment she'd been savoring her small victory, conjuring up a semblance of happiness, and the next ... How utterly absurd.

At least Benedict hadn't worn his spectacles to the table. Did that mean he couldn't see her clearly? With any luck, she could give her eyes another dab and count to five, and he wouldn't notice a thing amiss when she looked up.

"Violet?"

The voice didn't come from across the table but from beside her, and then, a strong weight fell upon her shoulder. She inched her head to the side, taking in the masculine fingers that rested atop the delicate blue silk of her evening gown. The sight was so incongruous, so unexpected. How had he ... *Why* was he ...

She muttered a pitiable comment to his hand about dust in her eyes, wishing the floor would open and swallow her whole. Even so, her nerve endings gave a frisson of protest when the pressure on her shoulder receded.

Foolish. It was best for the length of the table to separate them again and for them to add this incident to the list of things they could pretend had never happened.

Except instead of leaving, he lowered himself to the chair beside her. His thumb went to her cheek, catching the moisture. Wiping it away.

Her breath hitched. Everything about him seemed so formal, so detached. However, his touch was warm and soft, the type of caress she could lean into like a needy lapdog demanding more. At least, that's what she'd do if she didn't know better. If she didn't recognize the need to keep her guard up, too, lest she encounter rejection yet again.

"Are there any shops in Dayleford you're fond of?" His voice was as gentle as the thumb upon her cheek. "Perhaps you'd like to take the carriage tomorrow and make a day of it."

A thick lump formed in her throat, and she studied the buttons on his waistcoat, unable to meet his eye. He was trying to distract her. To make her feel better. For some reason, the notion made her chest ache and her eyes sting more potently than ever. "Thank you, but no." She squeezed her fingers into the napkin on her lap, willing her words not to waver. "There's nothing I need."

He withdrew his hand, but his body remained close, his gaze lingering upon her. "Maybe you'd prefer a visit with your sister, then. You're welcome to invite her to Aldercombe. She can stay the week, or longer if it would please you both."

If only. Memories of her afternoon in the woods came rushing back. The frosty stares. Lord Frederick's dismissal. Arabella skipping away, her hand in his. "Thank you, but that won't be possible," she said, unable to prevent bitterness from seeping into her tone. "Arabella has other things to occupy her time. I'm afraid a visit here won't fit into her schedule."

She glanced up just in time to see Benedict's brow knit. "Surely, if you asked her—"

"No." She shook her head, hating how brittle she sounded. How *weak.* Yet there was something about his proximity, his concern, that made her keep going, letting the lamentable truth burst free. "I saw her today, and it became clear where her priorities lie. She doesn't have time for me. None of them want me around."

"None of them?" The line in his forehead grew deeper. "To whom, exactly, do you refer?"

An acerbic taste filled her mouth. "To Lord Frederick." Ugh, why did that man have the ability to plague her so? He was such a toad that his opinion didn't deserve to have any bearing on her in the least. However, her mind flashed back to the other faces in the woods. Those who blindly followed his lead because he was the son of a powerful duke and she was naught but a scandal-plagued woman. She blew out a breath, fighting against the sharp ache in her chest and the burn in her eyes. "To all the guests at his dratted house party."

How strange that as the admission poured from her body, her thoughts returned to the hand on her shoulder. The thumb on her cheek. And strangest of all, she wished they would come back because, inexplicably but undoubtedly, they would help make her feel better.

Benedict no longer leaned toward her, though, but sat upright in his chair, his arms crossed and fingers clamped tightly around his coat sleeves. "I'm sorry the day was distressing to you." He spoke not like a husband offering comfort but like a stranger. As if the embrace were a mere figment of her imagination and the length of the vast dining table still separated them after all. "If there's anything here at Aldercombe that could add to your happiness, you're welcome to it."

She could find no fault in his offer; it fairly dripped politeness. However, it was like an invisible door had sprung up between her chair and his, then been slammed in her face and locked, creating an impassable distance between them.

A distance that quickly transformed from imaginary to real, for he rose from his seat, turning not to his former place at the head of the table but toward the doorway.

"Where are you going?" She tracked each of his movements—the bend of his fingers while he tugged invisible creases from his coat, the subtle tic in his jaw—as her spine became rigid, and her head spun too fast to think straight.

He shot her a glance, although it was clear his attention had already wandered beyond the dining room. "I have correspondence to attend to that will occupy the remainder of the evening. I'll bid you goodnight."

Goodnight? So, this was to be the end, then? Coming on the heels of the unexpected warmth he'd bestowed upon her, the sudden wave of frostiness was enough to chill her to the bone. "Do you not still want the main course?" she asked feebly, making a halfhearted motion toward his end of the table. As deep as the encounter in the woods had cut her, it suddenly felt secondary to the ache of watching him walk away with renewed aloofness.

He paused only to give the paltriest shake of his head. "The ice was sufficient. Goodnight."

And then, before she could utter another word, he was gone. Leaving behind nothing but a near-empty bowl of melted lemon ice and the memory of a touch that no longer felt real.

She grabbed the napkin from her lap and tossed it onto the table, letting out an aggrieved sigh. Only for it to dawn on her that she remained under the watch of two attentive footmen.

She motioned to Thomas, making her best attempt to appear collected but certain she failed miserably. "That will be all for this evening. Please see that the duck is shared at the servant's table."

Mercifully, the footmen obeyed without question, sweeping in to collect the dessert dishes and vanishing through a side door before she could count to ten. Then, in the vacant room, she well and truly let her elbows slump against the table, her head drop to her palms, and her breath come in deep, shuddering exhales.

What on earth had just happened? Why had her husband

come close merely to retreat? And why had she craved that closeness?

Because she was a ninny, that's why. As for Benedict, he was a ... a ...

An enigma. An uptight, infuriating, contradictory, compassionate, handsome enigma.

She shifted her bleary gaze to the doorway through which he'd departed for his study. Had he gone there to pen a note to his land agent about irrigation or sheep-shearing? Or did his quill hit paper to craft another story about a wanton widow who surrendered herself to pleasures of the flesh?

She clamped her thighs together, her mouth becoming a tight line. What he wrote in the solitude of his study hardly mattered, did it? It wouldn't change the fact that they'd moved a step forward eating ices at the dinner table. And then promptly stumbled two steps back.

10

Dear Benedict,

I'm pleased to hear you've formed a favorable first impression of Aldercombe Grange. Forgive me if I neglect to pose additional questions on the subject, though, and instead ask: what's this about a <u>marriage</u>???

Rockliffe

B en had slept poorly in the nine days since his wedding. Consequently, his brain was slow to absorb the copious information within his agricultural pamphlets. He sometimes had to ask Mr. Hayward to repeat himself during their meetings. And his quill could no longer create the appropriate combination of words to craft a suitable missive.

He crumpled his tenth attempt at a letter to his uncle, letting the quill slip from his ink-stained fingers and slouching back in his leather desk chair. Ideally, he would send word to London that improvements were underway at Aldercombe and that his precipitous marriage was both satisfactory and harmonious. But while he could confidently provide a positive report of the estate and Mr. Hayward's management of it, what truth could he tell of his marriage besides that his wife seemed miserable?

His gaze shifted to the window overlooking the back garden where, every once in a while, Violet appeared in the distance, out for one of her lengthy walks. However, there was currently nothing beyond the glass but the lush green lawn and trees bursting with new leaves. She hadn't yet returned, then. With plenty of daylight hours left, perhaps she was still enjoying the grounds next door.

He glanced back at his desktop, clenching his fingers as a familiar pang stabbed him in the gut. Right from the beginning, he'd told her he didn't wish for her to be unhappy, and he meant it. As his unskilled attempts at cheering her had gone nowhere, he should be glad for her to seek enjoyment where she could find it. Only, why did that place have to be at Lord Frederick Denham's house party?

Hadn't she already suffered enough humiliation and rejection on that account? Hadn't George Metcalfe already proven himself a faithless cad? Nonetheless, she walked in the direction of Watley every day, slipping into the trees near the river and disappearing. Leaving him to watch from the opposite riverbank where he oversaw repairs to the water meadow. Did she hope to reconcile with her former suitor, marriage vows be hanged?

The knife in his gut twisted a little deeper. He could still see the fire in her eyes when she insisted he not take a mistress. He could also see the moisture in them as her bravado over lemon ices melted into poorly concealed sorrow, and it became impossible not to sit by her side and wipe her tears away. To fix a problem that needed a solution.

Except there was no solution. Not if the only thing to make her happy would be reacceptance by the so-called friends —and the suitor—who'd abandoned her because of a misunderstanding. He couldn't give her that, damn it. And more importantly, he *refused* to give her that. Yes, he might be a poor excuse for a husband, but that didn't mean he could sit by, uncaring, while she did the very thing she'd demanded he not do.

And so, because he couldn't solve the problem, he did the next best thing: he avoided it. Held himself at a distance. She still came into his study sometimes to ask what he was reading or writing, and they continued to have dinner together each night—with the soup course notably absent. However, their conversations never strayed much beyond his farming manuals, or work being done about the estate, or household arrangements she discussed with Mrs. Wheeler.

You could talk to her, for Christ's sake. Truly talk to her and determine what in hell you're both supposed to make of this marriage. The thought came to him sometimes at night while he lay sleepless atop his mattress, listening to the rustles on the other side of the wall as she prepared for bed. However, he kept the connecting door between their rooms locked, and by the time morning's light arrived, the idea always felt a little too exposing, too uncouth, and so it remained behind in the shadows.

Which was why he instead poured himself into the estate, casting aside his trepidation on the subject and learning everything he could about agricultural matters and management. While he failed as a husband, he could still act as a dutiful nephew, at least for the time being.

He reached toward the edge of his desk with a sigh, taking up the pamphlet on crop rotation that rested there. If nothing else, he could see that Aldercombe—which had fallen on hard times after last year's abysmal weather, followed by the sudden death of the former land agent—thrived again. For whoever's hands into which it fell in the end.

Yet no sooner did he flip to the first page than an incessant string of murmurs wafted in from the front of the house, the voices growing increasingly louder and more heated.

Achilles lifted his head from where he'd been dozing on the rug, cocking it to the side, and Ben found himself doing the same. As it rose in volume, one of the voices distinguished itself as belonging to his butler, Pearce, but why in blazes was the man yelling? And who was the man that shouted back?

Ben was just rising from his chair when a red-faced footman appeared in the doorway, making a hasty bow. "Sir?" The footman drew a few quick breaths, then stepped forward. "Arthur Ruddle is here to see you. Pearce wonders if he should be allowed in."

Arthur Ruddle. Ben knew the name well, for Ruddle had been one of the more vocal tenant farmers, demanding reparations after an autumn flood destroyed part of his barn. But while Mr. Hayward had immediately orchestrated the repairs neglected by Mr. Morris, the former land agent, along with promising that improvements to the water meadow would help prevent flooding farther downstream, it would seem Ruddle's satisfaction with the arrangement had waned.

Ben frowned at the doorway, beyond which Pearce barked something about respecting one's betters. "I take it he has a grievance to air."

"It would appear so, sir."

What else was Ben to do? While technically, there were two solutions to the problem, only one stood out as being correct. "Tell Pearce to send him in."

He remained standing by his desk as the footman hurried away, one palm resting against the polished mahogany. The palm by his side suddenly grew wet as Achilles came up and shoved his nose into it—his way of demanding ear scratches.

Ben obliged, absently running his fingers through the thick fur. He made his spine tall and shoulders taut, just as his uncle did when looming behind his desk at Rockliffe House in London. The only thing Ben lacked was a signet ring.

Some people found the sight of a hefty bulldog off-putting. However, no sooner did Pearce appear and announce Arthur Ruddle than the farmer stormed into the room and rushed forward, not so much as batting an eye.

Ben regarded him levelly, nodding as the short but robust man ground to a halt on the other side of his desk, nostrils flaring and breaths coming in noisy pants. "Ruddle." He didn't wait for an answering bow or tip of the hat, for it was clear none would be forthcoming. "What seems to be the trouble?"

Ruddle planted his fist on the desktop, his knuckles cracking with the effort. "When I said something needed to be done to stop the river from flooding, I didn't mean for you to dry it up completely."

Ben's eyebrows twitched. Had the man just visited the alehouse? It didn't smell like it, although his words made no sense. "I'm afraid I don't comprehend your meaning."

"The river's been dammed!" Ruddle stomped his foot, his face turning the shade of a newly sliced beet. "When I saw the state of the riverbed, I followed it all the way over to Watley, where Lord Frederick Denham's got the water dammed and diverted back through his own woods."

What? That made no sense, either; it wasn't possible. Yet Ruddle's incensed countenance suggested he spoke the truth.

"I assure you, I did *not* condone it," Ben snapped, close to shouting himself. His head spun, his eyes darting to the hefty stack of correspondence on his desk. He'd been so distracted this week. Was there any chance he'd read something in haste without understanding its significance and unknowingly agreed—

No. Thoughts of his wife may have filled his head, but he

was certain he hadn't done anything so reckless, and he needed to call for Mr. Hayward at once.

Except he couldn't call for Mr. Hayward. Everything had gone so well with the estate over the past fortnight that he'd granted the man three days off, and Mr. Hayward was using them to ride north to visit his parents. *Hell and damnation.*

Ben squared his jaw, forcing himself to keep looking at Ruddle and not begin pacing the floor. "When did you first make this discovery?"

"Just now," Ruddle huffed, "and I didn't waste a minute before coming here to say that if you fail to change course, I don't know how you think any of us, yourself included, are to water crops or livestock—"

"I know." Again, Ben's words came out terse and overloud, although to his credit, his urge to shout obscenities at the top of his lungs and hurl a vase or two remained clamped deep inside him. Ruddle clearly saw him for who he was: an impostor. *Not* the marquess. But while Ben could fill tomes on the things he had yet to learn about estate management, he'd be damned if he let whatever had happened with the river go unchecked.

"If you'll excuse me, Ruddle." He broke the man's irate gaze, abandoning his desk and marching toward the door with clipped, purposeful strides. "I'm going to fix this."

Ben drove the old curricle to Watley Hall, racing over the stretch of deserted road and up the tree-lined drive until he arrived at the manor's front entrance. He'd taken a quick detour before departing Aldercombe, just long enough to head to the riverbank and witness the weak trickle where water had previously flowed in a healthy stream. Thus stoking both his confusion and ire—sentiments that burned into a full-fledged inferno by the time he jumped from the curricle and bounded up the steps to knock on the door.

Fortunately, a groom was swift in coming to tend to his horses, just as the Watley Hall butler wasted no time in opening the door and regarding him with mild curiosity.

"Mr. Benedict Prescott here to see Lord Frederick Denham," he bit out, forgoing good manners and stepping into the entrance hall the instant the man made a slight movement to the side. "It's urgent."

The butler's graying brows shifted closer together, giving him a subtle air of disgruntlement. "Allow me to check if Lord Frederick is available." He shuffled away, Ben's claim of urgency not prompting him to hurry. But at least he made the effort, disappearing down a corridor from which came a steady hum of voices. A feminine giggle.

The house party. Ben's chest tightened, and he clamped his hands into fists, pressing them against his sides. He didn't know which was worse: picturing Violet laughing amongst the guests, or imagining her back at Aldercombe alone, silently bemoaning her fate. For Watley Hall was where she wanted to be. With Denham, and her sister, and *George*.

But he couldn't think about that. He couldn't afford the distraction when a pressing estate matter required his full attention. The sound of footsteps began resonating in the corridor, slowly growing louder. Until suddenly, a man in shirtsleeves appeared, strolling into the corridor with a glass of brandy in hand.

"Mr. Prescott, I presume." The man, who couldn't be much different in age from Ben himself, assessed him with cool gray eyes, running a hand through disheveled hair and bringing it down to the lazy knots of his cravat. He may be a duke's son, but he either didn't employ a valet or had partaken of recent activities to undo his valet's efforts.

"Lord Frederick." Ben stiffly inclined his chin, raising it just as a shriek emerged from a room deep in the corridor, followed by a torrent of laughter.

Denham emitted a small chuckle of his own. "A game of kiss the monkey has grown somewhat boisterous." His eyes momentarily filled with mirth, and he gave a longing glance down the corridor before abruptly seeming to remember himself and sobering again. "I understand you have urgent need of an audience, so you'd best come with me to my study. I can spare you but a minute of my time."

Ben swallowed back a retort about idleness and idiotic games, following Denham as he crossed the entrance hall and approached the first door on his right. Hopefully, the lordling wasn't foxed, or this would be nigh on excruciating.

But disorderly appearance aside, Denham walked in a straight line and opened the door without fumbling, leading him into a sunlit study that overlooked the front drive.

Much like Ben's study, the room contained a pair of chairs in front of the master's desk, along with two wingback chairs near the fireplace. However, Ben ignored them all, standing rigidly in the middle of the Aubusson rug while Denham went to the sideboard and fetched a decanter.

"Brandy?" The young lord splashed some of the amber liquid into his tumbler before turning to Ben, decanter outstretched.

"No." Ben swallowed, his throat like sandpaper. He'd best just get on with it before the man did, in fact, grow tipsy. "Why did you dam the river?"

Denham laughed, although the sound rang cold. "Really, Prescott. Did you not want to discuss the weather first? Or perhaps you'd rather we swapped stories about our days at university." A knowing glint appeared in his eye. A glint that left no doubt he'd heard about Ben's expulsion from Cambridge—and the reason for it.

Ben planted his feet more firmly against the floor, forcing his chin to remain high. "I didn't intend this as a social call. It's strictly a business matter. Namely, why you interfered with a water source that's the lifeblood of Aldercombe Grange."

With an infuriating shrug, the lordling took a long swig of his drink. "Have your land agent arrange a meeting with mine."

My land agent, who isn't even in the county at present. "No." Ben took a clipped step toward the sideboard, fire raging between his ribs. "I want to hear it from you. Now."

Perhaps Denham was unaccustomed to having his directives contradicted, for the spite in his gaze swiftly darkened to ire, and his brandy-coated lips twisted into a scowl. "Very well. Everyone knows the river was a devastating source of flooding last year. If you've failed to speak with your tenants on the subject, I suggest you do so without delay, for I'm sure they'd regale you with plenty of tales about how that doddering old Morris neglected to do anything to prevent it. In any case, the flood forced Morris to recognize his grievous error, and he agreed that Mr. Gingell—my *capable* land agent—should take control of water management."

What bollocks. The words rose in Ben's throat but then died on his tongue, a seed of doubt catapulting its way in. His uncle had acquainted him with the unfortunate story of Mr. Morris, Aldercombe's former land agent—the man who'd rejected the marquess's suggestions of retirement, insisting he remained capable of doing the job until an apoplexy had taken him in late winter. Uncle Rockliffe said he'd noticed slight oversights in Mr. Morris's correspondence in the weeks leading up to his death, signs the man's impeccable shrewdness was maybe beginning to fade. However, omitting a figure or two from a letter was a far cry from making an agreement that proved deleterious to the estate. Even if Mr. Morris had suffered from occasional bouts of forgetfulness or confusion, surely he wouldn't have done such a thing. Would he?

"Do you have proof of this arrangement?" Ben asked tightly, hating that the question warranted asking.

Denham gave a contemptuous snort. "Of course I do. We drew up an irrigation deed." He flicked his wrist, then brought his glass back toward his lips. "As I said, have your new land agent take it up with mine."

Bloody buggering hell. Ben stared at the swirl of amber liquid as Denham drained it in one swift gulp. His thoughts spiraled backward to his own study, to the numerous ledgers, letters, and deeds that sat on bookshelves and lined his desk drawers. He and Mr. Hayward had been perusing them thoroughly, familiarizing themselves with matters that for close to four decades had rested in the hands of another man. They'd encountered nothing so preposterous as an irrigation deed granting control of the river to Watley alone. But was that merely because they hadn't discovered the document yet? Because in his distraction, Ben had somehow overlooked it?

Damn, damn, damn. How infuriating to lack answers. To be unable to denounce the lordling's words as rubbish because there was the smallest chance they held merit.

He stiffened his shoulders, forcing them to remain high despite how they felt laden down by boulders. "I'll be sending a solicitor as well to verify your claim."

Lord Frederick's empty glass clattered back to the sideboard, and something in the air suddenly shifted. A heightened tension, a heaviness, that left his countenance dripping with renewed malice. "Do as you see fit. But who are you to question my word as a gentleman?" He abandoned the decanter, taking a few ominous steps toward the center of the room. "*I'm* the son of a duke. You may be an heir presumptive, but no one would ever mistake you for bon ton. Not with your lowbred mother and that tart Violet for a wife—"

"Don't you *dare* speak of them." Fury uncurled in Ben's chest, squeezing his ribs, propelling him forward until he and the lordling were eye to eye. "Don't you *ever* let me catch you with my wife's name in your mouth again," he snarled, his lungs on the verge of exploding, his fists quivering at his sides.

"Or what?" Denham jutted his chin upward, the hiss of his words ensconcing Ben in a liquor-scented cloud.

It would be so easy to raise his fist. To wipe the sneer off that cocky face, because *no one* should get away with speaking of his family—and his wife—that way. The few seconds of gratification would nearly be worth it.

Except what would he prove? His fists wouldn't make Denham renounce his claim to the river. Indeed, they would only demonstrate the lordling's point: that Ben was inferior. Uncouth. Out of control.

Maybe his father had been right in his insistence that they all remain far from the aristocracy. That their place in the world was elsewhere. Yet his father's beliefs couldn't change fate. They wouldn't make Ben feel any less bilious about writing another letter to his uncle, the marquess, and explaining his lack of self-restraint. His failure.

He took a brusque step backward, assuaging the violent tempest between himself and Denham just before it delivered a catastrophic deluge. However, his insides continued to churn, his bones feeling brittle enough to crack. "You'll hear from my solicitor directly," he choked out, already pivoting, no longer able to peer at that defiant chin or breathe the brandy-infused air.

Denham's boots thumped against the carpet in the opposite direction. Liquid splattered against glass. "I look forward to it." The lordling's caustic retort hit him just as he reached the doorway, but he didn't look back. He didn't turn when a round of boisterous cheers echoed from the room farther down the corridor, followed by another burst of feminine laughter.

Let the lordling have the last word. Let them all have their games, their frivolity, their dalliances.

Ben was finished here.

11

Benedict wasn't in the dining room when Violet came down for dinner that night.

Every evening thus far, he'd always been standing near the doorway when she appeared, ready to accompany her to her seat at the foot of the table before making the long march to the opposite end to take his. The only person awaiting her at the moment, however, was Thomas.

He did his duty as efficiently as ever, inclining his head and then pulling out her chair as if not a thing were different. But Violet hesitated, the difference proving so stark in her mind that her body refused to sit. "Has there been no sign of Mr. Prescott?" she asked, feeling a slight crease form in her brow. Surely, Benedict Prescott would never do anything so careless as run *late*.

"Mr. Prescott sends his regrets, madam. He's been detained by an important business matter."

Humph. She didn't know why her stomach pinched at the news. Not from disappointment, certainly—for how did it make sense to miss a dinner partner when their conversations never strayed beyond the most mundane topics? Perhaps it was because, once again, the chasm between them displayed itself to full advantage, alerting the servants just how superficial their marriage continued to be. She often tried to hide it, to make it look as though *husband* and *wife* weren't sham titles and that they actually knew something of one another's whereabouts and well-being.

Tonight, though, instead of pretending she and Benedict shared a confidence they did not, she swallowed her pride. "Is he not at home, then?"

"He is, madam. In his study." Thomas paused, the next word coming out lower than the others. "Alone."

Violet's eyebrows arched. *Odd.* Why would the footman add such a clarifier?

But no matter. She'd learned everything she needed to know. "Thank you, Thomas. My apologies for the delay, but please hold dinner a while longer." She turned away from the vacant table, waiting just until she heard his assent before slipping from the dining room.

The study was only a few doors away. Not nearly long enough of a walk to give her time to ponder why she was the one suddenly craving structure and routine. In fact, she didn't think at all; she simply stood before the carved oak door and knocked. And then, when no answer came, she pushed the door open and entered.

Dear Lord, had there been an *explosion*? Her eyes trailed around the room, her mouth gaping.

Typically, Benedict kept his study in perfect order, with books arranged by size and color lining the shelves and correspondence stacked in two neat piles atop his desk. Over the short course of their marriage, she'd sometimes stopped in unannounced to say goodnight—always hoping to catch him in the act of authoring a salacious story, although it had never happened—and the room was equally pristine on each occasion.

Presently, however, tomes of all sizes were scattered across the shelves and cast onto the floor, and Benedict's ancient bulldog lay dozing on the carpet, surrounded by a flurry of discarded papers. As for Benedict himself, he stood hunched over one of his desk drawers with a ledger in hand, rapidly flipping through pages before tossing it to the floor where a small pile had already accumulated.

"What in heaven's name has happened?" She crossed the floor—careful not to tread on any papers—until she stood near the chaos that surrounded his desk.

He didn't seem to have heard her come in, although the question caused him to dart the paltriest glance upward before his focus returned to the drawer. "I'm looking for something."

Yes, I gathered. She placed her hands on her hips. "Would you care to provide a touch more detail?"

"A document ... a letter ... a deed ... *something*," he mumbled. He hauled out another ledger, giving it a shake to check for loose pages before pushing his spectacles up his nose and reading anew.

Well, that was frustratingly vague. She sank her fingers deeper into her hips, racking her brain for a question that might produce a real answer. Until Benedict abruptly straightened, his gaze going to hers and remaining longer than a fleeting moment. "Violet." He sounded surprised, as if he'd truly taken stock of her presence for the first time. "Did no one relay the message that I wouldn't be at dinner this evening? Please, go ahead without me."

He tapped his fingers against the open page, clearly anxious to get back to his task. Yet Violet remained where she was, taking stock of him, too. She hadn't thought it possible for his starched cravat to move an inch out of place, but lo and behold, the knotted linen rested askew. There was even—*gasp*—a wrinkle in his waistcoat. As for his hair, several of the locks he kept carefully contained with pomade had sprung free, falling in unruly curls across his forehead.

She didn't think he had it in him. What on earth had transpired to make him look so … undone? Whatever it was, a flicker of heat uncurled low in her belly.

She shook her head, going to the opposite side of his desk and waiting, not unlike the day they'd solidified their marriage arrangements. "I don't want dinner. I want to help you. Although I confess, I remain unclear what you're seeking."

"I'm searching for something I hope to God doesn't exist!" His voice was rough, unmeasured, and he pitched the ledger to the desktop, letting out a beleaguered sigh. "A written agreement, signed by Aldercombe's former land agent, stating that due to issues with flooding on tenant lands, Lord Frederick Denham can take full control of the river intersecting our properties."

She frowned, the loathsome name causing its usual stab of resentment within her. "But why would the land agent have signed such a thing?"

"I don't know!" He shoved a hand through his hair, although it did little to tame the errant curls on his forehead. "There were questions about his competence during his final days, but even so, I highly doubt he ever did. Regardless, Denham has taken it as cause to dam the river and divert the water flow back to his own land."

"He *what*?"

Benedict's jaw looked rigid enough to snap. "You didn't notice?"

"Something amiss with the river?" Her brow rumpled. "No, although I haven't gone past it today. I took my walk into the village instead so I could procure new trimmings for a bonnet."

For an instant, the tension marring his features softened, and she could nearly imagine she saw something approaching relief. Nearly, except the lines around his mouth returned as quickly as they'd waned, and it was impossible to perceive him as anything less than ruffled.

"Surely, Mr. Hayward would know about the arrangement if it truly does exist," she said, her mind whirling a hundred miles a minute. "Or have you conversed with a solicitor?"

"The solicitor is exploring the matter as we speak. He judges the claim to be drivel, but we need proof." Benedict swallowed, the cords in his throat tight. "I have to believe Mr. Hayward would have spoken up immediately had he known anything about this. However, I cannot verify my belief until he returns from Gloucestershire in two days' time. I granted him a sojourn because I thought everything with the estate was going so blasted well!"

His tone rose and then fell, his vehement words fading to something indistinguishable but having the distinct air of another oath. She hadn't imagined he'd allow himself to say such improper things—not outside his secret writings, in any case. Yet this version of her husband differed from the one she thought she knew. He was rawer. Realer. All because he was distraught.

A small twinge tugged at her chest, and her arm began creeping forward. He'd held her ankle once. He'd brushed his thumb over her cheeks as she'd let emotions get the better of her at the dinner table. Did that mean she could touch him, too? Lay a palm on his shoulder, perhaps, or allow their hands to intersect.

But before she could make any further moves, he slid his fingers beneath the temples of his spectacles, releasing another exasperated breath. "Denham may deem me an ignorant land manager, but I'm not so daft that I fail to recognize the consequences this will have for our crops and livestock." His fingertips pressed tightly against his forehead. "Uncle Rockliffe is considering selling Aldercombe," he mumbled, more to himself than to her. "Perhaps I'd best tell him to do so and be done with it."

What? The revelation crashed into her like a pack of wild horses. She'd had no idea the estate wasn't entailed and that selling the property had ever been a consideration. To what purpose, then, did he traverse the land and toil over farming pamphlets at all hours? And if he let the numbskull next door drive them away, where did he mean for them to go instead?

"This is absurd," she snapped. "I'll visit Watley Hall this moment and find out just what Lord Frederick thinks he's doing."

"No." Benedict's face was a thundercloud, his eyes black as flint.

"Yes." She squared her shoulders, giving her foot a determined stomp against the rug. "I've confronted that toad before, and I have no qualms about doing so again. He believes himself to be so high and mighty because of his parentage, but I won't let him get away with—"

"Leave it, Violet. I've already spoken with Denham today. There's nothing more you can do."

Ugh. Why was the world filled with so many *cannots* and *should nots*? Especially for women, who continually found themselves underestimated. She folded her arms across her chest, refusing to let her chin drop as she looked at him. "Do you think I lack the cleverness for such an undertaking?"

A strangled sound shot from his throat, one she would have called a laugh if she didn't know any better. "God help the man foolhardy enough to make that assumption." He gave his head a quick shake, and his hands went to his sides, his body somehow more unyielding than ever. "This has nothing to do with cleverness. I simply do not wish for you to charge over to Watley in the dark and become involved in a confrontation."

He's right. A tiny part of her brain had the wherewithal to recognize as much. However, the knowledge failed to lessen her urge to yell at Lord Frederick Denham until his eardrums burst. Or if not that, at least to understand the purpose behind his whole water diversion scheme. She'd seen nothing of the river today, just like she told Benedict. Her mind raced backward, though, to the muddy hole that was Watley's back garden. To the argument between Lord Frederick and the laborer beside the riverbank last week. Could it be that—

"Violet." Benedict's voice was sharp, containing an unmistakable note of warning. "I won't have it. I ... I forbid it."

She snapped back to attention, a fiery prickle shooting down her spine. More denials. More dismissals. More decisions made on her behalf where she didn't get a say. She wouldn't stand for it!

Her feet moved without another thought, rounding the desk so she, too, stood behind it like a master did. Benedict had the obvious advantage in height, his body long and lean where hers was short and curved. However, that didn't stop her from getting so close that the front of her gown nearly brushed his coat, nor from raising her head and displaying her fiercest glower. "You cannot order me about."

His eyes flashed, something turbulent stirring in their dark depths. "I'm your husband."

The air between them was heavy, the word like a lightning bolt illuminating a stormy sky. *Husband.* The man with whom she'd stood in a church and promised to obey. The man who now towered above her while holding her stare, his chest rising and falling, each exhale sending a tiny lick of warmth onto her skin.

How maddening. How unjust.

How utterly perplexing that she couldn't shake the urge to tear off his crooked cravat and throw it on the floor. To tug and twist his waistcoat until the buttons were undone and every bit was wrinkled. To run her hands through his hair so not a single curl stayed in place.

She squeezed her thighs together, willing the ache between them to abate. Her heartbeat was a rapid thump; her blood simmered with the heat of her frustration. And even so, she was cognizant enough to know she couldn't win like this.

She sucked in a breath, her words coming out as a hiss. "Very well." Her gaze remained locked with his, for she kept her chin in the air, refusing to let it tremble. "*Husband.*"

And then, because the fire she played with seemed on the verge of scorching her, she whipped away from him, marching over to a bookshelf he'd so far neglected and taking up a manual on Wiltshire Horn sheep. After all, she'd said she wanted to help him, and in this matter, she could keep her word.

She shook out the pages to check for secret papers tucked within, just as he'd done with the ledger. And when none appeared, she took another lesson from him and cast it to the floor. She repeated the process with one book after another, each one landing with a satisfying thud, until the full shelf was bare.

Only then did she glance over her shoulder, meeting the gaze whose weight had rested upon her the whole time. "The document you seek isn't here," she said tartly, trying to ignore how very intense his eyes appeared behind his spectacles. Then, she returned to work, scooping the discarded books into her arms and tossing them back on the shelf in an arrangement that was decidedly *not* by color or size.

She could keep going with the rest of the shelves he had yet to check—there was something cathartic about the thump as each cover hit the floor and careful order became dishevelment. However, this was a fool's errand. Land agents, even confused ones, were unlikely to tuck contracts into the pages of random books.

The answer to the river dispute lay next door. The place she'd been forbidden by her husband to go. Yet when said husband remained closed-off and secretive about his life, it seemed only fair for her to have a secret of her own.

And so, she abandoned the shelf and walked out of the study without another word. Without a single backward glance.

Beginning to plan.

12

Ben wasn't in the habit of throwing things on the floor while behaving like a raging arsehole. Nonetheless, it would seem after his abomination of a day, that's what he'd been reduced to.

He slumped onto the edge of his bed, shrugging the coat from his shoulders and starting to work on unfastening his cravat. *I've proven myself a madman,* he reflected ruefully, wincing as he envisioned the disarray he'd caused in both the muniment room and the study. He'd torn open drawers without method, casting aside everything that proved useless until he was surrounded by chaos and no closer to answers.

He couldn't say exactly which unfruitful book or piece of parchment had snapped him back to some semblance of logic. Only that a point had come where he'd surveyed the disorder in his study and recognized everything he made a habit of avoiding. Sloppiness. Impulsiveness. Emotionality. All the qualities that ran through his blood but he kept tightly under control, for he knew the consequences when one left them unbridled.

A tight band squeezed his chest, and he tossed his cravat to the side, forcing in a lungful of air and breathing out until the feeling passed. The important thing was, he'd brought himself back to order. Had recognized that he'd done what he could—speaking with the solicitor, writing to his uncle, sending a note to Mr. Hayward's abode for when the man returned—and now just needed to wait. Easier said than done, certainly, but the estate wouldn't flounder overnight. Especially not now that light rain tapped against the windows, which meant it filled the drying riverbed, too.

The lordling's idiotic claim will be renounced soon enough, and all will return to the way it was. Ben repeated the incantation within his head as he unfastened the buttons of his waistcoat, trying to put himself in a frame of mind for sleep. No amount of rational thinking, though, would untangle the knot low in his abdomen. Nor could any attempts to do otherwise prevent his gaze from continually flicking to the connecting door between his room and Violet's.

He'd put his study back to rights with the help of some industrious chambermaids. However, his relationship with his wife remained an elaborate mess.

He sighed, his fingers stilling on the final button. He hadn't meant to ignore or dismiss her. Hadn't meant to command her, either. It was just so blasted unsettling to think of her barreling through the dark alone, only to wind up at Watley Hall once again. To imagine one of the sonorous giggles from behind closed doors as belonging to her.

Not that she'd given any indication she secretly meant it as a social call. On the contrary, she'd seemed earnest in her desire to help him and had blatantly spoken out against Lord Frederick Denham, despite the man being her sister's intended. Yet there were so many other guests at the house, including one who'd held—who still held?—her affections. So many unknowns ...

He stood abruptly and, on second thought, replaced the

buttons he'd unfastened on his waistcoat. His mother always told his two youngest brothers—and had told him and Alexander, too, when they'd been squabbling youths—that they should never let the sun set on their provocation. Well, there was no question of Violet's anger. No question, either, that his words to her had been terse and unyielding. That wasn't the right way to leave things between them. He should speak to her. Explain his concerns. Apologize for his brashness.

He slunk toward the connecting door, putting his knuckles to the wood and giving a few gentle taps before he could talk himself out of it.

So often, he fell asleep to the sounds of her moving about her chamber, readying herself for bed. The swish of fabric. The splash of wash water. The quiet creak of a mattress dipping. Noises that always left a slight throb in his chest because they were so close, so intimate, but also so far away. Tonight, though, the space beyond the door was silent.

He waited a moment for her voice, for footsteps. Even for an irritated huff signaling she had no interest in speaking to him. However, nothing came back to him but the echo of his own knock.

Strange. Before making his way upstairs, he'd told the footmen to extinguish all the main floor sconces, for the housekeeper informed him that Mrs. Prescott had retired for the evening. Had Violet already fallen asleep? It wasn't yet ten, earlier than when she normally began preparing for bed. Then again, he well knew that ire could be exhausting.

"Violet?" He called her name softly, giving the door another few taps. He didn't want to disturb her if she was sleeping soundly. But at the same time, how could he retreat while this uncertain void remained?

His call went unanswered, and he hesitated, his fingers hovering above the door handle. Perhaps he could ease the door open an inch. Not enough to wake her, just enough to ensure she wasn't glowering in the direction of his bedchamber, punishing him with her silence. Would that be overstepping? Improper of him?

For once, he didn't take the time to ponder the matter too carefully; he simply unlocked the door and cracked it open, giving himself a partial view of the bedchamber he hadn't entered since Violet moved in.

The bedside lamp was lit, casting a faint glow over the flowered counterpane. Enough brightness to reveal that the bed had been turned down for the night but otherwise remained untouched.

"Violet?" He pushed the door aside and stepped over the threshold, hastily scanning the space. It smelled like her, soft and floral. Held physical signs of her, too, like the silver hairbrush atop the vanity. The silk slippers beside her bed. However, no feminine form sat at the vanity bench or appeared from behind the dressing screen.

Quite plainly, Violet wasn't here.

He spun back into his own bedchamber, his mind beginning to race. Perhaps she'd forgotten her book in the drawing room or had gone to the kitchen to fetch a drink before bed. There were plenty of explanations for her absence that didn't warrant his pulse quickening the way it did.

Yet the ground floor of the house remained empty and dark, and his encounter with Mrs. Wheeler as he bounded down the servant's stairs toward the kitchen revealed that no, Mrs. Prescott wasn't there. She hadn't been seen since she'd announced her intention to retire for the evening.

He dug his fingernails into his palms, forcing out the question he loathed to give voice but couldn't avoid. "Is there any chance she requested a carriage or horse?"

"N-not that I know of, sir." For all her outward attempts at maintaining decorum, the housekeeper couldn't fully rein in her expression of shock. "Shall I summon the grooms to ask?"

He took a split-second to contemplate, then gave his head an abrupt shake. "No." What was the point of wasting time waiting for answers from the stables? Regardless of what the grooms said, he already knew Violet had absconded. *And* he knew where.

He pivoted so he could race back up the stairs, calling out as an afterthought, "Have someone check the back garden and see that the terrace door remains unlocked." Whatever entrance Violet had used to flee, he could at least ensure it stayed open so she wasn't barred out in the rain when she chose to return.

Yet that wasn't good enough. He couldn't simply sit back and turn a blind eye to the deception, nor to the danger involved with her being out at night alone. What if the ground became slippery? What if she lost her way in the dark? The headstrong, defiant, *infuriating* woman.

He rushed through the corridor and into the entrance hall, where Achilles was pacing uncertainly, awaiting his reappearance. The dog's tail perked up when Ben neared, giving several enthusiastic wags, but the ear scratches Achilles clearly sought would have to wait until later.

Ben couldn't stop. Not until he'd burst out the front door and gone down the stone steps to the drive, putting himself in the midst of the night rain, did he pause. The moon had been reduced to a blurred glow behind the clouds, and the lamp beside the door did little to provide illumination to the grounds beyond.

What now? How was he to proceed most logically when the world had turned into a black abyss?

Should he summon a horse? Having spent most of his life in the city, he'd had few opportunities to become a skilled rider, but that would be the quickest way to traverse the road to Watley. But what if she hadn't taken the road? What if she'd opted for the familiar trail along the river and gone on foot, regardless of the rain and darkness?

Damn. He muttered a string of oaths under his breath, raindrops soaking through his shirt as he stood helplessly, attempting to make a sound decision despite the lack of a clear path to follow.

He was just about to sprint toward the stables and try his luck on horseback when Achilles's broad head pushed against the clenched fist at his side. However, instead of lingering to remind Ben how he'd neglected his ear-scratching duties, Achilles bounded forward with a rare burst of energy.

"Achilles, come," Ben called sternly as the dog rushed down the drive, his paws churning up gravel in his haste. The elderly animal belonged indoors where it was warm and dry, and this was an exceedingly poor time for antics. But oblivious to Ben's sense of urgency, Achilles continued racing away with the vigor of a pup, emitting a series of eager barks.

"Achilles!" Ben shouted the name again, following the sound of the dog's barking as he raced blindly into the shadows to catch up to him.

Which was when he detected the other noises that made him sharply halt. Feet—not paws—hitting gravel. The rustle of skirts.

And then, beneath the weak light of the obscured moon, an outline appeared near the gate. A voluminous cloak. A face framed by a mass of unbound hair.

Achilles ran to the figure, doing an inquisitive circle around her back before coming to stand guard at her feet, his barks turning to uneasy whines.

"Shh, it's all right." Her voice, though breathless, was like a bell in the darkness, and she leaned forward, putting a soothing hand atop the dog's head. "What are you doing wandering outdoors by yourself? I didn't think you ever left your master's side."

For the briefest moment, Ben could do nothing but watch. She clearly hadn't seen him yet, not in her absorption with giving Achilles the scratches that had so far proved lacking. Yet the word *master* caused the dog to glance back in his direction. That, and Ben shifted, his boots crunching against the gravel. And whether it was from Achilles or Ben's own movement, Violet snapped upright, taking a few tentative steps forward and then sucking in an audible breath.

"Benedict?"

13

Ben was in motion at once, reaching Violet in less than a dozen brisk strides. Despite how the duskiness rendered her features indistinct, the subtle floral scent left no doubt it was his wife who stood before him.

He was uncertain how to name the sensation tossing about in his gut. It was both warm and icy. Airy and cloying. But suddenly, it didn't matter.

It didn't matter because the clouds above drifted enough to allow an extra sliver of moonlight through. A brightness that revealed the rivulets running down Violet's face weren't just raindrops, but blood.

He easily distinguished the resultant cold wave that washed over him: *fear*. The type so potent that he didn't think before scooping her off the ground and into his arms, hugging her damp, cloak-clad body tight to his chest.

She gasped in surprise, her body wriggling within his grasp. "What are you doing?"

He marched forward, keeping his gaze trained solely on the faint wisp of light from the lamp at the front of the house. "You're injured."

"Merely a scratch or two," she protested, her limbs continuing to flail. "Nothing to prevent me from walking."

She said something else as well, he thought, although he ceased registering the words. He could concentrate only on getting her indoors. On making the blood go away.

Somewhere in the midst of his unrelenting march forward, the wriggling stopped, her body becoming a soft, immobile weight in his arms. Her hands clasped the back of his neck, a sensation he could almost imagine as being pleasant. At least, he could if his heart were not pounding so thunderously. Were her skin not wet and cold, and his nose not filled with the scent of mud from her cloak.

Finally, they arrived back at the front steps—the short distance seeming to have taken a lifetime—and he climbed them two at a time, shoving open the door and bursting into the entrance hall.

"We need hot water. Linens," he barked at Mrs. Wheeler, who was hovering in the corner, trying to make sense of the chaos that had descended upon the house. But perplexed or not, she obeyed without a moment's hesitation, disappearing at the same time a footman emerged from the shadows with a lamp, ready to provide further assistance.

Due to its proximity, Ben opted to rush into the drawing room, the footman and Achilles close on his heels. Beneath the lamp's muted glow, he placed Violet on the settee and kneeled before her, working to unfasten her muddied cloak. Filled with alarm over what injuries it might conceal.

"I'm all right. Truly." Suddenly, her wet hand came atop his, stilling it, and her eyes turned to glinting orbs that assessed him in the dimness. "I fell and scraped my palm, and when I touched my face to check for additional cuts, I fear I may have spread the blood." She colored a little at that part; he could detect the change upon her countenance even in the low light. "I'm certain it's not as bad as it looks."

Pushing his hand gently out of the way, she finished untying her cloak herself, letting it fall to the settee. Whatever horrors he'd expected, he didn't find them. Her simple dark gown wasn't torn or bloodied; it wasn't even wet.

A slight relief, in any case. In the next moment, though, the industrious footman had the first of the wall sconces lit, its light revealing her damaged palm. The angry red smears on her face. The leaves in her hair, the dirt caked on her hem.

How had she come to be in this state? His mind swerved in myriad different directions, each one bleaker than the last. He both needed to know the details and dreaded them.

But before either of them could broach the subject, Mrs. Wheeler came hurrying in with the supplies he'd ordered, pushing aside an ormolu vase to make room for them on the end table beside the settee.

He bolted to his feet, standing back and nodding for the housekeeper to take his place. "Mrs. Prescott has cut herself. Please help her tend to the wounds." Yes, that was the best thing to do first. He and Violet would sort whatever the hell had transpired *after* she was no longer covered in blood.

As always, Mrs. Wheeler was quick to comply, but Violet held up her uninjured hand just as the housekeeper reached for the linen. "Thank you, Mrs. Wheeler, but that won't be necessary. I'm sure I can manage on my own, and you're free to go. I'd like a private word with Mr. Prescott."

Her eyes drifted to his as she uttered his name, the blue startling in its intensity. Christ, was the woman determined to ignore her well-being altogether and heed *nothing* he said this night?

Mrs. Wheeler did him the courtesy of looking his way for added direction, but she waited for only half a beat before bobbing a curtsy and scurrying away, with weak instructions to ring if they needed anything else. As for the footman, he followed close behind with a reluctant Achilles at his side, muttering something indistinct about washing the dog's paws.

With that, the drawing room door clicked shut, and Ben found himself face-to-face, alone, with his injured wife. His errant wife.

She wasted no time in shuffling down the settee and plunging her hand into the basin Mrs. Wheeler had brought, but whatever the housekeeper had put in the water made Violet wince and snatch it back out. She opted instead to bury her palm in her skirts, fumbling with her good hand for the roll of linen but inadvertently knocking it to the floor.

"Oh!" She made a little sound, her body shifting again so she could peer under the settee, the action causing a splatter of mud to spread as she jostled her discarded cloak.

"Stop." Ben's voice broke out, unable to hold back any longer. They would get nowhere while he stood here, watching her struggle.

He stepped forward, retrieving the linen from beneath the settee and pushing her soiled cloak to the floor with one long sweep of his arm. It was far too late to spare the settee from dirt, twigs, and leaves, but he ignored the mess, lowering himself beside her and taking her hand from the cradle she'd formed with her skirts.

Her eyes widened, and she made another of her soft noises, drawing in a quick puff of breath. She must not trust him, for she began squirming again, trying to free herself from his grip as he reached toward the basin. However, her efforts merely caused him to hold tighter.

"This will only hurt if you don't cease moving. Sit still," he ordered, dipping an edge of clean toweling in the water and bringing it to rest just above her palm. He waited for her to meet his gaze before proceeding any farther.

Comprehension flashed in her eyes, and with the realization that her sensitive palm was safe from another dousing, she nodded, giving up the struggle. "Very well." She flinched a little when the towel first hit her cuts, but true to her word, she kept her palm within his, allowing him to dab away the dirt and blood. However, her feet tapped rapidly against the floor, and she seemed to be swallowing excessively. It was as if her body were a coil, winding tighter and tighter. Until all at once, the tension became too much and words sprang out. "I'm trying to sit here as still as can be, but I can't wait another second to tell you about the river. About Lord Frederick's lake."

Ben's muscles tensed, his fingers momentarily faltering with the towel before he got himself back in line. He'd never been uncertain about where she'd snuck off to, but hearing her admit it aloud made the truth hit with particular harshness.

Violet, though, appeared far too eager to notice his disconcertment. She took the slightest pause for breath, then leaned forward, her face flushed with animation. "Any excuses his lordship makes about diverting the river for flood prevention are falsehoods. He's doing it to fill his new ornamental lake."

A *lake*? An ornamental lake. Ben let the words percolate, a vein in his neck beginning to throb.

"I should have realized it sooner," she continued earnestly when all she received from him was silence. "I knew he was undertaking a huge landscaping project, which included adding a lake. I suppose I just never imagined he'd be so nefarious in how he chose to fill it. Sure enough, though, when I went to the site of the dam and followed the diversion channel, it led me right to the new lake's shore. I meant to take a closer look so I could discern the exact configuration, but when the guard heard me, I—"

"A *guard*?" Ben snapped. He hadn't thought his chest could contain another ounce of ire, but he'd apparently been mistaken.

"Yes." She frowned, catching her bottom lip between her

teeth. "Lord Frederick undoubtedly knows he's done wrong, but I'm afraid he's committed to his scheme, for he's hired a big, burly fellow to stand watch by the river. You'd best warn your staff and tenants to stay clear of Watley for the time being. The guard merely fired into the air and caused me to startle and fall, but I'd hate to think what could happen if when the next person came along, he adjusted his aim and—"

"*What?*" Ben's voice was sharp and ragged, his lungs on the verge of bursting. How could she sit here and so blithely tell him she'd been *shot* at? As if she had no care for the danger she'd imposed on herself.

Somehow, he managed to set aside the towel and open the jar of salve Mrs. Wheeler had brought without shattering it in his fist. Somehow, he dotted the concoction over Violet's cuts while keeping his touch steady and featherlight. And somehow, he both evened and quieted his tone when he announced, "I'm going to murder Lord Frederick Denham."

"You mustn't say that." She shook her head emphatically, neglecting her promise of stillness and curling her fingers tight around his. "Responding to his threat with violence will do nothing to help your case."

He glanced up from his task to meet those big, crystal-clear eyes, letting his hand remain temporarily captured. She was right, of course. It was just exceptionally difficult to maintain his hold on reason when his pulse kept thundering the way it did.

"Meanwhile," she added as he retrieved the linen and coaxed her fingers to relax, "I have no qualms about riding over to Watley tomorrow and demanding he explain himself."

His hand, warmed by the heat of her bare skin, suddenly felt frigid, and he stumbled again, the linen nearly slipping from his grasp before he caught it with stiff fingers. She was trying to help; logically, he knew that. However, the icy pinpricks that stabbed him to the core cared nothing for logic.

They cared only that every dilemma Violet encountered was met with the same solution: a visit to Watley. Even after she could have been bloody well killed, she had no inclination to stay away.

"No." It was the only word he could manage, spoken with a clipped, ominous quality. What would it take to rid her of her wish to keep returning to the site of that blasted house party? To keep crossing paths with the man she'd hoped to marry? Was such a thing even possible, or would the desire remain with her for the rest of her days?

He focused on dressing her palm with almost fanatical precision, refusing to let his thoughts settle anywhere but on wrapping the linen with perfect folds. Not that his determination could stop his gut from roiling.

He could feel her eyes watching him as he worked. Could feel his insides clench and sputter, as if they contained a flame ready to burst into an inferno. And then, in a hesitant murmur, her words came. "You're angry with me."

He didn't turn away from his task to answer. Perhaps she was hoping for a denial, for a return to their habit of exchanging only banalities, but he couldn't comply. He *was* angry. He was fucking furious. Because Violet was bleeding. Because Violet wanted George Metcalfe.

"I know I went against your wishes," she said, "but I was trying to help—"

"Perhaps, but I find myself wondering something." He abruptly looked up, the frostiness of his tone ringing in his ears. Every nerve ending a combination of ice and fire. "Were you trying to help on all the other occasions you slipped away to Watley land, or did your visits have another purpose?"

Even while his body felt on the verge of combustion, he kept her hand secure within his, careful not to jostle it. Yet suddenly, she flinched as though he'd doused her palm in vinegar. She tugged it out of his grasp, scrambling to the opposite edge of the settee so an obvious gap rested between them. "What could you possibly mean by that?"

There was still time to douse the flames, to tamp down the ugly emotions coursing through his veins and return to a state of detached composure. However, every unspoken shred of doubt he'd harbored since the day of their betrothal, every unwanted pang of envy, swelled within him until he was powerless to hold back. "You insisted I not stray beyond the bounds of our marriage. Did you never think I would want the same courtesy in return?"

Her lips parted, her brows rising high on her forehead. "You cannot be implying ..." She sat with the declaration, unmoving, for several long, torturous seconds before her eyes narrowed, the vivid blue flashing dangerously in the candle-light. "As husband and wife, you and I have done pitiably little conversing, so let me make something clear. I haven't stepped foot in Watley Hall since the day of our encounter in the hut, nor would I have *strayed* if I had. I don't hold anything close to amorous sentiments for the gentlemen at that ridiculous party, least of all George Metcalfe, who was so appalled by my shocking behavior that he quickly hied back to London with no plans to return."

Now, Ben was the one who felt he had wounds drenched in vinegar. Or perhaps as though he'd been slapped to alertness. He'd ... he'd been *wrong*. A realization that proved equal parts relieving and horrifying.

On second thought, the *horrifying* part took precedence. He'd been an idiot, too cowardly to talk to his own wife. And now, she was bolting to her feet, glaring down at him with unrestrained fury. "How dare you question me?" she demanded. "How *dare* you, when *you're* the one who keeps shutting me out? When *you're* the one who's keeping secrets."

She may as well have barreled over him with a gelding from the stables, for the air rushed from his lungs, and he couldn't seem to refill them properly. Nor could he think in a coherent sequence.

To what did she refer, exactly? She'd said her mother enjoyed the gossip rags, where matters concerning the Prescott family had often appeared throughout the years for anyone's perusal. He'd never asked Violet which tidbits of gossip she'd read, but he hadn't outright lied about any of it, either. He'd partaken in omissions of truth, perhaps ...

In any case, he could do nothing but rise from the settee and give his chin a stiff shake. "I don't know what you're talking about."

Somehow, that seemed to be the worst thing to say of all. The thing that brought the glint in her eyes beyond outrage to somewhere dark, intent, and threatening. She stepped forward, erasing the gap she'd created between them, standing so close that her bodice brushed against his waistcoat. So close that he heard her trembling inhale before she opened her mouth and said, in a voice as expressive and clear as any Covent Garden actress, "'*You've misbehaved, Mrs. Rumpteaser. And with disobedience must come punishment.*'"

Oh.

Oh.

He remained upright, his muscles achingly taut, although she could have knocked him over and broken him with a tap from her index finger.

And still, she didn't relent.

"*Her loins ached, quivering with a need that only he could satiate.*" Violet's words gained momentum, vanquishing the short-lived silence. "'*Fill me, my lord, fill me—*'"

"Cease this at once," he rasped, trying to move back but finding his legs had nowhere to go beyond hitting the edge of the settee. His heart was pounding out of control, an errant hammer against his ribs. This problem required an immediate solution, but he couldn't concentrate, could scarcely even see straight.

Her lashes fluttered with feigned innocence. "You don't care to hear those passages recited?" And instead of retreating, she rose to her tiptoes, her breath a hot stream, her words a maddening siren's song, against his bare throat. "I'll choose another, then. *He breached her where she was hot and slick, her welcoming cunt enveloping him—*"

"I said stop it." His demand was rough. Raw. "You're being obscene."

"Obscene?" she hissed, her hands flying to his chest, the touch searing through his waistcoat and shooting to the marrow of his bones. "You damn well wrote the words!"

Stupid, stupid, stupid. He should have realized the scandal would follow him to Wiltshire, that there would be no avoiding it. Should have thought of what he would say, he supposed, even though he'd never anticipated having a wife with whom he'd share his confidences.

He *hadn't* realized, though. Hadn't thought. And now he *did* have a wife whose face nearly touched his as she waited for him to say something, and he didn't know, didn't know …

He didn't know anything beyond that her flushed cheeks contained dirt and dried blood, that her eyes looked ready to burn a hole through him, that her mouth, which had so candidly narrated the explicit text, was very near to his.

His heart hadn't ceased thundering, but for the first time, it occurred to him that maybe the frenzied *thump, thump, thump* originated from her chest as well as his own. The air was so heavy, so hot, as if it contained invisible sparks, and he needed to get away but also couldn't stop breathing it in—

Except then, she pressed her palms harder against his waistcoat and shoved away from him, and instead of her pattering heartbeat, he had only a cold void. Her accusing stare. "I'm through here," she muttered, her tone laced with ice. "I won't stay to listen to your self-righteous denials. If you refuse to be honest with me, I don't want to hear another word."

He staggered, blinking inanely while she spun away and marched toward the door like an unstoppable tempest. But he had to stop her, couldn't leave things like this. "Violet—"

"Don't." She spared a fraction of a second to look back and bestow on him a venomous glower. A warning. And then, she was gone, her mass of tangled hair and mud-stained hem disappearing into the corridor.

He took a step forward. Backward. Forward again. "Fuck!" He pressed his fingers to his temples, striving for clarity, sanity, any scrap of reason to which he could cling. But there was none to be found. Nothing to do but stumble blindly into the corridor and toward the stairs, his head violently whirling. Blood pounding through his veins.

Never let the sun set on your provocation.

He'd *wanted* to make things right with her before the evening was through. Except then she'd gone missing, and the night had taken so many chaotic turns that he no longer knew which way was up.

She must have run all the way up the stairs, for no sooner did he reach the top landing than a door slammed shut, leaving no doubt as to where she'd gone.

Which was good, perhaps. He could do just as he'd intended earlier and knock on her bedchamber door. Try to explain.

Were he a better man—a sensible man, a genteel man—he would have chosen that path rather than bypassing her door completely and bursting through his own, kicking it closed with his boot and turning the lock.

But he wasn't a better man right now. He was a goddamn mess.

He strode across the floor to his washstand, the mirror

above it catching his reflection and revealing his disgrace. The skin at his throat was dotted with his wife's bloody fingerprints. His white shirt had turned dingy, his waistcoat wrinkled and dirt-stained. And his muddy trousers had become far too tight, for it would seem he'd developed a rampant cockstand.

'*Fill me, my lord …*'

Hot and slick …

Welcoming cunt …

The words wouldn't stop circling back to him. Neither would the glimmer in her eyes, the flash of her pink tongue as she'd uttered them so unabashedly.

He plunged his hands into the basin of tepid water, splashing it over his face and neck. Staring at the disheveled image of himself, watching the water run beneath his shirt.

Until suddenly, he pivoted, his fingers tearing at his fall, sending buttons flying to the carpet until his erection sprang free. He took himself in hand, stifling a groan at the first stroke of relief. He quickly established a rhythm, pumping up and down the turgid shaft.

What had she done to him? He'd never felt like this before. Desperate. Unhinged.

"Violet," he choked out, the name rising unbidden from some place deep inside him. His current existence was composed of golden hair and full breasts pressing against him. Of floral perfume and hot breath and parted lips. '*Fill me, my lord.*'

His yearning spiked, ready to crash over a precipice. Which made it astounding, really, that the low sound from next door managed to reach his awareness.

It was a cry, soft and feminine. Wounded, perhaps. A cry that made his hand drop to his side and shame pierce his gut. What sort of husband induced his wife to weep? He was a reprobate, the worst kind of fiend—

But then, the cry sounded again. And again. Not the wail of a woman in distress but a needy, increasing moan.

Oh, God.

Oh, God; oh, Christ; oh, blistering hell, his wife was in the next room *pleasuring* herself. Not attempting to hold anything back.

He scrabbled frantically behind him for a towel, grabbing it into his fist at the same moment his other hand returned to his cock. One more stroke was all it took for his seed to spill out in thick jets and heady waves to inundate his body. Violet's moans led him through every one of them until, at last, both his shudders and her temptress's voice faded away.

He hastily cleaned himself, then staggered to his bed on legs that felt boneless, stopping just long enough to remove his boots before tumbling atop the counterpane, muddy clothing and all.

What in hell had happened? He stared at the plaster ceiling in a daze, satiated warmth running through his limbs. Proof it hadn't been only a feverish dream, even though Violet's bedchamber was now silent.

He could lie to himself and say that after this rare lapse in self-possession, he would spend all his days going forward level-headed and restrained.

The truth was, though, that beneath the vague aftershocks of pleasure lay a new and potent need he hadn't even begun to address.

14

I t took Ben a moment to get his bearings when sunlight first pierced his eyelids the next morning.

He'd gone to sleep in his bed last night, the same way he always did. However, his mouth was dry, filled with an odd taste. His limbs tingled but also felt oddly constrained. And his pulse thrummed a beat or two more quickly than usual, almost as if in anticipation. In warning?

His eyes flew open, falling upon the sight of his fully clothed body sprawled across the dirt-stained counterpane. He hadn't washed properly last night. Hadn't even brushed his teeth. Instead, he'd tumbled into bed wearing his muddied shirt, waistcoat, and trousers, which was how he remained now. Another cockstand poking through his damaged fall.

He scrambled upright, memories of all the events that had led to this moment inundating him like a deluge. The injured palm, the argument, the erotic recitations, the breathless moans.

Hellfire and damnation.

His gaze darted to the wall between the master's and mistress's chambers—the bit of wood and plaster that kept his wife just out of reach—and a sharp blow swiftly pummeled him in the gut.

The connecting door between the two rooms was open. Not shut and locked the way he always left it, but inched *open*.

He sprang from bed to fetch his banyan, his mind racing backward to the moment he'd discovered Violet missing last night. Yes, he *had* opened the door to check for her, but he'd closed it again afterward. Hadn't he?

Well, no, perhaps not. But even if not then, he'd surely done so later in the night. Or if he'd neglected the task, Violet would have remembered. Right? Yet sunlight streamed directly onto the polished wood and illuminated the space where the door stood ajar.

God, did that mean ... could Violet have *seen* him? Heat flooded his face, creating a fiery prickle that spread down his neck. He tried to focus on other possibilities: Violet had opened the door at dawn to check if he was awake. Achilles had nudged it with his nose. A draft had blown it askew in the middle of the night. Were any of those likely alternatives to the scenario he'd first imagined?

He supposed there was only one way to find out.

Wrapping the banyan tightly around his body, he gave the door a single tap before easing it the rest of the way open and peering inside. However, the only person to greet him was the chambermaid in the midst of making Violet's bed.

He halted and cleared his throat, uncertain if the muscles clenching in his chest signaled relief or disappointment. "Where's Mrs. Prescott?"

The maid stared at him a beat too long but ultimately dipped her head. "Last I saw, she'd just finished breakfast, sir. I believe she was preparing for her daily promenade."

Damn, how long had he slept? He was accustomed to rising with the sun, keeping his days ordered and productive.

But this was no time to focus on the position of hands on a clock.

He made a gruff noise of acknowledgment and hastened back to his own chamber, *very* certain to close and lock the door before shedding his banyan. Then, he cast off the rest of his sorry clothing, rummaging in his clothespress for replacements to make him look presentable again. It was impossible to fully return to a state of refinement without the proper bath and shave he needed, but he forwent both in the interest of time.

Confronting his wife may not be easy, but it was necessary. And he didn't have a moment to lose.

By neglecting pomade for his unruly hair and tying the knots in his cravat not quite evenly, he made it downstairs just in time to encounter Violet in the entrance hall with Achilles at her heels. She was adjusting a vibrant crimson shawl about her shoulders and murmuring something to the dog when his footsteps caused her to look up.

Her eyes widened at the sight of him, not unlike the chambermaid's, but at least Violet didn't appear openly repulsed. "Good morning." It was hardly the warmest greeting he'd ever received, but neither did it contain outright contempt. "We're just leaving for a walk."

Achilles's tail swished eagerly at the word, and while he trotted over to give Ben a polite sniff, he then returned to wait by the door beside the mistress with whom he'd apparently found favor.

Ben swallowed, willing his voice not to crack. "I'll come with you."

She pursed her lips. "I'm sure you have more important things to do."

"I don't."

Her brows scrunched, her hands going to her hips. "What about breakfast?"

"I'm not hungry." Indeed, how could he care about food when his wife was ready to abscond yet again with everything between them still jumbled and unresolved? At its core, the matter went far beyond the unlocked door and what they'd each heard or seen. He owed her an apology for his behavior earlier in the evening, and while he may have been too addled, too frenzied, to address the situation last night, with morning light came clarity. A little of it, anyway.

She let out a long sigh, not trying to hide her irritation. "Very well." Her pert chin bobbed. "But take care to keep up."

He hurriedly accepted the invitation, however unenthusiastic, following her brisk footsteps as she strode outdoors and turned toward the back garden. Her face was pinched, her gaze remaining far in the distance, refusing to drift in his direction even the slightest bit. But at least they were here, together. That had to count as a small victory.

Ultimately, he let her take the lead, slowing his footfalls to match Achilles's tottering pace and keeping at her back. They needn't speak immediately if she wasn't ready. He could be patient.

He passed the time staring at the figure in front of him. Brilliant golden hair pinned neatly beneath a straw bonnet. An airy white dress, decorated with tiny embroidered flowers, that wafted behind her in the breeze. Dainty gloves, flawless except for a faint bulge in the left one that must be covering the bandage on her palm.

She'd put herself back to rights, so bright and lovely it was difficult to envision her as being dirt-stained and battered mere hours ago. He *did* envision it, though. He imagined the weight of her body as he'd cradled her in his arms. The softness of her ungloved hand as he'd wiped it clean.

His musings risked driving him to distraction again until, with a sharp jolt, he discerned the path on which she led him. They'd skimmed past the formal garden and gone down to the river, but she didn't stop there. Instead, she continued her path into the woods, heading toward Watley without missing a beat. Just as he'd seen her do on countless days prior, as if not a thing in the world had changed.

He and Achilles followed—doing otherwise wasn't an option—but his throat became acrid, and tight bands constricted his ribs. What was the meaning of this? After the incident with the guard, and her avowal that she had no interest in going to Watley, she couldn't possibly intend to—

She whirled around to face him, the shrewd glint in her eyes daring him to question her. To his benefit, perhaps, he was so taken aback by her apparent ability to read minds that he neglected to turn his thoughts into an interrogation.

Yes, his speechlessness was a fortunate thing, indeed. For after a single moment's pause, she pivoted once more, taking a sharp turn away from the double-trunked oak that marked the property line and striding north. Not east to Watley, the way he'd always imagined her doing. She started up an incline, along a faintly marked path through the trees he hadn't noticed before. Whether or not he followed didn't seem to concern her.

His boots froze to the ground beneath him, his jaw slackening as the meaning of what he witnessed hit the surface of his awareness. Permeated. Then besieged him with a hot torrent of remorse.

There was no getting around it: he was a dunderhead. Inventing false scenarios in his mind, accusing her of wrongdoing because he hadn't been clever enough to imagine anything but the most nefarious possibilities.

He jerked himself back into motion, ignoring the heaviness that settled into his limbs and starting up the path before he could lose sight of her. While the surroundings remained unfamiliar to him, she forged ahead with more speed than ever, dodging tree trunks and hopping over felled logs as if she'd traversed these woods all her life.

"I regret to say, your master is an ass," he muttered to Achilles, hefting the elderly dog into his arms so he could spare the creature's legs on the slope. With that, he tramped up the hill, keeping his eyes on her crimson shawl until the trees thinned, the ground leveled, and an open field appeared up ahead.

She bolted into the clearing, and he found himself running after her, faster and faster until he burst from the shadowy maze of oaks and into the brilliant sunshine.

They'd arrived in a large swath of grass, liberally sprinkled with wildflowers and with a single prominent beech tree growing in its midst. A picturesque sight, although it was merely a precursor to the scenery beyond. From this vantage point, they had an unobstructed view of all the fields and pastures, all the low stone walls and tiny cottages, below. Everything gleamed beneath the morning light—green, crisp, and vivid. It was laid before him as pristinely as a painting, this land he'd been charged with overseeing, that was so far removed from London but could be his home if he accepted it.

Yet suddenly, the idyllic scene was secondary to the view of Violet striding to the beech and sinking to the grass against its trunk. She kicked off her shoes and tossed her bonnet aside, revealing delicate silk stockings and a full head of golden curls. And then, her eyes met his, as blue and clear as the sky.

"This is where I come to read," she said tartly, the gaze lasting only an instant before she busied herself with her reticule, rummaging within and pulling out a book. "Please feel free to carry on your way."

She located the page she sought, then held the book close to her face and quickly became absorbed in its contents. Ben, however, refused to *carry on*.

He set down the wriggling Achilles and cautiously approached the tree, ducking into its shade and squinting so he could make out the title on her book's spine. *A Vindication of the Rights of Woman*. Mary Wollstonecraft. A particular favorite of his mother's; he should have known Violet would esteem it, too. Clever, determined woman she was.

She grew so caught up in the text that her focus never wavered, although did she truly not notice the figure looming above her?

"Violet." He cleared his throat, feeling large and ungainly, but he forced himself to remain where he was, arms planted stiffly at his sides. "I wonder if you would forgo your book for the time being so we can speak."

That, at least, enticed her to look up and assess him. Were he not mistaken, a faint flash of pink spread over her cheeks, and she bit down on her lip, not saying a word.

Her chin moved, though, a slight gesture inviting him to sit on the ground beside her. After another moment, she set her book down, releasing a quiet puff of breath.

He accepted without hesitation, lowering himself onto the shaded grass while taking care not to crowd *too* close to her. Maintaining a respectable distance was best, so he wouldn't become distracted by the brush of her skirts or the sweet scent of floral perfume. He needed to think of last night logically, without envisioning her sliding her skirts up her thighs or circling her fingertips over intimate flesh.

He squeezed his hands into fists, forcing the thought to dissipate. Before he could start making veiled inquiries about the connecting door—*without* letting the discussion affect him—something else more pressing required stating. Something there was no easy way to address, so he'd just have to come out with it.

"What I said to you about respecting our marriage vows ... When I implied you did not ..." He paused, watching the flicker in her eyes, a sharp pang stabbing him in the chest. "I drew the wrong conclusion. For that, I profusely apologize."

She let a long moment of silence fall, her fingers idly sweeping over the lush blades of grass. "It's difficult for two strangers to build trust when they scarcely communicate," she said at last, her hands returning to her lap. Her gaze becoming pointed. "Nevertheless, I do forgive you ... for that."

Relief turned to trepidation in his gut within seconds. Not that he'd been so naive as to think that with one apology, the other issues at hand would vanish.

She forgave him for his inane assumption. That was good, very good. However, there was still the matter of his secret that wasn't a secret. Her knowledge—how long had she harbored it?—of his *literary pursuits,* which left her feeling deceived and appalled.

He knew no easy way to broach this subject, either. No way to make a confession that had implications far beyond his own person. Yet to say nothing would be to ensure that the distance between them always remained an untraversable void. That their marriage never progressed beyond a couple of signatures in a parish register, scrawled in haste, out of necessity. He didn't want that. Not for the rest of his life, not anymore.

And so, he took a breath, peering into blue eyes, at pursed lips, and refusing to look away. "May I ask where you procured the literature you quoted to me last night?"

Her fingers curled into the folds of her muslin skirt, and while another hint of color shaded her cheeks, she, too, held the gaze without faltering. "It would seem it's quite popular amongst the servants, as is the tale of the anonymous author's identity and his expulsion from Cambridge for his efforts. Or so I was told by my lady's maid on the night before our wedding."

Damn. Why did gossip have to be so blasted virulent? He'd imagined this idyllic countryside, far from both

Cambridge and London, would offer a haven from it. He certainly *hadn't* imagined his household as being all-knowing, tittering over their new master's licentiousness when he was out of earshot.

But there was no use dwelling on it and little he could do to change what had come to pass. In this moment, he simply had to make a choice based on the cards he'd already been dealt: to lie, or to trust her.

The former being the safer choice, certainly. But the latter being the right one.

"I didn't write those pamphlets." He let the words fall before he could think better of it, their echo a heavy weight that sliced through the springtime breeze.

Violet's body stiffened, a severe line forming at the bridge of her nose. She thought he was prevaricating, giving the false denials she'd warned him against.

Which meant he still had far more explaining to do.

"I claimed it was me," he said, taking a key and unlocking the truth he'd so fervently guarded, forcing the story to pour from his throat. "But the real author is my brother, Alexander."

The hand on her skirts jerked, the line between her brows deepening. "But … why would you do such a thing?"

He pressed his palms against the grass for support, weariness leaching right to his bones. *Why, Ben?* The question his family had also asked when he'd returned from Cambridge in disgrace, as if the answer weren't perfectly obvious.

Violet, though, was a stranger to the intricacies of the Prescott family. What else was left but to enlighten her?

"Because." He unclenched his jaw, blowing out a breath from too-tight lungs. "Alex needed to stay at university more than I did."

He had to look away, then, to turn instead to the sweeping landscape beyond the tree. Rolling hills, fertile fields. So far removed from King's College at Cambridge, although he could imagine his brother as plain as a pikestaff, clad in his silk robe and mortarboard with the tassel forever hanging askew.

"I told him his writing would get him in trouble one day. Especially when, during his second year at Cambridge, he turned the subject of his published works to ... to *that*." Ben tried not to sound perturbed as he uttered the revelation. He'd never wanted to appear scornful of Alex's literary endeavors, despite how his brother's ever-increasing interest in penning stories and inhabiting their parents' printshop left a niggling sense of dread in his gut. However, when bundles of the erotic pamphlets made their way from London to King's College, exploding in popularity with the same fervor as gunpowder tossed on a bonfire, he couldn't help but voice his disapproval. He'd always envisioned the consequences, even when Alex remained immune to such worries.

"He did stop publishing for a while." Ben shifted his rigid shoulders, recalling the faint surge of relief he'd felt. The months when he'd tried to pretend that Alex was settling down and would be content to focus solely on his studies. It wasn't to last, of course. "At the beginning of this year's Lent term, though, the pamphlets returned. More coveted and widespread than ever after their temporary absence, which was their downfall in the end."

The grass rustled beside him, and he could sense Violet's body drawing nearer, all warmth and sweetness even more aromatic than the wildflowers surrounding them.

"One day, Alex and I were summoned to the provost's office," he said, continuing to look into the distance at the boundless sky. "I don't think it was ever a mystery to our classmates where the pamphlets came from. Alex distributed them at the start of each term, and when anyone questioned him about the anonymous author, he simply gave a roguish smile, neither confirming nor denying anything."

The memory of that smile hurt. So carefree and easily given, whereas Ben had always stood back with his jaw clenched, unable to shake his sense of impending danger.

"It got to such a point that the administration had had enough of the depravity. It didn't take the skill of a private detective to trace the pamphlets back to Robinson and Clare, our mother and stepfather's printshop in London. Nor did it escape anyone's notice that new issues always appeared when Alex and I returned after visits to London with our family." He gritted his teeth, still able to feel the walls of the provost's office closing in on him. The weight of Dr. Thackeray's scrutiny.

"I think I was summoned as a formality. Alex and I always traveled to and from Cambridge together, so it would be wrong to accuse him alone. The provost knew, though. He knew the truth." Ben struggled for air, his voice cracking, intensifying. "He knew the truth, and I lied to him. I said it was me. I *insisted*. I told him my brother was blameless and that I wanted Alex to leave so I could accept my punishment privately."

"And your brother was happy to go along with this?" Violet's words were a soft murmur. Not horrified, just somewhat incredulous.

He shook his head stiffly. "I didn't let him speak. I made my voice louder than his, and I gainsaid him every time he opened his mouth. I fought with everything I had until the provost finally allowed him to leave. And then, I walked with Alex to the door so I could whisper that if he dared contradict my claims to anyone, I would never forgive him."

Alex had been dumbfounded. Alex, with the black tassel hanging haphazardly behind his ear, had looked at him with a mixture of confusion and anger. But most importantly, Alex had done as he was told and left.

"Why were you so insistent that the blame fall on your

shoulders?" she asked, and he didn't have to turn to detect the perplexity twisting her features. "Did you not have a care for your studies? Your reputation?"

A thick lump rose in his throat. "I—didn't need to stay at university. I'd already obtained my bachelor's degree, I ..." *I only remained at Cambridge because for as long as I was there, I didn't have to choose between betraying my past or denying my future.*

He didn't give voice to the last part, to the buried truth within him that cut far too deeply for words. He skipped it instead, forcing himself to carry on with the remainder of the story.

"Alex needed it more," he said roughly, and that part cut, too, gnawing at another longstanding ache. "He ... requires a purpose, somewhere to focus his attention."

Images of his brother flashed through his memory once more. Alex sneaking away from the college after curfew, meeting Ben's admonitions with a lazy grin. *Ah, Ben, don't be such a prig.* Alex with a quill in hand, scribbling furiously to get the latest tale he'd invented onto the page. Alex refusing to rise from bed for the tenth day in a row, Alex with a brandy bottle in hand, Alex with the same sharp azure eyes as their father—

"He requires somewhere he'll be safe from his own vices," Ben choked out, digging his nails into his palms before the lump in his throat could get the better of him. "I had it in my power to give him that. Doing otherwise was never an option for me."

He stared at green grass. Cerulean sky. He inhaled the strengthening scent of wildflower perfume, although his mind was spiraling backward, hurtling him into a dim study. Assaulting him with the harsh odor of gin, with the image of an overturned bottle. A limp hand.

"You understand, don't you?" He spun his head to face

her, finding she'd inched very close, and he didn't recoil but drew closer still, his insides knotted with a strange desperation. She must understand, this woman who'd sacrificed—who'd forgone her own desires and bound herself in marriage to him —on account of her sister.

And Violet—his unintended wife, a recent stranger, a woman with whom he might have more in common than he thought—nodded, her plush lips gently parting. "Yes."

Yes. The knots within him snapped, a wave of tension draining from his shoulders. Her face was in front of his, sunlit and placid and beautiful, and she understood. She *understood.* He'd been right to trust her with his brother's secret. Perhaps he could even consider her ... an ally?

If only he hadn't wasted so much time avoiding the subject, pretending it would magically disappear without consequence.

He released a long breath, sinking his fingers into the knees of his trousers before they got better ideas and clung to her gown instead. "I'm sorry to have brought this scandal into our marriage. I should have made you aware of it before we spoke our vows, so you weren't unknowingly subjected to shame."

"But I'm not ashamed. Quite the contrary, actually." She shifted, her skirts sweeping against his leg. Her eyes were so bright, so inviting, studying him more intently than ever. As if she saw what rested far below the surface. "Perhaps my initial instincts about you were correct, after all."

His ears, his entire body, pricked. "What instincts?"

"I thought you were as rigid as a ramrod." She said it unflinchingly, although the wry tilt of her mouth made it impossible for him to take offense. Especially not when her bandaged hand reached out, her fingertips lightly falling atop his sleeve. Lingering for an instant. "But I also suspected you were honorable. Good."

He shut his eyes, the words seeping into his chest, closing around his heart. He tried, he tried so damn hard, to be honorable, but he often felt lately like he failed miserably and got everything wrong. But Violet still recognized his intentions. She *saw* him.

She saw him, and when his eyelids drifted open, he saw her, too: the woman who shared his home and his name. The woman who was all color and light, strength and passion. The woman who sharpened his senses and made him want things he never had before.

He dared to raise his hand, to let a lone fingertip skirt against the curve of her chin, and to utter words he hadn't thought he'd say. "May I kiss you, Violet?"

Her breath hitched, the quiet sound hitting like a shower of sparks upon his skin. Her lashes fluttered; her face tipped upward.

And all at once, their lips were aligned, pressing together in a gentle embrace.

He'd known she was soft, had recognized it from that first day when he'd held her ankle within his palm. However, he couldn't have anticipated how her lips would be like pillows, plump and inviting. How he would wish to sink into them and never emerge.

He brought a hand to her nape, splaying his fingers across her collar, her skin, the tendrils that hung from her coiffure. Everything was warm and delicate, and he absorbed the sensation, lightly holding her against him as he explored the wonder that was her mouth.

She held him, too, her hands running through his hair, drifting down his back. And the more they each took, the more he wanted. She was sweet, *so* sweet, and he let his tongue emerge, carefully tracing over the edge of her lip. Her body flexed, a keening noise rising in her throat.

Which made him halt, his fingers stiffening against her nape.

Had he overstepped? There was such a thin line between pleasure and pain. Between sounds of distress and sounds of yearning.

Good. I needn't be inconvenienced, then. Her words on their wedding night, when he'd informed her he wouldn't visit her chamber. She'd been prepared to do her duty in the marriage bed, but ... but did she *want* to?

He'd gotten carried away, letting newfound desire trump reason. God, he hadn't even finished what he set out to do and solve the mystery of the open door. The moment for that, though, had passed.

"Forgive me." He drew away, allowing his fingers a final brush over the soft flesh at her nape before returning his hands to his lap. "I should get back. I have another meeting scheduled with the solicitor."

"Benedict ..." He didn't know what to make of the way she said his name. It was part breath, part admonition, part ... plea? But whatever it meant, she followed it with a brief sigh—not angry, only resigned—and repositioned herself against the tree trunk. "All right. I'm going to remain here for a while and read. Achilles can stay with me if he'd like." She glanced toward the sleeping dog who lay sprawled out beneath the sunshine, then turned back to him, her lips kiss-swollen and pink. "Will I see you at dinner?"

It was a simple question, yet the answer gave him pause. Instinct demanded he remain in his study until nightfall, shielded from the matter of uncertain kisses and of another type of uncertain intimacy, forged beneath the veil of darkness as a door—possibly—hung ajar.

Except he didn't want to stay shut away from her. Something between him and Violet had altered, broken free, and if he could trust her with the truth of the pamphlets ...

well, maybe those other subjects were also worth confronting, when the time was right.

"Yes," he said, straightening his spine, and he didn't regret his answer, even as it made his stomach flip.

"All right," she repeated gently. She reached for her book, finding the place where she'd left off and immersing herself in the text. Not looking up again.

He did as he said, rising from the comfortable place they'd created beneath the tree, brushing off his trousers, and turning to leave. At least, that's what he did after taking one last moment to survey the unparalleled beauty of the scene.

The last thing he saw before striding away was the hint of her smile.

15

For the first time since moving into Aldercombe Grange, Violet was grateful for the ridiculous length of the dining table.

From her usual seat at the table's foot, she speared a carrot slice with her fork, popping it into her mouth and chewing delicately. However, as much as she tried thinking of little beyond the contents of her dinner plate, her eyes kept darting upward, sneaking glances at the clean-shaven, neatly attired, perfectly coiffed gentleman sitting across from her. The gentleman who may be put back to rights, but that did nothing to make her forget how he'd looked with his hair curly and wild, his jaw darkened by a new beard, and the skin at his throat exposed in the absence of a cravat. Nothing to erase the feel of his palm clutching her nape, the scent of his shaving soap mixed with something else undeniably male, the sound of his rough groan—

She took a hasty sip from her wine goblet, squeezing her thighs together as a frisson radiated from low in her belly. If there was any providence to be had, her cheeks wouldn't flush and betray the nature of her thoughts.

Her head hadn't stopped spinning for a good twenty-four hours. Not since their argument in the study, followed by their confrontation in the drawing room and then their encounter in the meadow this morning. One thing after another, all challenging her preconceived notions and shattering them like crystal beneath his heavy boots.

She set down the goblet, although she hesitated before retrieving her cutlery, taking a moment to swallow back the dryness in her throat. Her husband—reserved, distant creature he was—had opened up to her. Trusted her with a secret. *Kissed* her.

And furthermore, he *desired* her. Her face became hot, and she could only hope the space between them would prevent him from noticing.

She inelegantly cut herself a piece of sole with lemon sauce, studying him from beneath her lashes. Yes, he'd returned to the picture of a gentleman, alternating between making nondescript comments about the day's worsening weather and busying himself with the vegetables upon his plate. Yet he was also the man who, in her mind's eye, stood in his darkened bedchamber with his fall gaping and his shaft in hand, pumping the engorged length as her name shot from his lips.

A clap of thunder shook the windowpanes, and she started, her fork wobbling as she brought it to her mouth. Was it a signal from the heavens for her not to think of such things? Unfortunately, that sort of restraint proved beyond her abilities.

From the moment she'd approached the cracked-open door between their bedchambers—thinking it a sign that perhaps she'd been too rash, that she hadn't fully given Benedict the chance to explain himself—and witnessed what she did, something within her had shifted. Snapped. Something that had made her desperate, that had caused her to fling herself on her bed and put her hands between her legs, crying out every bit of her frustration, her confusion, her lust. She hadn't cared if he heard. In fact, she'd *wanted* him to hear, wanted him to feel the same desperation and torment she did, but tenfold. Maybe even enough that he'd burst through the door and confront her.

Yet in the light of day, beneath the pleasant breeze on Skylark Ridge, she realized something: Benedict Prescott wasn't a man to be pushed. In his own time, he'd sat beside her in the beech tree's shade and told her the truth about the pamphlets. (She should have guessed he had a noble purpose in claiming authorship.) Of his own volition, he'd pressed his mouth to hers.

The intimacy, though, had seemed to scare him. His drive to remain the impeccable, reserved gentleman must be strong. And while his hesitancy made her want to scream a little, she saw him in a new light: as a man who did everything he could to protect his brother. A man who strove to do his best in an unfamiliar place and position. A man who would let himself be close to her again if she only gave him time.

She chewed thoughtfully, watching his throat work as he swallowed a piece of artichoke. The same throat that had emitted her name like a guttural plea, and—heavens, the dining room was getting hot. At least from this distance, she didn't have to contend with the crisp male scent of him. Nor was his rigid body close enough for her to reach out and touch.

Patience. A wind gust rattled the windowpanes, as if reminding her, insistently, of the necessity of the sixth virtue.

Biting back a sigh, she moved to retrieve another piece of fish, pondering a comment she could offer that went beyond the weather.

However, before she could say a word, another burst of noise echoed through the dining room. The wind again, picking up in intensity as the thunderstorm drew closer, but also ... voices. Footsteps.

Shouting.

Running.

She dropped her fork, her body instantly straightening to alertness. Benedict did the same, the dark slashes of his brows drawing together with apprehension.

"Mr. Prescott." All at once, a red-faced Pearce was in the doorway, his shoulders strangely hunched and his mouth dragging downward. "Forgive the interruption, but one of the grooms, Jem, is here with an urgent message."

"I'll see him at once." Benedict got to his feet in an instant, already starting toward the door. Despite his haste, he made it only halfway across the dining room before Pearce vanished and a young man, windblown and soaked through, appeared in his place.

"Oh, sir." At Benedict's clipped gesture, the disheveled groom—Jem—stumbled into the room, attempting a bow but ending it while remaining stooped and visibly winded. "It's the sheep ..." he panted between heaving breaths, his hands clutching the drenched knees of his trousers. "And the mud ... And the river ..."

"What about them?" Benedict's question was severe, the word *river* seeming to poke him like a thorn.

Jem attempted to straighten, his face flushed and despondent. "We think the dam at Watley must've burst, and now the river's flooding. Gushing right over the meadow, and the sheep ... The sheep've got down there somehow, and a few have become stuck in the mud. If something's not done, they're bound to be swept away!"

Violet heard herself gasp at the same moment Benedict emitted an oath she hadn't known was part of his repertoire. She watched, momentarily dazed, as a muscle ticked in his jaw and a shadow passed over his features, making him appear especially stony.

"Go to the kitchen to dry off." He abruptly issued the command to Jem, then strode past him, his rapid footfalls heavy with purpose. He made it as far as the doorway before Violet's lingering presence seemed to occur to him, and he spared a split second to glance at the foot of the table. "Please, excuse me."

That was the last she heard from him before he disappeared into the corridor, his footsteps echoing in the direction of the entrance hall. But by that point, she'd recovered her senses and was on her feet, scrambling into the corridor behind him.

She ran until she was at his side, earning a frown for her efforts. "Violet." He said her name as a warning, his pace momentarily slowing.

Oh, not this again. She charged ahead to the entrance hall, where Pearce stood in anticipation, already holding his master's greatcoat. "My cloak and boots, please, at once," she called to the footman who waited alongside the butler, at the ready for whatever task Benedict might require of him. Fortunately, he was equally prompt in accepting a request from her, and once he disappeared to fetch her things, she spun around, confronting her flinty-faced husband. "Clearly, I'm coming with you."

"No, you're not." Benedict seized his greatcoat from Pearce, the worried lines in his forehead deepening as he hauled it over his arms. "There's a bloody thunderstorm raging outdoors. Not to mention the fact that you were injured just last night."

"A few scratches, Benedict, nothing more." She kicked off her slippers, staring in his direction until those dark, anxious eyes locked with hers. "Haven't you realized by now that I *want* to help you? Not every burden pertaining to the estate needs to fall on your shoulders alone."

His mouth was severe, his creased brow showcasing every ounce of his discontent. Yet something flickered in his gaze. A sort of ... softness, almost. He released a quick huff of breath, his shoulders giving the slightest dip. "I don't have time to argue this."

Did that mean ... he conceded? She darted forward to meet the returning footman halfway, hastily accepting her proffered outerwear. She shoved the boots onto her feet and tossed the cloak over her shoulders. "We won't argue, then. Let's just go."

Whatever he muttered in response—she thought she detected the words *death of me*—was swallowed up by a gust of wind as Pearce threw open the front door. The world beyond was indeed ominous, the tree branches swaying violently and the clouds a purple-gray color that purged the landscape of brightness and cast it into artificial night.

Yet if Benedict believed the scene would deter her, he was wrong.

She moved to the threshold, steeling herself against the elements, preparing to give another rebuttal. Instead of words, though, she was met with the brush of kid leather against her palm. Fingers entwining with hers, clasping tight.

She squeezed back, taking a single instant to peer at the sight of her hand joined to her husband's, to let the spark of warmth shoot through her veins.

And then, in tacit agreement, they raced outdoors, placing themselves beneath the rumbling sky.

The wind was pitiless, tearing the hood from her head the second she raised it and making raindrops hit her face like pinpricks. It fought to push her backward, to send her tumbling to the wet ground and prove to her how she'd been wrong to think herself capable.

She didn't let it. She couldn't, not when the prosperity of the estate was at stake. This was their home, and she refused to sit back and watch it suffer another blow.

She used Benedict's hand as a guide when the downpour obstructed her vision, and she forced her legs to power forward without relenting. They ran over gravel and grass, through the small formal garden and into the field that traveled down to the river, an ever-increasing roar pounding in her ears.

A flash of lightning broke through the sky, casting the riverbed, which had been so callously drained, into stark illumination. It wasn't dried up now. Turbulent water swelled and gurgled, cresting over the banks and drawing precariously close to the bridge that led across to the irrigation channels. It was there that the hapless flock of sheep had situated themselves, bleating plaintively as farmhands hovered amongst them, everything a mixture of rain and chaos and so much mud.

Violet's heart sank to her boots. The scene was just as the frantic groom had described it, but witnessing it firsthand made the danger that much more imminent.

She felt herself being pulled to a halt as Benedict slowed beside her, his grip on her hand tightening. The grim set of his jaw relayed his despair, but she could sense his hesitation, too. He didn't want her down there, not where the ground was muddy and slippery, where thunder cracked and the river raged.

Yet she could no more turn around and abandon the flock —abandon *him*—than she could cease breathing.

"Come, we don't have a moment to lose." She squeezed his fingers, then gave a powerful push forward, twisting free of his grasp and rushing toward the imperiled bridge. She couldn't wait to ensure he agreed with her actions; they simply had to get to the water meadow and fix this before it was too late.

If he offered a reply, it was impossible to distinguish above the storm's cacophony. All she knew was that he caught up to her on the bridge, grabbing her by the waist and helping her across the slick stones until they stood upon the water meadow on the other side.

Now that they were immersed in the scene, the sound of yelling amongst the four farmhands became mixed with the noises of sheep and rainwater, amplifying the dissonance. One man circled anxiously behind the flock, while the others remained occupied with freeing two hefty ewes from their prison of mud, seemingly in disagreement over the best way to do so.

Benedict drew their attention by emitting a sharp whistle, loud enough to prove a match for the howling wind. "What in hell happened?" He freed Violet's waist, plodding over the sodden ground toward the four dripping faces that suddenly peered back at him with alarm.

"We don't rightly know." The eldest of the farmhands—a wiry gentleman with graying hair plastered to his head and weathered cheeks flecked with mud—momentarily released his hold on the trapped sheep's flanks to gesture to the tightly huddled flock. "Seems the wind must've freed them from their hurdle, and the witless creatures wandered down here, where they're used to grazing."

Even amidst the turmoil, Violet detected the bristling of her husband's body beneath his drenched greatcoat. "Where are Green and his dog?" he shouted, posing the question that plagued her, too. Why hadn't the shepherd noticed the flock's escape? Why had he—or the great shaggy dog who accompanied him in his work—done nothing to stop the situation before it reached the point of calamity?

The farmhand's shoulders quickly rose before he resumed his attempts at liberating the ewe, his face straining with effort. "No one's seen a trace of 'em. I sent a lad up toward his cottage, but there's nary a sign."

Benedict's curse began an instant before thunder reverberated across the landscape, as if reminding them of impending doom.

With the help of a final determined push, the ewe came free of the viscous puddle, eliciting a collective groan of relief from the farmhands who'd come to her aid. However, when the creature took a few tentative steps away, any hint of relief on Violet's part promptly crumbled into dust. The ewe strayed toward the newly repaired irrigation channels, where more thick mud created hazards in every direction.

Invigorated by their success, the farmhands set to work on freeing the second ensnared ewe, heedless of the remaining sheep. Violet saw them, though. Saw how hooves shifted against the wet grass. All it would take was one agitated ewe to start running, and suddenly, the entire flock would be racing across the water meadow, farther into mud and danger. If the sheep panicked, they had no way of herding them to safety. Not enough power to free them if they all became entrapped.

"Wait. Stop." The sharpness in Benedict's command suggested the looming risk had hit him, too. "Before you do anything else, we need to construct barriers. Something so the sheep will be driven back toward the bridge rather than wandering farther onto the meadow."

Yes, barriers ... She scanned the dismal scene, the unrelenting torrent of water and muck. There was nothing here but bleakness, but hopelessness and failure—

Nothing but the spades and shovels the laborers had left behind when making repairs to the irrigation channels, still resting on the banks.

She bolted forward, ignoring how her feet slid haphazardly beneath her, until she reached the edge of the channel, pulling two of the wooden handles into her grasp. That accomplished, she took another quick survey of the landscape before darting over to where the river curved inward toward the channel, creating a narrowing of the land. It was as good a place as any to start.

She drove a spade into the ground near the riverbank, the soaked earth yielding easily and providing a base so the tool could remain upright. Satisfied it wasn't in immediate danger of getting toppled by the wind, she rushed to the edge of the channel and repeated the process, fashioning another makeshift fencepost. There was no way her creation would last any length of time, not in these conditions. But if it could only last long enough.

She tore the cloak from her shoulders, shuddering as rain seeped through her silk evening dress. Yet the rest of her was already soaked; what difference did a little more rainwater make?

The evening was warm, at least, and her fingers remained nimble, making quick work of tying her cloak to each of the handles. A rickety fence rail if ever there was one, although the wet fabric flapped robustly in the wind, providing an adequate deterrent to sheep. Hopefully.

She spun away, ready to erect the next barrier in front of the footbridge leading across the channel. However, Benedict was already there, securing his greatcoat between the two remaining shovel handles he'd pitched into the ground.

We're partners in this, she realized, blinking away raindrops so her vision clarified, putting the rigid lines of his body —each adept motion he made—into sharp relief. *If determination plays any role, we* will *make things right.*

Access to the east side of the meadow, just beyond where the flock huddled, remained unimpeded, and they had no more shovels to serve as posts. However, water was over-flowing the banks and pooling across the land, forming a large enough puddle that the sheep should avoid it. As long as they didn't become frenzied.

She dragged her feet through the cloying mud, hurrying toward Benedict so she could share her observations. A jagged flash lit the sky, followed by another rumble that momentarily overpowered all other noise.

Even so, he turned to her, seeming to sense her approach. His face was dark, rain-streaked, severe. Yet in those harsh angles, she saw not despair but resolve.

"Will you stand here?" He reached for her hand, helping her come the final few steps until she stood before him, his body a sudden blockade against the wind. "Make sure no errant sheep attempt escape in the wrong direction."

She nodded swiftly, meeting the intensity of his gaze, allowing herself the briefest moment to savor the shelter he provided. And then, because they weren't presently bound by careful words and restrained gestures but propelled by urgency and vehemence, she placed a hand on his jaw. A motion that, for a sliver of time, shut out the chaos and grounded her. A motion he answered by squeezing his fingers against hers for a fleeting moment before rushing away, back to the cluster of waiting farmhands and the final trapped ewe.

"Let's continue." His voice had an undisputable tone of authority, clear even amidst the unrelenting storm. He positioned himself beside the eldest farmhand at the ewe's flanks, then gestured to the other men. "I need one of you to come take the ewe's shoulders. The other two stand to the side and prepare to drive the sheep back if they venture to the east."

The farmhands scrambled into place, a duo of them keeping guard near the ever-growing puddle in the meadow, while the burliest of the men took his spot in front of the bleating, quivering ewe.

"As soon as we free 'er, sir, we'll turn 'er," the man shouted, his voice hefty enough to carry across the wind. "See if we can't get 'er moving away from the river."

Benedict dipped his chin in acknowledgment, shoving a mass of sodden curls away from his forehead. Then, in an unspoken agreement, they began pushing and pulling simultaneously, the ewe's body jerking with the remaining strength she possessed.

The mud was a ruthless captor, determined to keep hold of the animal's legs. Yet suddenly, with a great heave from the back, timed with a tug beneath the chest from the farmhand in front, the ewe broke free, her hooves finding purchase on the grass.

This time, the men were prepared, not pausing to celebrate victory but hastily lifting the ewe away from the riverbank and back so she faced her flock.

The startled creature eyed the scene suspiciously, testing her newfound freedom with one step. Another. Another. Until all at once, she was off like a shot, barreling away from the humans who intruded upon her space.

The flock stirred, and Violet steeled herself, warily glancing at the flimsy barriers they'd made—still upright, for now.

Yet the ewe—praise the poor, wonderful creature—avoided the barriers altogether and made straight for the bridge from whence she'd entered the meadow. An action that provoked the entire flock to disband from their huddle and bolt, accepting the ewe as their trusted leader.

Oh, thank heavens. The promise of safety dangled so close, and Violet stared a moment, anticipation bubbling in her chest as the flock raced in unison, the bridge mere feet away.

Only when the first set of hooves hit the bridge, rapidly followed by an influx of others, did she deem it safe to leave her post. Did she dare to breathe again.

Benedict was already coming for her, and she rushed to meet him partway, the mud that had crept up her ankles and seeped into her boots no longer registering. Hang the mud; hang the rain; hang every calamity that plagued them this night, for Aldercombe Grange hadn't been defeated in the end.

Yes, the shepherd was still concerningly absent, and yes, the sheep could run any which way once they returned to the fields, but at least they'd be safe from flooding on the water meadow.

They'd be safe.

Safe ...

A concept that would have comforted her had a flicker of white, separate from the flock, not caught her eye. She shielded her brow from the rain, squinting until the object became a lamb. A lamb who skidded along the riverbank, one wrong step away from meeting the hazardous waters.

She didn't think; she simply bolted and then dove to the ground, her arms flying outward—

Where they connected with a soaked bundle of fleece at the same moment someone grabbed her from behind, hauling her upward.

Her heart, which must have stopped for a beat or two, skittered back into action as she was whirled around to find Benedict towering over her.

"Jesus, Violet." His breaths came in heavy gulps. While she'd witnessed a great many sentiments wash over his face throughout the evening, this was the first time she'd seen him look so pallid. So ... horrified.

What could she say? She drew in several lungfuls of air, clutching the lamb's wooly body to her chest. "The poor thing would have drowned." As might they if they didn't vacate the weakening riverbank and get across the bridge before water overtook it, too.

She didn't know what to make of the choked sound that rose in Benedict's throat. Or the tic in his jaw. There was no time to ponder it, for they were suddenly running again, darting over mud-slicked ground and onto the bridge, the river churning angrily below.

Their boots slapped in unison against wet stone, each step an eternity, until at last, *at last*, grass appeared beneath their feet on the other side.

They'd done it. The farmhands, the sheep, and the lamb had all made it across, and when thunder rumbled again, the sound came from farther in the distance, suggesting nature might show them mercy, after all.

The sound, once so intense, was overpowered by something else more distinctive: a long, two-toned whistle, followed by a hearty baritone call. "Sheep!"

Her gaze darted upward, her heart thrumming anew. A man, just as battered by the elements as the rest of them, rushed down the gentle slope toward the flock, wooden crook in hand.

The effect on the sheep was instant, causing the lead ewe to change course and bound toward the voice, the remainder of the flock tumbling behind. Apparently, their shepherd had them well-trained, even without the help of a dog.

"Green." Benedict muttered the man's name under his breath, his tone part relief, part incredulity, part fury. For a moment, he simply stared at the flock as she did, their fluid motion creating a strange, almost-captivating effect. The spell shattered quickly, though, and he marched forward, giving her a brief backward glance before he left. "Wait here. I'll return momentarily."

For once, she took no objection to heeding an order and staying where she was, for her chest still heaved, tangled with exhaustion and thankfulness and other emotions she couldn't quite name. She released the wriggling lamb from her grasp so it could rejoin the flock, then let herself observe from a distance as Benedict made his way to the shepherd.

The two began an animated exchange, soon joined by the farmhands, although the precise nature of what they discussed got drowned out by the wind. Whatever it was, the group quickly disbanded, the shepherd giving another whistle and leading his flock across the field.

Whether the man's timing was exceedingly fortunate or exceedingly poor, Violet couldn't decide. Either way, the mud-coated sheep were back in order and returning to safety, just as her mud-coated husband was returning to *her*.

How odd that her heart clenched at the sight of him—lean figure, drenched shirt, wild curls—and her stomach fluttered as if anticipating a surprise.

How much odder still that he drew close, and her insides kept quivering, and he didn't stop where she expected. Didn't stop until he'd pulled her into his arms, his forehead resting against hers.

The wind was miserable and her dress was soaked, but an instant shot of warmth burst through her veins. She clutched him tight, sinking her palms into his shoulders, half-waiting for him to remember himself and retreat. He didn't, though, and after another beat, she dared to nestle herself against his chest. "Benedict." His name came out breathy. "Is everything all right? What happened with Green?"

She felt his inhale. Turned her gaze down and watched his lips part. "Yes, it's all right now." He exhaled, long and wavering. "Green says the thunder made his dog run off, resulting in a chase around the fields. By the time he captured the animal and they returned to his cottage, the sheep were already gone."

"Oh." The word sounded inane, but it was the only one she could produce. She closed her eyes as a strange torrent washed over her, unsure whether she was about to laugh or weep.

"He's bringing them to the barn for the night." Benedict's voice was a low hum in her ears, reducing everything else to insignificant background noise. "He'll make sure none of them have suffered any ill effects. I'll go check up on them directly, and I'll need to survey the estate for damages, and—"

"After you've dried yourself." She cut him off gently, sliding her hand down to the wet waistcoat clinging to his chest. "You don't even have a coat."

A muscle in his torso twitched. "Yes." She heard him swallow. Detected the urgent rhythm of his heart beneath her palm, each beat proof of his steadfastness, his fervency—of all the emotions that had burst out in the water meadow that he hadn't yet packed away. "Yes, you're right. I'll see you back to the house at once, and I'll fetch proper attire. You don't have a coat either, and we're bound to catch our deaths if we remain here like this."

And still, they didn't move, just clung to one another with their foreheads still joined. Her eyelids drifted open to find that his had now shuttered, faint lines tugging at the corners.

"Violet?" He uttered her name as a rasp, little more than a whisper. It was if they were under a spell, held transfixed in a place where rainstorms and mud didn't exist—where there was nothing except the two of them—but one wrong word would shatter it.

Which was why she was equally quiet, scarcely daring to blink, when she said, "Yes?"

His hands pressed into the small of her back, sure and sturdy. They were both mud-stained and drenched; any overwhelming sense of comfort could be nothing but an illusion.

She felt it, though.

She felt it.

She'd twirled around ballrooms in a waltz, walked arm-in-arm with gentlemen in Hyde Park, let George Metcalfe catch and explore her in a game of blind man's bluff. However, she'd never experienced anything like the sensations coursing through her body, filling the most guarded parts of her.

Never felt her heart swell and her stomach flutter, so much so that tears stung the corner of her eyes, the way they did when he spoke again. "Thank you."

16

The hour had grown late when Ben at last made for bed that evening.

With great relief, he cast off cravat, waistcoat, and stockings, folding them haphazardly atop the bench at the bottom of his bed and basking in the warmth of the low fire. An extravagance he could enjoy now that his responsibilities around the estate had finally ended for the night.

He stood beside the sleeping Achilles and held his fingers —the tips still slightly wrinkled—near the flames, ridding his weary body of the dampness that had permeated to his bones. He'd found it no easy task to forgo this comfort earlier, when he'd run up to his bedchamber to throw on dry clothing before dashing off again into the blustery twilight. However, ignoring the turmoil wreaked by the storm had never been an option for him, and he could rest that much easier knowing there had been no critical losses on his lands. Not tonight, anyway.

He brought his warmed fingers to the buttons on his shirt, just slipping the top one free when a murmur gave him pause. He tilted his head, and sure enough, the muffled feminine voice sounded again from the other side of the wall, followed by the gentle splashing of water.

Violet. It had been no easy task to leave her, either. Only after her lady's maid and Mrs. Wheeler had flocked around her, promising fires and baths and tea, had he managed it, stealing one last glance backward before he'd slipped out the door. Even water-logged, mud-stained, and exhausted, she remained his spot of light. The *only* brightness on a miserable night.

She should have long since gotten herself dry and warm, then slid into bed to sleep off the effects of the chaotic evening. It was for fear of disturbing her that he'd been keeping his footfalls soft. However, if Violet was still awake …

His feet moved toward the connecting door of their own volition, and his hand curled into a fist that tapped the carved, polished wood. He wouldn't bother her overlong and cling to her as he'd done outdoors, like she were the flotsam keeping him from drowning in a turbulent sea. He'd merely lay eyes on her. Ensure she was well.

"Come in." Her voice drifted through the door, containing an almost dreamlike quality. Had she been on the verge of slumber?

He took hold of the door handle and entered her bedchamber with a careful step, where he was immediately enveloped in a humid, fragrant cloud. He blinked, his eyes darting to the small fire that burned in her grate, in front of which stood the large copper tub.

A tub that Violet currently *occupied*, her blonde head angled back against the edge and her bare arms resting atop the rim to each side. He couldn't see her face from this position, only knew that she lay very still as her lady's maid tiptoed around her, pouring a can of steaming water into the bath.

"Forgive me." His throat went arid, his words cracking as they emerged. "I—I didn't mean to intrude."

"It's not an intrusion, Benedict." She spoke just as he returned his fingers to the door handle, ready to make a hasty retreat. "I said you could come in."

He froze, watching as she made a gesture to her maid and uttered a few words he couldn't distinguish. Whatever they were, the maid bobbed a curtsy and scurried into the corridor, shutting the door behind her with a quiet click.

Well. It would seem they were alone. That his wife had no qualms about him being here. Even though she was in the bath.

Did that mean ... he should approach her? For it dawned on him that he could cower beside the door—the door *he'd* knocked on—for only so long before looking ridiculous.

He crept forward, trying not to think about what he did and whether it was right or wise. The tendrils of steam beckoned to him, the rich scent becoming stronger—lavender and orange blossom, and something else creamy and sweet that he couldn't put his finger on. Whatever concoction had been added to the bath, it turned the water murky, concealing Violet's body within its depths.

Yet that only made the rest of her more captivating. Arms dotted with tiny droplets. Loose hair spilling across her shoulders and disappearing below the surface of the water. Cheeks flushed pink with the heat, blue eyes drifting open to take him in as he stilled at the head of the tub.

He swallowed thickly, praying he remembered how to speak. "I ... wanted to make sure you were well." He peered down at her slackened lips, her heavy eyelids, the delicate spikes of her lashes. "Were you sleeping?"

His voice sounded pinched, the question absurd, although it didn't seem to rattle her state of tranquility. "No, not sleeping. Luxuriating." Her mouth curved into a small smile. "It feels wonderful to no longer have mud in every crevice."

Yes, to be sure. Her skin was pristine, bearing no evidence

of the earlier catastrophe. Except now, he was thinking about crevices. The creases in her elbows. The point where her neck met her collarbone. The cleft between her breasts, just visible above the water's surface.

"I thought you would be abed by now," he choked out, his neck constricting despite his lack of cravat.

The comment caused her to sit up a little straighter, and her tongue slid over her damp bottom lip. "I couldn't rest until I went back out to see the sheep settled in the barn. Don't be angry," she added quickly as his jaw began twitching. "A footman accompanied me, and we waited until the rain lessened. I thought I might see you there."

He reminded himself to breathe, in and out. He'd wanted her safe, wanted her warm and dry—the thought of her in danger *did* make him angry. Yet he should have known Violet would never reduce herself to a passive bystander while matters remained unsettled. She had too much determination for that. She *cared* too much for that.

"I was in the barn only a short time before riding out to inspect how the rest of the estate fared," he said, something intense and spasmodic hitting him between the ribs. "I was concerned that the tenant farms closest to the river may have come to harm."

"And did they?" A small pucker formed at the bridge of her nose.

"No." He unclenched fingers that had tightened into fists, creating a small release of tension. Despite his alarm as they'd rushed into the storm to confront disaster, and despite his ongoing outrage with the idiotic lordling next door, he could relay one encouraging development. "The newly repaired water meadow was able to contain the brunt of the flooding."

"That's wonderful news." The lines on her brow eased, her lips curving upward once more. Her perfect, plush lips, sprinkled with tiny beads of moisture from the bath. Why did he suddenly feel like he needed to kiss them as urgently as he required his next breath?

He'd ascertained that she was well; consequently, it was time for him to retreat to his bedchamber and leave her in peace. Yet just as he clamped his mouth shut and thought to step away from the bath, her hand shot out to clutch his, trapping it against the rim of the tub.

A beat of unadulterated stillness passed, in which the room turned silent but his mind raced with what should come next. He could divert his eyes, wrench himself free, run back to his bedchamber and replace the lock on the connecting door.

Instead, he found his knees loosening, his body dropping to sit on the narrow edge of the tub.

"Violet." Her name emerged from some deep, raw place inside him, and he didn't know why he was saying it, what he was asking of her. He knew very little beyond that her skin was flushed and wet, that her eyes glittered as she watched him, that his heart thudded like great claps of thunder.

And then, he knew nothing at all besides that their lips had collided, and everything he yearned for came to fruition.

Wet hands clasped the sides of his face, water dripping down his neck and below the collar of his shirt as he explored her lips. They were fuller than he remembered, softer, warmer. And while he'd cursed the biting rain outdoors, desiring nothing so much as to be rid of the dampness, each droplet of bathwater created a spark against his skin, and he wanted more. Wanted to drown in them.

He cupped her nape, her sodden tendrils of hair draping over his fingers like a cloak. What if he followed the pathway of her curls into the water and down her back? What if his fingers discovered what his eyes couldn't see? The ridges of her spine, the cleft of her buttocks, the curve of her hips.

His cock stirred to attention, pressing insistently against

his fall. All those secret parts of her were just beyond his fingertips, his to reach out and explore—

I needn't be inconvenienced, then.

The memory of her words shot back at him, making his fingers stiffen. His lips pull away.

He knew he longed for her. Knew it to his core. However, where did logic fit into the equation? He'd become overzealous and wasn't thinking clearly. He hadn't thought of how far this would lead. Of how far she *wanted* it to lead, or if he had the ability to please her.

She shrank back, just enough that their eyes locked. Her hands didn't leave his face. "Do you desire me, Benedict?" Her voice was almost a whisper, floating in the air alongside the fragrant wisps of steam. "I thought you did when I heard you call my name last night. I saw you in your bedchamber through the crack in the connecting door."

His heart jerked, missing a beat before reestablishing its tempestuous rhythm. So, she *had* seen. When her cries of pleasure had echoed through the wall, it was because she'd seen.

Logic fought for purchase, telling him he should be ashamed of his lack of control and needed to apologize. But instead, his cock only grew harder in his trousers, the force of his want igniting his veins.

"Don't hide from it. Don't tell me what you think is decorous." Her fingers curled, the scrape of her nails on his jaw bringing something close to discomfort. "I *want* you to desire me."

Her eyes—those boundless, summer sky eyes—had grown large enough to look dark. Dark with yearning, with promise, with an intensity more powerful than the electrified sky.

The glint in them was the last thing he saw before their mouths crashed together once more, and he was tasting her, parting her lips with his tongue, slipping inside.

He'd spent most of his life dedicated to restraint. And yet, he wasn't infallible. Wasn't immune to the sweetness of her, to the glide of her tongue each time it connected with his.

He was holding onto her for dear life, he realized as his palms pressed tight to her shoulders, and she was clinging to him, too, wrapping her arms around his torso and pulling, pulling.

With a conspicuous splash, his world turned sideways, and he found himself dazed, spluttering. *Wet.*

His legs hung haphazardly outside the tub, while the rest of him lay half-sitting, half-floating in the water, still contained in Violet's embrace.

His brain tried to tell him a great many things. That he'd fallen, that he was clothed, that he needed to scramble upright and remove himself from the bath.

Except he didn't move.

She peered at him, her face dripping with the water he'd splashed, her beaded eyelashes fluttering coyly. "Goodness me."

And then, they were tumbling together, water rippling over the sides of the tub. He dragged his legs below the surface and shifted her weight until he was the one who reclined against the bottom with Violet atop him.

She splayed her legs to each side of his thighs, using his shoulders for support as she straightened her spine and brought her luscious arse to rest in his lap. With her body sitting upright, her breasts emerged from their concealment beneath the clouded water, giving him an unobstructed view of each plump globe. Of the berry-pink nipples.

How was it that despite his body being saturated, his mouth could go so dry? He *had* to kiss her again. To pull her against him and feel the moisture of her tongue.

"Will you touch me?" she murmured just as his lips neared to within a hairsbreadth of hers. Her voice was mainly breath, the sound curling in his chest, shooting to his groin. How could he resist when he had a bloody invitation?

He pressed his mouth against hers, his tongue stroking her lips as he raised a hand, testing the weight of the underside of her breast. It was round and full within his palm, the skin silken from the bath oils. He spread his fingers, reaching over the delectable curve until he connected with the pebbled bud in the center.

She hummed appreciatively, arching into his touch, and his fingertips closed around her nipple. Flesh that was soft but taut, that seemed to grow firmer as he gently caressed.

He brought up his other hand and stroked both breasts in tandem, relishing the sighs she made from deep in her throat. Yet it wasn't enough. He had her mouth; he had her perfect nipples beneath his touch. What would it be like to taste them, though? He wanted to find out if they'd be as sweet as her tongue, to discover the sounds she'd make while he sampled her.

He withdrew his lips, and before she could finish her groan of protest, he repositioned them on her neck, kissing down the delicate column. His hands slid to her hips, his mouth traveling lower and lower. To the notch at the base of her throat. To her collarbone.

His tongue lapped at the droplets along the swell of her breast, then hovered for an achingly long moment above her hardened nipple while he paused to look up at her. Violet's head was tipped back, although her eyes flew open to meet his, assessing him with an urgent hunger.

He'd wanted to be certain he had this right, and there was the proof he needed. Without further delay, he captured her nipple between his lips and carefully sucked, causing a breathy moan to fly from her throat and her entire body to twitch. He shuddered in return, for her mound brushed his arousal when she shifted in his lap, creating a lightning strike of pleasure. A coveted spark of friction.

He knew it was yearning, not pain, that made her fingernails sink deeper into his shoulders while he laved her. It was for pleasure, too, that her hips lifted again so she could drag herself along his length, emitting another cry.

His shirt and trousers clung to him maddeningly, although they didn't stop his need from spiking each time she moved. In fact, the unwanted barrier seemed to render him more desperate, the fabric rubbing him where instead he craved her flesh. He couldn't pause to undo buttons and free himself of wet linen, though, not without releasing her from his mouth and halting the up-and-down rhythm she'd established against his cock. And he didn't want that, even for a second.

Water splashed onto the floor in waves, as meanwhile, torrents of pleasure swelled within him. Neither able to be contained. His body was tightening, spiraling, sensitive to every lap of the water, to every touch. He had sweetness upon his tongue, bare skin beneath his fingertips, and he couldn't hold on much longer, couldn't—

"Violet." He half-groaned, half-choked out her name, for that was the only word he could form, the only thought that hadn't vaporized within his head. He didn't even know for certain what he meant by it—whether it was a caution for her to stop or a plea to keep going.

Whatever it was, she didn't cease moving, and her hand was suddenly at his fall.

His body tensed at the contact, his lips clamping around her nipple far more forcefully than he intended. There was no escaping it—his last thread of composure snapped, and release hurtled over him.

Everything was reduced to a stupor of pleasure, although

he still heard the moan that crossed her lips. Still felt the pinch of her fingernails, the final thrust of her hips, the weight of her head collapsing against his shoulder, her body trembling and breathless.

It took a long time before he could properly inhale again. Longer still until he untangled his limbs from hers and analyzed the circumstances. Such as the fact that the water had grown tepid. A great deal of it was on the floor. And he was still wearing his damn trousers.

"As I've dismissed my lady's maid for the night, I wonder if you might pass me a towel," Violet said at last, her words cutting through his thoughts and lingering in the floral-scented haze. A haze that now contained a trace of something heady and primal, too.

A towel. Yes, he could fetch one. Because they could hardly stay here all night, despite that seeming to be the easiest solution.

Much to his relief—and surprise—his legs obeyed when he bid them to stand. As such, there was nothing to do but step onto the soaked floor and retrieve the towel lying on the nearby stool.

She accepted it with a word of thanks, and he had the sudden inclination—if not the genuine desire—to divert his eyes. Why did he feel the same way as when he'd first stepped into the room: like an intruder?

His body had never been so boneless, so replete. And yet, his mind failed to make sense of anything. What did this all mean? What was supposed to come next? These were the conundrums that arose when one acted without thinking.

"Benedict." Once more, her voice broke through his web of contemplation, and sleek fingers lifted his chin, prompting him to look at her. "We should go to bed."

She'd wrapped the towel around her torso, covering the

most intimate parts of herself. However, not for one second did he forget the image of those glorious breasts, nor the succulent taste of them in his mouth. She was the most exquisite thing he'd ever beheld.

And now, she wished to go to bed. Did she possibly mean ... *together*? He couldn't stop his eyes from drifting toward her counterpane, which her maid had turned down for the night to reveal clean white sheets. Couldn't help the vision of laying her down, removing the towel, and letting his tongue discover every inch of dew-dotted flesh.

Yet here he was, dripping puddles on the floor. Uncertain. Undone.

"Yes," he managed, but God, the word came out husky. "We should ..." He paused, his heart and his head tugging him in a hundred different directions, water continuing to trickle from his shirt and trousers. What did she want? What did he want? What was right, what was wise, what was best?

Ultimately, it was the safe, logical direction that gained voice. "We should get some sleep."

There was a beat of silence and then, her gentle words. "Goodnight, husband." She leaned in to press her lips against his. Not with the urgency they'd shared earlier, but as a soft, barely there caress.

It was still enough to stir sparks in his chest. Especially when she lingered an extra moment, her fingertips continuing to rest on his chin and her mouth curving into a tender smile that promised him the world.

"Goodnight, wife," he managed, giving himself the briefest moment to squeeze her fingers before turning away.

It was decided, then. His feet squelched against the floor all the way to the connecting door, and his hand slid around the handle. Yes, it was decided. She would go to her bed and he would go to his, the same way they always did.

However, something undeniable had shifted between them. Something that would require a great deal of contemplation. For while he may be woefully inexperienced, there was one thing of which he was certain: he longed for her.

Oh, Christ, he longed for her.

17

As Benedict was occupied with meetings, Violet spent much of the next day touring the estate by herself.

She hadn't felt a stab of disappointment—mostly—when word had come, just as they'd both reached the breakfast room, that Mr. Hayward had been spotted on the road north of Aldercombe. Knowing how anxious Benedict was to converse with his land agent, she'd even encouraged him to make haste when he said he'd ride out immediately and meet the man.

The fact that their encounter from last night hung uncertainly between them, and would remain that way for the foreseeable future, was the unfortunate consequence of Mr. Hayward's sudden return. However, she would be selfish to regret the interruption, and it wasn't as if she lacked her own tasks to attend to. Namely, surveying the water meadow and then locating the sheep where they'd been brought back out to pasture.

She took her time, and only once thoroughly convinced that the meadow was properly draining and the flock seemed no worse for wear did she make her way back to the house, strolling beneath the warmth of the high afternoon sun.

Would Benedict and Mr. Hayward have concluded their business by now? She was eager to hear of any new developments with the river dispute. With any luck, Lord Frederick would be forced to abandon his ill-fated dam before he inflicted further damage.

And then, once they were through discussing estate matters, and if she and Benedict ended up alone in his study ...

Despite the heat of the day, a small shiver darted down her spine as she stepped onto the gravel drive. Why could she not stop imagining him? Wet linen clinging to his chest, his arousal brushing her sex, his mouth on her breasts.

She'd realized from the moment of their first kiss that prompting Benedict to lower his guard—and leave it lowered—would take care and patience. That didn't prevent her from experiencing an anticipant pang at the thought of kissing him again. At the thought of what else could happen between them if the spark they'd created could only be nurtured.

She rushed up to the house, taking the front steps two at a time. However, before she could reach for the door handle, her foot stumbled over something uneven, and her body pitched.

"Oh!" She shot her arms out to steady herself, narrowly avoiding disaster. Had she become so distracted that she'd almost tripped on her own boots? The thought left her red-faced.

When she glanced down, though, a large stone rested on the landing, printed papers of some sort nestled beneath, the edges lightly flapping in the breeze. What on earth was all that doing here?

She nudged the stone aside with her foot, bending over to retrieve the pages.

No, not just any pages. A pamphlet.

Her heart dropped even before her gaze fell upon the title:

The Salacious Solicitor. Printed in the same bold font, with the same scalloped border, as the other pamphlets that had become so familiar. And then, her eyes darted to the bottom of the cover, revealing the worst thing of all. *By an author of the initials A.P.*

She blinked rapidly, because surely she'd misunderstood something and this wasn't what it appeared. No matter how many times her eyelids flickered, though, the text wouldn't say anything other than what she'd already discerned.

Did Benedict know about this? He couldn't have this morning; there was no way he would have entered the breakfast room so coolly had that burden weighed on his mind. He mustn't now, either, for he never would have left his brother's erotic literature upon the doorstep for anyone to see.

Regardless, somebody was determined he find out about the newly published—and initialed—pamphlet. Somebody clandestine and nefarious, who'd taken advantage of the fact that most servants had been given a half-day off for Whitsun and went right up to Aldercombe's front door undetected.

An unladylike oath tumbled from her lips. She could hazard a guess as to the detestable toad who would like to see Benedict lowered and humiliated—a toad whose household was familiar with this series of pamphlets. The mere thought filled her mouth with bile. But what was she to do when he'd left behind no evidence to prove her assumption? And more importantly, how was she going to approach Benedict and reveal what she'd found?

Before she could decide one way or another about how to proceed, a low rumble started on the drive. The unmistakable clip-clop of hooves, the turning of wheels.

She put her hand to her brow, squinting into the afternoon sun. Sure enough, a post chaise was barreling toward Aldercombe, the postilion working the duo of matched bays at a near-gallop.

She knew those horses. That postilion. She recognized the carriage as surely as she knew her own name. It belonged to her mother, the Collingwood crest a colored blur upon the door.

Her heart began pounding with fresh vigor, the pamphlet flapping within her clenched fist. Of all the times her family could have selected for their first visit to Aldercombe, this was among the worst. But oblivious to its poor timing, the post chaise continued its journey up the drive until it ground to a halt near the front entrance.

She could do nothing but watch as the accompanying footman leaped down from the bench seat at the rear of the carriage and pulled open the door. He barely had the opportunity to extend his hand before the viscountess tumbled out, falling against him as though her legs lacked the power to keep her upright.

"Oh, Violet, it's terrible," she moaned as Violet darted down the steps to meet her, quickly taking hold of her mother's arm to offer added support. "But I never should have undertaken this journey. I haven't the strength; I'm going to swoon."

"Shh, Mama, it's all right," Violet uttered helplessly, her knees also feeling weak. Could her mother have somehow found out about the pamphlet debacle even before she did? Did the whole neighborhood know? She crumpled the pages into a ball within her fist, willing her voice not to tremble. "Come inside and rest a while."

After exchanging a pointed glance with the footman, she worked with him to half-guide, half-drag the viscountess into the house, where they were greeted by a wide-eyed Mrs. Wheeler.

"Gracious, madam. My lady." The housekeeper dropped into an inelegant curtsy, the ribbons on her fine Whitsun bonnet bobbing against her shoulders. "What can I do to assist?"

"Perhaps just a pot of tea before you depart for the festivities." Violet tried not to sound miserable, although it was difficult when her mother trembled next to her, emitting a pitiable moan. She swallowed, an ever-growing sense of dread closing in on her. "Is Mr. Prescott at home?"

"No, madam. He and Mr. Hayward were here in his study for a spell, but they left again about an hour ago."

Well, that was one stroke of good fortune, at least. Having him here—having him find out about the pamphlet like this—was beyond what she could bear.

She uttered a hasty word of thanks, and she and the footman continued on their way, depositing her mother upon the drawing room sofa. After dismissing him with a nod—he was only too happy to shut the door behind him and flee—she rushed to the side cabinet that held a bottle of sherry. She deposited the pamphlet behind a vase, then shakily poured two glasses.

"Here, drink this." She whirled back toward her mother, extending her arm to pass her one. However, the viscountess was occupied with digging through her reticule, paper crinkling against her gloved fingertips as she clasped the item she sought.

This was it, then. Her mother had somehow gotten ahold of *The Salacious Solicitor*, had somehow determined its connection to Benedict—

Except the paper that emerged from the reticule wasn't a pamphlet. It was a copy of that horrid gossip rag her mother liked, *The London Tattler*.

A sensation approaching relief slackened her limbs, and she stumbled forward, sherry splashing over the rims of the glasses as she set them on the end table beside her mother.

The viscountess didn't even seem to notice, for she busied

herself with unfolding the paper, pointing forlornly to the text at the top. "It's the first story, Violet." Her pale eyes turned misty. "The very first one."

Violet lowered herself onto the sofa, coaxing the paper from her mother's grasp and placing it in her own lap so she could read what had made the viscountess so distraught.

A certain Lord C, whose wife and daughters have been notice-ably absent from London of late, seems to be alone no more. A Mrs. F—along with another lady of unknown origin, who is decidedly __not__ Lady C—has been seen coming and going from his Mayfair abode at all hours of day and night. Were one not apprised of the rules of church and country, one might almost think he had forsaken his lady wife and taken two more in her place. But given Lord C's noteworthy endeavors at the Theatre Royal earlier in the Season, one can hardly be surprised.

Well. Wasn't that something? Their town house overtaken by mistresses, as if the viscount's own family had ceased to exist.

She let the words sink in, a dull throb beginning in her chest. However, the sensation didn't carry with it the tightness of despair or the burn of indignation. Truthfully, she was accustomed to her father's humiliating antics and recklessness by now. Was it very wrong of her to prefer one more story about him in the *Tattler* over a fresh catastrophe involving the pamphlets?

Her mother, of course, didn't see it as anything less than the end of the world. Her eyes continued shining with unshed tears, and she threw a hand to her chest, emphatically clutching her fichu. "He has no shame! He has turned us all into laughingstocks." At last, she took notice of the sherry beside her, and she drained the glass in one long swallow before drooping against the arm of the sofa. "You married just in time, but what of Arabella? Lord Frederick has been forgiving of the gossip thus far, but his tolerance is bound to run out. Where will she be then but destitute? Alone. A spinster."

"No. No, it will not come to that." Violet patted her mother's arm gently but kept her tone firm, her thoughts turning at a breakneck pace.

So many of their actions lately had been driven by a desire to please Lord Frederick. Heavens, it was the entire reason for Violet's marriage. However, what if this was a sign that the union between Arabella and Frederick wasn't meant to be? What if a path existed in which her sister could learn to love someone other than a pompous duke's son who kept proving himself increasingly heinous?

"Lord Frederick is not the only unwed man in the world," she said, the idea gaining more clarity by the second. "There are others who will recognize Arabella's charm and not care a whit for what the gossip rags say. I'd never wish to see her heartbroken, but she's still so young, and if she's only given more time to meet another suitable gentleman—"

"I beg your pardon?" Her mother straightened a little, staring at her as if she'd begun speaking in a foreign tongue. "But ... but she's decided on Lord Frederick. The son of a *duke*."

"He's a numbskull! He's hardly the best she can do," Violet burst out. At least, she started to before the door swung open and Mrs. Wheeler appeared with the tea tray—followed, a single step behind, by none other than Arabella herself.

"Violet! Mama!" Arabella almost skipped into the room, giving no sign she'd detected the harsh words. In fact, her cheeks glowed a charming pink, and her lips curved into a wide grin.

Their mother sniffed, casting a doleful glance at Arabella

and then the approaching tea tray before deciding she had the strength for neither and slumping her head against the sofa.

Arabella, though, was unperturbed. She waltzed right up to the aggrieved viscountess with a giggle, fetching her limp hands and clasping them in her own. "I rushed home to tell you, Mama. Only, Davis said you'd left to pay a call on Violet not ten minutes prior, so I got the pony cart and drove here as quickly as I could. I'm fairly bursting with the news."

The viscountess snapped to attention, her eyes becoming large and intent. "What news? Tell me *what*? My poor nerves cannot handle you keeping me in suspense."

"It's wonderful!" Arabella laughed again, releasing their mother's hands to give a little twirl. "Lord Frederick has proposed marriage."

No. Violet had sat by silently to watch the scene unfold, and continued to do so even now, but all she could think was *no.*

The viscountess, however, clapped delightedly, jumping to her feet and joining Arabella in a spin. "That's wonderful indeed, my dear. Brilliant news. The best news." She reached for Violet's untouched glass of sherry, tipping it to her lips and releasing a contented sigh. "Two daughters successfully married. I shall have a modicum of peace at last."

No, no, no. Violet knew she should be thankful that her mother's fears had been assuaged. Knew she should congratulate her sister. The only idea to fill her head, though, was that nothing about this felt right.

"Violet?" Suddenly, a slender hand fell upon her shoulder, and she raised her eyes to find Arabella peering down at her, her pale brows knitting in confusion. "Aren't you pleased?"

Violet caught the warning glance from her mother, but it did nothing to quell the bile rising inside her. She'd started imagining a future that was different, *better*, for her sister, so to have it snatched away so quickly, to know that detestable coxcomb would soon become a relation—

"I begin to doubt Lord Frederick's character," she said, the words tumbling out like a wave, impossible to keep contained.

Arabella made a startled sound, and their mother's features darkened, her expression going from cautionary to downright murderous.

Even so, Violet was unable to hold her tongue and stop what she'd already set in motion. "He's diverting river water, without a care for the disastrous impact upon Aldercombe's crops and livestock, for the sole purpose of supplying his ornamental lake."

"Goodness, girl, that's a *farming* matter," the viscountess snapped with distaste. "It's not something over which you should trouble yourself. Whatever's amiss, leave it to the land agents to sort."

Violet's body stiffened as if she'd been struck, and something simmered in her belly, hot and furious. She was no stranger to handling her mother's moods and nervous complaints. She'd grown accustomed to fetching vinaigrettes and speaking platitudes in a soft voice so as not to make things worse. However, never had the temptation been so strong to shout her frustration at the top of her lungs.

None of them—not her mother, or Arabella, or even the land agent—had been outdoors last night in the driving rain as thunder crashed around them. None of them had tried to drive a flock of sheep without a shepherd or dog, leaped into the mud, or clutched a frightened lamb's wooly body to their chest—and all because of Lord Frederick's thoughtless, asinine scheme.

"Surely, it's a misunderstanding," Arabella said, a slight tremble in her voice. She worked her lip back and forth between her teeth, her eyes glittering. Hopeful. Pleading, almost. "I realize you and Frederick have had your differences recently, but I trust him to be honorable and true. If some sort of trouble has arisen, he'll see that it's rectified. I'm certain of it."

Violet did her sister the service of not retching at the declaration. In fact, she sat painfully still, not trusting herself to do anything at all. Arabella was so bright. So carefree and lovely and delicate. How could Violet yell at her during the happiest moment of her sister's life? What was she to say when one set of eyes shot daggers at her and another stared eagerly while awaiting her response, the taintless joy in them showing the slightest sign of dimming?

"Congratulations." The word felt like nails as Violet forced it from her throat. There was no merriment in it, no false excitement she pulled from some shallow place within her. Yet it seemed to be enough.

"Thank you, dearest." Arabella's smile broadened, and her slippers tapped a little dance against the carpet. "And I haven't even told you the other marvelous news. Frederick says he'll host a grand ball at Watley to celebrate our betrothal."

Their mother let out an excited gasp. "A betrothal ball and then a wedding?" She grabbed her discarded reticule from the sofa, the offensive gossip rag beside it entirely forgotten. "With so much to plan, we haven't a moment to lose."

"Indeed. I don't know where to begin!" Arabella pressed her palms to her flushed cheeks, another of her giggles ringing through the drawing room. "I should do up my portion of the guest list. Oh, and do you think I could have a new gown made? My pink silk might do if we had it retrimmed, but there's still the matter of slippers, and then what jewels I'm to wear, and—"

"Yes, we'll return to Meadowleigh at once so we can get these things in order," the viscountess declared, starting across the room with considerably more vigor than she'd displayed upon entering it.

"Come with us, Vi." Arabella extended a hand toward the sofa, where Violet remained watching the intensifying flurry she was powerless to stop.

Violet accepted the proffered hand, pushing rigidly to her feet. However, she went no farther, flashing a stony look toward the doorway where her mother waited. "I cannot. I'm afraid I have more of my silly *farming* matters to attend to."

Even then, Arabella's grin was unflappable. "Well, you must come to Meadowleigh as soon as you have the time. Perhaps you can have a new gown made, too."

Poor, naive Arabella really did mean it as a kindness. She appeared to have nothing but delight in her heart as she uttered a distracted farewell and flitted away, surely dreaming of all that awaited her.

In the end, it was the viscountess who turned back, meeting Violet's humorless stare with one of her own. "I'm sorry you did not make the match you hoped for. Still, you mustn't begrudge Arabella her happiness."

Violet gaped, an invisible fist pummeling her in the chest. "It's not—"

But the viscountess had already spun away and was out the door, leaving Violet in solitude.

"It's not that," she muttered, collapsing back onto the sofa as if she were the one who suffered from weakness and poor health.

She blew out a long breath, the ceiling swimming above her. What a proper mess this was. A mess she knew no easy way to fix.

Perhaps she could have prevented it weeks ago. Perhaps if she'd refused to get married after the shepherd's hut incident, Lord Frederick would have cried off before Arabella's attachment to him grew even stronger, and her sister, somehow, would have found another eligible gentleman to take his place.

Perhaps someday far in the future, a gentleman would

have come along who'd forgive Violet's sins and fall in love with her, too. Except suddenly, nothing about that possibility felt right.

She put a palm to her chest, where her heart thumped with a strange rhythm. She *did* want Arabella to be happy and loved, would never begrudge her that. If only there was a way for it to come about that didn't involve such a duplicitous toad.

As for her own happiness ...

I'm sorry you did not make the match you hoped for.

The words cut because no, she hadn't. She hadn't wanted the match in the least.

Only ... what if the match she'd once hoped for was wrong?

What if the things that truly mattered—loyalty, honor, goodness—came from somewhere and some*one* far different from what she'd expected?

18

Violet was in the study, leafing through the pamphlets she'd discovered on foot scald and fleece rot, when Benedict finally returned home that afternoon.

He was dusty and a little rumpled, with dark curls poking every which way atop his head. Quite honestly, he appeared exactly as she most desired him.

"How did your meeting with Mr. Hayward go?" She set down the pamphlets on his desk, leaning against the sturdy wooden surface as he came forward to greet her. Of all the matters swirling through her head, that one currently took precedence.

"It was productive, I suppose. He confirmed as I suspected: he'd never heard tell of any river diversion arrangement." Benedict joined her at the desk, his long limbs uncharacteristically slack as he, too, rested his weight against it. "We spoke again with Mr. Clark, the solicitor, who produced Denham's so-called irrigation deed. It was signed by Aldercombe's former land agent, Mr. Morris, and witnessed by another solicitor who just so happens also to be deceased. How convenient for the lordling that the men supposedly involved in this deed are no longer around to refute it."

His mouth took on a sardonic tilt, and his fingers tightened into a ball before splaying across the thigh of his black trousers. "Nonetheless, Mr. Clark thinks he'll be able to disprove its validity. Hopefully before Denham makes much headway with dam repair."

He set to work on removing his gloves, then raked a hand through his disheveled hair—not that it did anything to contain the one curl hanging over his forehead.

"I hope so." She managed a small smile. "That's a promising development."

He nodded, his hands suddenly back in his lap. His brow became tight with concentration as he peered at her, his eyes very dark. "Is everything well here?"

"Yes." She spat out the word quickly. Too quickly. She had so much to tell him—the news of her sister's betrothal announcement, the story of the pamphlet on the doorstep. However, looking into his solemn face, inhaling the outdoor scent of him—air and earth and a trace of something masculine—she didn't want to reveal any of it. As soon as she uttered the words, this moment of tentative calm would be blasted to pieces, and she couldn't bear setting disaster upon him. Not yet, when he'd just stepped foot through the door, on the verge of feeling optimistic.

She summoned another half-smile, forcing lightness into her tone. "Quite well, although I'm afraid there won't be much on the dinner table this evening. Most of the servants have already gone to enjoy the Whitsun festivities." Off to Dayleford, where they'd be immersed in merriment, their responsibilities out of mind for the night.

An idea began turning in her head. "We could go, too," she said. "There will be music, games, dancing, and more ale than anyone has a right to drink."

Perhaps unsurprisingly, Benedict frowned. "I'm not certain."

No, he wouldn't be, would he? He didn't drink ale. He likely didn't dance, either, or play mindless games, or do anything that could be considered unrestrained or frivolous.

Not usually, anyway.

The memory sprang forward of him tumbling into the bath. Of the hardness of his manhood, her nipples between his lips.

Why did she think of that now, when this fragile moment of peace was about to get pulled out from under them? Why, despite everything that had happened this day, did the curl on his forehead cause heat to pool between her legs? Why did even the hint of sweat on his skin have to smell appealing?

"We can stay home if you prefer." Her voice came out throatier than she'd imagined it would. Her lashes flickered maybe a touch too coquettishly. "We're very nearly alone in the house."

Had she really spoken that last part aloud? She hadn't intended to, although the subtle twitch in his jaw revealed that yes, in fact, she had.

His spine became taller. His shoulders more rigid. Yet instead of backing away, he stayed very near.

Very near, very dark and alluring and male, and while she'd vowed she wouldn't push him, that she'd let him come to her on his own terms, she needed just a taste.

She brushed her lips against his, the severe line of his mouth surprisingly soft to the touch.

That was all she took before drawing back so she could see his face and examine each sharp angle and contour. Had she startled him? Pleased him? She didn't know what his expression meant, only that he remained still. Studious. Only knew that the air in the study suddenly felt cloying, and she heard him draw in a breath, detected the slight movement of his chest.

It was the last thing to hit her awareness before his mouth crashed into hers, and he was stroking her, nipping at the edges of her lips, pulling her close.

Lord, he felt good. The pressure of his mouth, the caresses of his tongue, the weight of his palm against her nape. She combed her fingers through his hair, losing herself in the pleasure of their embrace. Moaning as his free hand skirted the edge of her bodice, and he dragged it down to capture her nipple amidst the layers of muslin.

She had no business wanting him this much. Not right now, when two disastrous revelations loomed over her head, demanding to be shared with him.

But if anything, wasn't that a reason to give in to desire? To keep the truth at bay for just a little longer? Suddenly, something burned even hotter than her own need: a need to give *him* pleasure, to see him loose and unraveled and sated before circumstances rendered him tense and distant.

She broke the kiss, pulling away from the blissful attention he bestowed upon her breast, so she could drop to her knees in front of him. It gratified her to lay eyes on the telltale bulge tenting his trousers, and an answering surge of desire pulsed between her legs.

Slowly, she brought her hands to his hips, then dragged her fingers inward to the top buttons of his fall.

He hissed out a breath, his thighs jerking against the desk, his fingers seizing her chignon and pulling her head up so her eyes locked with his. Those glittering depths filled with raw, insistent need.

"Will you let me touch you?" she whispered, her fingertips hovering over the buttons. So, *so* close, but just above the polished silver surface. "I *want* to touch you."

There was a moment of silence, of anticipation, for his lips were clamped together far too tightly for speech. After another beat, however, came the motion of his chin. A brisk, barely there nod.

With her heart pounding, she recaptured the buttons, her attention returning to what was right in front of her. Deliberately, carefully, she slipped each one free—giving him the opportunity to stop her if he had second thoughts.

He didn't stop her, though. Didn't do anything but grip her hair and take ragged breaths, the muscles beneath his trousers visibly tight.

She was unsure where the sound came from when she undid the final button and his fall dropped. Was it his gasp? Hers? She'd never seen a man's ... *manhood* in real life, and the sight robbed the air from her lungs. He was swollen and ruddy, thick—

Hot. She placed her hand near the base of him, the heat setting her nerve endings ablaze. His skin was like fire, like silk, and so very hard beneath.

She curled her fingers, tentatively stroking toward the tip. *He likes that.* At least, that's what she took the hitch in his breath to mean. Emboldened, she slid her fingers down and back up again, squeezing a little harder. That's what the women in the pamphlets had done. An act that had caused the men in the stories to shudder and groan and shout all manner of adoring—and salacious—words.

Benedict could be brought to completion this way as well; she was nearly certain of it. Except she didn't wish to stop with only her hands. He'd granted her the searing pleasure of his mouth upon her breasts, and she wanted him to experience that pleasure, too. Wanted, for herself, to know how that combination of velvet and steel would feel beneath her lips. How it would taste.

Thanks to the pamphlets, she knew such things were done. In Benedict's—no, Alexander's—story of the three merry kitchen maids, the groom they favored had liked the act very much, indeed.

She stilled her hand at the base of his shaft, leaning forward to press her mouth to the head and give it the tiniest caress with her tongue.

"Jesus, Violet." His body jolted, his erection springing free of her lips. "*Fuck.*"

She recoiled, heartbeat stuttering, stomach plunging. "Did I hurt you? Do you not like it?"

"No, but ..." His face tautened with hard creases, making him appear as if in agony. "It's ... it's the middle of the day. In the study. It's ... not honorable for me to want such a thing from you."

So, *that* was the problem. The last tattered thread of his restraint, fighting to maintain its hold.

As far as she was concerned, restraint could go hang. There would be plenty of time for that later, when she revealed the truth of what she'd discovered today. For this one brief span of time, though ...

"It's what I desire," she said, drawing near to him again—close enough that he would feel her breath upon his shaft. "What I want to do for you. But if you think it unsuitable ..." She shrugged as if her thighs weren't wet with her arousal. As if every inch of her body weren't buzzing with the force of her need. "Perhaps I should leave. Perhaps I should get off my knees, retire to the drawing room, and spend the rest of the day perusing the agricultural pamphlets I found. Do you think I should do that, Benedict?"

His eyes were huge. Black. His thighs quivering. She could see the battle within him, the way he grappled with the potency of primal desire.

Could see the moment when that last thread snapped, and his lips parted, emitting a choked sound. "No."

The rawness of it shot to her core, coiled in her belly. She dropped her mouth, giving him a languid swipe with her tongue.

He shuddered again but didn't draw away. Instead, one hand returned to her hair, the other clinging to the edge of the desk as if he were trying to prevent himself from drowning.

"Shall I keep going?" She gave him another slow lick before looking up at him, her tongue tasting of salt and musk. Of male. Of her *husband*.

"Yes." He didn't hesitate before the gravelly sound tore from his throat. "God, Violet, *please*."

Another heady wave of pleasure burst through her veins. She'd never felt like this before. This needy, but also, this powerful. *She* did this to him. Made him tremble and groan and want. And while maybe it was wrong of her, she couldn't help but test that power, just a little more, as she murmured, "Please what?"

His fingers sank deeper into her scalp, his eyelids shuttering. His head tilting back. "Put my cock in your mouth."

Oh, my God. She couldn't have imagined the frenzy the words would ignite in her blood. The surge of longing that would pulse between her legs.

She did just as he said, taking him between her lips, drawing him toward the back of her throat. And this time, she didn't stop to tease or make certain; she simply caressed and sucked the way she'd read about in the pamphlets, letting the guttural sounds he made be her guide.

"Violet." Her name was cracked and strained. Desperate. "You need to stop or I'm going to ... to—"

To spend. She knew what he meant, even when he broke off into a garbled curse.

She didn't stop, though. Couldn't stop. Not until she saw this to completion. He may be desperate, but she was desperate, too, propelled by a need to witness—no, to cause—the culmination of his pleasure. To also drive her own pleasure so that nothing else existed in the world.

Her lips moved faster, her fingers tightening around the base of his cock. Meanwhile, her other hand grappled blindly with her skirts until she shoved them out of the way and plunged her palm between her thighs.

Mmm. She heard herself moan. Heard, at the same time, another fragmented version of her name that sounded like a warning, although it came to her as if from far away. She was drunk with pleasure, impossibly aroused. Just as Benedict was impossibly harder, hotter—until his desire reached a breaking point, and his body jerked with the spasms of his climax.

Warm liquid salt burst into her throat, and she continued lapping at him, taking in the heady, unfamiliar taste. Continued working her fingers against her sex, tracing the bud that contained the heart of her yearning. She'd become a mixture of agony and bliss, was both taut and soaring—

Except all at once, fingers tightened in her hair, and she felt herself being pulled away from him. The weight of a heavy gaze fell upon her, and she froze, startled, as Benedict tilted her face upward.

He was staring down at her, skin flushed, jaw slack, eyes like molten onyx. What was she to make of that, other than he looked ominous enough to devour her whole? What was she to say when her head was too fogged to form a coherent thought, when her body hummed with unfulfilled need, when she hadn't a clue what he was thinking or feeling?

She said nothing, only yelped in surprise, for she was suddenly being lifted and spun, her backside connecting with the desk. Papers rustled; books thumped against the floor. However, Benedict ignored the disorder as if it didn't exist— he was too busy hiking up her skirts.

Her thighs splayed of their own accord, and she whimpered as his palm cupped her sex, his fingers parting her folds.

She fairly screamed as his thumb found the peak she'd been circling, and he applied tentative pressure.

"Yes, right there." She was too needy to be subtle. "Keep touching me there. Don't stop."

And oh, sweet heaven, he listened, his fingers stroking her the same way her own had done. Almost the same way, that was, but different, too, for his were a little sturdier, a little rougher. A little more intoxicating, simply because they belonged to *him*.

Her eyes screwed shut, her world reduced to nothing but the pulse between her legs. To sensation.

And then, when she thought she couldn't handle any more, that the yearning would drive her mad, his mouth fell upon her breast, his tongue finding her pebbled nipple through her bodice.

Release washed over her like a deluge, making her intimate muscles throb with torrent after torrent of bliss. Her hands flew up to clutch him, fingers twining in the thick waves above his nape, giving her an anchor while she floated as if weightless. And he kept her floating, kept lavishing her with tiny flicks of his tongue and caresses of his thumb until her sensitized flesh, at last, had taken all it could bear.

Even then, his hand lingered against her thigh, his head by her breasts, and she left her arms draped loosely around his neck, loath to let the moment pass. Could they stay like this indefinitely? There were far worse ways to spend a lifetime.

She'd grown dazed and sated enough that his words, when they came, possessed an almost dreamlike quality. "Shall we go to the Whitsun festivities now?"

She blinked, hazily stirring as he lifted his head and the warmth of his palm slid away. *The Whitsun festivities*. She'd forgotten she'd even proposed such a thing and certainly hadn't thought he was inclined to attend.

They shouldn't go. They'd taken their interlude, and it

was time to tell him what she'd learned today, while the aftereffects of pleasure lingered to soften the blow.

Only ... why couldn't it wait a little longer? Would it be so terrible if they took the rest of the day for enjoyment and she waited to reveal what she knew until they returned home at nightfall?

Surely not.

Surely, they deserved more than just a fleeting moment to be carefree. Happy. Together.

"Yes." She dragged her hand through his hair, pushing the errant curl off his forehead. Smiling as it immediately flopped down again. The muscles between her legs continued to tingle faintly. Her heart pattered in a way it hadn't before.

"Yes," she said, "that sounds wonderful."

19

The village green in Dayleford had become a veritable maelstrom of merriment. From the children who shrieked delightedly as they chased each other between the trees, to the food vendors who called out their offerings from the stalls they'd erected, to the band of white-clad dancers who spun about with bells jingling on their legs, everything was alive and boisterous.

Ben stood at the edge of the throng with Violet on his arm, not quite certain which way to turn first. Twilight had fallen, and a few young men began climbing up to light the lanterns hung in the trees, which cast the scene in a golden glow. Every part vivid. Radiant.

Although not so much as the woman beside him, her mass of flaxen curls twisted into a loose knot. Her skirts adorned with delicate silver threads that caught the light.

Something peculiar rattled in his chest when he gazed at her. Something that might make the whole of the chaotic scene vanish and leave only her behind, were he to stare long enough.

"Shouldn't you be accustomed to crowds?" When he

didn't move, Violet's elbow jabbed lightly into his side, and she gave his arm a gentle tug forward, her smile brighter than any lantern. Brighter than the sun. "Coming from London and all."

He looked away, concentrating his attention straight ahead of him lest he grow distracted and tread on any feet. Yes, he'd grown up amidst the bustle of London. However, that wasn't the same thing—didn't hold the same significance. The crowds on Fleet Street or in Hyde Park weren't composed of people to whom he held a responsibility. People who relied on his management and judged his actions accordingly. People he would count as tenants, servants, and neighbors for the rest of his life, if that's the path he chose.

His throat tightened at the thought, a new sensation he couldn't name fighting for purchase in his chest. Fortunately, Violet didn't seem to expect an answer, for she'd turned toward the food stalls, standing on tiptoe to survey what was available.

"I think I spy apple tarts," she said excitedly, her gloved hand slipping away from his coat. "Let me go buy us some refreshments."

She was gone a moment later, weaving through the throng, following the aromas of spices and wood smoke. And while he could have easily joined her, he found himself holding back. Watching. Taking everything in.

He was still half in awe he'd agreed to come. He likely wouldn't have, had he not been afraid the urge to plunge his cock into his wife right on his desk would get the better of him. Yet now that they were here ... he didn't think he was sorry.

He inhaled deeply, tracking the glint of her hair as she hurried up to one of the pie sellers, the cheerful lilt of fiddle music accompanying her steps. Everything was chaotic but bright. Everything just seemed to fit.

What had he expected on the day his uncle came to him, after his expulsion from Cambridge, and requested his help with Aldercombe Grange? Certainly not this. Not *her*.

"Mr. Prescott." A hefty body brushed past his shoulder, the deep bellow tearing his attention away from Violet. In front of him stood Arthur Ruddle, the tenant farmer who'd marched into his study with news of Lord Frederick's dam. But whereas the confrontation in the study had been filled with ire and accusations, Ruddle's stout face now danced with gaiety.

"To you, sir." Ruddle thrust the mug he held into the air, white foam spilling over the side. "For setting the land right."

Ben felt his brow quirk and jaw loosen, although surprise rendered him unable to say a word.

Apparently, he didn't need to, for a younger man stumbled up beside Ruddle, tipping his wide-brimmed hat in Ben's direction and then raising his mug high. "To your health."

"To the prosperity of Aldercombe," cried another, spinning around to clink mugs with the duo.

"And *not* to that weasel Lord Frederick," shouted a fourth, causing a bevy of raucous cheers to burst from the group.

Ben couldn't stop the choked laugh that rose in his throat. *Not to that weasel, indeed.*

Something cool pressed against his palm, and he turned to find that Violet had come back and was passing him a mug of his own. "Small ale," she whispered close to his ear. "Is that all right?"

He nodded, mouthing his thanks as he took hold of the handle and joined the men in their toast. "To all of you, too, for your patience, hard work, and dedication," he said, touching mugs with the group—including Violet, who'd also procured a mug for herself. *Especially* with Violet.

Everyone took a drink, and after another round of jubilant cheers, followed by a series of emphatic bows to Violet, the men disbanded. Leaving Ben alone—or at least, alone in the middle of a crowd—with his wife.

"What was all that about?" She looked at him brightly, her cheeks an even more pronounced pink than when she'd left him several minutes prior.

He glanced into the throng, unable to fully fathom what had just happened. "It seems they're pleased with recent developments to the land. Mainly, I suppose, on account of the water meadow preventing their farms from flooding." He shrugged. "That, or they're addled by the effects of drink."

She shook her head, the curls framing her face slightly bobbing. "It's not just the drink." She lifted her mug, giving it another light tap against his. "To you, Mr. Prescott, and the fine job you're doing with Aldercombe."

His heart clenched, then felt very light. "And to you, wife." *Because I wouldn't have done half as well were you not there, too.*

He took another swallow of small ale, watching over the rim of his mug as she tipped hers to her mouth. Watching as she pulled her mug away, and a coating of moisture remained on her lips. He'd best not think about her lips—about where they'd been, what they'd done, how incomparably pleasurable they'd felt—or he'd be certain to go mad.

"I've brought you a meat pie and an apple tart," she said, reaching into the small sack that hung around her arm. She was utterly unaware of just how much she'd captivated him. Of how the air around them felt different and something in the world had shifted in a way he'd never experienced before.

He forced himself back to his senses, setting down his mug so he could accept the two pastries she offered. One sweet, one savory.

He could hardly claim surprise when, of the two she kept for herself, she bit into the apple tart first, a satisfied grin tugging at the edges of her mouth. As such, his cock did *not* twitch in his trousers when she sighed contentedly, licking a bit of apple from her fingertip.

Very well, it did. But how could he help it? She was beautiful, alluring. To frame it from a logical standpoint, his body desired hers.

Yet it went beyond that. He didn't just crave those lush hips and rounded breasts but also that smile. There was something brilliant about it. Something infectious.

Something that made him smile uninhibitedly in return, take a large bite of his apple tart, and feel as if he hadn't a care in the world.

They stood in the grass eating their makeshift dinner, soon approached by other revelers, for the scene with Ruddle and the men had drawn attention. They spoke with tenants, servants, and villagers, meeting infants, the elderly, and people of all ages in between. An undertaking that was surprisingly easy when everyone was so merry.

They conversed so long that his voice grew hoarse from shouting to be heard above the din of the celebration, until eventually, the crowd shifted, many going to take part in a country dance now that the troupe of jingling dancers had finished their performance.

Violet watched eagerly, her foot tapping against the grass as the fiddle began a new, lively tune. "We should dance, too."

He joined her in peering at the joyful procession, his brow and his stomach knotting simultaneously. "But I ... I cannot." A lifetime of caution wouldn't disappear in a single evening. "I don't know how."

She was undeterred, her hand falling upon his shoulder. Her eyes met his and glimmered with the purest, most dazzling blue. "It doesn't matter if you cannot execute every step. You'll keep up. I'm confident."

She released his shoulder and held her palm out as an offering, her grin wide and brilliant. Her golden lashes lightly fluttering.

It would appear he was powerless to refuse, for his hand slipped into hers, and he let her pull him along, right to the center of the dancers.

"Ready?" She mouthed the word as she spun herself to face him, lips quirking.

And then, there was no time to do anything but step and clap and whirl along with the music, to keep up with the flurry of dancers alongside them.

Having spent his youth neither in the country nor in ballrooms, he had precious little dance experience of any kind. The steps were foreign to him, and he stumbled while he tried to get his bearings.

But there was something freeing about it. Lightness rushed through his head each time he spun, and dizzying sparks of pleasure flared when he arrived back at his starting position to find Violet there waiting, flushed and smiling. Silver and blue and pink and gold.

He was certain he looked ridiculous. And yet, the knowledge didn't trouble him in the least.

Ben was uncertain of the hour when they returned home that night. Then again, he also didn't care. What difference did the time on his watch make when his feet were satisfyingly weary, his ears hummed from the memory of fiddle music, and Aldercombe Grange was bathed in the light of countless stars and a moon nearly full?

What difference did anything make when Violet clutched his arm, her silhouette framed by golden curls that had come loose to spill down her back? There was no more crowd. No more food stalls, games, or entertainers.

There was simply the two of them, standing on a silent drive on a tranquil spring night.

Naturally, he kissed her. Pressing his lips to hers was as seamless a progression as taking his next breath. She sank into him as if she belonged in the shelter of his chest. As if their lips were meant to be joined.

He ran his hands through her wild curls as their tongues twined, relishing the sensation of her arms wrapping around his back. Of her fingers stroking up and down his spine, lingering near the waist of his trousers.

His cock inevitably stirred to attention, mild pulses of need sparking in his veins. He'd been so afraid. Afraid of his own desires, afraid of what she wanted or didn't want, afraid of his inability to please her. Yet here in the moonlight, fear became less.

Instead, his mind seized on possibilities. What would happen if he let himself be free with her? If instead of analyzing, he simply let himself trust?

He broke the kiss, reaching for her hand and posing a silent question with his eyes.

She answered by squeezing his fingers, and they started toward the front door in unspoken agreement.

They would go inside. Go upstairs together. No connecting door would separate them.

His heart hammered as visions flashed of her lying across his bed. Of pulling off garments until he could gaze upon her rosy nipples, the curls between her legs, the intimate flesh he'd caressed with his fingertips. Of removing his trousers and letting that flesh envelop him, if that's what she desired.

Their footfalls became more urgent as they ascended the front steps.

Except then, he abruptly stilled.

A pamphlet of some sort was wedged against the bottom of the door. Another two tucked behind the pillar. A fourth, fifth, and sixth placed on the edge of the landing, held in position by small rocks.

He bent down to grab one, an odd feeling settling in his stomach. Straightening, he shifted so he stood directly beneath the lantern above the door, wrenching his spectacles from his pocket. Violet's muttered words reached him just as he perched the spectacles on his nose: "*Not again.*"

However, her voice faded into nothingness. Everything disappeared but the pounding of blood through his ears and the words, suddenly clear, on the pamphlet he held.

The Salacious Solicitor.

By an author of the initials A.P.

The air fled from his lungs as if he'd been kicked. *Initials A.P.* It made no sense. *Initials A.P. …*

Violet moved in a flurry around him, paper rustling as she swept the remainder of the pamphlets into her arms. Meanwhile, the door swung open, a bleary-eyed footman granting them entry.

Ben, though, was frozen. Numb.

The pamphlet in front of his face couldn't be real. There was some other explanation; Alex would never …

But the pamphlet *was* real, printed in the same style as all the others. And Alex had.

Alex had.

As if a bonfire flared under his feet, he bolted into the house and toward his study, not even stopping to acknowledge the waiting Achilles. He marched all the way to his desk, his wobbly legs collapsing into the leather chair but then popping up again, for he could never sit still at a time like this.

He paced across the carpet with the pamphlet clenched in his fist, the cover illuminated by the stark slashes of moonlight pouring through the windows. *The Salacious Solicitor. Initials A.P.*

"Benedict?" Violet's soft call was accompanied by a subtle

glow, and he turned to find her approaching his desk, lamp in one hand and pile of pamphlets in the other.

He wished he could think only of the glimmer the lamp cast across her features. How she was lush, radiant, and unequivocally *his*.

Yet the thought was merely a flicker, quickly doused as he hurried to meet her, throwing out his hand to claim the pamphlets she held.

She passed them over without resistance, although her face appeared strained, and he flipped through the atrocious things, each one the same as the last. *The Salacious Solicitor. The Salacious Solicitor.* The anonymous benefactor had taken no chances that Ben would fail to notice the gift they'd left.

Except suddenly, the gift remained anonymous no longer, for a calling card slipped from between the thin pages, its lettering so bold that Ben would be confronted with the name even if he ripped off his spectacles. *Lord Frederick Denham.*

Where in hell had the lordling summoned the gall to litter Aldercombe's doorstep with erotic literature? With *this* erotic literature, specifically, because he wished to flaunt its connection to the master of the house. Did he think it only fitting that after his embarrassing failure with the broken dam, Ben suffer humiliation, too?

Ben should feel irate at the blackguard for the prank he'd played. No doubt he *would* feel irate once the truth had an opportunity to permeate. However, his present fury shifted to only one target: Alexander.

What in God's name had his brother been thinking? Ben had given up so much to protect him. He'd bought him another chance. And Alex had wasted it. He'd bloody well thrown it away.

Ben crumpled the pages, his fingers like a vise, and pitched them onto his desk. Despite the warmth of the night, he would have to start a fire so he could reduce the entire works to ash. He couldn't bear looking at the damn things any longer, each one screaming danger. Betrayal.

"Benedict?" Violet tried his name again just as he was about to pivot toward the hearth. However, he stopped abruptly, a thought seizing him. The flash of a memory. *Not again*: her words while they stood on the doorstep and he pulled the pamphlets into the light.

"What did you mean?" With a single sharp motion, he abandoned the hearth in favor of whirling toward his wife, knots tightening between his ribs as he peered at her. "When we were outside, you said *not again*."

It was impossible to miss the way her eyes shifted so they didn't quite meet his. The way her lip slid between her teeth and her fingers curled into the gauzy fabric of her skirts. He recognized her expression. Knew it meant she was contemplating, calculating, searching for the right answer to give him.

In the end, though, her joyless gaze went back to his, and she settled on the truth. "I found a single copy of the same pamphlet lying on the step when I returned home this afternoon."

Hell and damnation. So, this incident was a repeat occurrence? And Violet had *known*? His jaw clenched painfully. "And you didn't think I should be informed?"

"I did. I planned to tell you." She blew out a weary sigh. "I just ..."

"You should have come to me at once," he snapped. "You had no right to keep this a secret."

Her spine stiffened as if she'd received an electrical shock, her eyes flashing with a sudden burst of wrath. "Is it so wrong that I wanted to enjoy one blasted evening with you before, once again, something came along to interfere?"

His head swirled, no longer with merriment but with foreboding. Everything from the day came rushing back: the ring of her laughter, the clinking of mugs, the tang of spiced apple. Did he wish it all away?

No. Of course he didn't. However, this wasn't the time for it. He shouldn't be in Wiltshire dancing—lovemaking—when Alex was off God knows where doing God knows what. No longer protected by the safety Cambridge offered, for he'd certainly been expelled when the pamphlet came to light.

"You should have told me," he reasserted thickly, the rapid pitch and sway of his thoughts making him so dizzy that he neared the point of casting up his accounts. He needed to fix this. Needed to find Alex.

"I'm sorry." Her hand fell upon his sleeve, the touch scalding enough that he snatched his arm away. He couldn't endure her caresses right now. He *couldn't*.

Her eyes—hard turned gentle—developed the unmistakable sheen of hurt. It lasted only an instant, though, before she blinked it away, not retreating from him but keeping her hands firmly at her sides. "I'm sorry," she repeated, so soft and compassionate that it hurt. "I know this is distressing news for you, but everything's going to be all right. I'm not afraid of any scandal that ensues, and if your brother needs our support, I can help to—"

"No." His voice sounded stringent, hollow. He was being dragged inward, forced into a spiraling abyss that contained all his worst fears come true. "I don't want your help."

The pain in her eyes flared back to life, and this time, it didn't retreat. "I'm your *wife*, Benedict. Why must you always keep shutting me out?"

Because it's all too much. Because I cannot share this with you. Because this is my *burden,* my *vulnerability,* my *family affliction of which I cannot speak.*

Even in his anger, he hated himself for hurting her. He'd no doubt do so even more once the shock of what happened wore off and all that remained was his self-loathing.

Be that as it may, he wrenched himself back from her, glowering so severely that his brow felt in danger of splintering. "For the love of Christ, just leave me alone."

Violet's lips—those plump, perfect lips—formed an *o*. A choked sound emerged. And then, without another word, she spun away, giving him merely the briefest glimpse of her granite-like face before she made for the door.

The retreat of her skirts—the silver threads glinting in the lamplight, just as they'd done outdoors when she traipsed about the village green—caused a fresh stab of pain in his chest.

He pushed it aside, pressing his hands to his temples so he could focus on the issue at hand. He needed to be alone and without distractions. Needed to think about the situation rationally so he could invent a solution.

Infuriatingly, no obvious answer came to him, no matter how hard he drove his fingers into his skull. How long ago had the pamphlet first been distributed? Had Alex been discovered, and consequently sent down from Cambridge, right away? Was he now back home in London? Or had he taken himself somewhere else entirely to dream up his next stories, changeable clodpate that he was?

There were too many unknowns, and Ben could choose how he proceeded based only on his best guess—along with the influence of the urgency, outrage, and terror that crashed through his blood.

Despite his near-lifelong vow to let logic guide him, he'd already allowed emotions to steer his actions several times today. It would seem he needed to keep with the pattern and do so again.

And so, Benedict Prescott—rational thinker, unskilled rider, heeder of caution—rushed to the stables, fetched a horse, and started toward London by moonlight.

20

A patchy fog had settled over London when a coach nearly barreled into Ben the next morning.

He'd just begun crossing Buckingham Street on foot—having left his tired horse at mews about a half-mile away—and was minutes from his family's terrace house when the hulking vehicle appeared from the mist. He jumped onto the pavement to avoid a collision, and the four cantering horses were rapidly pulled to a halt, their whinnies mixing with the clamorous screech of wheels.

While his sleepless night on the road may have dulled his wits, the effect wasn't so great that recognition failed to sink in. He knew that coach. He'd watched it pull up onto the street before his bedroom window countless times, always with a strange mixture of awe and dread.

Yet when the door, proudly emblazoned with the flames and phoenix comprising the Rockliffe crest, flew open, it wasn't his uncle who appeared.

Rather, it was his mother, her lithe frame leaping to the ground, her dark eyes like saucers.

"Ben?" She cocked her head, staring as if he might be an

apparition crafted by the fog. An idea he half-wondered about himself, for it seemed so incongruous that his mother would suddenly be standing before him, sprung from the marquess's carriage.

However, after another beat of stillness, she launched herself at him, her arms circling him in a tight embrace. "Ben. You cannot even imagine how relieved I am to see you."

He let his hands go stiffly to the back of her traveling cloak, taking in the fact that yes, she was very much real. A tiny bit of familiarity and safety when nothing else in the world was right.

But all too soon, the comforting embrace was gone, and she stood back to stare at him once more, brows knitting. "Now, give me a moment while I fight the urge to strangle you. How could you show up in London without saying a word about it? Imagine if I hadn't happened upon you in the street at just the right time. There would have been so many wasted miles between us, and our paths might not have crossed for days."

His weary brain fought to keep up. "What do you mean?" He jutted his chin toward the opulent carriage—the conveyance his mother made a habit, like most things Rockliffe, of avoiding. "And what are you doing?"

"What am I *doing*?" Her mouth dropped incredulously, and her eyes flashed, making her appear especially keen to follow through on her threat of strangulation. "I accepted a loan of your uncle's carriage so I could go to Aldercombe Grange to see what in blazes is happening with you! Have you forgotten that you wrote a letter saying you were getting *married*?"

No, he hadn't forgotten. Not even remotely. However, the two distinct parts of his life—his family and childhood home, and the new home he'd established in Wiltshire—had yet to combine, and he could presently focus only on the former.

"I've been beside myself, Benedict Prescott," she continued at his silence, his full name a telltale sign of her exasperation. "First, you sent that infuriatingly vague letter about your betrothal at the same time I couldn't leave Timothy's bedside. Then, your missives all but stopped, and just when I thought I could get on the mail coach to come to you, the ague passed to Oliver. Do you have any idea how worrisome it was when I was confined to London and my letters went unanswered? Can you possibly imagine the torment a mother feels when she wishes she could divide herself in half but cannot?"

A thick lump formed in his throat. He'd been sorrily remiss with his correspondence, and in all his preoccupation with Aldercombe, he hadn't known that his youngest half-brother, Oliver, had also fallen ill. He swallowed, a bitter taste filling his mouth. "Are the boys both all right?"

His mother placed a hand on his shoulder with more gentleness than he deserved. "We had a few difficult days, but they're fine, Ben. We're all fine." She blew out a beleaguered sigh, her soft touch becoming a finger that jabbed him between the ribs. "Which is why we're now going to talk about you and this precipitous betrothal. Is it true? Did you really get married by license?"

"It's true," he managed, a quick blast of relief trickling through his insides at the news his young brothers had recovered. His mother and stepfather were well, too. With that established, however, his mind raced back to the task at hand —the entire reason he'd ridden all night. "Where's Alex?"

"Oh, no, no, no." The accusing finger pressed deeper, his mother's mouth twisting into a frown. "You cannot drop such a revelation on me and provide no other details."

He gritted his teeth, trying to rouse patience he didn't have. "It's just as I wrote to you: I encountered Miss Violet Collingwood upon my arrival at Aldercombe, our meeting was witnessed and misinterpreted, and I proposed marriage to salvage her damaged reputation. She accepted, I procured a bishop's license, and she proceeded to become my wife." That didn't begin to cover everything that had developed between him and Violet over the past weeks, but he couldn't contemplate, let alone articulate, any of that at present. Only one thing held his focus: "Now, where's Alex?"

His mother's jaw slackened, her dark brows shooting high on her forehead. "That's *it*? That's all you plan to tell me?"

She'd never been the swooning type; however, the way she stared disbelievingly made it look like she was about to do *something*. Yell at him, perhaps? Order him to go sit in a corner?

Instead, her mouth snapped shut, and she looked at the pavement, muttering more to herself than to him. "*Don't worry about Ben*, Jeremy insisted. *He's always had a level head. And when I spoke with Rockliffe about it, he said the same. Benedict is more rational than any of us. I trust him not to go astray.* Ha! What do they know?"

He shot his arm out to resummon her attention, unable to keep the frustration from his tone. "I cannot speak about it right now. Where's Alex?"

Her gaze darted back up, and he recognized what he saw there: an unmistakable flash of understanding. She knew why Ben had come. Knew what Alex had done.

"He just returned from the printshop," she said quietly. Soberly. "He's inside."

Oh, thank God. Ben's instincts had steered him right. There'd be no more frantic excursions on horseback because Alex was *here*. He was in London, just steps away, and Ben was going to ignore his stab of unease at the mention of Alex and the printshop and fix this asinine mess his brother had made.

His foot lifted and then stilled, for there was one more

thing he needed to establish. "And where are Jeremy and the boys?"

His mother crossed her arms, her lips squeezing together in hesitation before she said, "They've gone to the park."

"Good." Another stroke of luck, although he gleaned no joy from it, only a heightened sense of urgency. He spun away, his sights set on the terrace house near the end of the street. "I need to speak with Alex privately for a moment."

"Ben ..." Her voice was a warning, trailing after him as he marched down the street.

However, it hit his awareness without even causing a waver in his step. Nothing short of an explosion could do that now, so determined was he to get into the house and lay eyes on his brother.

"I'm staying away only as long as it takes to give the coachman a message for Lord Rockliffe," she cautioned, her unease plain even though he could no longer see her face. "I imagine he'll be curious to know why I'm not taking his carriage to Wiltshire after all."

"I just need a moment," he repeated, calling the words without looking back. With any luck, a moment would be enough time to talk sense into Alex and determine how to undo this pamphlet debacle.

He was practically running now, boots pounding against the pavement until he arrived in front of the familiar blue door. Finding it unlocked, he burst inside, taking the stairs two at a time and racing to the entrance of the sitting room.

Where he abruptly paused.

Alex, the blunderbuss, had ignored all furniture and was sitting in the middle of the floor, scribbled pages surrounding him. With a quill in hand, he stared at one of the sheets, tongue pressed into his cheek as he concentrated. It was a scene so uncannily reminiscent of their childhood that Ben's chest tightened with a sharp ache.

He cleared his throat, walking into the room with exaggerated footsteps—for his brother, when lost in thought, could fail to notice an apocalypse.

The boot stomps did the trick, though, and Alex snapped his head up, his quill tumbling to the floor and leaving a black splotch across the page. "Ben?"

Alex—the spitting image of their father with his wild russet curls and cobalt eyes—looked well. His color was high, his features animated. He'd even taken the time to put on a crisp green coat and properly knot his cravat, and the glass by his side appeared to contain lemonade instead of a stronger beverage. Ben wasn't sure what he'd imagined he'd find. Something more sinister, he supposed. Consequently, the sight of his brother prospering should inundate him with relief.

Yet it wasn't enough to make fear release its angry talons from his heart.

Wasn't enough to prompt him to do anything but snarl, "What the fuck were you thinking?"

Alex's cheeks paled, and he hurriedly swept his papers out of the way so he could push to his feet.

"You ruined everything with your bloody recklessness," Ben snapped, ire swelling like a high tide, sending an incensed wave crashing upon his brother. "Did you not stop for a second to think of the consequences your damn publishing venture would have if you chose to continue it? I gave you another chance at Cambridge, and you pissed it away."

Alex braved the tempest without flinching, although his face was shadowed. His mouth tight. "I'm sorry, I—"

"Don't apologize." Ben clenched his hands into fists, reminding himself to breathe. This was bad. This was horribly, exceptionally bad. However, he'd get nowhere if he lost his head to anger. He needed to think. Needed to be unflappable.

"Let's not waste time on *I'm sorry*," he continued,

working a touch more levelness into his tone. "I care about nothing but how we can make the university undo your expulsion. Perhaps we could find someone who would accept coin to claim responsibility, or—"

"I wasn't expelled." Alex kept his voice low, but it shot through Ben like a bullet. "I left of my own accord before it could come to that."

The room began spinning as the blood rushed from Ben's head. He couldn't have heard his brother correctly; there was no bloody way ...

Except Alex continued standing before him, his words a mocking ring in Ben's ears. *I left of my own accord.*

Not only did the room pitch as if it were a ship in a storm, but Alex's figure blurred into an indistinct mass of russet and green. So convoluted that it was impossible for Ben to tell whether he stared at Alex or their father. *Overturned bottle. Limp hand.*

"Are you an imbecile?" Ben shouted, because restraint and logic had deserted him, leaving only fiery, turbulent emotion in their wake. "Do you have a death wish?"

Alex shook his head, maddeningly unruffled. Oblivious to peril. If anything, he looked a little sad. "I don't know what you mean by that. You might not approve, but they're only stories. There's nothing unlawful about them."

Nothing unlawful, but there was everything to lose. A future in which Alex's stories consumed him until there was nothing left of him. Nothing at all.

Overturned bottle.

Limp hand.

"You were supposed to be at Cambridge!" Ben's reply was a roar, and with it, something ripped inside his chest, letting an animalistic sound break free. A growl? A sob? He forced air into his too-tight lungs; spat words in his brother's face. "You were supposed to be safe."

"Ben." Alex's features gentled, and he extended a hand, nearing Ben's sleeve.

Ben recoiled instantly, shirking the impending contact. "Don't you fucking touch me." He held every muscle taut enough to snap, pouring the force of his fury—his terror—into a lethal glower.

He wished he could hate his brother. Wished he didn't care what happened to him one way or another. How much easier it would be if he could return to Aldercombe and not give a good goddamn. Yet caring embedded itself at the root of him. Caring was the reason he couldn't lose again, for he'd never be able to withstand that pain a second time. Not if it pertained to Alex.

His brother held his hands up in surrender, his mouth opening to utter what would no doubt be placations. Platitudes.

"Don't you say another fucking word," Ben hissed, cutting him off before that could happen. Why couldn't Alex see? Why was he too much of a clodpole to recognize that if he didn't take care, history would repeat itself? *Like father, like son*.

Ben's legs turned to putty, making him stagger backward. He smelled his mother's perfume. Detected her voice from somewhere behind him, although her words were muffled by the pounding in his ears.

Alex spoke, then, just as something crunched beneath Ben's boot and trickled against the floorboards. *The glass of lemonade*, he registered vaguely, but he couldn't get it to mean anything. Couldn't think of anything but the voices in his head screaming danger and the pain tearing across his ribcage.

He'd become vulnerable and raw—prey being hunted by a fate he was powerless to quell. And so, he did the only thing any creature with a shred of self-preservation would do: he fled.

He bolted down the stairs and out the door, scarcely hearing the shouts that followed him. He ran until they faded to nothing at all, replaced by the indistinct hum of a bustling city and its nameless passersby.

He traversed both familiar streets and those he'd never walked before, plodding along until the mist turned to rain and then cleared to sun.

He strode haphazardly until his feet were as weary as his heart.

And then, he entered an alehouse, where he proceeded to get raging drunk.

21

E ven the lambs, with their downy fleece and tiny bleats, couldn't cure Violet's poor mood.

In the three days since Benedict had disappeared from Aldercombe without a word, she'd visited the sheep pastures enough times that Green was likely tired of seeing her coming. The animals were well, after all, continuing to show no ill effects after their misadventure on the water meadow.

Yet she was desperate to keep busy in any way possible. There'd been daily tours of the estate. Walks with Achilles. Cloudless afternoons spent underneath the beech on Skylark Ridge with her book. Nothing, though, felt right. None of it would take away the ache in her heart.

With a sigh, she lifted her hand from her favorite lamb's woolly head—*Petunia*, she'd named the little thing, adamant that the creature would *not* appear on the dinner table come autumn—and hopped over the stone fence. It gave her no joy to return to the house and eat dinner at the massive table alone, nor did it help that all food had come to taste like sawdust. However, the sun, gently sinking in the sky, indicated that the hour had come, and Mrs. Wheeler would worry if she didn't return.

Violet wouldn't do that to the kindly housekeeper. Benedict had already caused enough worry for them both.

She plodded through the grass, kicking at a small rock that appeared in her path. Drat Benedict Prescott. If not for the grooms, she wouldn't have even known that he'd hied to London, for he'd shut her out as soundly as if he'd slammed a door in her face.

And drat *her* for caring. Drat her for staying up at night and wondering how he fared. Drat her for thinking they shared a confidence they clearly did not.

He wanted to be angry with her? Well, she was angry, too. But that was the most damnable part of all: she missed him, nonetheless.

She pulled off her bonnet to let the sun stream upon her face, trying to push out the chill that had seeped to her bones. However, no sooner did she turn her face to the sky than a low rumble started in the distance—the pounding of hooves churning gravel. The faint echo of a whinny.

A frisson of hope shot through her chest, although it vanished the instant her eyes focused on the front drive. Even from afar, it was plain to see that the approaching horse didn't come from Aldercombe's stables. Nor was the rider the same exasperating man who'd dashed away three nights prior.

The figure on horseback was indeed a gentleman, but he was broader across the shoulders than Benedict. The hair that crept below the brim of his top hat glinted auburn, not black.

She began running at a breakneck pace, lungs burning, until the stranger's identity became obvious. And then, she ran even faster, arriving at the top of the drive just as Lord Rockliffe handed off his horse to a groom.

She'd encountered the stern-faced marquess only once or twice at ton events over the past few years but had a clear enough memory to recognize him as Benedict's uncle. A strange sense of unease churned in her stomach. He didn't seem the type to ride about the countryside for the purpose of spreading joyous news.

"Lord Rockliffe." She ground to a halt in front of him, folding herself into a breathless curtsy. She knew she looked a fright, and that her apprehension was likely plastered across her face. Unfortunately, there was little she could do to change that.

"Mrs. Prescott, I presume." He dipped his chin, uttering her name almost like a question. When she didn't refute it, he quickly straightened, his mouth pressing into a severe line. "Has Benedict returned?"

"Returned to Aldercombe?" Her insides did a flip. "No."

"Damn." He muttered another string of curses under his breath, his gaze drifting beyond her to survey the drive he'd just traversed.

Her heart, the foolish thing, battered against her ribs like the wings of a moth trapped beneath glass. "Where's Benedict? Has something happened?"

He shook his head, turning toward the entrance of Aldercombe Grange. "We should go inside."

"No." She rushed in front of him, using every bit of restraint she possessed not to grab the marquess's dusty coat sleeves. "Whatever news you bring, tell me here."

Lord Rockliffe—for all that he could cast her aside like the impertinent chit she was—stilled, his ice-blue eyes filling with reluctance. The following silence lasted an eternity, bringing her toward the point of pleading. But just before she could do that, he finally spoke, the words low and terrible. "Benedict hasn't been seen since Monday morning when he had a confrontation with his brother at their home on Buckingham Street. We thought he might have returned to Aldercombe without telling anyone."

"He hasn't." Violet had to swallow down a lump before she could force out the clipped phrase.

He removed his hat, pressing a hand to his dust-stained brow. "I should have suspected as much. He changed horses in Reading during his ride to London early Monday, but none of the coaching inns have heard tell of him since."

So Benedict had simply *vanished*? It wasn't possible; he was far too ordered for that. He followed rules, adhered to responsibilities, and he couldn't suddenly be missing. He just *couldn't.*

She didn't know how long she stood there, legs trembling beneath her skirts, her head trying to reconcile a shock that made no sense. She only knew that after an indeterminate amount of time passed, Lord Rockliffe strode away, making for the front steps. "If you don't mind, Mrs. Prescott, I'm in desperate need of a chair and a brandy."

With a start, she raced into action, grabbing his forearm just as he reached the landing and forcing him to look back at her. "But Benedict," she said thickly. "Where is he?"

The marquess, despite his foreboding mien, peered at her with gentleness, not shaking off her brash touch. "I have men out searching for him. Although I doubt any are so fierce as his mother." He shook his head, his lips twisting into a humorless smile. "Between us all, we're bound to find him somewhere, eventually."

Eventually. Somewhere. Those weren't good enough! Benedict may well infuriate her, but that didn't mean she could sit back and merely hope he would turn up.

"I'm going to London," she said, her path forward suddenly as clear as the blazing sun above.

However, Lord Rockliffe didn't look convinced. "He might return to Aldercombe within the next day or two, but none of us will know if there's no one here."

That was indeed a fair point, but she dismissed it after a

few seconds of thought. "London was the last place he was seen, so that's where I'm traveling," she asserted. "If he is, in fact, returning to Aldercombe as we speak, our paths are bound to cross on the road." Whether they'd have a happy reunion remained to be seen, but she'd worry about that after she found him.

"If you're certain, Mrs. Prescott." He appeared weary—and not altogether certain himself—although as a man with a wife and two daughters, he was likely used to the tenacity of a woman who'd made up her mind. "If you'd like to go in and see to your packing, I'll arrange for the coach to be made ready for you at first light."

"I'm not taking the coach." She shook her head, the mere thought of all those extra hours of waiting causing her skin to bristle. "I'll go on horseback. And I'm leaving now."

He raised a severe auburn brow. "Shall I remind you that darkness will soon fall?"

Sunlight, moonlight. It was all the same to her. She shrugged a rigid shoulder. "I'll bring a groom. We'll stop a few hours at a coaching inn if need be."

"There's no dissuading you, is there?"

"Indeed not, my lord."

He gave a clipped sigh before drawing his elongated spine even taller. "When you arrive in London, go to Rockliffe House and seek out my wife. She's being kept apprised of the search efforts throughout town, and she can also show you to Mr. and Mrs. Clare's residence, should you require it."

"Thank you." After sparing a moment to express her gratitude, she hurried to the door, about to run inside to gather a few items for the road. However, his next question caused her to freeze in place.

"Should I take this to mean that the union between you and Benedict is more than a necessary arrangement?"

A lightning bolt shot down the center of her chest, the

accompanying thunder a rumble around her heart. "Ask me again once we find him," she murmured, placing her fingers on the door handle, unable to look back and meet the marquess's eye.

Then, she burst through the door, running all the way to her bedchamber so she could throw on a traveling dress and locate the small satchel at the bottom of her clothespress. She grabbed a spare frock, chemise, and stockings, each action mechanical and unthinking, until a faint whine caught her notice.

Her eyes darted around to discover Achilles sitting in the doorway, his dark gaze eager and his tail swishing tentatively against the floorboards. The poor thing was lonely without Benedict. Keen to find attention wherever he could get it.

She snapped the overstuffed satchel closed, pulling the strap over her head and going to kneel beside the waiting dog.

"Your master is a pudding head, a numbskull, and a clod-pate," she announced crisply, causing Achilles to cock his ears and watch her with those intent eyes. She sank her fingers into the fur atop his broad head, giving him a few farewell scratches before leaning close to whisper the truth that kept thrumming in her frantic, frightened heart. "I believe I'm falling in love with him."

Ben's mind had become a sieve, unable to hold an intelligible thought.

What time was it? What day was it? He blinked, brilliant sunlight assaulting his eyes each time he turned them up from the pavement. It was morning, then. Or afternoon?

How long had he been walking? His knees wobbled from the strain of his weight, as if he'd subjected them to cruel overuse. But it hadn't really been that long, had it? Fragments of memories darted through his head like slithering eels. His arse on a rickety stool beside a barroom counter. His body toppling to the ground, shards of gravel digging into his palms.

What the hell had happened? And where *was* he? He blinked again, forcing his heavy eyelids to stay open and meet the merciless sun.

God, he was tired. The type of tired that made him crave sleep for a week, if only he had a safe place to rest his head.

He could imagine that place. Fresh springtime grass beneath his palms, beech leaves swaying above his head. A soft, floral-scented lap for his pillow, a golden curl that tumbled down to brush against his jawline, and fingers that stroked him, letting him know everything wrong in the world could be put right.

But that place was in a countryside far away. Maybe it had only been a dream.

A horse's hooves clip-clopped beside him, the deafening rattle of the cart it pulled making the vision evaporate. He was in the city. In London. Life bustling around him in every which way.

And the building in front of him—the sunlight catching its red-gray brick and gleaming white stone as if it were favored by the heavens—was goddamn Rockliffe House.

He staggered forward on aching legs, a bitter laugh rising in his throat. He was desperate for shelter. For home. And somehow, he'd ended up here, at his uncle's Mayfair town house. The place he'd been dragged as a child after his father's death had left his mother penniless. The place he'd be dragged again someday, permanently, assuming he lived a long life and that the pain coursing through his body didn't signal his imminent demise.

He laughed harder, each peal smarting his ribs, although

the situation seemed far less amusing than unequivocally pathetic.

This was the place on which his father had turned his back so he could marry a woman of lower birth and follow his dreams of poethood. The place he'd deemed oppressive and disparaging, swearing the family he created would have no association with the house, its occupants, or anything else linked to the peerage.

And yet, Ben kept stumbling toward the edifice's polished front door. A hapless creature venturing right into a predator's open jaws.

"Oh, thank the Lord." A sharp rasp pierced his eardrums, followed by a rhythmic *tap, tap, tap* that grated on his skull.

He squinted, and although the world swam before his eyes, he could see that a figure had appeared on the doorstep. A swath of gray fabric. Crepey skin. A silver-handled cane that glinted in the sun.

Laughter seized his insides as he stumbled toward the steps, for this was the funniest thing of all: his dragon of a grandmother standing here to welcome him to hell. The elderly dowager marchioness may look frail, but he'd be a fool to forget all the times she'd been calculating and ruthless. How when a rift occurred in the family, she could usually be named as the cause.

But it didn't matter. He went up those steps anyway, propelled by a power that didn't seem his own.

The snare snapped closed the instant he arrived on the landing, sharp nails digging into his arms like claws and refusing to let go. "Whatever you've done, don't you ever do it again; you hear me? You're better than this." Icy eyes glared up at him venomously, the gruff voice an echo in his pounding head. "You have Rockliffe blood in your veins. Marquess's blood."

She shook him, her fragile body surprisingly potent, and

he was forced to grab her arms in return before her efforts made him crumple to the doorstep. He wanted her to stop talking. Wanted her to cease jostling him before he vomited on her shoes.

But the dowager, who rarely behaved as desired, grew louder and more forceful, the cloudy blue of her irises transfixing him as everything else continued spinning. "I've come to realize something over the years: fate didn't grant sons to your uncle because *you* are the one built for the title. You always have been. Even the circumstances of your upbringing couldn't take that away from you."

He trembled violently, his nerve endings freezing over despite the sun that beat down on him. *You're wrong*, he tried to say. *You're wrong*. He couldn't have been built for the title; it was an accident. Something that never should have been.

A betrayal of his father.

However, it would seem his tongue had forgotten how to do anything but loll about inside his mouth. And his legs, which had held him upright for too long, didn't care to do so any longer.

He was bone-weary. He wanted to go home.

Marquess's blood. They were the final words to tumble through his head before his body gave up and everything went black.

22

Violet nearly cried with relief when a somber-looking butler admitted her into Rockliffe House after the longest continuous ride she'd ever done in her life. As for when Lady Rockliffe appeared in the entrance hall, taking a moment to confirm her identity before revealing that Benedict had been found and was under this very roof—well, relief was too weak a word.

The sensation made her stumble, forcing her to grab the nearest side table before she lost her balance altogether. It caused her breath to hitch and her eyes to sting, for everything to turn light and surreal.

Yet no sooner did the cathartic wave wash over her than reality pushed its way back in, leaving her with a hundred questions and far too much fatigue to articulate them properly.

"What happened?" she managed after a beat, continuing to grip the table for support. "Where was he?"

Lady Rockliffe's cheeks flushed, her slipper tapping quietly against the carpet before she answered. "He ... we don't know, exactly. The truth is, he fainted upon the doorstep before anyone could speak to him, and he has yet to awaken."

Violet's mouth dropped in alarm. "Are you saying he's ill?"

But before the marchioness could respond to the question, another figure rushed into the entrance hall. A woman whose curly ebony hair and intense dark eyes could make her no one but Benedict's mother.

"Theo." The marchioness beckoned to her, then tilted her head in Violet's direction. "This is Mrs. Violet Prescott."

Violet's new mother-in-law appeared before her in an instant, her expressive face hinting at so many emotions that it was difficult to determine how, precisely, she must be feeling. She looked Violet up and down, her stare shrewd and assessing, and whether she planned to welcome her unexpected daughter-in-law to the family or chide her for the hasty marriage, Violet couldn't say.

Ultimately, Benedict's mother—Theo—crossed her arms over her chest, keeping her gaze locked with Violet's but showing the tiniest bit of softening around her eyes. "As you can probably imagine," she said, "I have more questions for you than I can count. However, I wonder if you should lie down first."

Violet blew out a breath, running a hand through her tangled mass of curls. "I don't need to lie down." She undoubtedly looked a travel-stained fright, but she couldn't bring herself to care. Couldn't give in to fatigue quite yet. She forced her shoulders to remain high as she peered entreatingly at Theo. "I just want to know that Benedict is all right."

"He's been drinking," Theo said without preamble, her mouth tight. "Excessively. There are signs he may have been in some sort of altercation."

Drinking? An altercation? "But ..." Violet let the revelation turn through her head, unsure whether it brought relief or dismay. "But Benedict doesn't …"

"Drink? Get into trouble? No." Theo closed her eyes for an instant, worried creases appearing at the corners. "I'm afraid recent circumstances caused him to act out of character."

Oh, did Violet know it. The pamphlets fluttered mockingly in her mind, illuminated by stark moonlight on the doorstep of Aldercombe Grange. The precise moment when everything had crumbled apart for her and Benedict both. The moment he'd dismissed and rejected her, furious with the secret she'd kept.

I don't want your help. For the love of Christ, just leave me alone. His words came back to shoot daggers at her heart, and she dug her nails into the side table at the sudden onslaught of pain.

What was she even doing at this house? Sitting idly in Wiltshire without knowing what had happened to Benedict had been unfathomable, but now that he was accounted for … He wouldn't want her here. He'd made it clear he was angry, that he wished for her to have no part in his family matters. She was, after all, an outsider. The woman he'd married out of duty.

She forced her stiff fingers to release the table edge, willing her voice to sound composed—or at least not to break into sobs. "I'm glad to hear he's been found and that his ailments aren't of the worsening kind. I won't impose on you any longer."

With speed she didn't know she still possessed, she whirled around to leave, unable to take the intensity of those dark, too-familiar eyes for another instant. However, Lady Rockliffe rushed in front of her before she could reach the door, her face filled with kindness. "It's hardly an imposition when you're family. Please, you must stay. I'll show you to a guest room so you can rest after your long journey."

"Thank you, but no," Violet said hurriedly, wishing she could smile but finding the effort beyond her abilities. Something about the marchioness's hospitality caused an extra ache in her heart. "I should really be on my way."

Where she'd go, she had no idea, given that her father had turned their nearby town house into a harem. But somewhere. She'd find somewhere to lick her wounds, succumb to her weariness, and try to forget how everything about the future looked bleak.

"I heard him mutter your name in his sleep," Theo murmured from behind her. "More than once. Whatever you wish to make of that."

Violet froze on the spot, then slowly made herself turn, a strange pulse throbbing in her neck.

Benedict's mother continued to evaluate her, expression unreadable. However, there was an unmistakable hint of gentleness there. "You should stay, Violet," she said softly. "Not that you're obligated, of course. But if you have any inclination to do so … you should stay."

Violet blinked swiftly, tamping down the burn in her eyes. *It's not what Benedict wants*, her brain shouted, unwilling to relinquish the hurt that spiraled through her chest. But … had he really called out for her? Did it mean anything more than drunken ramblings? Was there any chance …

"May I see him?" she burst out, ceasing to think, simply letting her heart lead in the direction it chose. "Only for a moment. I won't disturb him; I'd just … I'd like to see him with my own eyes."

Theo exchanged a fleeting glance with Lady Rockliffe before the marchioness came to take Violet's arm, offering a small smile. "Certainly. Come with me."

After a quick nod of thanks to Theo, Violet let Lady Rockliffe guide her up the stairs and down a corridor, weariness overtaking pride and prompting her to lean on the marchioness's arm. Downstairs, a multitude of voices had hummed from behind a closed door close to the entrance hall, but up here, it was quiet. The type of place where one could sleep for a very longtime.

"He's in here," Lady Rockliffe said, stopping beside a door near the end of the corridor. She carefully released her hold on Violet and, after ascertaining that she remained upright, gave her dusty sleeve a reassuring pat. "I know you refused it, but I'm going to have the bedchamber directly across from this one made up for you in case you change your mind. In the meantime, are you certain there's nothing else you need?"

"Perhaps some coffee," Violet conceded, glancing at the door as if it were a rival to be vanquished. Her body was a mixture of exhaustion and nerves, and she'd be best served if she accepted fortification.

"I'll have it sent up right away." The marchioness flashed her another sympathetic half-smile. "Ring if you require anything else."

"Thank you," Violet murmured, setting her fingers against the door handle with a small swell of gratitude. She hadn't anticipated this sort of welcome. An automatic acceptance as if she were one of the family.

She'd use the tiny triumph to steel herself for what came next. To prevent her fears from roaring back to life and her body from running away.

She pushed into the room before additional thoughts had a chance to plague her, her eyes adjusting to the dimness created by the drawn curtains. They fell on him almost at once —the figure sprawled out in the vast tester bed. He breathed heavily, his chest rising and falling beneath the twisted blanket that covered him. As she crept closer, it became clear that his skin was ashy and sheened with sweat. An angry purple bruise marred his jaw. His shirt contained splatters of mud, and his hair was matted into an unruly nest.

He didn't look like Benedict Prescott at all—not the pristine, buttoned-up man she'd come to know. Not the man who rescued sheep in the rain or danced at Whitsun, either. This was the battered version of him. The rawest version. Yet he was still, undoubtedly, her husband. And he was safe. He was going to be all right.

No thanks to his own efforts.

She put her hands on her hips, glaring down at the sleeping figure. "It's like I said to Achilles," she muttered. "You're a pudding head."

He stirred, a faint sound crossing his lips that made her heart skip a beat. What if he awoke only to show her the same dismissive coldness as before he'd rushed away to London? She couldn't abide it; she had to leave—

Except he merely turned his head on the pillow and kept on sleeping, his eyelids lightly twitching as if he dreamed.

She let out an unsteady exhale, and all the energy seemed to seep from her limbs along with it. It was like everything— the sleepless night on horseback, the weight of her worry, the ache in her heart—caught up to her at once, and she didn't have the strength to sustain it any longer.

Thank heavens there was coffee coming to bolster her and a guest room being made ready as well. She may just give in and use it, if only to refresh herself for a few minutes.

In the meantime, though ...

She flopped onto the bottom of Benedict's bed, the plush counterpane too great a temptation to resist any longer. The mattress was soft, large enough for her to stretch out widthwise, and that's exactly what she did, nestling her body beneath the lump that was his feet.

What a reprieve to be off her legs. It couldn't last long, of course—only until a maid arrived with her coffee. But with

Benedict sleeping like the dead, there was surely no harm in lying down while she waited and absorbing just the smallest bit of heat from his body. She didn't have to be on good terms with him to appreciate his warmth.

"Pudding head," she repeated to his feet with a yawn, and whether the sensation darting through her chest was exasperation, relief, or something else entirely, she couldn't say.

She didn't find out, for in the next instant, her eyelids involuntarily closed. And then, she was asleep.

23

Benedict had both crashed his head into a brick wall and swallowed a jar of sand. At least, that's what the throbbing in his skull and dryness in his mouth would have him believe.

He pried open his heavy eyelids, the narrow stream of light peeking through the crack in the curtains searing his vision like he stared into the sun. Where in the hell was he? What had he done to make everything in his body hurt?

And why, amidst the misery, did he smell flowers? An airy perfume that was light and comforting. Familiar.

He struggled to right himself, but the effort of rising made his head swim and collapse back down onto the pillow. However, not before he caught a glimpse of golden curls fanned across the bottom of the bed.

"Violet?" he croaked, his thoughts swirling at a dizzying pace but blanketed by a thick layer of fog. He knew that hair. That scent. Yet Violet was in Wiltshire and, last he recalled, he was in London. Had he begun to experience delusions?

Something rustled and shoved into his feet, causing a momentary dip in the mattress and a flurry of color to burst before his eyes. He tilted his head in the direction of the movement, ignoring the shot of pain in his temples and focusing on the figure that had scrambled from his bed. Emerald green fabric, white lace, pink cheeks. That brilliant blonde hair.

"Violet," he rasped again, because it was really her, it must be. However, she was backing away from his bedside like a stalked animal ready to bolt.

Reluctantly, she stilled at the garbled sound of her name, and after a moment's hesitation—a moment where blue eyes bore down on him, and a few more scraps of his memory returned—she abandoned her retreat. Instead, she busied herself with something at his bedside table, the loud clatters and clinks tolerable only because her body shaded him from the light, filling his view with swaths of green skirts.

The shadow lasted only a minute, though, before she shifted to grab his pillow, jostling him into a semi-seated position. "Here." She shoved a mug into his hand before he could even utter a groan of protest, and when his fingers curled reflexively around the warm surface, she helped guide it to his lips. "Drink this."

His stomach roiled at the thought of consuming anything. However, when the first splash of strong, sugarless coffee hit his throat, it went down with surprising ease, taking away a little of the dryness. Giving him a tiny jolt of clarity, too. He was in a guest bedchamber at Rockliffe House, reclining beneath a brocade counterpane and surrounded by gilt-edged furniture.

Of course, how he'd ended up here with Violet at his side remained a mystery.

He accepted another mouthful of coffee, waiting for it to lift the haze from his brain. Everything came at him in flashes, little bits of memory that wouldn't form a whole. Yet the longer he glanced around—at Violet's pursed lips, at the cracked spectacles on the bedside table, at the bruise upon his knuckles—the more he could piece together.

Suddenly, his physical discomfort was secondary to the surge of shame coursing through his gut. What had he done? How had he allowed himself to so spectacularly, terribly lose control?

The coffee cup disappeared, replaced by a damp cloth pressed to his brow. He was perspiring, wasn't he? His skin pricked, feeling both fevered and chilled, the not-so-gentle motions of the cloth doing little to ease the sensation.

Over the past weeks, he'd come to crave Violet's caress, but this was only making things worse. He wrinkled his nose, a pungent odor cutting through the pleasant mist of flowers. Good God, was that *him*? When had he last bathed? His linen shirt, which had once been crisp and white, contained mud stains, and it clung to his body from sweat. He didn't need to pull back the counterpane and observe his trousers to realize they fared no better.

"My clothing," he muttered, shrugging away from her brusque ministrations. "You shouldn't be near me. I smell distasteful."

She arched a sardonic brow. "Your boots were covered in excrement the first time we met. Think nothing of it."

The cloth came back toward his forehead, but he recoiled, clamping his arms tight across his chest as if he could squeeze himself into non-existence. He was in no state to be touched or looked at. He didn't deserve her care, however snappishly given.

And perhaps she came to her senses and agreed, for she threw the cloth onto the bedside table, her face becoming stony. Her feet taking a clipped step away.

He closed his eyes, trying to wade through the monumental mess he'd created. Thanks to his own idiocy, time and circumstances had become a blur, leaving him with an onslaught of questions regarding what had happened during his drunken stupor.

"Where's Alex?" he managed to say, opening his eyes before visions of pamphlets littering the doorstep could add to his malaise. But where once there'd been an irate, panicked sense of doom, he experienced only a dull ache.

"I don't know." Violet looked at him blandly, her voice ringing hollow. "Your mother was downstairs when I arrived. I'll request that she come up so you can ask her."

She whirled away, feet marching one methodical step after another toward the door. In seconds, she'd be gone. And while he didn't know how she'd gotten here, he knew, with a certainty that made his stomach plummet, that once she left, she wouldn't come back. There'd be no more coffee, no more cloth against his throbbing brow. Not just today, but for every long, miserable year to come. This was the moment he'd look back on as the one that had shattered their marriage beyond repair.

And no, he didn't deserve any of what she had to give, not even a little. However, he also wasn't noble enough to watch her walk away. Not if it meant forever.

"Violet," he said, grit returning to his throat, making his voice dry and broken.

She kept walking, his pathetic call getting swallowed up by the determined rustle of her skirts.

"Violet." He drew air into his aching lungs and forced her name to reemerge with more power. Forced his body to scramble upright, fighting against the sudden blast of dizziness that made the room spin.

She turned, the tap of her slippers against the carpet momentarily halting. Her face was clouded, the soft lines of her features melding into one another. Nonetheless, he knew she was watching him expectantly. Knew her eyes were blue and cool, and he had only a speck of time before they grew impatient and didn't look his way again.

He grappled the bedpost, squeezing with all his strength in an effort not to crumple to the floor. "Violet I ..." His body was shaking, jaw clattering, but he had to make himself speak. Had to compel her to stay.

"I don't know what I've done," he choked out, the words coming from some deep, secluded place inside him. "I don't know who I am anymore."

His chest was being ripped in two, his legs on the verge of collapse.

Yet he couldn't stop, not until every jagged piece came free. "I'm so afraid. So ashamed." His eyes burned, and a raw, desperate sound tore from his throat. "So bloody sorry."

He couldn't stand any longer, could scarcely even breathe. But suddenly, he didn't need to stand, for gentle arms encircled him, guiding him back to the bed. Without letting go, Violet helped him get his head on the pillow and lie on his side amidst the tangle of sheets. And then, she lay down next to him, tucking her chest against his back like a comforting blanket.

She stayed there as uncontrollable shudders racked his chest and his inhales fell more like sobs. She stayed with him— one hand splayed across his abdomen, the other rubbing circles against his shoulders—as years of bottled-up emotions poured to the surface, leaving him stripped and undone.

Not once did she try prompting him to speak. She remained there simply as a silent foundation of support, giving while taking nothing in return. However, as seconds stretched into minutes, and he slowly recalled how to breathe without trembling, he knew he couldn't leave it this way.

He may have garnered her sympathy enough that she wouldn't prod him, but he couldn't spend the rest of his life holding her at a distance, keeping his family skeletons tucked in a closet. If he was to atone for his actions, he had to let her in.

He gingerly rolled to face her, finding that his head didn't throb nearly so much as it had before. Nor did her features swim before his eyes. Everything had become clear: pink lips, flushed cheeks, milky skin. Blue eyes that shone like the Wiltshire sky, serene and bright and lovely.

"I need to share some things with you," he said, driving the words from his tongue before they could retreat. "About Alex. About ... about my father, too."

She reached for his hand, her fingers curling tightly around his. Her body drawing a little closer. "I want to understand. I desire so much for you to be open with me."

It occurred to him, in the back of his mind, that he sorely needed to change his shirt. To brush his teeth. That perhaps he should be standing up for this, rigid and solemn, keeping a careful distance.

Yet the moment had arrived *now*, on this bed, with Violet embracing him regardless of his dishevelment. He couldn't risk losing his resolve and letting it pass them by. Besides ... something about lying next to her felt right. Like maybe it would make what he had to reveal just a fraction easier.

He took a breath, using the warmth of her hand to ground him. "I assume you know the scandal of Lord Samuel Prescott eschewing his family, and society as a whole, so he could marry a woman they disapproved of and start a new life as a working man—a poet."

She kept looking at him, her expression measured. "Yes."

"I assume you're also aware that he died unexpectedly about a decade later."

Her eyelids twitched at his frankness, and she paused a moment before giving a grave nod. That the estranged and rebellious Rockliffe spare had dropped dead was hardly surprising news to anyone familiar with ton gossip, after all. It was the intimate details of the situation—the ones he'd never uttered aloud in his life—that would prove the more difficult revelation.

"He drank. Excessively." Ben didn't shrink from the truth, as much as it poked a blade in his chest. "Not at first, when I was very young. However, as the years went on, he would get frustrated with his poetry sometimes. He'd have periods where he was so zealous, his words flowing from his quill without relenting, but then, inspiration would leave him, and he'd plunge into despair. Listlessness. Alcohol became his means of coping. Near the end, he often paired it with opium."

Violet's face looked as grim as he felt, and he wondered if she'd known that part, too. The gossip rags had speculated, no doubt, and rumors had circled and swelled. However, none of the gossipmongers had lived in his home. None of them had been there to hear what he'd heard and see what he'd seen.

"I used to overhear my mother pleading with him at night," Ben said tightly—as emotionlessly as he could manage. "She'd insist he stop before he brought about his own ruin. But he didn't stop. I think he arrived at a point where he just couldn't. And one day, I found him."

He paused for air, cold beads of sweat forming at his nape. He was heading down a dark path filled with memories that begged to remain concealed. Yet he wouldn't stop now. Wouldn't do anything but clutch Violet's hand and force himself to continue. "It was a sunny afternoon, and Alex and I thought that perhaps we'd convince him to go to Hyde Park with us before dinner, the way he'd always done ... *before*, when we were very young. He was sitting at his desk in the study the same way he always did, except ..."

He halted again, the scent of gin assaulting his nostrils even after all these years. Images hitting him as sharply as the day they'd been branded into his memory. "Except the curtains were drawn to make it dim, and he was slumped over in his chair, and when I got close to him, I knew ... I knew he was gone."

Overturned bottle.

Limp hand.

He could see it all. Could see his ten-year-old self frozen with shock, then terror, then gut-wrenching sorrow. Unaware of how drastically his life would soon change.

"I'm so sorry." Violet's fingers came up to cup his jaw, gifting him with a tender caress. "No child should ever have to witness such a thing."

He tried to hold onto the sight of her face in front of him, to let it lead him away from the bleak cluster of memories. However, his mind remained half in the past, half in the future. Grieving for what he'd lost. Agonizing over what he still could lose.

"Alexander is so similar to him," he said, his voice quieting to a murmur—closer than he'd like to breaking. "The spitting image, but it's more than that. He gets so caught up in writing his stories, it's as if they run through his veins. Like our father, he's vivacious, quick-witted, and talented. But also like our father, he's had moments of growing low-spirited. Apathetic. And I can picture him following that same path where his writing consumes him, where misery overtakes his spirit, where he feels he has nowhere to turn but a bottle, and I don't"—he choked on the thick lump that rose in his throat—"I don't want to lose him that way."

"Oh, Benedict." Violet's eyes glimmered with unshed tears as she brought her hand to his temple and tenderly stroked his hair. For a moment, there was only silence between them, the soothing motions of her fingers taking the edge off the pain that poured through his bloodstream. But then, she squeezed her tears away, her face taking on a look of steadfast resolution. "I understand your fear, and I ache for your loss. But while I may not know your brother, I do know that his similarities to your father haven't predestined him to share the same fate. An inclination to write, in and of itself, isn't a curse."

Her words flowed through him, hitting him in places that had long been untouchable. He supposed he already recognized the truth in what she said. After all, his stepfather, Jeremy, was a longtime novelist whose work provided him with happiness and fulfillment, secondary only to that which he gleaned from his family. However, Ben couldn't shake the vision of Alex's vibrant eyes. His father's lifeless ones. Couldn't shake the feeling they were one and the same.

"May I ask ..." She hesitated, her mouth forming a serious line. "Has Alexander already displayed signs of excessive alcohol consumption?"

He considered it a moment. "No more than the other boys at Cambridge." And then, another realization began to unfurl. One he'd never reflected on before. "If anything, I believe he drinks less when he's at home in London. When he's busy at the printshop and focused on his writing."

Her lips gave the faintest twitch, and she moved her hands to his shoulders, clasping tight. "It seems to me the best way to ensure his long-term happiness is to let him choose the path that calls to him without interfering. Yes, he may stumble sometimes, just as we all do. He may have dark moments. But you'll be there to pick him up and help him see the light again. I believe your entire family will, too, from what I've witnessed. That type of love is a powerful thing."

Ben's heart thumped at a strange tempo, the pulse of it echoing in his ears and mingling with his thoughts. He'd spent so much time trying to control. To protect. But what if Violet was right? What if he needed to step back and let Alex find his own way forward—even if the way involved him dabbling at the printshop and writing erotic pamphlets in the middle of the night? An adoring wife and children hadn't been enough to save their father from his demons. However, that didn't mean the care and support of his family would never be enough for Alex.

That type of love is a powerful thing. The statement hit Ben square between the ribs, filled with a significance he couldn't fully comprehend. It felt like the answer to a question he hadn't asked, that he didn't even know.

A question that may be worth pondering in further detail once he regained all his faculties.

"I want to do right by my brother." He let out a long sigh and flopped onto his back, the crush of the other weight he carried sinking into his chest. "And as much as I've denounced following in his footsteps ... I want to do right by my father as well. To honor the memory of the man he once was."

Violet raised herself on one elbow, gazing down at him with those open, earnest eyes. "I'm certain you do. You have so many qualities that any father would be proud of."

"No." His answer came immediately, accompanied by a prickle down his spine. "I cannot do him proud. Not when I'm in Wiltshire playing the lord."

Her brow knit in concern, and as much as he was exhausted—as much as he'd bared enough of his wounds for one day—he needed to share this with her, too. To make certain she understood every piece of him.

"Did you know that Aldercombe has always been given to the Rockliffe spare?" he asked, a hint of bitterness creeping into his tone. He thought of it often with a humorless smirk: how, under different circumstances, Aldercombe could have been his home from the start. How Violet might have been a childhood friend. "Had my father wanted the estate, he needed only to say the word. However, he renounced it, and the house sat empty for years. All until my uncle approached me, after my expulsion from Cambridge, about selling it."

The crease at the bridge of her nose deepened. He'd spoken of selling Aldercombe—*her* new home, too—once before, and it was no wonder the idea caused her worry. However, he'd come too far to shy away from the truth in its entirety.

"I could have rejected Aldercombe like my father did," he continued, gloom wrapping itself around him like a cloak. "I could have told Uncle Rockliffe to get rid of it and not given the matter another thought. Instead, I chose the second option he presented: that I travel there myself to assess the new land agent and see if I thought the estate worth keeping in the family. I *chose* to go to Wiltshire. I *chose* to care for the property as if it were my own."

"And do you view that as a bad thing?" She gaped at him, and it was difficult to tell whether the edge to her voice signaled perplexity or frustration.

"No," he answered swiftly, because the idea of never having gone to Wiltshire—of never having met her—had become unfathomable. However, his certainty couldn't erase the pang of guilt that stabbed him between the ribs.

He was going to have to entrust her with the family secret that had been cast upon him three years after his father's death. A matter the ton speculated about but that had never been confirmed.

He clenched and unclenched his jaw, then let the truth spring free. "I chose to do it because, unlike Alexander, my fate cannot be altered. On account of an injury, my uncle cannot sire more children. Unless I meet an early demise, the marquessate *will* fall into my hands one day. And so, I decided to do my duty and start preparing for the role, despite how it denigrates my father's wishes to stay far away from the peerage."

Traces of awe flickered on Violet's countenance, although they were quickly vanquished by the slight narrowing of her eyes. "You should hardly chastise yourself for fulfilling an obligation. Regardless of his thoughts on the peerage, your father would be pleased to know you possess such a strong sense of honor, would he not?"

"But it's more than an obligation." Remorse stretched and swelled within his chest, squeezing tight to each muscle and nerve. "I've come to realize that I want it," he said, the admission falling like a boulder he'd pushed from a mountaintop, gaining momentum and unable to be stopped. "I want to manage lands. I want us to have a home that lasts a lifetime. Someday, I want to speak in Parliament and have my voice help shape the country. I want every goddamn bit of it."

Suddenly, he was no longer on the mountain's summit but flailing at the bottom in the boulder's path, powerless to keep it from crushing him. He was a betrayer. A son who took what his father discarded as vile and clung to it instead.

However, in the face of his guilt, Violet remained unfaltering. "Accept it, then. Embrace your position as heir, and remember that belonging to the peerage isn't inherently bad." She sat up straighter, not so much as blinking while she gazed down at him. "I can appreciate your father's disillusionment with his family. I've witnessed my father behave in ways that make me wish to be estranged from him and everything he stands for. Yet that doesn't need to be *our* legacy. With your sense of honor, rightness, and dedication, I know you could do so much good with the role. I think we both could ... together. Not because of—or despite—our titles, but simply because of the values with which we conduct ourselves."

He tried to push himself upright, but in the next instant, Violet was back on the pillow beside him, her hand a soft weight against his sternum.

He turned his head to face her, a spark sputtering to life within him. A spark that wanted to take what she said as truth, to flare and ignite until he believed nothing else.

But he didn't know. Didn't know if it was safe to undo a lifetime of principles, didn't know if his judgment remained

impaired by alcohol, didn't know, didn't know, didn't know …
He was weary again. So weary. Yet Violet was beside him, her
small puffs of breath warm on his skin. Her palm on his chest
kept the world from breaking apart.

"Think about it, Benedict," she murmured, nestling
herself close to his side. "Sit with it a while. You needn't determine your entire future today."

He closed his eyes, his body feeling like it had been run
over by a chaise and four. However, beneath the ache, there
was also a whisper of relief. His burdens were no longer his
alone to bear. She'd shared them with him. Tried to assuage
them. She'd been there from the moment he opened his eyes,
even though his brow perspired and his shirt smelled.

Which begged a question. "Why are you in London?" he
asked, fighting through his exhaustion to look at her once
more.

Her eyelids, which had become even heavier than his own,
momentarily lifted. "I came to find *you*, of course."

Of course. She said it as if it were a foregone conclusion.
Like everything he'd done could be forgiven. Like they were a
true husband and wife.

He put an arm around her waist, holding her close. *Stay*,
the gesture said, a wordless entreaty. But even before he did it,
he already knew: she wasn't going anywhere.

No, they needn't determine the entire future today.
However, his mind drifted, envisioning tiny slivers of it. All
containing golden curls. Hilltops shaded by beech trees.
Rosebud lips that smiled at him.

He may not know many, many things. Yet he knew the
sensation in his chest to be hope.

24

Ben and Violet stayed in London another three days before deciding they'd return to Aldercombe on the morrow.

Ben's ribs—which he had vague, rueful recollections of getting kicked in a drunken brawl—needed time to heal before he was jostled for hours in a swaying carriage. He also required a visit to the optician to have his spectacles repaired. As for Violet, she grudgingly went to Bond Street and ordered a dress for her sister's betrothal ball—an event she'd told him about with a persistent scowl, although they both tried not to dwell on the conflicts their future brother-in-law was apt to cause.

Instead, they devoted all their spare time outside their errands to his family, allowing Violet to get to know them better. Perhaps unsurprisingly, she got along with everyone— even his dragon of a grandmother—appearing equally at ease in the Rockliffe House drawing room as in the printshop on Fleet Street when he brought her for a tour.

They spent their final night in town having dinner at the terrace house on Buckingham Street with his mother, stepfather, and two half-brothers. It was a merry affair filled with lively conversation and ample food—his mother even ordered a tray of his favorite sweets from Gunter's—and they all assembled in the sitting room afterward with high spirits and full stomachs.

Ben sat in an armchair leafing through his childhood copy of *Robinson Crusoe*, half-listening to his mother ask Jeremy's opinion of the sketch she worked on and half-listening to Violet and his brothers engage in a zealous game of spillikins. He'd found it difficult, after his unhinged escapade, to look any of them in the eye. However, no one had been angry or disdainful upon seeing him. If anything, they'd greeted him with warmth and expressed gladness for the unexpected visit. And if they could all forgive him for his lapse in judgment and control, he'd try very hard to forgive himself, too.

He flipped the page of his book, glancing up when Timothy shouted eagerly, waving a stick above his head, and Violet gave a delighted laugh. However, instead of stopping to gaze at her head of golden curls and her soft profile illuminated by candlelight, his eyes caught motion in the doorway and froze.

Alex was here. Alex, with their father's wild russet curls and blue eyes. With a crooked cravat and navy coat.

Ben swallowed, his throat suddenly tight. His brother's absence had been his one lingering point of remorse over the past few days. His mother had been frustratingly vague about it, assuring him Alex was well but that he'd recently taken his own lodgings and had much to occupy him. And as much as the matter plagued him, Ben hadn't pushed it, accepting that Alex would need time to forgive him for the things he'd said.

Except Alex was here and meeting his gaze, putting a finger to his lips to request silence.

For a moment, they simply studied each other, as if they were each an exhibit in a museum that neither knew how to decipher. But then, Alex mouthed a question: *Might we speak alone?*

Wordlessly, Ben set down his book and slipped from the chair, undetected by the engrossed spillikins players on the floor near him. He crept to the doorway, giving his brother a brisk nod, glancing at the staircase. And in a silent agreement, they made their way up to the top floor, to the bedroom they'd shared before their departure to Eton and then Cambridge.

Their mother and stepfather had left it untouched, so it still contained a scattering of Ben's old books. Alex's journals rested upon the small desk. Even the blanket Achilles used for a bed remained folded on the floor.

It was in this familiar space that they faced each other once more, Alex pacing a few times before stilling. Looking at him with hangdog eyes. "I was afraid you wouldn't consent to see me."

Ben took a rigid step closer to him and unclamped his jaw to let the truth come out. "I feared the same," he said gruffly.

Alex tilted his head; then, his whole body loosened with an audible rush of breath. "Jesus, Ben, I'm sorry. You said you didn't want to hear it, but I need to tell you all the same. I know you gave up Cambridge for me, and I was wrong to be wasteful of your sacrifice. But you have to understand: I didn't ask you to do it. I didn't *want* you to do it. I attended Cambridge because apparently, that's what marquess's nephews are supposed to do, but while I did try, it never felt right, and I—"

"Stop fretting." Ben held up a hand, for his brother had begun pacing again, his words getting faster with every step he took. "I know you disliked Cambridge. Consider what I did my misguided attempt to keep you out of trouble."

He sighed from deep in his chest—God, why did he have so much fondness for a brother so exasperating?—and remembered Violet's words and the conclusions he'd drawn as a result. "You're capable of making your own choices, and it's not my place to interfere. My only duty is supporting you in whatever path you decide to take and lending a helping hand whenever you may need it."

Alex's mouth opened, his eyes growing large. Twinkling in the dimness.

And suddenly, he was launching himself at Ben, nearly knocking him over as he wrapped his arms around Ben's shoulders in a rough embrace. "Thank you, brother," Alex said against his coat. "Thank you so damn much."

Ben regained his footing, his body stiff from the unexpected assault. After an instant, though, his motionless arms unclenched from his sides to circle Alex's back and give it an affectionate thump. "Clodpate," he grumbled, holding his brother tight for just a few seconds longer.

Alex chuckled as they broke apart, then drooped down to the edge of his old bed, pressing his hands into the counterpane. "I didn't publish the last pamphlet for my own benefit, you know. If it makes any difference." He shrugged, but his eyes quickly became solemn. Intent. "I'm telling you this because I trust you with my life. And because you're a married man now, so perhaps you'll understand that the pamphlet ... it was authored by someone else. Someone who needed my help in distributing it. Someone I care for deeply."

"*What?*" Ben's jaw dropped close to his boots, his head spinning as he sank to his own bed across from his brother's. His shock couldn't have been any greater had Alex grown wings and flown out the window.

"Please appreciate that I'm not at liberty to disclose further details," Alex rushed to say. "Only that I wouldn't have done it were the lady not in dire straits."

The ... the *lady*? Ben continued gaping nonsensically, his

brain not yet acclimated to this rapid turn of events. Was Alex trying to say ... Christ, was Alex in *love*?

Ben took a breath so he could speak, although his brother's withering glance made the words die on his tongue. Right. No further details. However, Alex had to know he couldn't drop that sort of revelation without evoking at least a modicum—but more accurately, a maelstrom—of curiosity.

That type of love is a powerful thing. Violet's words came back to him, and he was nearly certain his quirking lips had turned up in a grin. Yes, Alex would forever have the love and support of his family. However, what if there was also a different sort of affection at work? The sort that would fulfill him and center him no matter what challenges came his way.

Ben was learning a thing or two about that himself.

"Thank goodness." The low voice from the doorway cut into his musings, and he turned to find his mother standing there, gazing upon the scene with a wry smile. "I'm glad to see you two together like this, *peacefully*. Especially because I no longer have the physical ability to separate your squabbles as I did when you were children."

"I'm sure I don't know what you're talking about." Alex rose from the bed and demurely dipped his chin, the very picture of civility. "We never gave you even a moment's trouble in all our lives."

"Ha!" Their mother rolled her eyes, stepping into the room to give him a swat on the arm. Yet they all grinned at each other, Ben's chest lighter than it had been in a long time.

"Well, Ben?" Alex lingered near the doorway with their mother, shooting him an expectant look. "Are you going to introduce me to your wife?"

Yes, it was high time they returned to the sitting room so he could do that. Was it absurd that in the span of minutes, he'd already begun missing the sight of her curls, the sound of her laugh?

Just as he moved to push off the bed, though, his mother rushed toward him, placing a hand upon his shoulder. "Actually …" She gazed at him with pensive eyes. "Would you mind very much if Jeremy and your brothers saw to the introduction? I was hoping we could have a private moment to speak, Ben, while things are quiet."

Ah. He should have known this was coming. Their conversations over the past few days had been almost too easy, for she'd been so concerned about his well-being that she hadn't questioned him on his drunken antics or his precipitous marriage. However, those matters couldn't remain unspoken forever. After everything he'd done, he owed her whatever explanations she sought.

He nodded, repositioning himself against the mattress, and she sank down beside him, telling Alex they'd see him in a moment. Alex flashed them a good-natured grin before spinning away, and together, they watched his retreat, waiting as his footsteps faded down the stairs.

Even when the last echo of boots against floorboards vanished, his mother continued peering at the empty doorway. "Alex is going to be all right," she said, voice contemplative. "I know we decided, many years ago, that it would be best for you boys to go away for school, but he never seemed happy at Cambridge. The move back to London will be good for him, I think."

Ben blew out a long exhale, allowing his taut shoulders to loosen. "Yes. I see that now."

"And you, Ben?" She turned to him abruptly, giving him the type of stare that seemed to permeate far below the surface. "Are you all right?"

Several days ago, he would have been hard-pressed to answer that question with anything favorable. However, so much had changed since then. Old pieces of him crumbled away. New ones went up in their place. Brightness appeared where it hadn't before. Which was why he could reply, confidently, "I am. Truly."

His assurance seemed to satisfy her, for she nodded, her expression softening. "Given the circumstances, I was worried about you when you went off to Wiltshire. I grew significantly more worried when I learned of your hasty marriage plans. However, now that you're here and I've seen you with Violet —I believe she's good for you."

"She is," he replied without preamble. Without hesitation. Perhaps he'd suspected it back at Aldercombe, but the profundity of the statement had solidified itself here in London in a way he could neither forget nor deny. Which led to another truth, equally glaring. "I ... I care for her. The way a true husband cares for a wife."

"I know. I can see that quite plainly." His mother's eyes danced, filled with the wisdom of one who'd married not once, but twice, for love. "And you're both happy at Aldercombe?"

"Yes, I believe so." Because while they'd had their share of trials with the estate—and no doubt had more to come—they suddenly all felt surmountable if he had Violet beside him. He remembered whirling her around the village green. Kissing her beneath the beech on Skylark Ridge. Laying her across the desk in his study. Moments that connected them to the place and made it all seem right. "It's starting to feel like our home," he answered honestly. "Almost as if it were meant to be."

The words rolled off his tongue so easily, but once they did, he hesitated, a knot forming in his chest. *Meant to be.* His father wouldn't have seen it that way. "Forgive me. I spoke out of turn."

Yet his mother only gave her head a small shake. "There's nothing to forgive."

He peered at the woman who'd fought to provide for him and Alex after she'd been left widowed and destitute. Who'd been fiercely protective, raising them, with Jeremy's help, far away from Rockliffe House. All until the day—not so long after his uncle had been in an accident that nearly cost him his life—that she'd sat down with him and told him the truth of his inheritance. A fact that had always hovered in the distance, but her words had turned a possibility into a certainty: no other heir would come before him. Thus taking everything his father had sought to avoid and casting it into his lap.

The doubt that Violet had helped put at bay simmered back to life. "It's not what Father would have wanted." His voice was shallow. Strained.

"Oh, my darling." Her hand gripped his where it lay on the bed, fingers clasping tightly. "Your father had many sentiments about the peerage, but none so strong as his love for you. He'd want you to be happy, however that happiness came about. And I know he'd be so proud of the integrity, determination, and strength you display no matter what twists and turns come your way. I certainly am."

Her eyes glittered with moisture; he could see that even through the blur in his own. The views she expressed were a close echo of Violet's. Did that mean he could truly let himself believe them? That he could embrace his desires, his future— his position as heir—without compunction?

"Thank you." He leaned into her, wrapping her in a firm hug and feeling her arms encircle him in return. Throughout his lifetime, they'd shared such gestures on far too many occasions to count. This time, though, it felt monumental. Like love and acceptance. Like permission to let go. Like the cusp of a new beginning.

"I hope you, Jeremy, and the boys will come visit us at Aldercombe even though my recklessness and lack of communication are no longer forcing you there," he said when they finally pulled apart, giving her a rueful half-smile.

"You can depend upon it." She pursed her lips, one brow

quirking. "Although perhaps not right away. You and your new wife are still in the period where you likely require much time alone."

His mouth opened and closed, heat flooding the back of his neck. He hadn't anticipated having *that* sort of conversation with his mother. Meanwhile, it brought to light a topic that had been increasingly on his mind as he lay alone in bed each night, sorting through memories and waiting for his ribs to heal. He missed Violet—*physically*.

He'd been given small tastes of how wonderful intimacy with her could feel. And while circumstances—along with his own reservations—had kept interfering with any sort of lasting closeness, it didn't have to remain that way forever.

When they returned to Aldercombe, and were back in the privacy and comfort of their own home, he wanted to make her his wife. In every sense of the word.

"Not right away," he agreed, standing quickly so she wouldn't detect the flush spreading to his cheeks.

With his mother one step behind him, he crossed the small room, reaching back to give her hand a final squeeze—the wordless conclusion to their discussion.

The origins of his trip to London had been nothing short of disastrous. Who would have thought it could end up being so productive? So revelatory. So cathartic.

In satisfied silence, they approached the stairs.

It was time to enjoy one last night with his family before he and Violet got in the carriage at first light. And then, it was time to enjoy a future with his wife.

25

Violet gave a contented sigh when her feet hit the gravel drive in front of Aldercombe Grange. After two long days of travel—including a night in a malodorous coaching inn, where shouts from a barroom brawl made rest close to impossible—it was a relief to have the journey behind them.

But it was more than that, too. Standing in the warm evening air, Benedict's hand in hers, she felt like she'd returned home. Not the place she'd been forced into hiding because of her father's antics in London. Not the place she'd been banished because of the appearance of impropriety in the shepherd's hut. *Home.*

She and Benedict ascended the front steps together, not so different from the day he'd first brought her to Aldercombe as his bride. Whereas her thoughts that day had been filled with trepidation, though, she currently felt nothing but lightness. Like maybe this was a new beginning as surely as their wedding day—except not one inflicted upon her, but one she wanted.

Unfortunately, her carefree sense of anticipation lasted only until they were admitted through the front door. Pearce, the butler, made the necessary polite inquiries about their journey, but his face was grim.

"Mrs. Prescott," he said dourly after taking Benedict's greatcoat and her pelisse. "You've had a most anxious visitor who has left you with a great deal of correspondence. I'm led to believe it's urgent."

She followed his gaze to the console table, her pulse quickening as she took in the stack of letters upon the silver tray.

"Thank you, Pearce," she muttered, racing over to the table and rifling through the pages. She recognized Arabella's handwriting at once, although it appeared she'd scribbled Violet's name in haste. And why had she done it so many times? There were four separate letters here, and even an old calling card, all from Arabella.

Violet hastily unfolded the first letter and began to read.

Violet,
I must talk to you. Please respond to me as soon as you're able.
Arabella

Well, that was maddeningly unclear. She tossed it aside, reaching for the next.

Violet,
Did you receive my note? It remains imperative that we speak.
Arabella

Still nothing to give Violet any clue about what had transpired, and the other letters were no better.

Violet,
Where are you??? Come see me the second you return.
Arabella

I'm wretched, Vi. Everything is ruined. Answer me, I beg you.
A

She threw down the final missive, an oath forming on her tongue. If Arabella was going to write with such urgency, did she not think she should include a detail or two as to *why*? How was Violet to know whether this was a matter of her sister's new ballgown not fitting as desired or something far more dire?

"What's wrong?" Benedict's voice came from behind her, and she spun to find him standing there, shoulders rigid, jaw tight.

It took everything she had not to grasp those shoulders. To sink into his chest and reclaim the contentment she'd experienced only moments earlier. Instead, she forced her spine to remain tall and her hands to clamp to her sides. "Arabella is in some sort of trouble and is demanding we speak at once. Regrettably, she offered no other details." She pressed her lips together, all the things she'd envisioned for the evening—a walk with Benedict and Achilles, a leisurely dinner at her husband's side, a bath where perhaps he'd join her—vanished like a candle flame set out in a tempest. "I must go to her at once and determine what's amiss."

"I'll come with you." His answer was immediate, his gaze already seeking Pearce, issuing a silent request for the return of his greatcoat.

However, she shook her head, holding up a hand to still the butler in his tracks. "No, you needn't do that." There was little she craved more than having Benedict remain at her side, but not under these circumstances. Not when the trouble might be nothing but a fashion mishap or some other difficulty with party planning. She bit her lip, forcing back a sigh. "Arabella and my mother are both prone to exaggeration. The last thing I want is for you to turn around just as we've gotten in the door, merely to discover our haste is all for a triviality. Better I be the only one to expend my time."

"I don't mind." His hand sought hers, leather gloves encircling her cotton ones. "Regardless of the reason for your sister's urgency, I don't wish for you to be alone."

She'd realized right from the beginning he was a man of honor, but there was something about the way he spoke in this moment—something about the way he looked at her—that made the knowledge hit her with fresh potency. He was good and noble, yes, but his offer seemed motivated not just by duty but by affection. Dare she think it went even farther than that?

Her heart gave a little leap, and although it thrummed with a desire to stay close to him, her mind was already made up. "Don't worry about me." She squeezed his fingers, relishing the shot of warmth they provided. "With any luck, I won't be gone long. Perhaps you can use my absence to attend to any pressing estate business that may have cropped up, for when I return ... well, I was hoping we might spend the rest of the evening together without interruptions."

A muscle in his jaw twitched, his eyes flaring in a way that caused them to appear particularly black. "If—" He stopped to clear the roughness from his throat. "If you're certain."

She was quite certain she did right by sparing him her family's theatrics—for she'd made up her mind that's all this was, ignoring the prickle of unease that suggested more nefarious possibilities. Besides, knowing he awaited her would give her something to anticipate. The promise of a reward.

"I'll ride to Meadowleigh as quickly as I can." She spoke with assurance, but a thought suddenly hit her that caused her to falter. A thought that made it hard to continue meeting his gaze.

In the span of an instant, she reached a conclusion she knew was the right one: it was better to voice her intentions than to keep them concealed. Nonetheless, her words became tight. "In the event Arabella is at Watley instead, I'll have to stop there on my way back if the matter remains unresolved."

His dark eyes narrowed, a crease forming between his brows. This was a test, she supposed. A moment to determine whether they'd truly moved past the misunderstanding that had driven a wedge in their marriage. Whether he'd truly learned to trust.

"Do as you must." His fingers gripped hers back, the pressure strong but welcome, lingering a few seconds before he let them go. He *did* trust her. The intentness in his eyes didn't signal anger or jealousy, but the same sentiment she'd detected before. The one that led her to believe he cared for her. Deeply.

She brushed her fingertips against his one last time before turning toward the door, his threadbare voice following her as she went.

"But come home soon, Violet."

The butler at Meadowleigh appeared no more eager to see her on the doorstep than Pearce had.

"Miss Collingwood—uh, Mrs. Prescott," he corrected himself, a crimson flush spreading over his weathered cheeks. "I'm afraid Lady Collingwood isn't receiving callers at the moment."

"No matter, Davis." She stepped around him and into the entrance hall despite the lack of invitation—this was her former home, after all—and shot him a pointed look. "I'm here to see my sister."

"Ah." He released a quick exhale, his body nearly drooping with relief. "Miss Arabella is not at home, but I'll certainly tell her of your vis—"

"No." She ignored the gnarled hand that beckoned her back outdoors, taking another step across the floor tiles. The viscountess's voice drifted out from somewhere down the corridor, high-pitched but not despondent. In fact ... was that a giggle?

Something odd was afoot, and Violet had no intention of leaving until she got to the bottom of it. "It turns out I do need to speak with my mother regarding a matter of great importance. It will only take a moment, and I'll assure her of your blamelessness if she's angry about the intrusion."

Davis let out an aggrieved wheezing sound, his brow shiny with perspiration. "Please, Mrs. Prescott, I really don't think—"

But Violet had already started down the corridor, following the direction of her mother's voice.

Unsurprisingly, it led her toward the drawing room, where the viscountess spent many hours upon her 'swooning sofa.' In a departure from the usual, though, the door was closed, another shrill giggle—followed by a yelp—emanating from within.

"Mama?" She tapped gently on the door, then let herself in.

And promptly froze.

Her mother was indeed on her preferred sofa, bathed in the glow of evening sunlight. The difference being, there was a *man* beneath her. A man who held her in his lap and whispered in her ear as he glibly hiked up her skirts.

"*Mama*?" Violet's eyes bulged, half in horror and half in awe. Heavens, she knew that man, even though she was unaccustomed to seeing him without his coat and wide-brimmed hat. It was none other than Barker, Meadowleigh's longtime gardener. With her mother. On the drawing room sofa.

Her mother's head snapped toward the doorway, her pink cheeks turning a deep shade of scarlet. "Gracious, Violet!" She and Barker both scrambled upright, the viscountess's hands flying to both her skirts and bodice. "What are you doing here?"

"Forgive the interruption, but I came to inquire about Arabella," Violet said thickly, looking to the floor so the duo—the *lovers?*—could right their clothing without an audience. In all fairness to Davis, he'd tried to warn her.

The rustle of fabric being shoved over limbs filled the room, and she tried *very* hard not to hear the words that were whispered in tandem.

Only when the door to the terrace creaked open and then shut again did she look up to find her mother waiting by the sofa, skirts more than a little rumpled.

"Shall I call for tea?" The viscountess brushed a stray lock of hair from her dewy brow before folding her hands primly in front of her and lowering herself back onto the sofa.

"Um, no." Violet inched forward, walking as though the floor might disintegrate beneath her feet. It wouldn't be the most shocking thing to transpire in this drawing room within the past five minutes.

However, she arrived before the sofa unscathed, leaving her to hover uncertainly as she stared down at her mother. So often, the woman on the sofa was pale and listless, fretting over health complaints and bemoaning her misfortunes. This woman, though, was different. This woman fairly glowed.

"I'll just come out and say it." The new version of the viscountess was sharp, too, meeting Violet's gaze with her chin held high. "You've gone off and married. Arabella is all but married. Your father's scandal has ended my days in society." She sniffed. "A woman cannot be expected to forgo companionship altogether."

Violet's lips parted, and after a beat of stunned silence, a sound rose in her throat that was nearly a laugh. "No. No, of course not. You should do whatever best pleases you." The viscount certainly did. Why should the viscountess not follow his lead? She'd resigned herself to life in the country; she had every right to take what enjoyment she could.

"Precisely." A sly grin tugged at the corners of her mother's mouth. "And Barker pleases me very much. He does the most delightful things with his—"

"Perhaps we should forgo discussing it in too specific of terms." It was Violet's turn to become crimson-cheeked. The rejuvenated viscountess was still her mother, after all, and there were certain details Violet didn't need to know.

Besides, now that the shock of her discovery had begun to abate, she needed to regain her focus and address the reason for her interruption. "As I said, I've come to ask after Arabella. Is she well?"

Her mother quirked a brow. "Certainly. Why wouldn't she be?"

"I've just returned from London to discover an entire tray of missives from her, all conveying an urgent need to speak. She said everything was ruined, whatever I'm to make of that."

"Oh." The viscountess flicked her wrist, giving a little laugh. "She and Lord Frederick had a lover's tiff or some such thing earlier in the week. She didn't reveal the cause, but it couldn't be anything serious, as she's gone back to Watley for dinner tonight. The *duke* is there now, you know, come to welcome her as his future daughter-in-law and attend the betrothal ball."

Violet shifted her feet, trying to summon the veneer of a smile. "I'm glad to hear it." However, instead of relief, unease snaked through her belly. Perhaps she allowed herself to be over-influenced by her loathing of Lord Frederick, but she despised the thought of him upsetting her sister, even if hurt feelings from the quarrel had already been repaired.

Because what if Arabella still carried troubles she hadn't shared with their mother? What if she'd finally recognized a glimpse of her betrothed's true colors and needed a confidante?

She pushed the idea aside, giving the viscountess a quick nod. "Don't let me keep you any longer. I know I caught you while you were otherwise occupied."

"Indeed, I was." Her mother tugged her slanted bodice a little lower, lashes flitting like a schoolgirl's. "Farewell, my dear. Do come visit me again." Her attention traveled to the terrace door, her voice taking on an airy ring. "Although next time, I suggest you knock both louder and longer first."

Violet made haste in departing Meadowleigh, eager to avoid witnessing the amorous moments whose recommencement seemed imminent.

Nonetheless, as she hopped back onto her mare, Vespera, in the stable yard, she found herself unable to race straight for home—and Benedict—without a second thought. Her mind kept returning to Arabella and all those dratted letters. Was everything truly well again?

Violet trotted with her horse down the drive and onto the west road, tilting her head so she could take a breath and better feel the clarifying sunshine stream upon her face. However, something was wrong. There was an acrid tang in the breeze. Smoke in the sky.

Her hand flew up to shade her eyes, and she blinked to bring the scene into focus. This wasn't wispy chimney smoke but thick gray puffs that swelled above the trees.

Coming from the direction of Watley Hall.

Her heart lurched, the only feeling of which she had any recollection before driving Vespera into a gallop over the fields.

What on earth had that dimwitted Lord Frederick done now? Had his drunken antics caused a fire in the stables? Had he planned an evening bonfire for his guests that somehow went awry? Whatever the case, she was certain this was *his* fault. Yet no matter how hard she tried to focus on her disdain for the despicable lord, her mounting pangs of dread just wouldn't cease.

In fact, the closer she drew to Watley, and the more she discerned of the scene, the deeper that terror embedded itself between her ribs, hitting her with the force of a cannonball. This was no barn or grass fire but a blaze in the manor itself, with angry orange flames licking the roof and shooting through the top story windows.

She pushed Vespera forward with as much speed as the animal could muster until she dared take her no farther for fear of spooking her. Then, she tethered the horse to a fencepost with trembling fingers and bolted the rest of the way down to the back garden of Watley, where a flurry of activity had broken out.

A bucket brigade, composed of servants and laborers, had assembled, drawing water from the stagnant lake and tossing it at the house, to little effect. On the other side of the lake, huddled on the muddy bank, were the partygoers dressed in their evening finery, murmuring frantically amongst themselves.

Her eyes hastily scanned the scene, falling upon Lord Frederick's dashing blue coat, Mr. Calthorpe's black boots, the ivory feather in Lady Kingsland's hair. But there was no bright, jaunty gown or golden ringlets.

There was no Arabella.

"Arabella!" she shouted, racing toward the group on aching legs, the smoke already making her lungs raw. It didn't matter, though. None of it mattered until she laid eyes on her sister.

"Arabella!" she cried out again, her scream causing the tight cluster of Lord Frederick's cronies to spread apart so they could assess the source of the commotion. Her gaze flew across the group once more, meeting every set of dazed, frightened eyes that gawked back at her. None of them were Arabella's sunny sky blue. It had become clear, beyond a doubt, that her sister wasn't among them.

She ground to a halt in front of Lord Frederick, using all the restraint she possessed not to scream at him when she asked, "What's happened? Where's Arabella?"

He seemed not to notice her fully, his stare traveling past her face and resting on the burning house. "The fireworks display." He sounded like a man half-asleep, uncertain what was real and what was a ghastly figment of his imagination. "I was testing it before dark. A rocket misfired."

She knew it. She *knew* this disaster had happened because of the man's bloody carelessness. But what difference did it make when he hadn't answered her second question? "Where's Arabella?" she demanded again, her heart on the verge of pounding out of her chest.

"She said she was going to the retiring room." It was Lady Kingsland—Arabella's, and formerly Violet's, chaperone— who responded, her words infuriatingly cool. Her countenance unruffled. "When the call of *fire* went out, we just assumed she would make her exit as we all did."

Violet's knees wobbled, the air rushing from her lungs in a horrified shudder. "And when she didn't emerge, none of you thought to go search for her?" She glared at Lady Kingsland, then trailed her wrathful gaze over the rest of the so-called noblemen. None of them spoke. None of them did anything but look at her blankly or ignore her altogether. Even that blasted Lord Frederick, for all his claims of heartfelt affection. His solution, when his future wife was in peril, was to do nothing at all.

"Damn you," she hissed in his face, just to make very

certain he heard. She didn't stay to gauge his reaction, though. There was simply no more time.

She rushed down the muddy bank, hauling her skirts to her knees so she could tear a piece of cotton from the hem of her shift and plunge it into the lake.

Lady Kingsland's appalled gasp was audible even above the shouts of the bucket brigade. However, the sound left Violet's awareness just as quickly as it entered it. Her focus had locked on one thing and one thing only: finding Arabella.

She pivoted toward the house, where fire continued blazing through the top windows and spreading across the roof. Despite the brigade's best efforts, they were fighting a losing battle.

Violet, though, refused to lose.

Not the flames in front of her, nor the shouts behind her, could stop her from sprinting to the terrace with her makeshift facemask and dashing inside the burning building.

26

As the minutes on the clock ticked by, it was difficult to say who grew more restless: Ben or Achilles.

While he'd spent much of the carriage ride from London dreaming of a comfortable seat—or better yet, a bed—he now found it torture to sit still.

His dreams in the carriage had of course involved Violet. How he would invite her into his bedchamber. Help her remove her traveling dress. See her sprawled across his counterpane.

However, Violet wasn't here. Her sister's letters had put an immediate end to any thoughts of relaxation or intimacy, and there was no clear time period for when the possibility might return.

She'd insisted on attending to the matter alone, saying it was likely nothing serious, and he hadn't wanted to force his presence where it wasn't needed. If there was one thing he'd learned about Violet over the past weeks, it was that she knew her own mind. Had he been right, though, to let her go alone when there was a chance of more serious trouble than she'd anticipated?

God, he missed his days at Cambridge when the answers he required existed in books.

But far more significantly, he missed his wife.

Achilles, apparently, disagreed with Ben's choice to remain in the study and wait, for he'd spent the past quarter hour pacing the floor and whimpering. Ben tried to console him with scratches behind the ears, but no sooner would the dog drop to his haunches beside Ben's desk chair than he'd be up and circling the room once more.

With a sigh, Ben tossed aside the ledger he'd been trying—and failing—to read, whistling to the disgruntled creature. "Shall we go for a walk?"

Achilles had already been for a walk in the garden after his dinner, so he shouldn't feel disgruntled on that account. However, mention of another outing made him perk up instantly, and he padded to the door, giving an impatient whine.

Ben followed with due haste, although he didn't know why he rushed. Running wouldn't make Violet come home any quicker or render him any less anxious about why she stayed away. Then again, perhaps a spurt of fresh air would help clear his head—to the extent such a thing was possible.

He let Achilles take the lead, for the elderly dog moved with purpose, giving only the briefest pauses to glance back and ensure Ben accompanied him all the way to the front door.

"Yes, I'm here." Ben's attempt at sounding reassuring was so pitiful that even a dog was apt to disbelieve it. "Let's go, then."

He swung open the door, Achilles slipping outside the instant the aperture became wide enough and hurrying down the steps. Ben, though, lingered on the doorstep, taking a quick breath. The air contained an odd, sharp smell.

The smell of smoke.

He rushed to the edge of the landing, his eyes darting up to the evening sky. The setting sun had become a glowing orange ball, the surrounding clouds a vivid pink. Yet in the midst of the picturesque scene, dark swirls of smoke billowed upward, as if an artist had overturned an inkpot upon his masterpiece.

A pit formed in his stomach while his mind raced to generate a map. The smoke was too far east to originate from Aldercombe land, which meant ...

Oh, Christ, which meant it had to come from Watley instead. From the direction Violet would be riding home. From the place she may have stopped.

He whirled to push the door back open, bellowing for a footman to see to Achilles. Then, he took off at a run, bounding toward the stables.

He made it only a little more than halfway before a stableboy came racing up to meet him, his youthful face flushed and harried.

"A fire's broke out in Watley Hall!" the boy shouted, pointing erratically in the general direction of the catastrophe. "The whole roof's ablaze. A footman just came with the news."

A fire at Watley. *In* the house itself. Damn it, why had Ben let Violet go off alone? She may not even be on Watley property, of course. But she *could* be. And that was enough to make his heart slam against his ribs.

"Go to the house and inform Pearce. I'll tell everyone in the stables that they are to go to Watley and offer assistance with battling the fire." Ben scrabbled for composure, fighting to maintain the dimmest scrap of rational thought while his mind screamed danger, screamed panic, screamed *Violet, Violet, Violet*. "But first, I need a horse."

Given the speed at which Ben traveled, the journey to Watley must have taken only minutes. Nonetheless, each moment that slipped by without Violet in his sight felt more like an hour. An eternity.

Even in his haste, he'd scanned both the road and fields, desperate for any sign of golden curls and a dusty blue carriage dress. He'd encountered no one, though, but a few anxious laborers. Had discovered nothing as he approached Watley but the thickening of smoke and the appearance of brilliant flames painting the sky.

Nothing, that was, until he got close enough to witness the chaotic scene in the back garden. A line of shouting people threw water on flames that were already beyond control, while a group of horrified aristocrats congregated near the lake. Despite the commotion, though, his gaze flicked to, and then held, a spot in the distance, where a dappled horse grazed.

While it was impossible to make out every detail about the creature from this far away, and there was no way to achieve complete certainty without further inspection, he *knew*. He knew with a sureness that turned his blood to ice and punched him in the gut: this was Violet's horse.

He jumped down and secured his own gelding within a matter of seconds, hurtling toward the mess that was Watley's back garden. His eyes flew over the scene, frantic to catch even a glimpse of the familiar figure who filled his world with brightness.

However, amidst the hazy, noxious landscape, no such figure appeared. There was no one in the bucket brigade but servants he didn't recognize. No one in the cluster of idle toffs but Denham and his apparent party guests.

With his chest on the verge of splitting open, Ben raced up

to the lordling, who was surveying the destruction of his home like a spectator might watch a play at the theater. "Where is my wife?" Ben demanded. "Was she here this evening?"

He barked the words, his alarm far too great to try for any sort of levelness. Yet Denham was silent, seemingly oblivious to anything but the flames whose light was reflected in his pupils.

"Damn it, Denham, answer me!" It took everything Ben had not to shake the man senseless. Did he have no bloody concept of how urgent this was?

Each second of silence boiled Ben's blood, made nausea churn in his gut. Until finally, the lordling spoke in a low rasp. "She's inside."

"*What*?" Ben roared, his breath, his heart, *everything* stopping before suddenly kicking back into motion at triple the speed.

"With Arabella," he muttered, the name stuttering off his tongue as if he didn't quite comprehend it.

Ben grabbed the lordling by the cravat, forcing the man to look him in the face. "*Where* inside?"

Denham's skin was pallid, his expression vacant. "I don't know."

With a snarl, Ben shoved him away and turned toward the blazing house, the glow of the flames stinging his eyes.

He'd been in Violet's position before. Thanks to a barn fire when he was a child, he knew what it felt like to have smoke siphon the air from his lungs. Knew the terror that came when flames closed in and there was no obvious escape route. When one could do nothing but pray for rescue.

His head screamed danger, warning him away from ever returning to that sort of peril. Yet his heart cried something different.

It was his heart that drove him toward the flames.

His heart that paid no heed to caution, not where his wife was concerned, because it knew how shattered it would be without her.

His heart that led him up the terrace steps and pushed him into the smoke-filled house with no other thought but *Violet*.

27

"Arabella!" With the soaked piece of her shift pressed to her face, Violet half-stumbled, half-crawled out of the drawing room and into the main corridor.

A pungent haze hung in the air, angry pops and crackles sounding ominously from above. But if there was any small mercy, the perilous glow of flames had yet to appear. Nothing prevented her from continuing.

She made a snap decision to turn left instead of right, taking the direction that would eventually lead her to the staircase. Would the stairs even be accessible if she had cause to use them? Something groaned and then snapped overhead, as if warning her away from the idea. She'd worry about that when —if—the time came, though. For now, she simply needed to make haste and keep going.

"Arabella!" She darted into the music room next door, crouching low to the floor and finding the space just as bleak and vacant as the drawing room before it.

Onward, then. One room after another, until she found her sister. Anything less wasn't an option.

"Arabella!" She momentarily hauled the muffling cotton away from her face, her throat stinging in protest and causing her to cough. However, as she righted the strip of fabric, willing her lungs to cooperate long enough for her to see her mission through, the faintest sound emerged from somewhere down the corridor.

"Vi?"

She froze, every nerve ending instantly alert.

"Vi, help!" The voice came again, weak but unmistakable.

Violet shot back into the corridor, her pulse skittering erratically. "I'm here. Where are you?"

She received a string of coughs in response, but the noise was enough to guide her in the right direction. Enough that, when Arabella croaked out "the study," Violet was already there, shoving open the door.

Her burning eyes tore around the room, scanning through the haze before landing on a sight that made her heart stop. A bookcase had toppled to the floor like a felled giant, leaving a scattering of leather-bound volumes in its wake. And lying next to it, limp and ashen—Arabella.

Violet bolted across the room and dove to the carpet beside her sister, terror slamming against her chest. Only when she took a second glance, realizing that both Arabella's arms and legs were visible, did she breathe again, her inhale becoming a choked sob of relief. No part of her sister had been crushed, although she'd come dangerously close. However, the bookcase had pinned a large swath of Arabella's skirts, rendering her immobile.

Violet's hands flew to the bookcase, giving it a shove, but the solid mahogany remained impervious to her efforts. She tried again, fear swelling anew when the furniture didn't move.

Arabella, though, appeared strangely unflappable. "I

found it," she rasped, turning her head over her shoulder to peer at Violet while she worked. "I found the deed."

Violet didn't have time to ask her what she meant. She scrambled to her feet, using the force of her legs along with her arms to push the bookcase, still to no avail.

"I'm so sorry, Vi. I should have listened." Arabella bit down on her lip, a lone tear sliding down her bloodless cheek. "You were right about Frederick."

Under any other circumstances, Violet would have celebrated her sister's declaration, offering a comforting shoulder to cry on while assuring Arabella how much better off she'd be without the toad. Instead, she strained helplessly, her physical strength unable to match her determination.

"Help!" she screamed toward the doorway, a fear-prompted reflex she couldn't contain.

She immediately clamped her lips shut, refusing to let panic overtake her even as she was forced to confront what she'd known all along: there was no one coming to help. Lord Frederick and his entourage had made their unwillingness clear.

Arabella shifted her arms against the carpet, her quivering fingers pulling a crumpled piece of parchment from her bodice. "Take the deed. You must take it."

Violet stared down at her sister's extended hand with stinging eyes. Blast it, did Arabella think she was *leaving*?

She snapped her gaze back upward, unable to look at that doleful, innocent face and the creased parchment—whatever it contained—any longer. Just as she'd done with the hisses and bangs on the floor above her, she needed to put them out of her mind and focus.

Exiting this room without her sister simply wasn't an option. And if she couldn't move the bookshelf ...

She bolted to the desk in three long strides, hauling open

the closest drawer and hastily rifling through the contents. If she couldn't move the bookshelf, she would instead need to free Arabella from her gown. Surely, Lord Frederick had a pair of scissors somewhere. Or a paper knife?

The first drawer proved useless, and she slammed it closed, starting to work on the next.

Which was the moment a stifled call reached her awareness, slightly louder than the blood rushing through her ears. "Violet!"

Her hand shook as she cast a pile of quills aside, her head instinctively darting up to face the doorway. The voice, though muted, was so close to the one she craved hearing above all else that she scarcely dared believe it was real.

"In here!" It was Arabella, harboring no such qualms, who cried out, her smoke-roughened voice gaining a burst of momentum. "In the study!"

Violet's heart pounded recklessly, the faintest strand of hope mingling with her panic even as the drawer proved devoid of anything sharp. She couldn't get distracted, had to keep searching—

Except suddenly, Benedict was in the doorway. Not just the suggestion of his voice or the image in her memory, but Benedict, wearing the same travel-rumpled attire as when she'd left him, his cravat pulled over his mouth.

"Arabella's skirt is trapped," she said without preamble, because uttering anything else—telling him of her dread, her relief—would surely melt her into an incoherent puddle from which there'd be no going back. "The bookshelf is too heavy to move, so I need to find scissors or a knife or—damn it, why can Lord Frederick not do something useful for a change?"

Her composure wavered upon discovering a third drawer filled only with papers, and she clamped down hard on her lip, fighting the urge to run to him and let herself dissolve.

However, Benedict moved with brisk, unflappable strides,

crouching at Arabella's side and assessing the bookcase. "We'll try moving it together, yes?" His eyes shot up to meet hers, dark and steady. Stalwart.

Yes. She had only a split-second to take in his gaze before abandoning the desk and rushing toward him. There was no way of knowing if they'd succeed or merely squander seconds she could have better spent continuing her search. Yet there was something about the way he looked at her. Something that made her trust him.

They each grabbed an edge of the bookcase, Benedict wasting no time in mouthing a single word: *Ready?*

At her hasty nod, they pushed in unison, the recalcitrant piece of furniture refusing to yield more than a fraction of an inch. However, it was a fraction more than she'd achieved previously. *Progress.*

"Again," she rasped, her lungs craving fresh air but finding only smoke. There would be no stopping—no fresh air—until they accomplished what they'd set out to do.

Benedict complied without hesitation, the cords in his neck straining as they coaxed the bookcase another sliver backward. Meanwhile, Arabella wriggled her body to the extent she could, her gauzy overskirt swishing against the floor as if demanding to be let loose.

"That's good, Arabella." Violet dared to glance at her sister's face, relieved to see it maintained its expression of almost unnatural calmness. She did her best to sound encouraging, knowing that if her sister panicked and became overcome with sobs, it would be difficult not to follow suit. "You're almost free." *Close yet far.* Lest they forget the dire urgency of their situation, fire consumed something directly overhead with a series of intensifying crackles.

"Let's see if we can lift the bookcase just enough for Arabella to pull her skirt loose." Benedict's command drowned out the flames' ire, the assuredness of his words a bolstering echo in her head. Making her believe they *could* do it, even though the bookcase had started to feel like her mortal enemy, determined to see her defeated.

She spent a final moment examining her sister, the resolute set of Arabella's mouth assuring her that yes, she'd heard the plan. She was ready.

And then, Violet had eyes only for Benedict. For the sturdy hands repositioning themselves against the bookcase. The brow furrowed in concentration. The swift dip of his chin telling her it was time to begin.

Her fingers gripped the shelf, creating an immediate ache in her muscles as she pulled upward instead of pushed. The wood was so blasted heavy. So blasted infuriating, just like Lord Frederick himself—

Except suddenly, there came the rending of fabric, an ardent cry, and Arabella rolled across the floor in a tangle of fabric.

Free.

She was free.

With Arabella's skirts clear, Violet abruptly released her hold on the shelf and sent it crashing to the floor, taking a few seconds to blink away the water from her burning eyes.

They'd ... they'd done it. Truly done it. Lifting the book-case hadn't been impossible after all—not with Benedict at her side to help.

He'd already scrambled to the floor beside Arabella to assist her in getting up, and Violet jolted herself back into motion, reaching out to grab her sister's arm and hauling her toward the door. Fortunately, Arabella's legs remained strong despite her ordeal, and while Benedict stayed at her other side to offer support, she had no trouble approaching the exit using her own strength.

If anything, her urge to escape would be more potent than any of theirs, for she'd been trapped in the burning house the longest. Abandoned there by her worthless excuse for a betrothed.

Whether Violet's sudden surge of energy was fueled by anger, fear, or desperation, she couldn't say. She only knew that they began running in unison, heedless of the pungent smoke trying to rob them of vision and breath.

She didn't need to see. Didn't need to inhale deeply. The way out was imprinted in her memory, and if they could just hold on a little longer, they'd be free of this cursed place and the uninhibited flames that promised to consume it.

Her heart pounded uncontrollably, knowing they were close to the drawing room and the terrace doors that would bring them to safety. Knowing, simultaneously, that the floor above could cave in at any moment, and fire could lurk around every turn.

However, when at last they burst into the murky drawing room and the terrace doors came into view, there was nothing impeding them. Nothing to do but sprint the final distance until Benedict shoved one of the doors open, and the heat and haze of the drawing room was replaced by a blast of cool night breeze.

Her lungs became greedy, sucking in great gulps of air as she raced down the stone steps and found her way onto the grass. Almost like they feared getting plunged back into the inferno that was Watley Hall.

There was no way on earth, heaven, or hell she would allow that to happen. She continued bolting away from the blaze, oblivious to the direction she traveled, to the shouts that surrounded them, or to anything at all but Benedict's and Arabella's footsteps beating in time with hers.

It was as if her legs were so desperate to remove her from Watley that they couldn't stop, even though fatigue made them wobble and the rawness in her throat caused her to cough relentlessly.

Every fiber in her exhausted body pushed and pushed, until a powerful grip encircled her waist, obliging her to halt. The force of it whirled her around, dragging her against a hot, solid surface.

That's when it truly sank in that she was safe. Benedict clasped her tight against his chest, his chin resting atop her hair.

At last, she could let herself melt. Let herself be held. He rubbed circles over her back while she caught her breath, and she leaned against him, relishing every bit of warmth, care, and security he provided.

When her coughing fit abated, she raised her head to look at him, needing to take in those features that had become so familiar—so dear—to her. Needing to be certain he was real.

Sure enough, her husband peered back at her, his chest still heaving from the aftereffects of exertion. "God, Violet, I ..." His words broke away, but she had only to examine his stricken face—jaw tight, eyes like obsidian—to guess at what he wished to say. *I was terrified. I thought I might never see you again.*

She knew because she'd felt the same way, the sensation creating a cavernous, throbbing ache. Tonight could have been the end for them. Her world could have culminated in an eruption of smoke and flames.

Except he hadn't allowed that to happen. He'd found her. Stayed with her. Hadn't relented until they'd freed Arabella from her fiery prison and were clear of Watley Hall.

This wasn't the end but the beginning. The start of a future with a man to whom she could trust her life. A man who made her chest swell and flutter in a way that could only mean she'd well and truly fallen in love.

"I know," she murmured in her smoke-tinged rasp, the realization—*love*— threatening to steal her breath once more. She pressed her forehead to his, closing her eyes as the notion danced through her head and trickled in her veins. *I love him. I love him.* She clasped his shoulders, her lips parting and curving upward. For despite the chaos surrounding them, everything wrong in the world—if only for this one intimate moment—had suddenly turned right. "Me, too."

28

V iolet could have easily remained in Benedict's embrace, oblivious to the flames raging behind them, for another hour. Rather, another lifetime. However, one thread kept her tied to the chaos of the present, giving a persistent tug she couldn't ignore. *Arabella*.

She forced herself to pull away, hastily locating her sister where she'd dropped to the ground nearby and was sucking in large mouthfuls of air. In an instant, Violet was at her side, throwing an arm around her slender shoulders and squeezing tight. Whatever terror Violet had experienced in the burning house, Arabella's must have been ten times worse. Sunny, delicate Arabella should never have been made to experience something so horrific, and Violet needed to offer comfort while her sister dealt with the emotions of all she'd gone through.

But far from swooning or sobbing in distress, Arabella's body stiffened, her gaze fixing on a spot straight ahead of her.

Violet's eyes followed, the taste of bile rising in her throat. Lord Frederick staggered toward them, his useless houseguests not far behind.

"Arabella." His voice sounded thin, containing none of the elation fitting for a man reunited with an almost-lost beloved. Nonetheless, he went through the motions, weakly extending his arms. "Thank goodness, my dear."

"Don't." Arabella's command was a cold weight in the darkness. A foreboding echo. Violet hadn't known her sister to be capable of producing such a tone.

Lord Frederick's arms drooped against his sides, his eyes narrowing. "I thought you'd recovered from whatever perceived slight made you run off in a huff the last time you were at Watley. I thought we'd reached an understanding."

Before Violet could blink, Arabella popped to her feet, her spine like an iron rod. "The only thing I understand is that you're a lying, dishonorable lout."

The lout in question gaped, appearing too stunned to display immediate anger at the insult. For once, he and Violet had something in common: she was stunned, too, that Arabella's adoration had taken such a drastic turn. Whatever the reason for the change, an anticipant hum fluttered through her abdomen.

"I heard every word you said to your father when you two locked yourselves in the study so he could yell at you for the hash you made of Watley's parkland!" Arabella jabbed an accusatory finger at her betrothed before planting her hands upon her hips, the ire in her voice continuing to grow. "You boasted about what a fine match you'd made with the woman who was sure to inherit Meadowleigh. How you endured her family's scandalous behavior—what a martyr you are—for fear Violet would inherit instead and spoil your great scheme to expand your lands."

Lord Frederick's eyes went from slits to bulging, his mouth quivering as he opened it to speak. However, Arabella silenced him with a cutting glare before he could get a word out. "I know the truth now, so don't deny it. You never loved me. You care only for your dratted estate." In a single swift motion, she reached for the paper she'd so staunchly guarded in her bodice, giving it a pointed flap in his direction. "And you're willing to use nefarious means to run it."

The houseguests chose that moment to assemble near their host, disregarding any need he and his betrothed might feel for privacy. On the contrary, this was prime material for the gossip rags, not to be missed.

Lord Frederick pulled at his cravat, his pale face turning even pastier. "You've had a harrowing experience. You're over-wrought."

"No." Arabella stomped her foot, shoving away his half-hearted attempt to reach for her. "In the countless hours I've spent at Watley of late, your conversation with your father wasn't the only thing I overheard coming from the study."

He shifted uncomfortably, his once-dashing figure becoming hunched. Arabella, on the other hand, didn't cower once as she gripped the paper close to her chest, staring at him with eyes like ice. "You were angry with your land agent one day. You shouted at him to get out and leave you alone until he had better news to relay. And then, when he departed, I witnessed you concealing a paper of some sort on the top shelf of the bookcase while muttering about a forgery."

Murmurs rippled through the cluster of gentlemen, while Lord Frederick himself was rendered speechless, perspiration accumulating on his strained brow.

"Even then, and even after Violet warned me about your misdeeds, I deluded myself into believing you noble," Arabella continued with a humorless laugh, her vehemence unrelent-ing. "*Frederick is so passionate about his estate.* But once I heard the heartless things you said about me, I began to recognize the truth of your character. That's the real reason I returned to Watley for dinner tonight. Not because I'd forgiven you, but because I needed to search your study and find out what you concealed there."

She flashed the parchment in his face for a lone second before snatching it away, motioning for Benedict to come and collect it from her. "This is an irrigation deed—a *true* deed—stating that Aldercombe Grange is entitled to control of the river intersecting both Aldercombe and Watley. Any damming of the river is unlawful, and any documents you've supplied to the contrary are forgeries. *Aren't* they?"

Violet had remained on the dusty ground throughout the exchange, too enraptured to move. At Arabella's biting accusation, though, she clambered to her feet, Benedict's eyes rising from the page he hastily scanned in the dimness to lock with hers. They'd suspected it the whole time: Lord Frederick's claims about the river, and the deed he'd presented as evidence, were all a sham. The problem being, they hadn't yet found a way to prove their suspicions.

Had Arabella really done that for them? Had she truly just risked her life in a burning house in pursuit of the truth?

Never had Violet been more in awe of her sister. The foolhardy, *wonderful* girl.

Once again, Lord Frederick remained dumbstruck, spluttering but unable to form coherent sentences. What could he say, after all, when defeat pummeled him from all angles?

And suddenly, he was spared from responding to Arabella's accusation, for an enraged cry rent the air, followed by an ear-splitting bellow. "Frederick! What have you done?"

A wiry, middle-aged gentleman bounded toward them, his face contorted with horror akin to if he'd been dropped into the brimstone of hell. Violet swiped a hand over her still-watery eyes and blinked him into clearer focus, recognition unfurling in her racing mind. She'd seen this man, looming in the corner with his severe brow and beaklike nose, at a

London soiree or two. It was the Duke of Hawkesbury. Frederick's father.

Where the duke had been this whole time, she hadn't a clue. Only that he stared at Watley Hall until the flames reflected in his gaze, his shock—and outrage—growing more apparent with every rapid step he took.

Ignoring the rest of them entirely, he pushed past Arabella to stand before his son, his labored breaths sounding more like snarls. "I depart for the village for a few hours' respite from the tomfoolery that's overtaken the house, and return to find ... to find ..." He gestured sharply toward Watley Hall, where the pop and snap of burning wood was now mixed with the clamor of exploding glass.

Lord Frederick visibly swallowed, his stooped shoulders beginning to tremble. "The fireworks," he said in the same dull, vacant tone he'd used to explain the catastrophe to Violet. "A rocket misfired."

"*Fireworks*?" the duke roared, grabbing him by the lapels before changing his mind and shoving him away. "Was it not enough for you to tear up the whole blasted park? Why did you have to destroy the house along with it?"

"I'll have it rebuilt." Lord Frederick stumbled a few steps before righting himself, his desperate attempt at confidence undermined by the continued tremor in his voice. "Watley will be better than ever, you'll see. A place that befits my new wife and your future grandchildren." He peered over his father's shoulder to flash Arabella a garish smile, the gleam of his exposed teeth wolfish, almost diabolical.

"That wife will not be me." Arabella glared at him stonily, folding her arms across her chest before he could do anything so repulsive as reach for her again. "In case I haven't made my intentions clear, I'm ending our betrothal. Our association is through."

The duke finally took notice of her, turning as though a

chirping bird had landed upon his shoulder. However, she received nothing but a glance of mild interest before he whirled back to his son, the glow of flames across his craggy features making him appear especially foreboding.

"I *knew* you didn't have the sense to manage an estate, but I went against my better judgment and granted you the opportunity, regardless. Well, no more," he thundered, a declaration that made Lord Frederick gasp with far more distress than he'd shown at the loss of his betrothed. "I said all along that a commission in the army would be the best path for you so you could learn some discipline ..."

The duke's diatribe continued, but Arabella turned away from the skirmish, reaching for Violet's hand. "I'm very tired, and I've seen more than enough of this disaster. No matter what anyone does, there will be no saving the house." She gave her head a rueful shake. "Shall we leave?"

Violet stole one more glimpse at Watley Hall, where the roof of the west wing had collapsed, and flames spread down to leap from the ground floor windows. The bucket brigade remained at work, but their movements had slowed, many of the participants pausing to rest. To observe the house's inevitable destruction.

A mild pang hit the center of her chest. How ironic that just a few short months ago, this was the house she and Arabella had viewed as their salvation. The place where they could put their father's scandal behind them and find husbands.

What a fool she'd been. Pinning all her hopes on a thoughtless cad—thinking it wise for them to share a romantic encounter in a derelict hut, for heaven's sake—because he could offer her an escape.

Thank the stars that fate had intervened and thrown a wrench into her plans. One she hadn't appreciated at the time but had come to realize was the best thing ever to happen to her.

She placed her free palm upon Benedict's sleeve, calling his attention back from the deed he'd resumed studying through his spectacles. Her forced retreat to Wiltshire had once felt like a prison sentence. Her marriage, an even greater punishment. Yet this man who peered at her—eyes intent, cravat mussed, untamed curls dangling over his forehead—had given her everything she wanted. Rather, everything she hadn't known she wanted.

He'd given her the things that mattered. The things that made her feel complete.

Arabella's broken betrothal was still so fresh, she hadn't yet had the same privilege. She would, though; Violet was set on it. Arabella's bruised heart would heal, and she, too, would realize that something far better awaited her elsewhere.

"Yes," she said, squeezing first her sister's hand, then her husband's. She steered them toward the path that would lead them out of the defiled garden with its choking air and stagnant lake. "We're quite finished here."

29

Ben desperately needed to shed his tattered clothing. To plunge his face into the washbasin. To slump across his bed and not rise for a very long time.

The problem was, he couldn't take his eyes off his wife.

He tried not to hover *too* closely while a cluster of maids prepared the tub in her room and she worked to remove the pins from her hair. However, after coming precariously close to losing her—his heart still stuttered when he imagined what could have happened had he not journeyed to Watley Hall when he did—he found himself anxious to remain in her vicinity, assured of her safety.

The small smiles she gifted him in her vanity mirror each time their reflections met offered a balm, of sorts, to his jagged nerves. They only took the edge off, though, leaving him with a deep-rooted need for more closeness. More reassurance.

"The bath is ready, madam," her lady's maid called to her from beside the tub, pulling Ben's eyes away from the mirror and making his shoulders stiffen. The time for lingering had come to an end, for he could hardly stay and gawk while the maid assisted her with so intimate a task.

His chest twinged in protest as he took a languid step toward his own bedchamber. But when Violet rose from her seat and approached the bath, it was to give her lady's maid a wave. "Thank you, Edith. I can manage from here. You're free to retire."

Edith bobbed a curtsy and was gone from the room within seconds, motioning for the others to follow her. It was late, after all, the maids having been roused from their beds when he and Violet had at last returned from seeing Arabella settled at Meadowleigh.

The door clicked shut behind the final chambermaid, leaving the room quiet and still save for the wisps of steam drifting up from the bathwater.

We're alone. The thought hit him low in the gut, sending a spark flickering through his veins. Because yes, he needed to leave her to wash her smoke-tinged hair while the water remained hot, to soak her weary limbs and rest. However, there was nothing forcing his immediate departure. No reason for him to go deprived of what he craved as much as his next breath.

He reached her in three strides, pulling her into his arms and lowering his lips to hers. A split-second's hesitation hit him as he realized he hadn't been careful, hadn't asked for her approval. Yet her lips returned the pressure almost at once, her fingers sinking into his nape, the delicious heat of her body curling into him.

His hands twined at the small of her back, savoring the plush softness beneath his palms. All his. All returned to him safe and well.

He'd intended the embrace as a farewell gesture before he left her to her bath. A taste to keep him going until he gazed upon her again. But the more he took of her, the more he wanted.

Logically, he knew she was real, knew she was unharmed,

knew she could go to sleep in her bed and still be there when he peeked in the next morning. His body, though, cared nothing for logic. His heart insisted he take one more stroke of her tongue, one more caress; except *one more* was never enough.

"Violet." He broke away from the kiss before it was too late, pulse thundering, voice as raw as if he'd inhaled another mouthful of smoke. God, he sounded unhinged, her name scraping from his throat like an admonition. An appeal. He didn't even know what he was asking. For her to remind him of their harrowing day and bid him goodnight? For her to sink her nails in deeper and never let go?

She remained with her hands around his neck, her voice a soft command. "Stay, Benedict."

Stay. The word hit him between the ribs, causing his breath, his fingers, to freeze in anticipation. *Stay.*

"Don't make me pull you in this time while you're still clad in your trousers." She quirked a brow before lowering her eyelids, lashes gently fluttering. "Get undressed and come into the bath with me."

Suddenly, the shadow lingering in his mind—of noxious smoke-filled corridors and ravaging flames—was pushed aside by memories of water splashing onto the floor as Violet moved atop him. Memories of the slickness of her wet skin, the fullness of her breasts within his palms.

No amount of logic or weariness could prompt him to refuse such an invitation.

He spun her in one deft motion, pushing the mass of unbound hair over her shoulder so he could obtain full access to her back. The tub beckoned, the wafting steam enticing them to enter before the water cooled. Nonetheless, he couldn't resist taking time to press his lips to the dimple in her nape before setting to work on the tapes of her gown, drawing the tattered fabric from her shoulders and letting it fall to the floor.

Next came her stays, a garment he unlaced while dropping a kiss against each exposed shoulder. Claiming her as his to revere. His to protect.

With the stays cast aside, he got to his knees, gliding his hands along her legs until he found the ribbons that held up her stockings. One by one, he slipped them free, rolling away the delicate material until all that remained was the silk of her skin. And as he cradled her foot to slide the final stocking off her toes, her arms rose to the neckline of her shift, rendering it, too, a puddle upon the carpet.

He silently returned to his feet, breath catching at the view. Milky white thighs, the plump globes of her arse, the perfect ridges of her spine. He could gaze upon her symmetry for hours, exploring the contours of those globes, tracing along the column that ran from the cleft between them all the way up to her neck.

But then, she turned to face him, and his wits were truly lost. Yes, he'd both touched and tasted her before, but never without some sort of obstruction. Never had she stood before him so gloriously naked, allowing him to see her rosebud nipples, her curved hips, the golden curls between her legs.

He heard himself make a sound. *Beautiful.* It didn't do her justice, but it was the only word he seemed capable of producing. He didn't have time to invent a more fitting alternative before her hands were upon him, pushing away his coat and waistcoat. Tugging the shirt over his head. Unfastening the buttons at his fall.

Prior to this moment, she hadn't seen him fully unclothed, either. No one had. But any nerves that cropped up were assuaged by an overwhelming sense of rightness. A feeling that he and Violet belonged like this. Together.

Unshielded. For whatever unknowns arose from intimacy, there was safety in it, too.

With his trousers and stockings kicked aside, he took her hand, her appreciative hum ricocheting straight to his cock. He was already in a state of increasing arousal, his previous exhaustion swept away like driftwood in an ocean swell.

But first things first.

He stepped into the tub and helped Violet in after him, settling against the curved edge and guiding her to sit between his thighs. The water was wonderful, sending a deluge of comforting heat into his overworked muscles. However, the sensation couldn't compare to that of Violet's back resting against his chest, the ends of her hair drifting through the water to tickle his abdomen.

For an instant, he closed his eyes and simply let himself *feel*. Until all at once, she slid forward to dunk her face below the surface, popping back up with her curls plastered to her head and rivulets pouring down from her jawline.

It took a great deal of restraint not to spin her around and lick the droplets from her lips. Instead, he contented himself with reaching for the soap and massaging it through her scalp. He dragged it across her shoulder blades and down her back, across to her belly. Allowing her to return the favor until every bit of dust from their ordeal had dissolved into the bathwater, and his cock had grown painfully hard.

She straddled his lap, her back arching, presenting her breasts to him like the most delectable gift.

It would be so easy to repeat their previous bathtub encounter. To take those pebbled nipples into his mouth and grasp her hips while she dragged herself against him, providing jolt after jolt of friction.

However, as much as his body desired relief from the ache pounding through his groin—and as much as her eyes glittered with longing, making demands without saying a word—

this moment called for something more. He wanted nothing to act as a barrier between them—not even water. Wanted her body not curled up in a tub but spread out so he could appreciate every inch.

"Will you come to my bed?" he murmured close to her ear, detecting the rapid beat of her pulse as he ran a finger along her neck. The rhythm of it matched his own, a constant *tap, tap, tap* that betrayed the force of his need. His nerves. He paused for fortitude, then posed the question whose answer would forever change him. "Will you let me make love to you?"

Her breath stuttered, creating a hot whisper against his cheek. "Yes." She drew back to look at him once more, pressing wet fingertips to his jaw. "*Yes.*"

His mouth crashed clumsily against hers, taking one more kiss before he rose to his feet, pulling her up along with him. They climbed out of the bath together, and he wrapped her in the waiting towel, rubbing warmth into the gooseflesh on her arms.

Then again, the reason her skin prickled didn't seem to be from cold, for every inch of her he touched was supple and hot. Slick and damp. As for his own body, it burned more intensely with each step they took, the water dripping from his limbs feeling more like sparks.

He led her as far as the connecting door between their chambers, pushing it open to reveal that the bedside lamp burned low and his counterpane had been turned down, awaiting their arrival. This was the place where they would truly become husband and wife. He hoped to spend a lifetime of nights here with her entangled in his arms. Entangled in his heart.

A lump rose in his throat as they reached the side of the bed, and he swallowed tightly, his pulse continuing to gallop. The towel he'd draped around her torso was one tug away from exposing every intimate part of her. Her body one gentle push from flopping onto the bed and lying sprawled out for his perusal. However, for every insistent nerve ending that snapped at him to hurry, a deeper part of him knew the occasion was far too important to rush. He couldn't unwrap her, couldn't lay her out on the bed, without first telling her the truth.

"You need to know ... When I asked to make love to you ..." Christ, his neck was hot, his voice sounding unnaturally tight. He'd never imagined he could feel this way about someone who, until not so long ago, had been a stranger. That interest could turn to affection, which could turn to something so profound it was difficult to express it in words.

Yet there was one word that would make her understand. One word to sum up the extent of his longing, his admiration, his adoration. He brushed a wet curl from her forehead and let himself make free with it. "It's because I do, Violet. I love you."

Her eyes widened, cerulean irises glittering in the candle-light. "I love you, too." Her voice was mostly breath, although loud enough to make the words plain. Loud enough to squeeze past his ribs and twist around his heart. "I trust you. I desire you."

She pushed onto her tiptoes, her lips falling upon his chin. His throat. The sudden motion caused the towel to slip away, leaving her bare. Willing. Ready.

He really was the luckiest man in all of England. Make that the world. Because all at once, he'd been granted bloody *everything*.

He guided her to sit on the edge of the bed and lowered her head to the mattress, the sight every bit as breathtaking —*more* breathtaking—as he'd known it would be. Instead of joining her, though, he sank to his knees on the floor in front of her, gently spreading her legs so he could nestle himself between them.

She wriggled onto her elbows, peering down at him questioningly with her lip caught between her teeth. In answer, he hooked a dew-dotted leg over each of his shoulders, pressing his mouth to the top of her thigh. To her newly exposed sex.

She gasped, her face going slack, her hand fisting in his hair.

"Do you like that, Violet?" Carefully, he moved along her folds, suckling her delicate flesh. God, a man could get drunk doing this. "Does it feel nice when I put my tongue on you?"

"I'm not sure that"—her words dissolved into a moan before she caught her breath—"*nice* does the sensation justice."

A heady surge of desire cascaded through his veins. If he had everything, he needed to be damn certain that she did, too. It was imperative he make this good for her. That he gift her the same pleasure she gave him.

He tried again, his tongue finding the bud at the top of her sex where he knew she liked to be stroked.

Fingernails sank into his scalp, her hips jerking against the bed. Her exhale became a whimper. "Keep doing that." She watched him for an instant longer from beneath the veil of her lashes before dropping her head back to the mattress. "Never stop."

He readily complied, lapping at the swollen peak while his finger slid up to explore near her entrance. No, *nice* didn't come close to describing how it felt to sample the essence of her, musky and sweet. To forget the step-by-step sequences to a woman's pleasure he'd learned from pamphlets and instead lead by instinct, adjusting his rhythm and position based on her movements, the sounds she made. To watch her eyes shutter in ecstasy and know her cries were because of *him*.

"Please, Benedict." She pushed forward as his fingertip

eased its way into the top of her channel, his cock enviously throbbing at the burst of wet heat. "I'm so ... I need ... I cannot ..."

Her body was tight, quivering. So close to bursting with pleasure; even his limited experience with her allowed him to recognize as much. She just needed him to bring her that final step, the one that would tip her over the edge.

He lightly stroked her inner wall while his lips closed around her clitoris. Tongue circling, laving, never relenting. And suddenly, the tension within her broke, her body pulsing beneath his mouth, intimate muscles clutching tight to his finger.

He lapped at her until her moans subsided and her body stilled. Until the fingers in his hair loosened, her eyes drifted open, and her lips curved into a languid smile.

Never stop. He'd be happy to oblige, to stay with his head in this exact position until he'd memorized every secret, sensitive crease. Yet now that she lay breathless and slick, perhaps the time had come to take it a step farther. To know her in the most intimate way of all.

He rose on limbs that weren't altogether steady, shifting her until her head hit the pillow and her legs extended along the length of the bed. Then, he allowed himself the luxury of joining her, settling between her thighs and bracing his weight on his forearms so he could lean down to kiss her forehead. The bridge of her nose. Her mouth.

He was *so* close to where he wanted to be, his body hovering over hers, the curls on her mound brushing against his erection. Yet with anticipation, *yearning*, there also came hesitation.

"I don't want to hurt you," he rasped, blood pounding through his ears, his cock. His nerves twisted into a bundle of knots. "I haven't ... I haven't done this before."

He assumed she knew as much, although there was something about uttering the statement aloud that made it feel particularly exposing. When he chanced to meet her eye, though, the peerless blue showed nothing but openness. Warmth. *Trust.* "Neither have I." She slid her palm up to rest against his hammering heart. "But we'll figure it out together."

They would, wouldn't they? Because he loved her. She loved him in return. And together, they could build something wondrous that they alone would share.

With his eyes locked on hers, he inched forward, the tip of his arousal nudging past her entrance. Oh, Jesus, she was tight, her walls clamping down on him as if staking a claim. He pushed a little farther, each motion bringing him one step closer to heaven. However, upon seeing tension knit her brow, he stilled, a weight knocking against his chest. "Are you all right? Shall I st—"

"Keep going. All the way." She curled her hands around his hips, setting her mouth in the determined line he recognized as a telltale sign there was no dissuading her. "You're not hurting me. It's just … fullness."

Thank God. At her reassurance, he traversed the final distance to seat himself fully inside her, the jolt of sensation causing his exhale to stutter. It was one thing to experience the headiness of exploring her with his fingers. It was another, even more blissful thing entirely to have her wetness and heat enveloping his cock.

He forced himself to remain still, not wanting this to end before it truly began. Wanting her to have time to adjust, too. After a few moments, though, his arms started quivering with the effort of motionlessness, his body demanding amendments for the friction it lacked.

"I need to move," he choked out, throat impossibly tight. Skin impossibly hot. "But you'll tell me if it's too much? If you wish for me to stop?"

She nodded, her hands giving him a slight tug forward. "I want to feel you move inside me. To know what it's like."

Her words created a fresh shock of longing in his bloodstream, invigorating him as he pulled himself up and sank back down. They both made a sound: hers high and breathy, his a low groan. The pure pleasure of the sensation went far beyond *nice*, or any other descriptor he could imagine.

Then again, he could think of very little beyond turning the motion into a rhythm. *Up, thrust, up, thrust,* each time a little deeper, a little faster. Violet's head was tipped back, the tension in her features melting into blissful, uninhibited slackness.

He *would* stop if she asked him, just like he promised— even though the effort may well cause him to expire on the spot. However, the more he plunged into her, the more she seemed to get lost in the cadence of it, her cries developing the same lilt as when he'd set his tongue between her legs.

"Violet," he ground out, kissing her throat, sliding a palm between their damp bodies to caress those plump, puckered nipples. His climax was bearing down on him at a pace he couldn't control, sending him hurtling, soaring—

And then, before he could say another word, release hit him like a tidal wave, drowning him in bursts of pleasure so intense that light flashed before his eyes.

His body shuddered and jerked, and he suddenly became aware that she pulsed along with him, the squeeze of her muscles drawing out his ecstasy until every drop had been wrung from his veins.

He had no words to describe how glorious she was. How damn beautiful, sensual, and altogether alluring. Instead, he had to content himself with dropping to the mattress and gathering her into his arms, holding her secure against his chest while they both waited for their breathing to return to its normal pace.

Ultimately, it was Violet who spoke first, her voice airy and dreamlike. "I think I might like to do that again sometime." Her fingers traced a languorous line from his collarbone to his navel and back again. "Preferably soon."

The grin she flashed him held all the brilliance of the sun, blinding him to everything but his impeccable fortune. Like a man dazed, he captured her hand and pressed it to his heart, his mouth splitting with an unconstrained grin of his own. "Have I told you I love you?"

"In fact, you have." She giggled, giving her tongue a coy swipe along her bottom lip. "But I don't mind hearing it again."

"I love you. I love you." He caught that lip between his own, the longing he'd thought sated already stirring back to life. However, he pulled away this time before the kiss could deepen, refusing to let desire take over before he'd collected his words.

"You're my light, Violet," he said, grounding himself in the brilliant blue of her eyes. "My courage. My desire. My everything. I came to Aldercombe feeling lost, like I had no means of finding my way again. But then, I met you. I *married* you. And before I knew it, everything missing and uncertain became whole and clear."

Her playful grin vanished, but in its place was a look of such intense, earnest joy that his heart leaped beneath her palm. "You changed everything for the better for me, too." She nuzzled up to his chest, bringing her free hand to rest at his nape. "I won't pretend that my sudden departure for Wiltshire, after my father's scandal, brought me any great enjoyment. But little did I know, I traveled exactly where I was meant to go at exactly the right time. For how else would I have encountered you in that ridiculous hut?"

He chortled in spite of himself, the memory that had once

made him cringe now seeming like the most fortuitous circumstance of his life.

"I couldn't picture myself ever being content in the countryside," she said, giving her head a rueful shake. "But now, when I envision my happiness, it's the only place I see."

Her smile returned, reaching up to her eyes and making them crinkle at the corners. "I'm sure we'll travel to London on occasion. The day may even come when Parliamentary duties require you to spend the Season there. But when I dream of the future, I imagine us here, at Aldercombe. I think of the river and the beech tree on Skylark Ridge. I think of Achilles and the sheep. And sometimes, I even imagine a child or two with spectacles and the wildest curls England has ever seen."

How could he describe the drumming in his chest? The feeling that he was somehow more alive than on any other night of his life? Perhaps the best word was *whole*. Or *hopeful*. Because he suddenly had a vision of what she described. Violet, heavy with his child. The patter of small feet, the ring of carefree laughter. A new generation—*an heir*—not bound by ghosts of the past but raised in the spirit of love, truth, and belonging.

"Yes." He closed his eyes, allowing the idea to percolate. His arms wrapped around her so they could fall asleep in each other's embrace and the vision would carry over to his dreams. "I know what I want from the future as well, and it's *you*. It's Aldercombe. It's everything we build together. It's any titles we inherit and any places we might dwell. Because as long as you're there, I'll always know I've found my home."

Epilogue

October, 1817

The autumn wind whipped through Violet's hair as she bounded across the field on Vespera's back, her sights set on the lone ash tree that drew nearer and nearer. The change of season had turned its leaves fiery, creating a yellow-red blur that beckoned to her like a flag. She was close. Very close.

With a burst of speed from Vespera's powerful legs, she flew past the mark she'd declared as the finish line, her shako hat tumbling to the grass as she pulled the reins to slow the horse's gallop.

Her breath heavy from exertion, she circled back around the tree just in time to see Benedict and his gelding hurtle past it, giving a strong finish to the race. Albeit in second place.

"I won," she announced gleefully when they'd both reduced their speed to a walk, the horses ambling side by side over the newly churned earth.

A dark brow lifted beneath the shadow of his top hat. "Don't you always?"

"Well, yes." She grinned, prompting Vespera to halt and vaulting from the horse's back. "But perhaps someday, you'll claim victory." He was getting more accustomed to riding, after all, taking daily trips on horseback to observe their extended lands. Riding out for pleasure, too, when she requested he join her, always indulging her whims to race.

"Perhaps." His lips twitched in return, and in the next instant, he was on the ground beside her, throwing his hat to the wind. He grabbed her by the waist, planting a kiss against the bridge of her nose. "Although I've already been victorious in the ways I most desire."

As usual, pinpricks of pleasure rippled over her skin, a spark low in her belly stirring to attention. Her husband was growing accustomed to doing this, too: reaching for her at unexpected moments, taking whatever occasions he could find to steal a kiss.

She *loved* those occasions. Loved how the delight of them only seemed to grow with each passing day of their marriage.

"So have I." She returned his caress with a peck on the lips, then turned to survey the endless stretch of field, ornamented by the vibrant purple and gold streaks of the twilight sky. "It's been a most successful month."

Indeed, evidence of their triumph existed as far as the eye could see, in all the freshly harvested fields. The last load of corn had been carted in with immense gaiety just yesterday, and she and Benedict had marked the occasion by hosting an evening of food, dancing, and merriment for the tenants and villagers. No, the crop yields hadn't been as prolific as records had shown from many autumns past, although they'd been a great deal better than those from the previous year and its abysmal weather. Benedict said they should view their first harvest as proprietors of Aldercombe as a starting point. A mere suggestion of what they could achieve with careful management and innovation.

To add to the cheer, Benedict's mother, stepfather, and two half-brothers had come for their first visit to Aldercombe, escaping life in town for a fortnight so they, too, could experience the excitement of harvesttime in the country. And because the house was already bursting with activity, Violet had followed the adage *the more, the merrier* and also invited Arabella to join them.

While her sister had fared remarkably well in recovering from her injured heart, Arabella often grew restless at Meadowleigh, and it was no big secret that their mother—still flitting about with a twinkle in her eye and glowing cheeks while she praised Barker's impressive gardening skills—sometimes wished for the house to herself.

Fortunately, Arabella had come to Aldercombe bright-eyed and vivacious herself, eager to tell Violet about the trio of gentlemen, newly arrived in Wiltshire for a shooting party, she'd met at the assembly hall the previous week. Given their experience at Watley, Violet was glad her sister made no love-struck declarations or postulations about wedding bells quite yet. But on the whole, the news gave them cause to feel optimistic.

The only drawback to the bustling house was the reduction of moments like this, when it was just the two of them, free to embrace whenever and wherever they wished. As they'd grown more comfortable with their marriage—with intimacy —she'd been surprised to discover how many locales could prove suitable for lovemaking if one used a little ingenuity. However, having a house full of guests, and overseeing a harvest home celebration besides, certainly impeded the extent to which they could put that ingenuity to the test. Then again, there *had* been that encounter in the linen room yesterday ...

"A successful month, to be sure." Benedict's mouth tugged into the suggestion of a smirk, almost as if he sensed the direction of her thoughts. Rather than allude to it, though, he offered his arm, and they made an unspoken agreement to begin strolling, the horses contentedly grazing behind them. "Although," he said, a sudden gust of wind causing his hair to tumble in all directions, "my victories began around the last week of April in a field not so far away from this one."

She grinned at the roguish curl that hung over his eyebrow. Grinned at his entire countenance, flushed and invigorated, because he really had no right being this handsome. "Funny, that's the exact week mine started as well." She gave him a playful nudge with her elbow, then curled her fingers tighter around his sleeve, peering at the landscape beyond. Changing trees. Brilliant, darkening sky. "And they've only continued to grow, haven't they?"

They reached a cluster of trees and a low limestone wall, Benedict stepping across before giving her his hands to help her climb over.

At one point, this would have marked a boundary: a section of border between Aldercombe and Watley. However, they were one and the same now, the Duke of Hawkesbury having sold his unentailed property to the Marquess of Rockliffe.

Perhaps it seemed a foolhardy purchase—a burned shell of a house and a razed park—but Benedict had insisted on its potential for farmland, and his uncle had readily trusted his judgment.

Someday, maybe—once grass and shrubs covered the scar of the ill-fated lake—they would look at rebuilding the house and putting it up for lease. For the time being, though, they were invested in establishing their new flock of Wiltshire Horn sheep in some of Watley's empty pastures.

"We have everything, Violet." Benedict's footsteps stilled, his gaze resting on the horizon a moment before abruptly turning to her. "Everything."

And then, before she could offer a reply or even blink, his lips were on hers, one hand fisting at her nape.

A dizzy burst of exhilaration exploded within her, and she returned the kiss hungrily, sinking her weight against his chest before her legs could make her stagger.

It couldn't last long, not with night fast approaching and family members back at Aldercombe Grange awaiting their return. For this stolen moment, though, they kissed while the evening breeze rustled their clothing and darkness swallowed the colors in the clouds.

And when they paused for breath, her lips hovering just below his, she voiced her agreement. *"Everything."*

THE END

Bonus Content

Thank you for reading!
Not quite ready to say goodbye to Benedict and Violet? Sign up for my newsletter to get a free steamy bonus scene. You will also be the first to know about special promotions and new releases, including what's coming next in the Rockliffe Dynasty series. Join now at:
www.janemaguireauthor.com/newsletter

About the Author

Jane Maguire is a Canadian author whose lifelong passions for history, writing, and love stories inevitably led her to begin penning historical romance novels. While her love of historical fiction spans all eras, she focuses her writing on high society in the regency period. She enjoys crafting stories with lots of angst, which makes giving her characters their happily ever afters all the more satisfying.

When she isn't at her computer writing and researching, you can find her vacationing in the Rocky Mountains, playing classical music on the piano, or simply curling up with a cup of tea and a good book. She lives with her husband, two kids, and a very floofy cat.

You can find Jane online at www.janemaguireauthor.com.

www.ingramcontent.com/pod-product-compliance
Lightning Source LLC
Chambersburg PA
CBHW030543190726
48283CB00006B/1994

A reluctant heir...

Benedict Prescott never wanted to be heir to a marquessate. Born to a father who rejected his highborn family and turned his back on the peerage, he can't help but feel that embracing his bloodline, and the title inevitably coming his way, is the ultimate betrayal. However, when an uncharacteristic scandal leads to his expulsion from university, he has few places left to turn but the countryside—and the flailing estate his uncle, the Marquess of Rockliffe, tasks him with managing. Little does Benedict know, his turmoil over the future is nothing compared to the upheaval that enters his life when he's caught in a compromising position with a viscount's daughter—and honor demands he marry her.

A lady trapped by circumstance...

If Miss Violet Collingwood learned anything after her father's dissolute antics prompted her exile to the country, it's never to rely on a man, and certainly not to fall in love with one. She's more than content to have found a suitor she esteems and who can offer escape from the taint on her family name. But just as her betrothal looks imminent, her path intersects with Benedict Prescott's, and an innocent encounter becomes misconstrued until she's embroiled in another scandal. With her reputation and her sister's own betrothal in peril, Violet has little choice but to accept a marriage proposal from the aloof stranger with whom she collided—even though he's the starchiest, most straitlaced man she's ever met.

A duty that becomes desire...

Thrust into an unwanted union, Benedict and Violet are bound by duty but divided by uncertainty and secrets. Yet as Violet's strong will clashes with Benedict's cool reserve, the tension between them evolves into something they never imagined: desire. As fragile passion blooms, a ruthless neighbor threatens the estate they share, and ghosts of the past linger around every corner. With their home and future at stake, they must decide if they'll take a risk neither thought themselves capable of: opening their hearts and letting each other in.